The Blade of Castlemayne

The Blade of Castlemayne

by *ANTHONY ESLER*

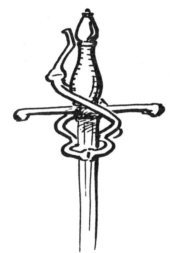

WILLIAM MORROW & COMPANY, INC.
NEW YORK   1974

Printed in the United States of America.

1 2 3 4 5 78 77 76 75 74

Book design by Helen Roberts

Library of Congress Cataloging in Publication Data

Esler, Anthony.
 The blade of Castlemayne.

 I. Title.
PZ4.E762Bl [PS3555.S52]   813'.5'4   74-7271
ISBN 0-688-00317-6

Contents

Elizabeth and Leicester
Beating oars
The stern was formed
A gilded shell
Red and gold
The brisk swell
Rippled both shores
Southwest wind
Carried down stream
The peal of bells . . .

—T. S. ELIOT, 1922

Tell men of high condition,
    that manage the estate,
Their purpose is ambition,
    their practice only hate . . .

—SIR WALTER RALEIGH,   c. 1600

The Blade of Castlemayne

~ *One* ~

The Kiss

i

"Dear sweet Lord Jesus!" The girl laughed, rocking helplessly
on her knees. "You will forgive me, I know—even for the witch's
broom!"

It was late, very late, on Christmas night. The Lady Arabella Traherne knelt beside the tall four-poster bed, her young
body swathed in an enveloping white shift. Her long fair hair
spilled freely over her shoulders, almost to her waist. Her hands
were clasped, her face tilted heavenward—and she was laughing
like a demented thing. Laughing till tears of joy sprang from
her eyes and she gasped for breath.

Her prayers were only just completed. She had prayed for
Elizabeth the Queen, whom she had never seen, far away in
London; for the Earl her father; for all beneath the roof of
Exmoor Castle; for the tenants on her father's lands; for soldiers
in peril and sailors on the sea; and for all good Christian souls
in that year of grace 1592, the thirty-fourth year of the reign.
And she had just realized that her mind and heart had not been
in one single prayer. She had invoked Divinity by rote, and she
knew that no one of her pleas had gotten any nearer heaven
than the dim, coffered ceiling of her own bedchamber.

From the first "Our Father" to the final "Jesus' name we
pray," she had been staring as though hypnotized at The
Hunting of the Unicorn, woven in green and yellow in a tapestry

across the back wall of her elegantly furnished room. A forest glade, unreal and dreamlike. The climax of the hunt—the horned head reclining in the lovely virgin's lap, the hunters closing in. A disgracefully worldly distraction. More disgraceful still, the reason for her fascination had suddenly dawned on her. The arras irresistibly reminded her of old Master Norton's merry tale —*sotto voce*, at the high table—of the modest maiden, and the witch's broom. The tale now struck her sleep-drugged mind as so hilarious, the association with the virgin and the unicorn's horn so ludicrous, that she could only rock with laughter, there on her knees.

"Oh Lord, oh Lord . . . what would Agnes say? You will not mind, dear Lord Jesus, I am sure. But poor Aggie would . . . would—" The image of her Puritanical old nurse's wrinkled face, mouth agape with horror, sent the girl off again into gales of laughter. She sank back on her haunches, arms now hanging limply at her sides, and surrendered herself completely to giggling, gurgling mirth.

The winter wind whistled outside the mullioned window, seeped in around the panes to flutter a candle. Far off through the labyrinthine corridors of the castle, other sounds of merriment echoed dimly. Mingled lutes and tambourines, distant roars of laughter rose faintly from the great hall where her father's guests still kept high festival. But the Lady Arabella was only just turned nineteen. A glance from the Earl had been sufficient to send her off to bed, secretly grateful for the chance to withdraw. To husband her tingling energies for the festivities that were to come.

It had been a glorious, unbelievable, exhausting day, the maddest Christmas Day she had ever known. And there were eleven more days of joyful celebration still to go, between this and Twelfth Night!

Her nervous explosion of laughter ended, the kneeling girl wiped her eyes and let her thoughts turn prudently toward bed. The curtains were pulled back between the bulbous, ornately carved bedposts, the coverlet and blankets turned down to reveal white sheets, inviting pillows on the bolster. The warming pan was in its place, she knew, cooling to no purpose while she dawdled. She shivered, feeling goose bumps on her body inside the nightdress. The fire had already died out in the marble fireplace behind her.

Three tall candles burned waveringly in a silver wall sconce, filling the chamber with soft light. Ripples of shadow ran over the surface of the unicorn tapestry. Blacker shadows shifted beneath the heavily carved table, behind the high-backed chairs and the wardrobe in the corner, in the depths of the curtained bed itself. It was very still. There was only the moaning of the wind over the moors, the half-heard music of the lutes. And farther still, a quarter of a mile beyond the castle, the distant roll and boom of the sea.

Had she heard something else? A faint step in the corridor. Then clearly the rattle of the latch. The hall door swung wide, and someone came striding across the antechamber, through the open doorway at her back.

Agnes would never enter in that fashion, she knew. And Agnes was asleep long since!

Arabella scrambled to her feet, clutching the loose shift close about her nakedness. She whirled around and saw Walter Castlemayne standing in the door.

His white-blond hair was wild, his eyes were two bright chips of blue, blazing with excitement. He wore scarlet still, as he had at supper, and that morning at the fencing—crimson doublet, scarlet breeches, hose and shoes of scarlet. He was smiling at her from the doorway—a bold, manic, daring smile that creased his long West Country jaw and glittered in his wild young eyes.

"Walter—Master Castlemayne—what is it?"

She had no time for more. Scarcely time, indeed, to register the shock of it—of this unbelievable, unthinkable intrusion into

the very bedchamber of the great Earl of Exmoor's only daughter.
Unspeaking, his blue eyes laughing still, Walter Castlemayne
swept across the room and caught the Lady Arabella in his arms.

Harry had tried to hold him back, to talk some sense into his
exultant heart.

"By Jesus Christ! You must be mad even to think it!" his
square-faced kinsman had hissed in his ear. Music was spilling
around them from the minstrel gallery above. Laughter was
rising in gusts and gales up and down the crowded tables.
Castlemayne had hardly heard the whispered, urgent injunction.
"Mad, or drunk, or both! Sweet Jesus, not twenty-four hours
under his lordship's roof—"

"And yet I'll have it, Harry! A kiss from that lovely mouth
this very night! I swear it on my sword's hilt, as the Crusaders of
old times used to do!" He did not actually have the weapon
with him, of course. No man wore a sword at the Earl of
Exmoor's table. But the oath had been no less sacred to his
chivalric soul.

His eyes were on fire, his lean face was flushed even beyond
his normal high coloring. But Walter Castlemayne was drunk
on success that night, not on Lord Henry Traherne's un-
exampled selection of wine and ale and good English beer.
Castlemayne had had a day of triumphs. He was intoxicated
with his own high destiny.

"Dear Lord," Harry Langland had muttered, running a freck-
led hand through his thick orange hair, "give me strength to
plant some prudence in this lunatic." And then, once more
against his kinsman's ear, "This is no Black Friars strumpet,
Walter! No French camp follower or tavern wench of Utrecht,
free with her kisses to any brave English hero that comes by!
This is Exmoor's daughter, the greatest magnate in all Devon
—did you not say so yourself? Aye, and the one man of all whom
you must *not* affront—"

"Tush, Harry, you make too much of it," Castlemayne had

answered cheerfully, waving off an obsequious servingman with a silver jug of wine. "The Lady Arabella is my old playfellow, remember. Maid Marian to my Robin Hood, on other Christmases at Exmoor."

"Maid Marian to your Robin! Jesus Christ, when you were a gawky lad and she in pigtails still—"

"Five years—seven years—what difference to such old companions?" Walter had grinned, remembering. "And Christ, Harry, if you had danced with her this night, had heard her voice, looked down into those eyes—"

Harry Langland had turned away with a groan. He had hooked a finger in his white ruff, loosening it about his thick red countryman's neck. He had heard this before. Walter Castlemayne was in love again.

But he had to make one more effort to save his kinsman from the maddest folly in a career of recklessness and folly.

"Walter, have you forgot your business here already? Why we rode so far from London in the dead of winter to accept his lordship's hospitality? Sweet Jesus, would you set all at hazard for a single kiss?"

He had not said, "From a green unfledged girl that will scarce know how to do it!" though he had thought as much. Harry was a stolid Cornishman with solid country tastes. He liked a more buxom beauty than the Earl's wand-slender daughter.

"Naught's forgotten—all shall be done!" had responded Castlemayne. "Indeed, have we not made great strides in the matter this very night? But I shall have a kiss for luck, good Harry! A kiss to seal this day's successes and give us good omen for the morrow! A kiss for an old playfellow too long away. . . ." One kiss, his heart had exulted, from that soft mouth that smiled so sweetly up at me this night!

And Walter Castlemayne had risen, shrugging off his kinsman's hand. Had bowed with all due deference to the dignitaries at the Earl's high table. And had swaggered out of the vaulted hall, followed by the eyes of half the drunken, joyful country squires and courtiers, gentlemen and gentlewomen, that lined his lordship's board.

Harry Langland could do nothing but curse and watch him go.

Her face turned toward him even as he entered. Her pale blue eyes, the lashes glistening still with laughter, were wide with fear. He saw her spring to her feet, clutching with one small hand to close her smock at the throat. He saw her lips forming the syllables of his name.

With hardly a pause he crossed the threshold and closed the space between them.

"Walter, what is it? What have you—" Then his arms swept around her waist and pulled her close against him.

His first laughing kiss caught only the corner of her mouth and the hollow of her cheek. She twisted her face quickly the other way—and he kissed her on the other cheek. He tasted a strand of her fine straw-colored hair against her skin, and chuckled in his throat.

"Walter—Master Castlemayne!" she whispered urgently. "You're mad to do this!" Her hands were on his upper arms, trying to push him away.

This time he captured her mouth. And held it.

Her lips were smooth and cool under his. At first her mouth was closed against him. Then she tried to speak again, and his tongue burst in upon her, eager and quick. His mouth moved against hers, and her lips grew soft, yielding. And was there a tremor of response there now?

He took his mouth away, and found that they had both forgotten to breathe.

"Oh, Walter," she said shakily.

His lips brushed her slender throat. He kissed her shoulder, warm and softly moving beneath the light fabric. He flattened one large hand across the small of her back and pressed her closer still against him, feeling the smoothness of her skin, the first steep swelling of a buttock under his fingers.

Her small hands were against his chest now, trying to push him away. But he was already rock-hard in his padded breeches, and the blood beat thickly in his temples. He crushed her gasping mouth beneath his own once more. His hands began to move, caressing her body, taut and twisting in his arms. Arabella, straining wildly away from him, tensed herself to scream. Then she felt her mouth invaded once again. She felt his hands upon her, caressing her with an ardor and a tenderness she had never known. Love, that had been a thing in books for her all her nineteen years, was suddenly, dazzlingly, overwhelmingly real. Not poetry, not romance, not even a bawdy tale. Not words at all, but tactile, physical beyond belief. The feel of a man's hands upon her body, of a man's mouth on hers.

Slowly her head fell back under the surging passion of his kiss. Back and back, vertiginous, her waterfall of golden hair spilling into emptiness, till only the rough band of his velvet-clad arm supported her above the abyss.

She was no longer struggling.

She heard herself whispering his name, again and again, as his mouth descended once more to the base of her throat. As his hand came up over her stomach to caress one small thrusting breast. As the touch of his palm and his fingertips, feathery through the cloth, sent waves of inexpressible pleasure radiating from one taut nipple.

Then his hand came up farther still, and made her shoulder naked, and slid down to cup her naked breast.

"Arabella, my lady—" he murmured thickly.

"Oh, Walter—No!" she cried out in sudden terror and shrank away.

Pious injunctions, frightful warnings clamored in her mind, the words of her aged nurse: Beware sweet words that lead to brute assault. Let no man kiss your cheek, nor touch your body with licentious hands. Preserve your maidenhead as woman's chiefest treasure. . . .

She was shuddering violently now, fearful of the new sensations that his caresses stirred within her. It was all too real, too starkly physical for her. With a sob, she broke away, staggered backward, fetched up against the foot of her tall bed.

"Walter . . . please . . . not now!"

She stood there a frightened little girl, her small breasts heaving, her eyes wide and swimming with blue. But Castlemayne's hands still tingled to the texture of her skin, his lips still felt her mouth moving under his. Her own face, flushed with passion, was so overwhelmingly at variance with her pleading words.

For a single instant he stood on the brink. Then he groaned and bowed his head to cover his eyes with burning palms. All his brash cavalier arrogance was gone. With disbelief and wonder he realized that—dear God!—he really did care for this girl.

"My lady, you must forgive a poor fool but newly escaped from Bedlam! Truly, I do not know what devil possessed me this night." He raised his head and contrived a rueful smile before he floundered on. "I came for one bold kiss, between old friends. One only. And then, when I beheld you there—"

"Sweet Walter, I know, I understand," she whispered fearfully. "A man is—but a man, and weak. But you must go now, quickly, before—I know not what—"

"One kiss more, my Arabella!" He was amazed at the trembling passion in his own voice.

She kissed him once more, coming quickly into his arms and slipping as swiftly away. There was a childish nervousness in her haste, but the coquettishness of young womanhood as well.

"Now go, sweet Walter, go quickly—"

One moment longer he stood looking at her small figure in the loose smock, outlined against the rich green hangings of the bed. At her tumbled hair and shy, uncertain smile. Then he wheeled abruptly, plunged across her chamber and the antechamber beyond, and vanished into the blackness of the unlit corridor.

Arabella heard the latch drop into place, heard one quick step away, then silence. She drew a deep breath that seemed to catch in her throat, and sat down shakily on the edge of her bed. Her pulse was still beating wildly, her mind spinning like a child's top. So wrong a thing, of course, she thought. Unthinkable—and God knew what might have come of it! And yet . . . and yet—She could not put her new sensations into words. But her body knew. Slowly she raised her hand to her own breast. Wonderingly she touched the nipple, still taut with passion beneath the chaste white shift.

From the pitch-dark hall outside the door that Castlemayne had closed not half a minute since, there came a sudden shriek of pain.

ii

Castlemayne swung the door to Arabella's apartments shut behind him and stood in total blackness in the unlit passage. He paused one second to get his bearings. He must move to his right, he knew, twenty paces down the corridor to the vestibule of the new wing, then left toward the older part of the castle. He turned, took two steps from her door—and froze again.

Something had moved. Perhaps six paces ahead of him, down the dark passageway. A quick scuttering sound, as of someone lurching against a wall in clumsy flight.

But even as Castlemayne paused to listen, the other also froze in his tracks.

There was a silence, while Castlemayne strove fruitlessly to see or hear. Perhaps twenty seconds passed before he caught the next signal that someone else was still there, crouched like himself in the blackness, waiting. It was the faintest of sounds: the hush of a tortuously indrawn breath.

Another moment Castlemayne waited, straining every faculty for some further sign of the exact location of that other croucher in the dark. His fists clenched tight as the seconds ticked over in his brain. The great muscles of his thighs bulged hard with tension.

Then something snapped in young Castlemayne. All the excitements of that unreal day and night balled up within him and exploded. Bending low like a pike-wielding skirmisher, breath bursting from him in a soundless battle cry, he charged up the passageway.

He had not taken half-a-dozen strides in the darkness before his left fist slammed into the meaty shoulder of a man, crouching close to the left-hand wall.

He felt his antagonist reel back from the glancing blow. He heard a low, hoarse oath, and the sound of scrabbling flight on down the corridor. Castlemayne raced after, the joy of wild pursuit flooding through him. Must close with the fellow quickly, warned his battlefield-conditioned brain, in the vestibule just ahead. Before he could disappear into the rabbit warren of the old castle. And quietly, for God's sake, lest some servant—

A moment later he glimpsed a squat, broad-shouldered figure, running low, but clearly visible against the grayness of the windowed parlor. Then, as pursuer and pursued burst through the open archway, Castlemayne leaped like a huge cat. He landed close on the other's heels and sent him sprawling with a vicious blow across the back of a shaggy neck and head.

The blow vibrated up the length of his right arm as the other fell rolling, tumbling. At the feel of it, a new kind of joy surged through Walter's veins. For Castlemayne loved the crash and thrill of battle. Fighting was strong wine to him, an alchemical mix of chivalric exaltation and sheer physical release that intoxicated his young heart.

But the other man rolled over and came up quickly, facing him. There was a rasp of metal on stiff leather. Castlemayne, weaponless, saw the dull gleam of a dagger in the other's hand.

They faced each other then, in the elegant, sparsely furnished room, two black shadows moving in pale starlight that filtered through the wide mullioned windows. Both breathing hard, bending low, circling for advantage.

"Will you draw upon me then, sir?" hissed Castlemayne.

"Will you indeed, my craven keyhole spy . . . cutpurse . . . whoremaster. . . spawn of a Cheapside dunghill . . . ?" He spoke in a low, steady whisper, smiling tightly in the dark. Insult by calculated insult, he drew his antagonist in, as a Spanish bullfighter calls in the bull, luring the beast close enough for the flicking thrust between the horns.

"Will you fight, rogue? Have you the belly for it then?"

The other lunged, slashed viciously with his long-bladed knife. Walter swayed to one side, avoiding the wicked, driving thrust. Then, before his opponent could recover, he swung his foot in a joyful, wide, upward-arching kick. Felt his toe slam into the other man's stomach, doubling him up with a grunt of pain. And saw his enemy crumple to his knees, clutching at his belly, mouth wide and gasping for air.

Castlemayne leaped in at once, yanked the man's head back, and dealt him a tremendous buffet across the face. The blow knocked the fellow over backward, his dagger flying into a far corner of the room. He did not rise this time but lay rolling on the floor, his arms still wrapped around his body, groaning.

Walter bent over, seized him by the front of his leather jerkin, and hauled him to his feet. Deftly businesslike, he jammed the fellow up against the nearest wall and thrust his own face close, striving to make out the other's features.

A sudden flicker of candlelight revealed the startlingly ugly face of his prisoner. Bearded, gap-toothed, and dirty, the man swayed drunkenly in Castlemayne's grasp. Through the matted hair that spilled over his sweaty forehead, a single eye glared venomously. Where the other eye should have been there was only an empty socket, hideously scarred.

Castlemayne had seen that face, seen it that very day, moving across the fringes of his vision. But where, and when?

"Luke!" gasped Arabella, standing in the arched entry way, a candle in her hand.

"You know him, my lady?"

"It is Luke Naylor, from the stable. My father's chief groom, these last four years and more. But did he hurt you? That cry—"

"His own, though his intentions ran clean the other way. But what did he here, skulking about your ladyship's apartments at this time of night?"

And what had he overheard? What had he seen, this hulking, unkempt lout, reeking of the stables?

One-eyed Luke twisted suddenly in his captor's grasp, struggling to break free. Castlemayne swung him around and flung him half across the unlit chamber into a far dark corner. Strode after him, caught him once more by his jerkin, and slammed him up against a tall oak cupboard, elaborately carved and decorated. And then at once, before Arabella could follow with her blowing candle, he dealt his panting prisoner three slashing backhand blows across the face.

"Well, fellow? How came you here?"

"Lord, young master!" whined Luke Naylor, wiping blood off a broken lip, rolling up his single eye. "Lord, sir, you wouldn't harm an old soldier like yourself, sir? A man that's trailed a pike in Flanders with the best of them, and lost an eye for England and our gracious Queen?"

Odds it was a brawl over some Flemish whore, grinned Castlemayne to himself. He smashed the cringing stablehand with his closed fist this time, and blood gushed from his nose.

Arabella gasped and shut her eyes quickly. This was nothing like the knightly combats in her romantic books of chivalry.

"What, good Master Luke," Castlemayne was saying, "no nosebags to fill, no straw to change, no dung to shovel, that you should leave your stables for a stroll about the castle at midnight?"

Luke simply goggled at him, blood trickling down into his beard. He saw the young man's hands eager to lash out at him again.

"What you most urgently need, Master Luke," Castlemayne went on, "is a stout cudgel or two broken about your skulking shoulders. And then," he added, grinning like a long-jawed wolf, "if even after that you should tend to be talkative, as well as restive in the night—perhaps something a bit more serious. Perhaps something much more serious indeed might happen to you, Luke."

He yanked the sweating, bleeding face up close to his own, fixed that one eye with an icy gaze.

"Do you follow me, old fellow soldier, or have I addled your brains already, with this little lesson in courtesy?"

With a roar and a desperate heave, the shaggy Cyclops broke loose. He came off the wall with a rush, slamming his burly shoulder into Castlemayne's chest. The young man in scarlet staggered back, the girl in white leaped aside with a stifled scream, and the dun-colored stablehand vanished down the nearest corridor.

Castlemayne lunged after him, made one wild grab at him as he disappeared. Then, with a shake of his head and a rueful smile, he turned back to Arabella.

"He—he surely had no honest business here, in this part of the castle," the girl whispered, staring wide-eyed after the vanished hostler. "But Walter"—she echoed his own thoughts—"what did he see?"

"Nothing, my lady," he soothed her quickly, calming the sudden terror in her wide blue eyes. "Nothing certainly, through two solid doors and the width of your antechamber, even if he progressed so far."

"But, Walter, even your being here—"

"And how of *his* being here, my lady—a stablehand crouching at his lordship's daughter's chamber door? Why, he'd rot in

Plymouth gaol from now till Gabriel's trump if he dared con-
fess to such a thing! If anyone believed him at all. For what is
the word of a sneaking groom against your ladyship's own? No
fear, my lady, the fellow will say nothing."

But his own heart misgave him as he said it. What had the
fellow been doing there, after all? And had he been lurking about
Lady Arabella's door? Or had he been following Castlemayne
himself through the midnight corridors of Exmoor?

Arabella nodded slowly, uncertainly, trying to believe him. In
the momentary silence, she heard a faint roar of laughter from
the great hall below. She felt bewildered and frightened suddenly, standing there before this strange young man with only
a single garment to cover her nakedness.

"Now quickly," he was saying urgently, "to your own room,
my lady . . . Arabella." He was still awkward with the name.
"Lest your ladyship should take cold. You are so thinly clad."

The girl flushed suddenly. Her chin went up and her eyes
sparkled. She felt her breasts grow taut again, and her body
pebbled once more with gooseflesh. But she remembered who
and what she was, and self-confidence flooded back into her.
She did not understand about Luke, or about herself and Walter
Castlemayne, or any of the miraculous things that had happened that strange Christmas Day. But she was the Earl of
Exmoor's daughter! What evil could ever befall the daughter
and heir of Lord Henry Traherne, the greatest magnate in all
the West Country?

"Good night, Walter Castlemayne," she said loftily yet softly,
her voice far more controlled than her quick-beating heart. Then
she turned and hurried off up the passageway to her own apartments.

He watched the candlelight fade, heard the latch fall, then
silence.

Only then did he turn and set out for the little room high up
in the ancient keep where he and Harry Langland were quar-
tered for those twelve days of Christmas. It had been a vivid

morning and a spectacular evening, even before he had set out so recklessly for the Lady Arabella's chamber. Remembering, wondering, he threaded his way through the corridors of Exmoor toward his bed.

~ *Two* ~

Clash of Steel

i

Walter Castlemayne had strode into the great hall of Exmoor Castle at eleven o'clock that morning, stamping the snow from his fawn-colored boots and shrugging the heavy traveling cloak back from his shoulders. Behind him in the snowy, gray-walled courtyard, servants unfastened baggage and led nickering horses off to the stables. Dogs barked and frisked in the powdery snow. Ahead of him, just through the dark screen passage, he could hear children laughing and shrieking in the great hall. They were welcome sounds to young Castlemayne—the sounds of warmth and life after ten weary days on the road from London.

Rubbing stiff, cold hands together, he strode up the short passageway with Harry grumbling at his heel. And then a new sound struck his ear. A sound that lifted the heart of Walter Castlemayne as no other could.

A clash of steel rang through the vaulted hall beyond the high, carved wooden screen before him. He heard heavy rapier blades cross and part, thrust and parry in the vicious, deadly dance he knew and loved. Feet slithered about the smooth stone floor. Edge scraped raspingly on edge till the basket hilts clanged one against the other, and a sudden panting silence fell.

Then a reedy old man's voice, slightly bored, formally declared:

16

"Nothing either way, gentlemen. No hit on either side."

Castlemayne swung round the wooden screen and stepped into the long, high-vaulted chamber.

Two rows of clustered pillars ran the length of the great hall, rising to a complex system of interlocking arches and free-soaring hammer-beam rafters high above. Faded tapestries covered the ancient walls in some places. Elsewhere there was only rough gray stone. Here and there a heavy piece of furniture stood back against the wall. On the dais at the rear end of the long chamber stood the high seat, where Lord Henry Traherne presided at dinner, when trestle tables were set up and half a hundred guests thronged the hall. Above the gleaming brass wall sconces, antique shields and coats of arms marched sedately around the walls. Higher still, narrow gothic windows admitted the wintry light of that Christmas morning.

Smocked, shag-haired children played and hid among the pillars. A lounging servingman or two dawdled at their work, polishing the brass wall sconces or sweeping up the hall. A favorite mastiff drowsed by the Earl's high seat. But Castlemayne had eyes only for the two locked sword blades, and the young men who held them.

To one side of the great hall, in the shadow of an open staircase a cluster of gaudily clad youths watched eagerly as the rapier fighters poised to resume their combat. A black-robed, slack-bellied old man with longish gray hair stepped forward gravely to interject his own blade between the two locked weapons.

At the first touch of the old man's sword, the two combatants sprang apart, both breathing hard. Their loose-flowing white shirts were plastered to their backs with perspiration. Their well-groomed hands, lacy at the wrist and glittering with rings, gripped their sword hilts moistly. Their padded trunk hose were brightly patterned and paned, their thigh-length stockings ribbon-gartered at the knee. They were courtiers to their fingertips, mirrors of the latest fashion, and as conscious of their finery as a pair of peacocks.

The young man nearer Castlemayne—a plump, soft-featured youth—paused briefly to dab at his forehead with a tiny handkerchief, which he then tucked back into the band of his padded breeches. The other man observed him narrowly, tensing for the attack. He was a sharp-featured gallant with small, rabbity moustaches and an elegantly embroidered shirt. A single jewel gleamed in his left ear.

The gray-bearded judge grounded his point with care, blinking rheumy eyes complacently.

Quick as an arrow striking to the butt, the ferret-faced youth closed the measure, lunging, driving in his blade. The thrust impacted solidly upon his unprepared opponent's rib cage, just below the heart. The blunted rapier, rigid as a poker, sent the other man staggering backward with a cry of pain.

"Hit!" intoned the aged judge, crisply official now.

A raucous cheer went up from the little knot of courtiers in bright doublets and particolored sleeves. But the children played on oblivious, and the servants did not bother to look up from their idling.

"You've broken the skin, Cousin Robert," said the short, pudgy gentleman petulantly. "Damn me if you haven't."

"I'm mightily sorry, Cousin Wilton," his elegant opponent responded insincerely. "Single rapiers are uncommon treacherous things. But let us have a bout or two with swords and daggers, and I've no doubt you shall have your revenge."

"A bout by all means, Cousin Robert," called Castlemayne, "though I'll lay cockfighter's odds on it the end will be no different."

The little group of gallants looked up as he strode toward them. Castlemayne's cloak was flung wide, his long rapier swung easily at his side. His thin cheeks were flaming from the winter wind. As he sauntered up the hall, glancing familiarly about him, there was more than a hint of a swagger in his walk.

"Walter Castlemayne," murmured the parchment-cheeked old man in academic black. His tone was low and oddly speculative.

"Good Master Norton!" Castlemayne returned the salutation cheerfully. "By God, there's nothing ever changes here at Exmoor!"

"Best things change least, Master Castlemayne." The aged scholar sniffed. "But you are welcome back to Exmoor nonetheless, I'm sure." He inclined his head with dignity to the newcomer's sweeping bow.

"And good Cousin Robert!" Castlemayne turned back to the ferret-faced fencer with the jewel in his ear, who was in fact no kin at all of his. "I have not seen you these half-dozen Christmases, coz. Five years ago at least, and in this very hall, accepting his lordship's hospitality for the season!"

Robert Naseby, perspiring freely from the exercise, cross at the interruption, controlled his irritation with an effort. "Indeed, sir, indeed, good cousin—" He launched into an elaborately flowery, courtierlike greeting.

He was not halfway through it when Castlemayne's riding companion followed him into the hall. The euphuistic salutation stalled in a tangle of alliterative paradoxes as everybody's Cousin Robert labored desperately to recall that unkempt orange hair, that square-cut countryman's face. For a courtier to forget a face—unthinkable.

Castlemayne allowed the would-be perfect courtier to flounder for a long unhappy minute before he let him off the hook.

"Cousin Robert, this is my kinsman Harry Langland. I don't believe you have the honor of his acquaintance. Harry and I," he added with a chuckle, "have done much hunting in each other's company of late."

"Hunting, sir?" said Naseby guardedly, now thoroughly confused and irritated.

"Aye—hunting of Spaniards in the Netherlands! Hunting of Leaguers in the provinces of France!" Then, with a quick ironic smile: "Harry, this is Robert Naseby. A young gentleman of high hopes and resolution."

Walter Castlemayne had been many days on the long cold

road, with no company but the glumly practical Harry to listen
to his sallies. He was glad to have an audience again. And he
had no great love for Robert Naseby, the would-be perfect
courtier.

Harry bowed, with more goodwill than grace. Cousin Robert
responded sourly, with impeccable form and no warmth whatever. Naseby had never been in the war-ravaged lands beyond
the seas, nor ever met a Spaniard in the field.

"Master Humphrey Norton," Castlemayne continued cheerfully, "the Solon and Silenus of this place, soul of wit and master of the revels. And—gentlemen!" He encompassed Cousin
Robert's plump antagonist and the garishly clad young spectators in one expansive gesture. He and his kinsman bowed
together, their right legs gracefully extended, extravagantly
flourishing their high-crowned feathered hats.

"But I see the noble art of fencing has penetrated even so
far into the country as this, Cousin Robert," he continued, his
eyes shining with sudden purpose. "Excellent, excellent. We
must have a bout before the holidays are over. And with you
too, sir, of course," he added, smiling broadly at the lumpish
Wilton, bedraggled in his sweat-soaked shirt, sword and dagger
dangling from his puffy, bright-ringed hands. "You'll make a
somewhat broader target than I am. But I'm sure your strength
is at least proportionate."

Wilton winced but could conceive no answer in time to in-
terrupt the smooth-flowing courtier's patter. It was a sort of aimless blarneying at which Castlemayne excelled.

"But tell me, Cousin Robert," Castlemayne went on, "what's
your school, then? Italianate? Spanish? Or even," he added with
mock horror, "even good old-fashioned English sword-and-
buckler play, perhaps?"

"The celebrated Master Silver still speaks loud enough for
swords and bucklers, sir!" snapped a ringleted dandy in a peascod
doublet leaning against the wall beneath the stair, supercilious
and superior. "He and his brother do most determinedly main-

tain the honor of the English broadsword and the cutting edge.
They teach it still in London."

"Aye, and your edged blade is a manlier thing," a stocky, hot-
eyed youth interjected, "than this needlepoint rapier or tuck
or however your Frenchmen call it now."

Nothing so lit up the faces of these tense, overdressed young
men in their gaudy doublets and garish neck ruffs as talk of
fighting. They clustered about the stranger, eagerly debating the
merits of the old broadsword and the new-fashioned rapier.

"Your rapier may prick a man a dozen times," snorted one,
"and he fight on. But a single blow with the cutting edge can
cripple a limb and end your fight at a stroke."

"Depend upon the edge," opined another, "and you'll live
to brag of it beside your grandchildren's fireplace. Your rapier
fighters do not live so long."

Castlemayne smiled broadly, one bony hand resting on the
hilt of his own long Spanish rapier as he spoke. "And how say
you, Cousin Robert? Will you also champion *mandritta* over
the *stoccata*, and good old ways over these innovations from
abroad?"

"Why, sir, there are many answers to all questions," Naseby
began cautiously, "and some questions that have no answers at
all. Yet in fine, when all is said and done, sir"—he bowed to
Castlemayne, who was cocking a quizzical eyebrow—"I must
admit to the view that the ancient style of striking with the
blade's edge has about it a chivalrous grace and a particular
efficacy—"

"Staunchly said, sir!" exclaimed Castlemayne, clapping him
on the back. "I like a man of conviction. Though as it happens,
my own opinion in the matter runs clean contrary."

"Indeed, cousin," said Naseby hastily, "an honorable dis-
agreement between gentlemen is no disgrace to either, but a
sign of breadth and toleration in both—"

"By God, I do like your spirit, coz! No disgrace at all, especially when the question may be so easily settled as this one."

"Your pardon, cousin?" Robert Naseby licked his lips.

"We'll have a bout or two right here and now, by our Lady! A friendly bout to test the two conflicting theories, do you see." Castlemayne beamed reassuringly at his audience, and began at once to unhook his sword and hangers.

"But you've been riding many hours today already," Naseby protested quickly. "A weary business in the snow—"

"Nothing like a few hours in the saddle to put a man in marvelous need of exercise," Castlemayne assured him. He flung his traveling cloak to his kinsman Harry.

The latter stepped close to mutter something in his ear.

"Is this your prudent conduct?" whispered Harry Langland irritably. "Is this the judicious new Castlemayne you boasted of from Exeter to Taunton? Is it even common sense, for God's sake?"

"Neither prudent nor judicious," Castlemayne confessed, still grinning cheerfully. "But I'll feel the better for it. And be so much the more able to put on a sober countenance for his lordship presently."

Harry shrugged and turned away.

In less than two minutes Walter Castlemayne stood stripped to his white silk shirt, his scarlet slops and hose. Passing his own weapon off to Harry, he accepted old Master Norton's bated blade. Hefted it, tested its balance and grip, accustoming his wrist and forearm to its lighter weight. Then extended an imperious left hand to his grumbling comrade. Harry filled it with his own dagger, which was of a length with those the fencers had been using.

Castlemayne turned quickly then to face his two antagonists, both still with bated weapons in their hands. Fell into a half crouch, flinging his unruly hair back out of his eyes. Slipped his thumb and forefinger over the crossbar onto the blade—a fencer's trick to increase control of the weapon.

And spoke, equally to Robert Naseby and to Wilton.

"Gentlemen?" he challenged.

At that moment, the Lady Arabella Traherne had come through the low archway at the stair's head and looked down on Walter Castlemayne.

ii

She stood by the doorway, gazing down at the tableau in the great hall below her.

The little group of gaily clad courtiers were familiar enough. Cousin Robert and his fencing friends had begun to arrive as much as a week before Christmas, eager to enjoy his lordship's hospitality. But the tall young man who confronted them with a rapier in his hand was another matter altogether.

Castlemayne's naturally high color, heightened by the chill December air, contrasted dramatically with the fierce mane of white-blond hair that curled above his forehead and lay thick on the back of his neck. His long West Country jaw was deeply cleft, the notch repeated in the lower lip, giving him a hard, dangerous look at times. But the wide mouth smiled easily, with much good humor and more than a touch of cheerful raillery. He was a man who would be noticed in any company.

But there was something else about him that held the Lady Arabella's gaze. A touch of the familiar in the eyes, the hands. Had she not seen that smile before? Years ago, when she—

Then suddenly the frozen tableau below her exploded into violent action.

With an unintelligible oath, young Wilton rushed upon Castlemayne.

Pummeled, laughed at, snubbed publicly, the plumpish youth had had enough from Naseby, and more than enough from this mocking stranger. Charging like a bear broken loose, he swung his blade up and in at his opponent's flank. He'd give this Castlemayne a bruise or two to sleep on this night, by God!

Arabella's hand flew to her mouth. She would have cried out, had there been time. But it was all over in three seconds of blurred action.

Castlemayne's dagger barely touched the flashing blade. His body swayed back no more than the necessary inch or two. Yet Wilton's stroke flashed harmlessly past him, and Castlemayne's own thrust drove in unopposed, to slam unmercifully into his assailant's chest.

Thin cloth and fatty flesh puckered about the impacting point. Wilton went flying back against the nearest clustered pillar, caromed off it, slipped, and fell in a tangle of sword and dagger and ungraceful limbs.

Shouts of jeering laughter burst from half-a-dozen throats, his boon companions loudly enjoying his discomfiture. The liveried servingmen looked up from their nominal labors at so violent a fall. The mastiff drowsing by the high seat was up and staring, stiff-legged, its wet nose quivering. Even the children paused briefly at their games to point and giggle.

Wilton scrambled to his feet, breathing with difficulty, and staggered off to sag against the nearest wall, his puffy face pink with chagrin.

"Master Castlemayne is a certified master of the art of defense, you know," Arabella heard old Humphrey Norton murmur grudgingly to the nearest spectator. "A student of Master Rocco, in London. Fought his master's bout at Hampton Court this past autumn, against the famous Italian master Saviolo. By my information, Castlemayne won seven of nine bouts."

"Master of fence!" the word went round below. The most urbane young gallant pursed his lips. None of these unfledged courtiers had ever seen a master of fence before.

Castlemayne! thought the girl at the stairhead with a rush of sudden warmth. Of course it was Walter. The same eyes, the same wide smiling mouth. But taller, and so much broader in the shoulders.

Castlemayne and Cousin Robert now faced each other in the rapier fighter's partial crouch, swords and daggers poised. They circled slowly, watching each other.

Robert Naseby's gaze was sharp, his points held steady. Yet he trembled inwardly. He was possessed of the courtier's greatest fear—the terror of public humiliation.

The blades were blunted; he need fear no physical wound. But embarrassment, disgrace, damage to that precious reputation he called his honor could destroy him far more surely than any wound. For his honor was his operating capital. Without his honor, the ambitious courtier was little better than a bankrupt in the devious world of influence and court intrigue in which he moved.

Behind his smiling eyes, Castlemayne's feelings were somewhat simpler—and far more sheerly physical. He felt pleasure in the strength of his own young body, quick and powerful as a hunting tiger. He exulted in the ribbed weight of sword and dagger hilts, loosely yet surely gripped in his long fingers and hard palms. His knees and shoulders tingled with the thrill of impending violence. Rationally, he had always known Cousin Robert Naseby for a fawning hypocrite, fair game for any better man. But his reactions now were largely visceral, the elemental joy of a fighting animal about to indulge its lust for combat. His white teeth smiled wickedly. The blood pounded in his veins.

"Come on then, sir," he said cheerfully, "and show us your *mandritta!*"

Like a metal spring suddenly released, Robert Naseby leaped at him. His left-hand weapon deftly deflected Castlemayne's rapier. With his right, he aimed a furious blow, half cut, half thrust, at his opponent's face.

The heavy steel blade, bated though it was, could have laid Castlemayne's cheek open to the bone. But with a quick step back and to the right, he was out of reach. The point whistled by, an inch or two beyond the tip of his nose.

Close in now, Naseby jabbed at Castlemayne's kidneys with his dagger. Castlemayne swayed easily back again, out of harm's way.

"Watch your distance, Cousin Robert, do," he murmured, like a teacher with a singularly inept pupil. Sidestepping almost casually, parrying with negligent ease, the master of fence seemed rather to be presenting a demonstration than fighting a serious bout.

Old Humphrey Norton chewed his gums and ticked off the strokes after his internal manual of theory. He nodded reluctant approval of their technical perfection. Master Norton was an admirer of expertise, even in the barbarous craft of swordplay.

The young men swore delightedly and whispered to each other as they watched. Such sport had never come their way before, here in the wilds of Devonshire.

Castlemayne dodged easily under an ill-timed swipe. He took two long steps back, opening the distance, and stood once more out of reach. Then he looked up and saw the Lady Arabella Traherne standing at the head of the stairs.

He saw a slight young girl in a burgundy gown. Honey-colored hair, piled high on ivory combs, gleamed in the pale morning light. Her eyes were glowing with excitement. Her lips were parted, bare of all cosmetics. She had slim shoulders, small breasts below an open ruff, and the tiniest waist he had ever seen on any woman.

To Walter Castlemayne at twenty-four, she was a vision of perfection.

Robert Naseby, seeing his opponent momentarily distracted, tensed for a sudden onslaught. Castlemayne simply ignored him. He lowered his sword and dagger and bowed very low to the Lady Arabella. The girl began a curtsey, then remembered her exalted position. She was an Earl's daughter, after all, and her father's official hostess for these holidays. She inclined her fair head regally instead.

"And now, gentlemen," the tall swordsman declared, turning briskly back to his audience, "the offensive mode, and the advantages of the thrusting point!"

The clang of swords, the thud of feet, and cries from the onlookers filled the hall as Master Castlemayne attacked. He seemed almost to surround his enemy, to be attacking him from all sides at once. In seconds Naseby was backpedaling wildly, reeling driven up the hall, with Castlemayne's rapier continually within inches of his eyes.

The young gentlemen whooped and followed, with children and servingmen scampering after, the mastiff barking about their legs. Harry Langland followed more slowly, looking bored and out of sorts. Last came Humphrey Norton, puffing and grunting, but as eager as the rest to keep up with the excitement. Even the Lady Arabella got halfway down the stairs before she remembered her dignity and came to a straining halt, her eyes still following the fencers.

The rout fetched up at the far end of the hall, against the great oak screen, with its paneling and linenfold carving and the antlers high above. Feeling his back come up against the barrier, Naseby lashed out and rolled off to his right, with Castlemayne in close pursuit. They passed between two pillars on the south side of the hall, still fighting, and came at last to a cul-de-sac, a blind corner of the room. Castlemayne feigned a thrust with his rapier and threatened with the dagger, and his victim was safely maneuvered into the angle of the two walls, hopelessly trapped.

Master Castlemayne stepped back again, breathing heavily himself, but smiling still.

In the momentary silence, the sound of voices and footsteps could be heard from the passage behind the tall oak screen. Then a stooped figure in a leather jerkin emerged, carrying a heavy traveling portmanteau on his back. One-eyed Luke the stablehand, Arabella noticed mechanically, her eyes still fixed on Castlemayne. Castlemayne himself did not look at the shambling servingman at all. Nor at the three black-clad figures— two men and a woman—who followed Luke into the hall.

"Now, gentlemen," the young master of the art of fencing said coolly, "for a final demonstration of the superiority of the thrusting point. In the following display, you will see not a single cut, nor any use of the edge at all for an offensive stroke.

This particular demonstration," he added mysteriously, "is known as the button ward."

He saluted his opponent jauntily with his sword's point, fell into the fencer's bending stance again, and in one quick stride closed the distance. Their blades clashed once more in the tingling silence, this time with a businesslike definitive ring.

Down the front of Cousin Robert's white silk shirt ran a row of four small emerald buttons. They were entirely functionless, simply sewn to the shirtfront for decorative effect, like the lace at the neck and cuffs. In his first uncoiling thrust, Castlemayne slipped his point above the other's desperate guard to impact solidly upon the topmost of these bright green baubles. Naseby staggered back against the wall. Shouts greeted the clear hit.

"*Imbroccata*, gentlemen," said Master Norton, irrepressibly didactic, "or thrust above the adversary's guard, in which—"

The husky groomsman shuffled slowly up the staircase, bowed under the portmanteau, bobbing his shaggy head obsequiously at the Lady Arabella. She realized vaguely that the black-clad trio to whom the baggage must belong had paused in the shadow of the oaken screen to watch the conclusion of the bout.

Castlemayne had opened the distance and lowered his rapier, allowing his shaken antagonist a moment to recover. Then, with a crisp announcement, he stepped in to reengage. In the uncertain light and tight, cramped quarters, Naseby hacked and parried furiously, his face dark with rage. But in three passes Castlemayne's blade again slipped through the other's defenses and clicked sharply against the second button, counting downward from the throat. Cries and a muffled curse greeted the startling duplication of his former feat.

"*Stoccata*," explained Master Norton, "the classic thrust beneath—"

A third time the rapiers crossed, blue-black streaks in the dimness among the pillars. The spectators, grasping Castlemayne's intent, hunched forward, rapt. Quickly now, Naseby's desperation betrayed him into error. Almost at once, Castlemayne's point came twisting in, backhanded, from the left, to strike the base of the third button. The button snapped off the sweat-soaked blouse and went rolling off across the floor.

"*Punta riversa,*" whispered Humphrey Norton huskily. And then fell silent.

The thinner of the two men in the shadow of the high carved screen bent to whisper something to the other. The woman's skirts moved restlessly.

Castlemayne allowed his victim a full minute to breathe this time. For Cousin Robert, the respite only prolonged the nightmare of his humiliation. But no one had any time to laugh at him now. The flushed, excited gallants, the children, the servingmen, even the gray-bearded judge, were as mesmerized as Arabella by Walter Castlemayne's wild talent.

It passed the point of bearing. Robert Naseby, galvanized to action, sprang out of his corner at last, thrusting with all the strength of his thighs and the reach of his arm at the maddeningly inviolate shirtfront of his foe. Once again his enemy eluded him, once again his rapier passed through empty air. He recovered and whirled around, glad at least to be out in the free space of the hall. He found Castlemayne politely waiting for him.

The arrogant young man closed in then, smooth and sure and deadly. With three feints and a single thrust, he hit the fourth button. An instant later, with a dazzling combination of sword and dagger play, he twisted Robert Naseby's rapier from his clutching hand and sent it arching down the hall to clatter on the stone floor, a dozen yards away.

There was no sound at all. Not the tiniest round-eyed child moved as Robert Naseby's rapier rolled to a stop and lay rocking tinnily on the smooth stone floor.

"I thank you, cousin, for the bout," said Walter.

He reversed his bated rapier and handed it back to old Master Norton, bowed briefly to the group in general, and turned upon his heel. They all watched him stride off up the hall, followed by his resigned kinsman with his cloak and doublet. It was pure theater, and Castlemayne, passing out through the wide arch at the far end of the room, relished every moment of it.

"How did he do that?" A dark-haired little girl in a blue gown broke the silence.

"Every single button," whispered the hot-eyed, stocky youth, whose voice could generally be heard half across the castle.

"The Italian masters of the art of defense," croaked Humphrey Norton, recovering his voice and his authoritative tone at once, "do boast that they will touch any man upon every several button at will. But I have never seen it done. Nor did I ever think to see an English swordsman do it."

"And Walter—Master Castlemayne has done it!" The company in the hall below saw their hostess for the first time, and there was a commotion of bowing and scraping. "I mean," the girl stumbled on, "that—that was Walter, was it not, Master Norton? The lad who used—"

"Master Walter Castlemayne, my lady," the old factotum assented with pedantic precision. "A young gentleman of Cornwall. Learned enough for a courtier—he has been to Cambridge. And to the court. And to the wars. A swordsman, my lady," he concluded dryly. "A swordsman by profession."

"Not too bad a swordsman either," murmured a flat, foreign-sounding voice. "For an Englishman."

A second time that morning, all eyes swung to focus on a party of late arrivals. The thin man who had just spoken stood now beside the restless woman. The other man, older and more solidly built, stood alone.

The couple, Arabella saw with some surprise, were in fact foreigners—Italians, by the look of them. Both olive-skinned and dark-eyed. Both dressed in the dignified black affected in the sun-bright cities of the south. But it was the other man who held her eyes.

"Sir Malcolm Devereux," intoned Master Norton, seeing him for the first time. "You are welcome, sir." And then, turning back to the Lady Arabella on the stair: "It is Captain Devereux, my lady."

Captain Devereux, she thought confusedly. Of course. Her father had said something. Baffled, blushing, she could not think what. She could only stare.

He did not seem particularly frightening at first glance. He was a thickset man of perhaps forty years with a black military spade beard. He wore a heavy traveling cloak and rapier, dark doublet and hose, wide-topped black boots with snow still melting on them. He stood in an oddly spraddling stance, deep-chested and hard-bellied, with powerful arms somewhat longer than his stature warranted. His skin, she noticed, seemed unnaturally pale, his beard and beetling brows as black as coal.

It was only as he approached the stairway where she stood, as he bowed heavily to her stammered greeting, that Arabella felt an icy tremor up her spine.

A striking face, she thought nervously, and then: a fearful face, dear Lord! The lips were thick and hard, set in a permanent expression of contempt for everything and everyone about him. The nose was hooked like a falcon's beak, the eyes harsh and arrogant, empty of all feeling. The eyes were strangely colorless beneath the thick black brows.

With a brusque gesture, Captain Devereux presented his lieutenant and the lady. "Messer Lodovico Marsigliano and his lady wife"—was there the faintest unnecessary stress on the title? —"Signora Bianca." Messer Lodovico bowed with that exquisite foreign grace no Englishman could master. He was a painfully emaciated, suavely elegant man with a thin goatee and pencil-fine moustaches. Signora Bianca seemed his polar opposite—a flamboyantly full-breasted woman, lushly rounded at the hips, her dark gown slashed and padded in the latest fashion. She curtseyed very properly to my lady, her dark eyes cast down.

"You—you are welcome to my father's house," Arabella heard her own voice stammering. "All of you—most welcome."

The somber trio made their calm obeisances once more and passed by her up the stair.

The Lady Arabella, vexed at her own foolishness, lifted her skirts and raised her chin and descended smiling into the hall, the hostess of Exmoor once more. The overdressed young men quickly clustered around her. The children shrieked and went back to their playing among the ancient clustered pillars. Outside the high narrow windows, thick wet flakes of snow began to fall once more over the castle and the forest, the moorland and the sea beyond.

Christmas was begun at Exmoor.

~ Three ~

Glitter of Gold

i

So Christmas Day had passed, and Christmas night had come.
That night, which was to end at the door of Lady Arabella's
bedchamber, had begun with a roar of high festival in her father's hall.

> "And all the bells on earth shall ring,
>   On Christmas Day, on Christmas Day.
> And all the bells on earth shall ring,
>   On Christmas Day in the morning.
>
> And all the angels in heaven shall sing,
>   On Christmas Day, on Christmas Day.
> And all the angels in heaven shall sing,
>   On Christmas Day in the morning.
>
> Then let us all rejoice amain,
>   On Christmas Day, on Christmas Day.
> Then let us all rejoice amain,
>   On Christmas Day in the *mo*rning!"

"Hoo! Hoo! More! More!" The din of pounding flagons, the
bray and shriek of laughter rattled windows far above. Tarnished
silver goblets tilted, sopping whiskers, sprinkling gorgeous velvet
gowns with telltale drops of wine.

Scores of joyful gentlefolk lined the long, feast-littered tables.

33

Children scampered underfoot, dogs quarreled in corners. Picked bones, scraps of meat and fowl were everywhere, with spatterings of tallow, sauces, blood. Silver dishes gleamed amid bowls of red berries and spiky leaves. Green-liveried servants passed quickly among the revelers with jugs of wine and brimming tankards of good English beer.

"O my lord—O my lord—" A helpless fat wench gasped with laughter at a jeweled, drunken courtier's antics. Her somber husband, in dim russet, stiffened his mouth, eyes opaque, hiding the red glow in the brain. A lantern-jawed country squire regaled his neighbors with a ribald jest. A fat merchant's face emerged from a silver tankard, hooting, squealing, hiccuping, dripping brown ale on a soiled ruff. Above the uproar, in the minstrel gallery, viols, lutes, recorders, and tambourines struck up another cheerful carol.

His lordship the Earl of Exmoor presided at the high table on the dais, smiling rather vaguely through his ginger-colored whiskers down upon his guests. As the meats were cleared away and the wine and ale went round again, Lord Henry nodded to his steward. The music stopped, and an unobtrusive hand roused old Humphrey Norton to his duty. Somewhat intoxicated, with purple stains on his lace collar, Master Norton rose a bit unsteadily above the joyful throng.

"My lords and ladies, gentlemen and gentlewomen—"

"Peace ho! Hear his royal highness, the Prince of Purpoole! Heed our venerable lord of misrule! Speak, old master of the revels—we all attend!"

"Welcome you all to Exmoor Castle," Norton proceeded serenely, "and to my lord of Exmoor's hospitality for these holidays. I shall not take your time and your attention from his lordship's bounty to expatiate long upon it—"

An isolated drunken cheer, a hush, a laugh.

"Let us simply begin then with an entertainment provided by some of our young gentlefolk." Written and choreographed by himself, though custom forbade his mentioning it. "It is a masque in the latest court style, entitled *Antique Chivalry,* or *The Nine Noble Knights and Their Ladies!"*

Master Norton bowed and sat. Expectant cheers and clapping filled the air. Flutes and viols played and then, to the beat of the tambourine, the masquers strutted into the hall.

Out from behind the paneled screen at the end of the great hall they marched, a brilliant cavalcade. Two by two parading in, fantastically costumed in plumes and furbelows vaguely suggestive of past ages and exotic lands. Gilded armor spangled with stars, bejeweled helmets and barbaric lion skins, floor-length veils, peacock fans, and a Turkish turban with a great green gem.

The wives of country squires gaped. Young gallants nodded familiarly at all this courtly magnificence. But all eyes were drawn to the gorgeous figures of Queen Guinevere and Sir Lancelot leading the procession, both costumed in crimson shot with gold. And many mouths whispered to briskly nodding ears: "The Lady Arabella—and Master Walter Castlemayne!"

The amateur entertainers began with a formal, stately measure, as became their noble theme. Plumed heads nodded, red-slippered feet traced the complex figures more or less precisely. The gentlemen's gartered knees and the ladies' swishing skirts, held stiff by farthingales, moved elegantly to solemn, pompous music.

The audience applauded. Solid country gentry murmured approbation. "Is it not lovely then?" "And so little time they had to set it out!"

The masquers ended the dance in a great square fronting the crowded tables, bowed and curtseyed, and began a lilting tune:

> "We speak for antique chivalry,
>   For noble knights of old,
> When ladies all were sweet and pure,
>   And knights were always bold.

We sing of better days than these,
  Of golden days long gone,
When love was always true and pure,
  And fields were always won."

Castlemayne and Arabella stood hand in hand in the center
of the first rank, swaying and singing to the melancholy music
of the lutes. And for that magical time at least, they believed
what they sang, that there had indeed been better, purer,
nobler days than their own Machiavellian age.

"When Lancelot died for his gracious Queen,
  The lovely Guinevere;
When Orlando ran mad for Angelique,
  That was his only fere;

When Caesar conquered a wide empire,
  And Alexander a world;
When Egyptian queen and Persian dame
  The banner of love unfurled;

When David the King loved Bathsheba;
  When Joshua's trumpet called;
When knights could fight and ladies would love . · ."

The music changed again, the tempo faster still, and Castlemayne and Arabella took the center of the hall to execute a
graceful galliard. As they stepped and turned and leaped to
the skirling tune, eye after eye lit up with admiration. Drunk-
ards forgot their cups to watch the dazzling couple. Babblers
staunched their flow of wit to stare. All the young girls envied
Arabella. Every courtier curdled with envy of Castlemayne.

The music whirled faster still. They were two flames spinning down the vaulted hall. The audience was rapt. Bustling
servingmen turned in surprise at the unaccustomed stillness at
the tables.

The music ceased with a clash of tambourines. Lancelot

bowed to Guinevere, and Guinevere curtseyed low. There was a moment of absolute silence. Then hanging shields rattled high upon the walls, and a solitary bat fled frantically among the blackened rafters as the jammed and joyful tables clapped and cheered and shouted.

The Earl himself started out of his meditations, blinked at the tumult, and joined in the applause. It was a triumph, complete and unalloyed, for Walter Castlemayne and for the blushing, happy girl on his arm.

ii

"Little Robert the Devil himself, by Jesus Christ," Harry Langland whispered in his kinsman's ear as Castlemayne sank into his seat midway down the second table. "Now what does he so far from London?"

His face still flushed with the exertion, the music and the cheering, Castlemayne turned to follow his kinsman's gaze.

Seated beside the Earl of Exmoor at the table on the dais was a dwarfish little man in black. Sharp-featured, with calculating eyes and a small pointed beard. And visibly, though not painfully, deformed—a slightly twisted spine, one leg seeming shorter than the other. Yet he sat with absolute composure, calmly certain of his preeminence. It was Robert Cecil, as clever and influential a man as the Queen's court knew.

Master Cecil was the son and heir apparent to the great Lord Treasurer Burghley, for two decades and more the Queen's chief minister of state. His father's brains, his father's patience, his father's unrivaled patronage and influence—all were his. And little Robert Cecil had made good use of his advantages. At thirty, he was a Privy Councillor already, and one of the fastest-rising men at Queen Elizabeth's court. Embittered enemies called him Robert the Devil behind his back. But no one called the little master of court intrigue anything but Sir or Master Cecil to his face.

And what does he here indeed, wondered Castlemayne, so far from the Council and the Queen?

Master Cecil was holding out two glittering artifacts for the Earl's inspection. In his right hand he held a heavy silver crucifix, fully a foot high. The cross was outlined in shining diamonds, each of the five wounds of Christ marked by a blood-red ruby. In his left hand he gripped a barbaric figure of pure gold, glowing in the candlelight. Its stubby arms and legs were gleaming semicircles, its eyes and mouth gaping holes through which Master Cecil's black velvet doublet showed incongruously austere. The blue-white radiance of the diamonds, the dull yellow glow of gold lit up every face at the high table. And more and more faces lower down were turning that way too.

"As you see, gentlemen," Cecil was saying, "there is good reason for my coming. It is surely intolerable that her Majesty, and those patriotic gentlemen who have invested with her in this expedition, should lose their shares of such returns as these —to common thieves."

Understanding clicked in Castlemayne's brain. "The Great Carrack?" he asked the grizzled squire on his left. He got a brief nod in return. Neither the young man nor the old took his eyes for an instant from the gleaming treasures that Master Cecil held up like sacred vessels in his pale slender hands.

All through the autumn, London had talked of nothing else but the capture of this huge treasure ship, the *Madre de Dios*. It was one of the richest prizes ever towed into an English port. Rumor swore that the cargo of the Great Carrack, as she was soon familiarly known, would run to several hundred thousand pounds. Fantastic profits for the Queen, and for the noblemen who had outfitted the privateering expedition that brought her in.

The Lords of the Privy Council, Castlemayne remembered now, had dispatched Robert Cecil, riding post to Devon, to protect those profits from thieving sailors and light-fingered landsmen. From Plymouth, where the great ship lay, it was no more than a day's ride to Exmoor Castle, even in winter.

"I confiscated this," said Cecil, raising high the jeweled cross, "this papistical icon, from an innkeeper near the Plymouth docks. He said it was a family heirloom!" General laughter greeted this absurdity. Such a piece would make any tavernkeeper's fortune to the third generation. "And this Indian idol from Peru I found in a Jew peddler's pack of trinkets. Said he had it of a seaman for forty shillings cash. Had no idea where the seaman got it." Louder laughter still. Wet lips and shining eyes. The yellow beaten gold, the silver, the sparkling gems seemed to illumine every face now, from the Earl's great seat to far below the salt.

Harry swore softly, passionately. And Castlemayne rose suddenly in his place.

"Truly it is a propitious omen for the success of your own enterprise in the spring, my lord!"

Lord Henry Traherne turned to stare uncertainly at the young man who thus thrust himself upon his lordship's notice. He blinked once or twice before he recognized the cavalier in scarlet. Then he smiled benignly, and responded. "Ah—Walter Castlemayne, is it? Welcome once again to Exmoor."

Castlemayne bowed very low and seriously. There was all due reverence in his manner, but cool self-respect as well. A self-confidence that was almost overbold.

Lord Henry Traherne, second Earl of Exmoor, was not a man of overwhelming presence—or even of any immediately discernible dignity. He was a portly gentleman in his fifties, of middle height and mild appearance, with an unimpressive gingery beard and almost scraggly moustache. His eyes were watery and lackluster, often vaguely out of focus, as if the person before him were hardly there at all. His mouth was small and pink, his small pink tongue forever darting out to moisten his lips. His round pug nose glowed a dull maroon, the effect of a perpetual sniffling cold. He always looked nervously uncertain, as though he had forgotten something and couldn't remember what.

Indecision was in fact the great Earl's besetting sin. When Saint Peter should fling wide the gates of heaven—so ran the jest—his lordship of Exmoor would debate the pros and cons of crossing the threshold of salvation. Lord Henry Traherne was never certain, never sure. Yet he always seemed to make the right decision in the end, and he grew richer year by year.

"I thank my lord for his kind welcome," said young Castlemayne, a sudden glitter in his eyes. "And I dare hope that next Christmas holy days I may come again to Exmoor, bringing some small recompense for your lordship's goodness. Some slight increase of honor to your lordship's noble name. And more also of those bright baubles yonder"—he waved almost casually at the golden idol and the silver crucifix—"to grace your lordship's hall."

Over the feathered hats and starched wheel ruffs of a dozen diners, he looked Lord Henry in the face.

"So much at least I dare to promise, sire, if the *Golden Fortune* should be mine."

Faces swiveled to stare at him in astonishment. Harry groaned softly at his elbow. But Castlemayne had already turned to Master Cecil. To Robert the Devil, the shrewdest intriguer at the court of Queen Elizabeth.

"His lordship," the younger man explained, quite unnecessarily, "builds even now a warship for the Queen's good service. The *Golden Fortune*—a name of good omen. You yourself may have seen the vessel rising in Deptford Yards, plank by plank and spar by spar, all this autumn past. I at least have observed her often. And to be short, I have fallen so in love with the sweet craft that I am come a humble suitor for her command. You will not think me presumptuous to hope for a happy issue?"

"By no means," said Cecil, polite but noncommittal. "A

gentleman of such skill and reputation as yourself would seem a natural candidate for such a post."

"I hope, sir," pursued Castlemayne, "that should his lordship's choice fall upon myself, her gracious Majesty may be of your mind. Since the Queen's Majesty alone can grant the requisite commission," he added, again with superfluous explicitness.

"I am sure, Master Castelmayne," Cecil responded dryly, "that her Majesty's judgment will prove as sound as it has ever been in such matters."

"I do not doubt it will be so, sir," said Castlemayne, with mounting excitement. "As sound as his lordship of Exmoor's unfailing judgment of affairs." He bowed to the Earl as he spoke.

"Undoubtedly," said Cecil—and bit his lip to silence. Too late, he saw where this exchange of pleasantries was leading.

"Why then," said Castlemayne, his face lighting up as though he just that moment grasped the consequence, "if I can but win his lordship's magnanimous consent to serve him, I may with some confidence expect a royal commission too?"

There was a stunned silence at the high table.

"I think you may depend upon it, sir," said Master Cecil finally, "that the Lords of the Council and the Queen will not contravene his lordship's judgment in the matter."

"Why, I thank you, sir," answered Castlemayne, bowing with a flourish. "And if you say it, Master Cecil, I am sure it will be so."

It was all beyond belief. Suits of this magnitude were never publicly discussed at all—let alone carried so far toward success before half a hundred pairs of eyes. Such petitions were pursued deviously and in secret, in very private talks, through confidential intermediaries and influential friends. One simply did not beard a great Earl in public or trap a Privy Councillor into a commitment before all the world.

"Madness!" and "My God, he's drunk!" whispered one courtier to another, one bluff squire to his neighbor.

And yet no thunder crashed, no lightning flashed from heaven.

Robert Cecil could not of course rebuke a man whom his lordship chose to let pass uncondemned. And then, in his shrewd courtier's mind, Cecil felt a grudging admiration for the other's stroke. A clever opening gambit, Master Castlemayne, he mused, settling back, reaching for his wine. Cleverly conceived and executed. Yet reckless too—perhaps that above all. Had his lordship so much as frowned, Castlemayne's career would have been set five years back—nay, more. And the odds were high against success . . . Cecil pursed his lips above the port. He was a calculating man. He never went against the odds himself.

The Earl, whose judgment now held absolute sway over the destiny of Walter Castlemayne, thought nothing at all definitive. He understood that Castlemayne had secured a fairly binding commitment from the royal government. He felt this gesture of support by so influential a Councillor to be a factor strongly in the young man's favor. But after all, one factor only. One among so many that must be weighed and balanced out before any decision—how he hated that word!—was finally arrived at . . .

Lord Henry sighed and turned away, nibbling at a bit of marzipan. He sniffled and wondered vaguely if he felt a cold coming on.

Walter Castlemayne sank back into his seat, realizing suddenly what he had done. He let his breath escape with a slow, silent *whoosh*.

He had intended to be circumspect, God knew. A mere distant glance, he had thought, at the matter of the Queen's commission. But a sudden wild impulse had swept him far beyond his original intent. Again, again, and even here—the grand, heroic gesture! He shook his head, his thoughts jumbled and confused. By God, it was a moment! exulted half his being. But Harry's right, countered the shrewder part of him, overboldness and a weakness for grand gestures are no qualities for a courtier.

And a courtier he must be, he knew, if he would ever sail the *Golden Fortune* down the Thames that spring and off for the Spanish Main.

"Good Master Castlemayne." Humphrey Norton's reedy tenor intruded on his tumbled thoughts. "Are you by any chance acquainted with Sir Malcolm Devereux?"

"Sir Malcolm Devereux?" repeated Castlemayne, only half hearing.

"Indeed, sir. Sir Malcolm—"

Castlemayne turned to stare at the wrinkled old face at his shoulder.

Devereux. He had of course heard the name. Everyone in England that had ever heard of Drake or Raleigh or Sir Philip Sidney had heard the name of Devereux as well.

Sir Malcolm Devereux was one of the authentic heroes. For twenty years and more he had been fighting England's battles from one end of Europe to the other. Even while the Queen had kept her country prudently at peace, Devereux had fought her enemies in the Netherlands and France, serving as a volunteer in other men's armies. Between these patriotic wars, he had fared south to fight the Turks, defending England's rich trade in the Levant. He had fought in Germany and Poland, in Portugal and even in Spain itself. He was a soldier's soldier, and one of the best.

All or some part of this passed through Castlemayne's mind as he stared up at Master Norton. Aloud, he said only, "I have not the honor of the gentleman's acquaintance, sir. Though I have of course heard—"

"Then, sir, I am sent to bring the two of you together. His

lordship feels that two such redoubtable men of the sword, both friends of his and good servants of the Queen, would be glad of each other's acquaintance."

The blood seemed to move more slowly through Castlemayne's veins. Devereux—here at Exmoor?

Whispers came clearly to his ears now, above the murmur and babble of the diners. Voice after voice took up the low refrain:

"Sir Malcolm Devereux—the great Captain Devereux!"

A new face had appeared at the Earl of Exmoor's right hand at the high table. A dark-browed, black-bearded face, pale in the candlelight, gazing impassively down upon the throng. A brutal face, hook-nosed, thick-lipped. The face of a bravo or a *condottiere,* thought Castlemayne, not of one of Queen Elizabeth's most celebrated captains!

"Sir Malcolm Devereux," Master Norton was announcing ceremoniously. "Master Walter Castlemayne."

Somehow he had followed Humphrey Norton up upon the dais. Somehow he was standing face to face with the Great Captain.

"Master Castlemayne," grated the heavy, spade-bearded face before him. "I have heard of you, sir."

"I am honored, Captain Devereux," said Castlemayne, speaking rather more rapidly than he had intended, "to have come to the attention of so distinguished a commander as yourself."

Both men doffed hats, bent the knee, and bowed. Then they looked each other in the eyes.

The eyes of Sir Malcolm Devereux bored into Walter Castlemayne. Hard, cold, colorless eyes, shadowed by thick brows. Eyes that defied the world to guess what thoughts moved behind them, what harsh passions burned beneath their icy impassivity.

But Castlemayne knew. Beyond any shadow of a doubt, he knew. What else could bring the great Captain Devereux to this desolate corner of Devonshire—but the need of a new command?

iii

The feasting, the music, and the laughter roared on into the night. Cooks, turnspits, kitchen maids labored before the great fires belowstairs. Liveried servingmen scurried up and down the broad stone steps. Casks of wine and ale were emptied out, bins of fruit and cheese and nuts, that the gentlefolk above-stairs might keep the first day of Christmas as befitted a great Earl's dignity.

In the great vaulted hall, old folks chattered and sang and stuffed their ruddy cheeks with still more food and wine. Children drowsed in corners. The young folk drank and laughed —and danced.

Harry Langland swung his partner high in a mighty *saltarello*. He laughed as he felt his strong fingers dig into the flesh of her waist. Drunk now as much with excitement as with his lordship's ale, he even ventured an awkward gallantry.

"By God, Mistress Marsigliano, you're quick as eiderdown in the wind," he said, drawing her to him for the next figure. "There's none to touch you here."

"My lord has such surprising skill in our Italian figures," smiled Messer Lodovico's lady. Bianca Marsigliano spoke in uncertain English, but with a voice of velvet. She looked up at him with dark eyes, the pupils soft with a feather's touch of belladonna.

"Aargh—it's a necessary skill for an Englishman these days, to know the foreign steps. I was not raised on such stuff, that's sure." Harry was an awkward dancer, and he knew it. He was drawn into masques and entertainments only as Castlemayne's kinsman, and to make up the number.

"Ah, but I'm sure Italia could learn much from England too."
The Italian woman's words were the merest courtesy, cover perhaps for his crudeness. Yet there was a boldness in her tone,
a hint of hidden meanings in her eyes, that kindled a sudden
urgency in Harry Langland's loins.

"Alas, mistress, I fear I'm not the Englishman for such a
task. I'm a plain country fellow, that knows only country
matters. All my wisdom is horseflesh and cattle and barnyard
doings, lady."

"But much can be learned, is it not so, from the doings of the
simple barnyard animals?" Again his high-strained ear caught
an ambiguous note. "The famous fablemaker Aesop, now . . ."
She told a risqué tale as they stepped to the spritely music.
Harry, burning with quickly kindled desire, scarcely heard a
word she said.

Bianca felt his lust for her and reveled in it. A strong stallion,
this Englishman! she thought, and dallied with his fingers as
she turned. To dally further would be folly, well she knew.
And yet, she mused, from time to time a woman must . . . be
foolish.

Harry hardly thought at all now. He felt the muscles of her
back slide beneath his fingertips as she swayed and glided to
the music. Watched her round breasts move beneath the
fashionable black satin of her bodice. Felt his own lips go dry
as her painted mouth smiled up at him.

And in so doing found some brief escape from this strange,
unreal world into which he had drifted in the wake of Walter
Castlemayne. Escape from pompous virtue and sententious vice,
from endless words instead of deeds, from involuted wit and
neither-yes-nor-no. Escape into the simple logic of his lust.

By Jesus Christ, come here against me, mistress, and let me
feel—Ah God, but you could bear a man a ways on that, my
sweet cockhorse. Aye me, a foul unnatural world it is where
two such barnyard creatures as we are kept from bedding—by
a spindleshanks Italian's stare!

For Messer Lodovico's eyes were on them, steady and malevolent. He sat at the head of the second table, in his captain's very shadow, skeletal and silent, watching them.

Harry, a famous village brawler and a veteran of two campaigns, was not worried.

"Mistress, you're light as a feather!"

"*Signore,* you are strong as a bull!

A cheerful grin suffused his square-cut face. Her full cheeks dimpled in a smile. They laughed together, in animal enjoyment, and jounced off down the hall in the quick five-step of the dance.

Someone from the buttery scurried up the stairs to the minstrel gallery, carrying wine for the musicians. Red wine in an earthen jar, to slake dry throats and strengthen limping fingers. For a time then, while they drank, the imperious music ceased to drive the young revelers below. The interlude gave Castlemayne and Arabella, flushed and breathing rapidly, time for a moment's quiet talk in the shadow of a clustered pillar.

For Castlemayne had no more thought for Captain Devereux this night than Harry had for Marsigliano. Tomorrow was soon enough to face the challenge of the Great Captain. Tonight he had eyes for Arabella only.

"Tell me then, my lady." He smiled down at her. "How has life fared at Exmoor, while I've been away in the world?"

"Why, as always, Master Castlemayne," she answered him serenely. "One day followeth on another, as the Preacher saith. My Agnes is a bit more grim for conscience, but a bit less strict, so that's all one. Master Norton babbles no more learned nonsense than before, but no less either. The Earl my father is more full of affairs than he was, perhaps, and probably twice as rich. The war makes markets, so he says. But he was always rich and full of affairs. All's the same, and nothing happening at all. Nothing ever really happens here," she said, and sighed extravagantly. "We are so out of the world."

"A quiet country life indeed, my lady, here in the hills of Devon. Idyllic, many men would say. Like shepherd lads and milkmaids in a poem."

He was merely making conversation. The words, he realized, were only an excuse to look at her.

Her face, her bearing, her whole being were so utterly transformed in half-a-dozen years—and yet they were so clearly Arabella still. The honey-colored hair, the delicately pale forehead he knew well enough. But her cheeks had lost their childish fat entirely, were higher and more pointed. He remembered the flaring Welsh nostrils and the wide smiling mouth. But the lower lip was fuller, the smile was different altogether. He knew her and he did not know her. He felt slightly giddy with a mingled sense of discovery and homecoming.

"My lady," he said, after a pause that had grown too long, "has grown up since last we met."

She curtseyed grandly, her golden head cocked up at him at the old familiar angle.

Arabella was struck more by the differences between the boy she had once known and the man before her now. The adolescent's scarecrow hair, the outsized hands and feet were gone. Or rather, the lean, muscular body had grown up to them. How tall he is, she thought, six feet and more, and so broad across the shoulders. His face is thin still, and the jaw as long and sharp. But the wild, haunted yearling look is gone. Or is it only faded, back into those blue, blue eyes of his?

At nineteen, the Lady Arabella was an ardently romantic soul beneath her new, untried sophistication.

"Oh, Walter!" she said suddenly, softly and intensely. "It is so dull here! Birds sing in the spring, bees buzz in summer, the trees turn in autumn, the fields freeze in winter and slow up spring planting! It is monotonous, it is tedious, it is utterly, unbearably, intolerably boring!"

Gone was the polite reserve proper to her station and her

role as hostess. Castlemayne grinned down suddenly at the little girl he had known, stamping a petulant foot at the rain that dared to fall when her ladyship desired to play out of doors.

"Arabella," he said, "you have not changed so much after all since I saw you last."

"Oh, but *you* have!" she said impulsively. "You've traveled so far and seen so much, in the years between! Oh, Walter, tell me about London, and the Queen's Majesty's court, and foreign lands, and the wars, and dueling, and Cambridge—"

"And Saracens and Amazons and the wild Indians of America, you'll be asking next! Little Arabella, your head's as full of fables and foolishness as ever."

She knew he patronized her, played the worldly courtier for her benefit. Such presumption would have infuriated her any day but this. Tonight, somehow, she did not seem to care at all. Her heart even beat more quickly, with something akin to pleasure, when he called her his little Arabella. How she had hated that fond diminutive when he was sixteen and she was but eleven!

The lutes and viols struck up once again, imposing their will upon young hands and feet. Castlemayne and Arabella danced, rediscovering each other.

She moved so gracefully into his arms, and so gracefully away. He looked into her saucy young eyes and remembered birdsnesting and hunting mushrooms and afternoons by the fire, hunched together over romantic tales of ancient chivalry, of King Arthur and his Table Round, of Camelot and Caerleon and all the unforgotten heroes of old times. Then she darted him a backward glance over her shoulder—a shoulder almost bare in the stylish scarlet gown—and a new fire kindled in his belly.

Then it was late, very late that Christmas night. Arabella was gone, withdrawn to her own chamber, obedient to her father's will. Castlemayne sat with Harry, laughing, drinking, talking low and eagerly, while the revelers about them shouted for more wine.

The soul of Walter Castlemayne was exalted with that day's unlikely doings. In the shouting and the laughter of the great hall, he conceived one final *geste* more incredible than any since he had set foot in Exmoor a dozen hours ago.

"A kiss for luck, good Harry! A kiss to seal this day's successes and give us good omen for the morrow! A kiss for an old play-fellow too long away—"

Harry Langland could only curse and watch him go.

∽ Four ∾

The Great Captain

i

"My lord has been out so long already," pouted Bianca Marsigliano. "Surely you will not go out again at once?" She spoke in Italian, as she generally did when the two of them were alone.

"It is necessary," Messer Lodovico answered tonelessly, not bothering to look at her. His mind was busy with the tour he had just made—Master Norton's quarters, the great hall where the fencing gentry gathered, the kitchens, the stables. "I must speak with my captain before supper. Not all of us," he added without emotion, "have leisure to lie abed all day."

Bianca Marsigliano lay half reclining in the narrow canopied bed she shared each night with Lodovico. It was early afternoon now, the afternoon of the third day of Christmas. She was naked beneath the blankets, her coarse black hair a hopeless tangle on the pillows. Her lusterless dark-brown eyes ruminated on the painfully thin figure of her lord, clad in white shirt and thigh-length velvet breeches, seated on a low chest across the room. He was exchanging a pair of damp black riding boots for shoes of soft cordovan leather.

"And what else is there for me to do but lie abed?" Bianca asked. She shrugged irritably. The blankets slid down from one soft-fleshed shoulder. "Besides, it is so cold here. You can feel the snow right through the stone walls. And the wind—

it comes through every door and window. It is a barbarous place you have brought me to."

Bianca was a child of Naples, in the warm far south of Italy. She had complained of the cold for years, ever since Lodovico's fortunes had taken them both north of the Alps.

"No more barbarous than another place," said Marsigliano, brushing the leather shoes carefully with a piece of cloth kept especially for the purpose. Lodovico was a Florentine, and all places that were not Florence were Barbary to him.

"You will be gone long?"

"As long as my captain wishes." His tone was flat and unemotional, discouraging further talk.

Of course, she thought, as long as your captain wishes. We must not vex the Great Captain. Never that.

Abruptly she remembered a time when Captain Devereux had in fact been vexed. Remembered and shuddered, though not with cold, at the vivid images that memory conjured up.

Devereux in shirt and slops, even as Lodovico was at this moment. Eight years ago, that spring when Messer Lodovico had first been taken into Sir Malcolm's service. At an inn in southern France, where the three of them had paused a night on their way north to join the captain's company. Sir Malcolm Devereux at his window—and terror down below.

She remembered the inn sign still, that warm blue morning, as they prepared to leave. A shield-shaped sign above the door, with a peeling ram's head on a golden ground. The smell of dust and lemons. And the tall dark cypresses behind the pink-tiled roof of the *auberge*.

Lodovico was in town, half a mile away, seeing to a horse that had cast a shoe on the rocky road the day before. Bianca sat on the edge of an old stone fountain in the innyard, slowly fanning herself, her body hot and moist already in the black gown, even at ten o'clock in the morning. She was aware of curious, hostile eyes upon her. Hostlers and other servants at the inn, peasants passing in slow carts. They were foreigners, the three of them, and foreigners were suspect everywhere.

She never knew what started it. She only heard the shout, and then the crash. *"Morbleu! Sacré!"* And then rending wood and shattering glass, and a thump that seemed to shake the yard behind her. She swung around in the stiff farthingales and the swathing gown, in time to see a glittering shower of falling glass settle about a man sprawling in the dust, his hulking body awkwardly entangled in the remains of a window frame. It was one of the inn servants—she had seen him the night before. He lay unmoving, face down, and blood began to show beneath his head.

She did not have to look up to know what she would see. A gaping hole where Captain Devereux's second-floor window had been. And the stocky, hard-bellied Englishman himself glaring down.

Some petty thievery perhaps, she thought numbly, or—

But she had no chance for further conjecture.

"Maudit!" roared a big red-faced hostler, shaking a slablike fist up at Devereux. *"Salauds d'étrangers—"*

Other servingmen poured out of the stables and the inn. Peasant laborers jumped off a passing oxcart and joined the yelling mob that formed magically in seconds in the dusty yard. Scythes glistened in the sunlight, hoes and mattocks waved in the air. The red-faced hostler was hefting a rusty pike now, shouting for blood.

Bianca slipped, terrified, off the fountain and bolted for the low inn door. The mob saw her then, knew her for one of *them*. Wrathful hands reached out. The host himself, a sallow, angry-looking man, appeared suddenly in the doorway, barring her entry. She screamed and froze, trapped between the furious innkeeper and the jeering horde behind her. For an endless moment, she stood in that sunny innyard, shaking with terror, snared in nightmare.

Then suddenly, Devereux was there.

She still saw that berserker charge. Mine host flung suddenly forward on his face, and the Great Captain surging out. Out with a roar, swinging a huge two-handed war sword, a relic she remembered above the fireplace in the public parlor. Out shouting oaths and insults as he rushed the mob of menials and peasant scum that dared soil the ears of Malcolm Devereux with their maledictions.

She shuddered again, remembering.

The dusty, sun-bright courtyard half full of men, and one single man confronting them. "What, villains—poltroons—will ye stand? Will ye fight, by the bloody wounds of God?"

And then the rush. The screams, the flailing arms and churning legs as they tumbled backward, tried to flee. The crunch and hiss of the great blade, and the new howls, the gouts of blood bursting from torn limbs and bodies ripped open by that whistling sword.

He had cleared the yard in half a minute, and a dozen men at least did not go home whole from that affray. Three or four lay groaning around the fellow Devereux had flung from the upstairs window.

"O God," she remembered gasping, "Mary Mother—"

"Stop that pestilent whining," Malcolm Devereux had snarled at her then, his massive chest heaving, swinging the big sword like a bullwhip. "You Italian bitch, it was your rutting scents drew the rogue in the first place!"

The harsh remembered accents still sounded in Bianca's narrow skull. She still saw the groaning men, blood spattered in the trampled dust. It was no wonder, she thought, that men feared Sir Malcolm Devereux as they feared no other captain of his age.

Give that man a single broadsword, and he would drive a dozen before him. Give him a regiment and the vultures would feed for days on the picked bones of his enemies.

She had seen them at Zutphen, at Coutras, at that horrid

place in the Germanies with the name she could never pronounce. Acres of dead and dying, cut down as by a gigantic scythe. Men with severed limbs and mangled faces. Men with white bones jutting through torn clothing and tattered flesh. The dead and the dying, frying under the noonday sun at Coutras, or heaped and tangled in ghostly windrows in the mists at Zutphen.

She remembered the terrible fogs that hung over the roads and polders around that Lowland city, where Sir Philip Sidney died. Sir Philip Sidney, brave and young and dashing—the Phoenix of his age, they said. Carried raving from the battlefield at Zutphen with a red-hot musket ball lodged in his shattered thigh.

And through the mists, the cold damp fogs of the Lowlands— the face of Sir Malcolm Devereux, watching the fallen hero carried from the field. The heavy face impassive, unmoving as though carved out of solid stone. The black breastplate and helmet, the black warhorse stirring restlessly under him. The square-cut beard, the craggy brows—and the pale cold eyes beneath. Eyes without pity or feeling. The eyes of the implacable commander they called the Great Captain from one end of Europe to the other.

He had lost battles—what commander had not, outside of poetry and chivalric fictions? He had left whole companies lying on the field. But he had come back for his revenge. Sir Malcolm Devereux, they said, always came back.

Remembering that face in the fog at Zutphen, Bianca believed it.

She trembled almost voluptuously and touched her own naked body underneath the covers.

"I shall return in time for supper," Lodovico was saying. "My lady will be ready." It was a statement, not a request. "Between now and then, do not disturb us. It is a matter of business."

"You spend too much time on your . . . business matters,"

Bianca answered crossly. She did not say, "And not enough on your Bianca."

"It is the nature of my profession. A good lieutenant's labors neither begin nor end upon the battlefield."

He turned his back upon her as he spoke and passed out of the little bedchamber into the even tinier anteroom.

Bianca shrugged her olive-tinted shoulders and settled into the blankets. For a moment a feline smile played about her lips, then slowly faded. Her faintly puffy features settled into an expression of flaccid discontent. She was well into her thirties now, and this look of sullen irritation was becoming more natural to her every day.

"Have them send me in a maidservant," she called querulously after Lodovico. "I must have a servingwoman to dress me."

No answer came back through the low arched doorway.

ii

The elegant, high-windowed gallery that stretched the length of the new wing was the Earl of Exmoor's pride. He had built it himself, to his own taste and pleasure. It was a long cavernous room, all gilt and marble and decorated plaster, with high mullioned windows down one side and family portraits on the other wall. It was so big that on days too cold or wet to venture out gentlemen might stroll and talk in the long gallery as freely as they did in the castle gardens in more pleasant weather. Half-a-dozen groups might promenade there, and no man overhear another's conversation.

Sir Malcolm Devereux and Lodovico Marsigliano spoke quite freely, in only slightly lowered voices, as they walked beneath the high windows in the fading light of that winter afternoon. Perhaps a score of other guests strolled there too, older, more substantial men than the young gentlemen who gathered for the fencing in the vaulted hall below. But these solid country gentry were too preoccupied with cattle and planting, land prices and the perils of the weather, to bother with the two dark men who walked in grimmer colloquy across the gallery.

Sir Malcolm and Messer Lodovico were talking about the *Golden Fortune*—and Master Walter Castlemayne.

A ship, thought Marsigliano. So much scheming, so much ingenuity—for the command of a single ship! The captain's urgency about the business baffled him. He had seen men lavish less intrigue on a regiment of horse.

Otherwise, the affair was familiar enough. The road to any great command lay through just such rich and powerful men as the Earl of Exmoor. Men like Lord Henry were the patrons and the financiers of war in the England of Elizabeth. Their favor was more essential to an ambitious soldier than anything else in life—except, perhaps, his rapier and dagger.

"This Master Castlemayne," said Devereux heavily at length. "He is a pricking fencing master, it appears."

"Even so, my lord. So dubbed by my compatriots in London." Marsigliano spoke with the faintest trace of scorn of those expatriate Italian tradesmen—for they were little better than that to the Florentine. Fighting was a legitimate profession: teaching it was a trade. "A year's service in the Low Countries, with some much-heralded heroics at the siege of Doesburg. Half a year at least in France, in the armies of his chivalric Majesty, the White Plume of Navarre. Time in between at one of your universities, and more time at the Queen's court. So much I have learned from his lordship's rheumy-eyed factotum, and from such other sources as I have been able to cultivate in so short a time."

"A young man of parts," said Devereux. "And a dashing figure too, in his doublet of the latest cut, making legs and flourishes so expertly. Is it not so, Lodovico?"

"It is, my lord."

"They're all of a breed, these carpet knights," grunted Devereux. "Spineless fops that would be soldiers in a season of campaigning. Dancing masters that would win their spurs for flattery and the fashion of their doublets."

"Indeed, my lord."

"And that rare performance night before last at his lordship's daughter's bedchamber? What make you of that, Lodovico?"

"Fortune favored him, my lord. If Master Luke had but come to me at once, instead of licking his wounds half the night, we might have taken the gallant gentleman hot at his amours!"

"Amours, Lodovico? Come, it is too strong. A quarter of an hour in my lady's chamber! That's a piece of cavalier folly, no more."

"Folly certainly, my captain. Yet there may be more to it than that. They are much together, these last two days. Sitting half the morning in a window nook together, and all the afternoon in the old solar. Reading poetry, dabbling at chess and draughts. Hands paddling accidentally for hands . . ."

"Pah—more courtlike nonsense." said Devereux contemptuously. "Mere lechery will not bring our paragon down." He took a slow turn and paced back up the gallery, his ensign moving more quickly at his side. "Mad for love of her he may well be, for aught I know or care. But press his overbusy prick upon an Earl's daughter? Spoil the heiress of Exmoor, upon whom all his future hangs? Come, not the most desperate cocksman would be so mad as that!"

"No doubt it is true, my lord. Nevertheless, if my lord permits—"

"Oh, proceed with your investigations, good Lodovico. Spread your web how you will, so you bring me my handsome bluebottle neatly trussed for stabbing." There's a special stench to this sort of intrigue, he meditated sourly, that your delicate Florentine nostrils sniff at once, where mine smell nothing.

"This Earl is most strict for the old virtues, my lord," said Marsigliano quietly. "Proper precedence, deference to one's betters, due decorum in all things. Chastity in women and some discretion at least in a gentleman. It would take far less than this 'cavalier folly' of Master Castlemayne's to strip him of all honor in his lordship's eyes."

"And none but a gentleman of stainless honor shall ever command his lordship of Exmoor's new-built vessel—eh, Lodovico?" Devereux pitched back his head and laughed, a short, barking laugh.

Honor is courage, thought Messer Lodovico mechanically. Honor is justice. . . .

Pacing beside his master, gazing coldly into nothingness, Lodovico saw suddenly a face. An old man's face, long since vanished from the earth. A narrow beardless jaw, a thin aristocratic nose, sharp hollows at the temples. Yellowed skin, wrinkled in vertical lines up the jaw, in crow's-feet all about the eyes. Silky, long white hair, receding from the elevated forehead, falling to the shoulders in the back.

He heard once again the prim, tight voice of that man of unbending rectitude and pride: "The Marsigliani are an honorable lineage, my sons, and have always been. Remember the formula, live by it absolutely: Honor is courage; honor is justice; honor is all virtue. And the *gens* Marsigliano have always been an honorable race."

All about that stern yellow face the great *palazzo* rose—columns, arches, pediments, ascending story after story to the soulless blue Italian sky. The *palazzo* itself seemed hushed in veneration of the aging giant that walked its halls. The three brothers would stand before him in stiff, respectful silence when he deigned to speak to them. Antonio and Sebastiano with their heads imperially high like his, their young eyes already arrogant with the rigid honor of the Marsigliani. He himself, Lodovico, with nothing in his eyes but smoldering resentment. For Antonio and Sebastiano were the heirs to all that bore the Marsigliano name—the farms and vineyards and ships, the villas and *palazzi*, obsequious bowing faces in the streets of Florence, silent power in the Signory. But Lodovico —Lodovico was the family's only error in four generations. The only bastard acknowledged by a head of the house of Marsigliano in this century.

He had been raised in Christian duty by a man who hated him. Raised side by side with two half-brothers who never bothered to conceal their contempt.

He had gone early to the bad. Dicing and drinking, street brawls and one stabbing affray too many for the family name to bear. Yet what should they expect, he had wondered more than once, flying in the face of nature as they did—to raise a bastard like another man? For it was well-known—and Lodovico believed it—that a bastard was an affront to nature, and bound to come to no good end.

He remembered the last word he had ever had from that parchment-faced, white-haired old man. A short note, delivered by his triumphant brothers personally, with a dozen club-armed servants at their backs—for Lodovico was a terror with his weapons even in his youth. A dozen lines on foolscap, informing him that the Marsigliano name was no longer his, nor Florence his city anymore.

He remembered the old man's face, and the great *palazzo*, and the villa in the hills above the Arno, with its geometric paths and falling fountains. He had not seen any of them for fifteen years.

But then, he mused bitterly, there in his lordship of Exmoor's ornately decorated gallery, a bastard may learn to make his way in this misbegotten world as well as a more honorable man. For what is a gentleman's honor truly, but the opinions of other men? That, and the certified ability to stab his enemies at will with rapier or dagger?

And that I have, he added grimly to himself. That I most

certainly possess. He smiled a thin-lipped smile, thinking of
the long Picinino rapier that hung in the cherrywood cupboard
in his chamber.

Devereux and Lodovico strolled on, continuing their conversation. More than one round-bellied country squire stared
after them. The dun-colored aristocrats of south Devon were
still not properly accustomed to these exotic black-clad strangers.

The inhumanly thin, impeccably dandified Italian was surely
different, with his swarthy skin, his smooth black hair and
hollow eyes, his perfect pointed teeth. And there were all the
tales one heard about Italians, about those sinful cities of the
plain beyond the Alps—very Sodoms and Gomorrahs, so they
said. These solid English gentry shook slow heads. Who could
tell what strange contagions, evil habits, awful deeds the foreigners might bring among them?

As for Sir Malcolm Devereux—there was a problem now.
They watched the famous captain stride past, a powerful, fierce-
looking man who had no doubt earned his awesome reputation,
his square-cut veteran's beard. And yet there was something
about him that they found oddly unpalatable.

There was an arrogance about his short-legged swagger, an
ill-concealed look of contempt about his heavy features. There
was the ostentatious simplicity of his clothing: all leather and
plain dark broadcloth, with the severest minimum of lace and
the smallest of ruffs about his thick neck. There was his silence,
and the clipped phrases and blunt words he affected when he
did speak. The manners of the camp and field, ill-suited surely
to the halls and galleries of a great Earl's country house. Some
of these portly men of wealth and power did not care for them
at all.

Messer Lodovico, the perfect ensign, was detailing his general
plan of operations to his chief. Captain Devereux always wanted

details of this sort. "Come, sir, tell me how your ambuscades are laid, where your sappers lay their mines . . ."

Lodovico told him, with elegant gestures and much slow stroking of his thin goatee. The diagramming of operations, military or political, always gave Lodovico Marsigliano a certain icy pleasure. It was the frigid joy of the school logician, following his chain of syllogisms through to the inevitable, irrefutable *sic probo*—thus I prove— It was one of the few pleasures in an otherwise coldly cerebral life.

Sir Malcolm had paused before a high-arched window, staring out through the diamond panes at the dying day. Bellying gray clouds, heavy with snow, hovered low over the huge round towers of the gatehouse. Another snowfall and the roads would be impassable. The castle would be totally cut off, even from the nearest village. Let alone the outside world.

Messer Lodovico, drawing to the end of his tactical exposition, felt his master's hand close upon his arm.

"My lord?" He paused.

The short, powerful fingers seemed to press through muscle and sinew, to constrict the narrow bone itself. Lodovico felt the nerves cut off, the whole arm paralyzed by that crushing grip. He felt Sir Malcolm Devereux's hard, colorless eyes boring into him, bending his will to the captain's purposes.

"He is a high aspiring mind, this Castlemayne?" The words came slow and metallic, impacting like physical blows on the Italian's brain. "He is ambitious, is he not, Lodovico? Thirsty now for glory, knightly honor, fame echoing down to future ages? Hungry later for more solid things—wealth and power and high place?"

"Most probably, my lord."

"Most probably, indeed! And Fortune has been kind, you say. Too kind by half to our mincing, smirking *caballero!*" Devereux smiled beneath the black moustaches. "We must help Fortune to see her way to a trimmer reckoning, Lodovico.

"A man of parts and high ambitions. A man for whom the

future waits. By God, we'll smash those panting hopes of his! We'll snatch that golden future from his clutching fingertips!" He paused, mastering his sudden passion. "And a man without a future, Lodovico—why, what's that but a man already dead? A shell, a husk, the outer semblance only of a man. A damned corpse that still walks the earth, searching for his grave."

The heavy dark head lowered, the black beard scraped the barrel chest. The Great Captain wheeled and paced off up the long room.

Messer Lodovico followed, nursing his arm, wondering.

～ *Five* ～

Dreams of Glory,
Dreams of Love

i

"Arabella!" snapped old Agnes Mayhew. "Sit up, lass. You're dreaming again!"

The Lady Arabella straightened up obediently. She sat at her little dressing table, docile and demure, while the gaunt Scotswoman ministered to her.

The old nurse clucked at the wild disarray the girl had gotten her hair into. Sighed over its coarseness. "So unlike your blessed mother's, child, her hair was fine as flax." And rapidly transformed the recalcitrant haystack into a high-piled glory, resplendent with ivory combs for the evening's festivities.

For nineteen years the essential routine had hardly varied. With her sharp northern tongue, Agnes had kept the girl from thinking too well of her precious self. For due modesty was a Christian virtue, and Agnes Mayhew was a Christian woman. At the same time, with aging hands that never lost their skill, she had tenderly cultivated the strange beauty of this child, whose only real mother she had been.

Arabella had been posing her wrists and hands at various elegant angles, alternately smiling and frowning over the effects. Now she took up the Venetian hand mirror and gazed in happy admiration at her own coiffure in the uncertain glass.

"Agnes," she said abruptly, "do you think I shall have lovers?"

The old woman snatched away the mirror and answered with tight-lipped propriety. "You shall have a husband, lady. When and as your father shall decide."

"Oh, that—" The girl shrugged her shoulders impatiently. "Indeed, I know my *husband* well enough—"

"Sit still for your stomacher, child," snapped the hatchet-faced old woman, beginning the complicated job of dressing her charge. "My eyes are not what they were for these hooks and pins and ribbon bows."

"My *husband,*" said Arabella, "shall be well-cousined at court, with the bulk of his estates somewhat closer in to London than this far corner of the realm. He shall be no more than two deaths from a peerage, and shall trace his lineage as far back as the Plantagenets—farther if may be." She recited the list of qualities in a singsong voice, like a litany long-known and of utterly no consequence. "His income shall be five thousand the year at minimum, more than half of it in land and cattle, which the Earl my father thinks are safe. His religion shall be impeccable Protestant, though Puritan extremism shall be frowned upon. And of course he shall offer a seller's market price for my hand. The daughter of the Earl of Exmoor should fetch ten thousand pound in marriage settlement, I'm sure."

She primped in mock hauteur. Agnes Mayhew's wrinkled lips stiffened again. "You know your father would never marry you against your wishes, my lady."

"Oh, certainly not, sweet Agnes. He would never be so barbarous. Why, I shall most certainly have every opportunity to meet the gentleman before the marriage contract is even signed." She winced as the last laces of the stiff brocaded bodice were drawn tight. Then, wriggling free, she whirled away in a quick dance step across the floor.

"But, dear Agnes, I may have lovers, may I not?" she pursued mischievously. "At least one paramour, sweet Aggie, at least one lusty gallant to solace me for a joyless wedding bed . . ."

Goody Mayhew told her sharply to act her age and station, to talk like a Christian maid, and for heaven's sake to stand still for her sash to be put on. Lady Arabella giggled and obeyed.

Arabella Traherne had grown up in a house full of men. Her quick, bright humor had readily absorbed the bawdy talk of the servingmen and the risqué wit of the high table. Nor had any questioned the propriety of a nobleman's daughter who could swear like a drover on occasion. The aging Virgin Queen herself, after all, was reputedly a bit rough-spoken at times.

But Agnes Mayhew was as much a Puritan as the strictest Presbyterian in Edinburgh, where she had grown up. She read the Gospels, the Psalms, and John Calvin's Catechism every day God brought. And she never failed to be horrified at her growing charge's casually ribald remarks. Not even the clear consciousness that she was being teased could keep the leathery old Scotswoman, who had heard John Knox's pulpit thunder, from reacting with horror to this sort of mockery.

"Why, I am old enough to take a lover even now, am I not?" Arabella swayed her hips voluptuously and drooped her lids behind the velvet mask she would wear in that evening's entertainment. "Why should I not have . . . Master Castlemayne, for a likely choice? There's a lusty cavalier surely, that would not disappoint a poor maid. Do you not think so, Agnes?"

Agnes looked up quickly from her task, narrowing her short-sighted eyes to peer into the child's face. The name had fallen too casually, too easily by half from the girl's lips. The old nurse smoothed her straight dark hair uneasily, but answered with her usual crisp authority.

"He was a troublesome lad always," she said irritably, "and he'll not be a comfortable man. I cannot count the times I had to call Ned or Dick from the armory to birch his rump for some wicked business or other, those other Christmases and Easters here. The Devil regularly found work for his idle hands to do. And still does, I don't doubt."

"Oh, Aggie—the Christmas Eve he slipped a toad in the parson's soup and spoilt that tedious long grace!" Arabella laughed delightedly at the memory. Agnes, adjusting the delicate open ruff upon the girl's bosom, snorted with disgust.

"At least he has good blood in him, Agnes," said Arabella, half teasing and half pleading. "His father was a Cornish gentleman. And his mother, is she not some distant kin of the Earl my father's?"

"A very distant, far too poor relation to matter in this world!" snapped the servant primly. "A shameless climber too, wheedling invitations from his noble lordship year after year. And as for the father, he was the meanest kind of Cornish squire, a man of little gumption and no consequence. Preferred his own fireside to the great world, and so cut no figure anywhere.

"In sum, no family worth considering at all, my child. No family, no fortune, no religion, I'll be bound—that's your gallant Master Walter Castlemayne!"

"But now he's been beyond the seas to fight the papists and the Spaniards. That should please you, Aggie, dispatching so many papist idolaters to Belial's gripe. And they say he's the greatest fencer in England, or almost. How beautiful he must be, tilting in the tournaments at Whitehall, with all the courtiers and ladies looking on, and even the Queen herself. Oh, Aggie, would it not be wonderful to have so handsome a cavalier begging for my favors?"

Her eyes sparkled, remembering his hands, his mouth on hers, his voice against her ear. Knowing it could not, must not happen again. Knowing true love was a thing of the spirit, a matter of pure platonic adoration, not carnal sensuality. But remembering nonetheless.

"He is a wild, foolish young gentleman," said the old woman with finality, "and he will come to an evil end."

"Oh, pooh," said Arabella. She tossed her head, spurning imaginary hordes of lovers swooning at her feet, and danced

out of the room, across the antechamber, and out into the hallway. And dancing as she went, she improvised new words to
an old song for Agnes Mayhew's benefit:

> "Give place, ye lovers, here before
> That spent your boasts and brags in vain.
> My lord his beauty passeth more
> The best of yours, I dare well sayn,
> Than doth the sun the candlelight . . .
> His name is Walter Castlemayne."

ii

"In sum, an excellent tall ship, my lord. One hundred five
feet at the keel, twenty-four at the beam. Five hundred tuns
burthen. Square-rigged on the main and foremast, lateen aft—"

William Hackett paused in his exposition to see what effect
these technicalities were having on his audience. One never
knew, of course. More often than not, the wealthy men who
hired him cared not a pin for such details, so long as his work
proved seaworthy. But there were peers of the realm who took
an amateur's interest in shipbuilding and were flattered to be
thus dealt with as a colleague.

Hackett glanced quickly at the two men before him. His
waxed moustache vibrated slightly as he smiled, puckering plump
cheeks. The Earl of Exmoor's dark-paneled, high-ceilinged library was hushed around him, heavy with oaken furniture,
ornate carving, rows of folio and quarto volumes in uniform
green bindings. Beyond the mullioned windows that lined one
wall, the snowy expanse of Dartmoor flowed away to the red
cliffs and the glittering sea.

"Rigged already, is she?" asked Master Cecil sharply, looking
up from the impressive array of drawings and plans strewn over
the long polished table. Lines, curves, dimensions, cross sections,
detailed drawings of assembled units. All meticulously made,

but more than the average layman would spend more than a few minutes thumbing through.

"Not yet rigged, my lord," said Master Hackett, bowing slightly. He had already conceived a wary respect for the twisted little man in black. "The ship was launched ten days ago, on the eve of my departure from the city, quite successfully despite some ice on the Thames. There would then be tests and adjustments of the hull and finishing of interiors—crew's and musketeers' quarters, cabins for officers and gentleman volunteers, powder and water storage especially. But of course the masts are stepped, and they will probably begin to rig her soon after the holidays."

"Um," said the Earl of Exmoor, bowed still over the table full of drawings, his nose twitching nervously. "And what about —ah—armament? Shouldn't the cannons or culverins or whatever be put aboard her soon?"

"Yes, my lord, within the month certainly. She'll mount fifty guns of all sorts. Drake's *Revenge* had no more in the Armada fight."

"Excellent, excellent," muttered the Earl, but without much enthusiasm. Shipbuilding jargon and shipwright's plans were all outside his province. And yet so much of his substance was bound up in this venture! He strove mightily to understand, required a constant stream of reports from his agents in London, and had positively insisted that Sir John Hawkins send down his master shipwright in the dead of winter for this interim report.

William Hackett was a short, plump man, slightly overdressed for one in his station in life. His tiny moustaches, the elegant short beard that ringed his faintly porcine face, the gaudy rings that glittered on his fingers all spoke of complacency and success. But there was shrewdness in his half-lowered lids, real skill and a craftsman's love of his work in the way he handled his plans and instruments.

Proud of his craft, judged Cecil. He'll labor to maintain his reputation, but also for the vessel's own sweet sake. For one reason or the other he'll make the *Golden Fortune* as fine as any ship afloat.

"The queen of the Deptford Yards," Hackett was saying somewhat pompously, as though reading the little hunchback's mind. "Tall and straight among a scattering of barks and pinnaces, like a stag among does and yearlings—if you'll pardon the figure of speech, gentlemen. The admiration of sailors and ship's carpenters that work there, and of no few young gentlemen that have ridden down to Deptford of set purpose to see her. Indeed, you'll hear her praises sung in half the inns and ordinaries of the city, and even at the court."

He paused, smoothing a thin mustachio with an elegantly manicured fingertip.

"The question everywhere," he continued carefully, "is, Who will have the command of her in the spring?"

"Ah," said the Earl, gnawing nervously at his underlip, "but surely a ship's company may be signed on without informing their worships the sailors and gunners who is to be giving their orders? Is it not their business to obey their commander, whether or no they care for the cut of his doublet?"

"Certainly, my lord, for the seamen. We shall in fact undertake to secure a full crew, to engage a master and mates, to find a full complement of soldiers—musketeers, pikemen, gunners. But for the officers to lead your troops, my lord—ah, there's the problem."

Lord Henry blinked, obviously uncomprehending.

"No worthy experienced officer, my lord, will sign on to follow a cipher. They must know who is to command before they will even consider service. Lieutenants, ensigns, even sergeants, all these swaggering professionals are as nervous as thoroughbred horses where their honorable reputations are concerned." Hackett laughed ingratiatingly. "Not to mention their purses, of course. And they base their estimates of the likelihood of loot and honor on what they know of the man who is to be their captain."

"It is so," Cecil assented shortly. "They are almighty jealous of their prerogatives and rights, these professional men of the sword."

The Earl sighed unhappily. With every word, the impending necessity for choice weighed more heavily upon him.

"Other ships are fitting out as well," Hackett continued, "and experienced men are more difficult to find every year. Many English bones bleach in foreign lands, as your lordship knows. Those men of proven skill and courage that remain can pick and choose amongst the companies that are being raised."

Master Cecil knew. He had seen his father the venerable Lord Treasurer draw up a list of all the experienced officers of captain's rank available in England—and then cross off almost half the names. Lord Burghley had sighed mightily and plucked his white beard in vexation, that men should vanish almost as rapidly as the money did in this endless war.

Cecil turned briskly to Lord Henry. "I think, your lordship, that we may dismiss this gentleman to his meal and rest?"

"Yes—certainly," agreed the Earl abstractedly. "We thank you, sir, and will have further speech with you upon the matter. Tomorrow, or soon thereafter."

William Hackett bowed to each, retreated down the room, bowed again, and was gone.

The nobleman and the politician were left alone in the wainscoted study, darkening now with the shadows of late afternoon. They stood at opposite ends of the long polished table, each busy with his own thoughts.

Robert Cecil thought of Devereux and Castlemayne. He weighed and judged their capabilities methodically, precisely. And he weighed and estimated too the drift of this uncertain Earl's judgment of these men, one of whom must sail his fine new vessel to glory or disaster in the spring.

The great Earl of Exmoor himself gazed out the mullioned windows over his vast, snow-shrouded lands, and thought about crops and cattle and spring planting. Plenty of time still to worry about the wretched ship, after all. It was only the fifth day of the holidays.

Walter Castlemayne stood alone in the dim cavern of the chapel, gazing raptly into his own future.

He stood just outside the communion rail near the old stone pulpit, holding Master Cecil's Indian idol in his right hand.

Beyond the railing, candles on a little table gleamed on yet more gaudy loot. There was the jeweled Spanish crucifix, all silver and precious stones. There were four ornately decorated silver cups. There were chains and bracelets and other treasures, row on row of them laid out for the delectation of the Earl's guests.

From Yucatán, thought Castlemayne, turning the heathen idol in his fingers. A satrapy of the golden Aztec empire the famous Captain Cortez conquered—sixty, seventy years ago, was it? Astounding there should be so much gold and silver left after so many years. He hefted the idol in his palm, thrilling to the mass and weight of the metal. He saw with pleasure how the nearest candle flame reflected in the lambent surface.

Every year a great fleet sailed from Havana, homeward bound to Spain, laden to the gunnels with such treasures. Every year the English sea dogs stalked and sniped at the closely guarded convoy. This spring, not six months hence, Walter Castlemayne would be with the ships that lay in ambush about the Azores to trap the treasure fleet.

This time, this spring, they would do it! Not a single isolated carrack, but the whole armada would be theirs! A thing never done before, the capture of the great plate fleet. A thing reserved, God willing, for this expedition, for these chosen men.

Castlemayne raised his eyes, stared clear and sightless into the seven candle flames upon the altar. He stared—and saw. He knew how it would be, for he had heard the scream of battle, the roar of guns . . .

Artillery like thunder, close up, stunning the eardrums. Splintering crash of shot, the Spanish broadside striking. Shrieks of maimed and dying men, of men trapped beneath a falling yard. Then the whole ship shuddering with the recoil of her own great guns, roaring all at once beneath their feet. A noise like the crack of doom that will one day split the world in two.

Then through acrid, billowing smoke, they glimpse the towering galleon, high-castled and ornate, not fifty feet away. See her reel beneath the onslaught of the English guns—bloody swathes across the main deck, carnage down below. See a mast come loose and fall like a tall pine tree, slowly down through tangled rigging and tearing sail to crash in a bedlam of screams athwart the Spaniard's deck.

Grappling hooks are out, lines fast. The two ships draw together, crash and scrape, separate and close again. Then over open water, through smoke and shouting, the English soldiers swarm to the Spaniard's shattered deck. Sharp steel on steel striking sparks, steel hacking hardened leather hauberks, steel carving the flesh of living men. Eyes tingling, arms and wrists untiring, and a tumultuous exaltation in the veins. The joy of absolute endeavor, of everything upon a single cast. The mad joy of battle.

The world of Walter Castlemayne. His for the winning, as real as the golden idol he held in his hand that moment. As heart-stoppingly beautiful to the young cavalier as the girl who waited for him even now in her father's high-vaulted hall.

~ *Six* ~

The Whore of Naples

i

"But Harry, *caro mio*," Bianca Marsigliano whispered with a lightness that her deep velvet voice belied, "how if my lord husband should find us here? How if my Lodovico shall discover we are not among the dancers anymore, and come in search of us . . . ?"

She drew away from his kiss and leaned back against a roughhewn pillar, arching one black eyebrow up at him. Her brown eyes seemed to glow like an animal's in the dark.

"Your evil-minded husband—damn his eyes—will notice nothing," Harry muttered gruffly, nuzzling her throat.

"Yet he is very jealous, my lord husband," she persisted half-seriously. "If he sees us together, just the two of us alone"—her fingers strayed across the back of his flushed neck—"he will not discuss the matter with you. He will not even propose you to defend yourself, as you English do. My Lodovico, he will stick his stiletto into the middle of your broad English back, *amore mio*. For an Italian gentleman, that is an honorable revenge, to kill the man that lays his hand upon your wife."

Harry turned away to spit a piece of meat, lodged between two teeth since supper, out upon the hard earth floor. All about them stretched the vast, low-beamed interior of the stables, lit only by a guttering torch or two.

"If that walking boneyard you call lord husband ever dares draw a blade on me, mistress"—he spoke with sudden ferocity—

"I'll carve him into giblets, by Jesus Christ! Never fear for that, lady." He laughed, relishing the prospect.

The woman in his arms said nothing. But *you* should fear for it, Englishman, she thought. Poor foolish Englishman.

Impatiently now, Harry pressed his greedy mouth against her own. Bianca responded with a laugh deep in her throat. Yet still, ruffling his thick orange hair, lazily accepting his caresses, she murmured protestations.

"And then there is my *purità*—how do you say it?—my matron's honor, sir! You English make such a virtue of a lady's wifely faithfulness, is it not so?" She bit one flaming ear, gently still, but with a raw sensuality that screwed his ardor up another notch. "I am a good wife, sir. I have my *purità* to think of too."

Purity! snorted Harry inwardly. You're a strumpet born if ever I tasted one, Mistress Would-Be Elegance. Offered up your maidenhead to the papist priest that baptized you, I'll be bound. And the lecherous shaveling probably took it too. Every man's whore, he chuckled silently, is no man's wife, that's sure.

Aloud, he went laboriously on with the pretense of wooing.

"But surely, sweet lady," he pleaded reasonably, still holding her close, "you would not have come to such a place at midnight if you felt no answering passion to my own." He waved a hazy hand at the low-raftered expanse of wooden stalls and hard-packed earth, the strong smells of stale manure and damp straw, the murmurous sounds of horses.

"And after all is said and done, mistress, why should you sweat for qualms and scruples? A beautiful woman, a lady of spirit and fire, yoked with such a paltry thing as that." That scarecrow, fine clothes upon a stick. Fine words in a toad's mouth. He smothered the epithets with difficulty, for he had conceived an implacable dislike for the cerebral Italian in the six days since he had first clapped eyes upon him—and upon his wife.

"Ah, *signore*," Bianca murmured, "you understand so well a woman's soul." She sighed and drew his face down to her high-bound breasts. His cheek and nose and seeking mouth pressed against her through the lace that bordered her décolletage. She moved luxuriously, feeling a slow stirring deep within her loins. And yet her smile, in the dim cresset's gleam, had none of the warmth that her rich body promised. It was a strange crooked smile, sour as the rind of lemons.

He poses me a good question after all, my big Englishman, she told herself. Why am I here after all? Why did I come to this place with him? And then, bitterly resentful: Why do I ever come?

He was kissing her breasts where they surged above the low-cut stomacher. "Bianca! Bianca!" he whispered, his need well-nigh unbearable. Soon he will pull the gown aside, she thought, with a mixture of excitement and disdain.

It is always the same, and still I always come. To silken perfumed sheets, or to a bed of straw. With some snorting bull of a man that seeks no pleasure but his own. Yet her soft fingers slid over the swelling muscle of his upper arm, thrilling to the strength she felt there. And her lips, purple as grapes in the uncertain light, curved in a warmer smile.

"Now, my sweet Bianca! Now, my lovely wench!" gasped her clutching lover, raising his face from her bosom. "Come with me now!" And come quickly, with no more court talk and quibbling, by Jesus Christ! I'm sweating like a blacksmith in this wintry night, and hot as a rutting stag!

She felt his thick arm about her waist, drawing her toward an empty stall. Her nostrils filled with a thickening odor of oats and straw and horses. He swung open the gate of the boxlike enclosure and drew her urgently in. Saint Mary Magdalene preserve me! she groaned inwardly. But I have slept upon worse beds, in thirty and more winters past.

With a faint grimace, yet a tremor of excitement too, she submitted to the pressure of his arm.

Bianca's mind, as she stepped across the splintered threshold of the stall, was a slowly turning pool of multicolored memories. This vortex of memory had moved before her half-closed eyes many times before on these occasions. Memories of other men, as she gave herself once more, past and present merging into one unending ambiguous event. It was the stuff and substance of her life, this tyrannous sensation eternally rekindled, illogical, unreasoning. For there were no meanings to it all for her. No lessons, consequences, moral or metaphysical significances. Only desire and what came after. What always followed after, like hot spiced wine spilled suddenly in the dust.

The olive-skinned Italian woman could no more stop the memories than she could keep the act itself from happening again. Inevitably, passions of the past swept clamoring before her empty dark-brown eyes as she took the step once more, leaning back to smile up, swaying in the crook of a man's relentless arm.

Naples. My Naples, where I lived.

The blue curve of the bay, the white tile-roofed city, the purple cone of Vesuvius beyond. Hoary Norman citadels, Spanish bullfights, polyglot crowds of traders, Christian, Moslem, Jew. And down near the harbor, the tangle of narrow winding streets and stinking alleys, the cheap taverns, cheaper bawdyhouses, shops of the moneylenders. And the small room with the one tick mattress on the floor, the scattering of straw for little Bianca. The room she shared with her mother, Beatrice, the pocky whore of Greek Street.

Life by day: Heat, flies, the sweetish smells of rotten fruit, the blistering heat of the far south on her eyelids. She felt it still, when she closed her eyes. The searing heat, the sunlight beating on her lids.

Life by night: Shrieks of pain and laughter, curses, drunken singing, thud of blows and scuffle of violence in the raucous street outside. And just across the little room, there in the blackness near her—sobs, groans, hissing breaths, and crackling of the tick pallet where men in monotonous succession plowed her mother's body.

She remembered the first time it had happened to herself. The first knowledge of the curse laid upon her life.

Paunchy, greasy Jew of Naples sprawling crushingly upon me
in that pitchy alley. Cobblestones the size of hen's eggs bruising
childish shanks. Stench of garlic and Chianti on his panting
whiskers, the stink of the open sewer flowing past my backward-
straining head. Then brief pain, and numbness, and the first
flame curling in the belly. And first despair at the retreating
footsteps of the man. And all the other men that could not
quench that flame.

Other cities for Bianca after that, and uncounted other men.

A dozen years of wandering, selling her warm southern body
from city to city up the length of the peninsula. Offering herself
in halting Neapolitan to papal pages in the shadow of the Vati-
can, to 'prentice painters in Florence, to gunsmiths and grimy en-
gineers in Milan. Fetching up finally in Venice, an established
courtesan at last, albeit of the second rank. With a clientele of
English and German gentlemen on the grand tour, of Venetian
shipmasters, of visiting *condottieri* from everywhere. With a
small two-story house, plane trees, and a courtyard fountain,
in a section of town houses and walled gardens on the outskirts
of the city.

But always, in the streets of Rome or in her brocaded, tas-
seled bed in Venice, the feel and smell and sounds of men.

Hands upon my body. Kneading, pinching, bruising my poor
flesh. Ah, but that first touch, the first touch and the rising
flame! The fire inside me that no man's water bullets quench.

No man, O Mother Magdalene, but one.

Taking stock in her midtwenties. House and garden, and
money to maintain them, for the time at least. Clients of the
middling sort. No scum any longer, but none of the cream
either—no prelates, Councillors, fat merchants of the Rialto.
Only the blond Lombard girls, their pampered hair bleached,
perfumed, and frizzed, drew stately members of the Council,
or the richest of the rich.

And what for the future then? An inexorably deteriorating
body that would sell for less each year. No head for business,

even the familiar business of the stews—hence no future as a madam. No future at all, that she could see, except her mother's fate. Giving herself in gutters, ravaged by disease, dead of old age in her forties.

All this rather felt than thought, over long nervous months one summer and fall. And then Messer Lodovico Marsigliano, with a crisp and clear solution.

Like herself, a man of the middle rank in his profession. A gentleman of ancient Tuscan stock, black sheep turned soldier, serious and dedicated to his work. An ensign or lieutenant, but never likely to be captain, though he would always serve the best. An occasional client, since his last mistress died—of camp fever, it was given out—before the walls of some barbarian town in the far north, beyond the Alps. A man of few peculiar needs and habits, of limited sexuality at all, in fact. She always thought he wanted her primarily to keep his clothes and quarters, and to maintain his status in camp or garrison. But there was established status for her too, as the mistress of an officer. And even she could see that Messer Lodovico was a man of brains and skill in his chosen trade, sure to provide ducats enough to keep her in some style.

So she had taken up her travels once again, now as Lodovico Marsigliano's lovely mistress, or as his lady wife.

But the curling flame still burned, and she must try and try again to quench it.

Burly sergeants, in his very tent, while he consulted elsewhere. Arrogant commanders who brusquely summoned her to theirs. More than one young cavalier with a haunted, feverish power smoldering behind the eyes. Irregular infidelities, and not many of them, but inevitable, compulsive, beyond her power to prevent. When the fire blazed up, she must give herself to the first strong man that crossed her restless path.

Must give herself—and risk each time the possessive fury of her lord.

The blade of Lodovico Marsigliano. Bianca shuddered at the

thought of it. Not the dress sword he wore in public, all gilt and silver fittings, but the killing rapier. The special sword he kept to gore her bulls.

Three inches longer than the average, almost a Verdun length, he said. But not quite so long as a true Verdun, that the unwary victim might not notice till too late. The deep cup hilt, a writhing snake's nest of rings and bars and metal filigree. The maker's name, of which he was so proud—"Antonio Picinino" of the famous Brescia family of swordsmiths—engraved in the hollow of the blade just below the crosspiece. And the edgeless blade itself, with only a needle-sharp point, a blade designed exclusively for thrusting. The blade of a professional rapier fighter, a confident master of the art of courtly butchery.

Three times she had seen him buckle on his Picinino, swing his cape about his narrow shoulders, and step out the door. His swarthy face death pale each time with the killing fever.

On a sandy, scrub-grown island in the swamps outside of Venice, there was a long, low mound, settling gradually with the years, where a handsome pikeman lay. Almost a head taller than Lodovico when he stood upon his feet. But a helpless babe before the stabbing fury of the Picinino.

Behind a hoary, famous church in an elegant *faubourg* of Paris, the young scion of an ancient house rotted under elaborately sculptured marble. Bianca had seen him die in the little park that brisk fall morning, formally and by the rules, wild-eyed at the last and bleeding at the mouth and nose.

And in the narrow, dank, beggars' back streets of Antwerp, all cobblestones and shrouding overhang, one might still stumble across a ragged crouching man. Or what remained of a man when Lodovico Marsigliano sheathed his blade.

The unquenched flame still smoldered in Bianca's bowels. Lodovico wrapped his sword away and returned to his trade, to tactics and maneuvers and logistics, coldly, rationally planned and executed. Until the fire blazed up in her, and the green fury swept over him again. The soft-fleshed woman and the living skeleton went on, bound by her lust and his obscurer passions, leaving a trail of death and horror in their wake.

Laughing her low, sensual laugh, swaying in the angle of Harry's sturdy arm, Bianca stepped across the hoof-splintered threshold.

"Now, my sweet wanton!" he whispered, pulling her hard against him in the shadowed interior of the stall. She said nothing, but returned his kisses with slow passion, almost tauntingly, using her tongue and teeth. An Italian strumpet's kiss! he exulted inwardly. Let Walter have his sapless virgin then, and bay the moon forever!

Her body began to move against his. She kissed him still more hotly. She bit his neck like an animal, till blood flowed. He clawed at her like a beast himself, swearing and sweating for her.

But when he tried to drag her down with him into the straw, she tore herself free.

"Wait, you evil man. Wait. Would you have me soil such a lovely gown, so costly, simply to pleasure you the more rapidly?"

She turned away with mock modesty and began the complicated business of undressing. Deft, ghostly movements in the darkness, with from time to time a half-seen smile flung back at him over one naked shoulder.

Breathing heavily, cursing like a drover, Harry stripped himself, flung his clothing about the stall. Then he fell on his knees to help the woman, fumbling with trembling fingers at her ribbons and laces, kissing her bare body as it was uncovered to his lust. And still at his touch or kiss, she swayed away, teasing, tempting, raising his passion to a shattering pitch.

So . . . so . . . steam with desire, my lusty thwacking stallion! And then perhaps—perhaps— Naked at last, she sank down into the stiff rustling straw, down upon his velvet doublet, and opened her embrace to him.

"Now cover me, my big Englishman. My poor southern flesh,

it is so cold in your English winter." Bianca stretched seductively
in the chilly dark, moving slow thighs. The warmth of nearby
horseflesh made it rather bracing than wintry cold, even for
her. Horseflesh, and the fires that now blazed high within her,
driving out all other feeling, all other thought but desire beyond
bearing.

"Aye, mistress, I'll cover you, by Jesus Christ!"

His body came heavy upon hers then, thick-muscled, bristling
with reddish hair on chest and limbs and groin. Farmer-quick,
with no preliminaries, he took her in the rocking, crackling, hard-
breathing darkness.

Release, revenge, and soaring triumph mingled for Harry
Langland in this moment of possession.

To lay the elegant Italian lady on her back. To lay her here,
where horses munched and snorted and filled the air with sharp
odors. To work his horny-handed will upon her, and turn her
courtly protestations to cries of an animal in heat. These were
sweet victory to him. Triumph over all her world of padded
clothes and glittering jewels, book learning and intrigue too
devious for an honest man to follow.

For the woman in his arms, he had scarcely a thought. A
whore, a foreigner, and a papist—what claims could such a one
make upon the sympathies of an honest Englishman?

One final moment of exploding nerves, release at last.

Then he sprawled over her, happily exhausted, grateful for
the soft fullness of her flesh, that made so comfortable a mattress.

For Bianca, moving expertly beneath him, it was all black
gall and bitter disappointment. As she had known it would be.
As it was always with all men. All men but one.

Against the blackness inside her lids, a red spot grew. In this
splash of pulsing crimson light, a face appeared. Not Harry's
square-jawed innocence, or Lodovico's baleful skull. The pale,
black-bearded face of Sir Malcolm Devereux.

The Great Captain, that drove whole armies from the field.

The only man that had ever quenched the flame that burned forever in her loins.

ii

Sir Malcolm Devereux sat up late in his chamber, in a quiet corner of the new wing. A wainscoted, smooth-plastered suite with polished furniture and heavy hangings on the bed. Finer quarters than Master Castlemayne's, though lacking the ornate elegance of the Lady Arabella's. The Earl of Exmoor had a nice eye in such matters.

Devereux sipped red wine by candlelight and thought of Walter Castlemayne. As he had done every night since he came to Exmoor, and found a rival waiting for him.

Castlemayne. A gaudy popinjay, in truth. But popinjays are in favor in these degenerate days, it seems. Your Raleighs, your Essexes, your Philip Sidneys! Devereux emptied his tankard and reached for the heavy earthenware pitcher. Aye, and in higher favor every year, the older the old Queen gets. A rival to be respected, then, for that if for no other thing. And dealt with accordingly.

Sir Malcolm settled his heavy frame in the low-backed chair, the replenished tankard ready to hand, and reviewed his information.

He put no faith in his lieutenant's hopes for further sexual indiscretions. There had been no repetitions of that first night's folly. Nor would there be, Devereux was sure. Only the dancing, the talk in quiet alcoves, the madrigals and laughter over the virginals.

Our Castlemayne talks court as greasily as all his kind, the dark-browed captain thought with a grimace, and no more than that. Lodovico saw lechery in every lady's smile. No doubt Signora Bianca's smiles were coming too easily to suit him once again. It was a tiresome business, the jealous passions of this otherwise passionless and perfect ensign.

But if not lechery, then what? What was the fatal weakness that would bring this Castlemayne down? For every man had his weakness, his flaw, the fissure in his character that, once detected, would split him open at a stroke. The problem, in politics as on the battlefield, was simply to find the fissure. Devereux shrugged irritably and reached for the brimming tankard.

The knock came a second time, low, almost hesitant, before he heard it. The captain swung around in his chair and stretched one long arm out to yank back the bolt.

A hunched, unprepossessing creature loomed across the doorway. His leather doublet was dirty, his woolen hose smelled dimly of manure. His hair was filthy, his ugly face still swollen with the beating he had taken from Castlemayne six nights before. His single eye glowed dully in the candlelight.

"Luke Naylor, at your service, sir," he began in a plaintive whine. "Chief hostler to his lordship. And an old soldier too, that lost this good eye in those same wars, sir, in which your worship—"

"You are out of place, fellow," snapped Devereux. "I have no business with his lordship's grooms."

"Aye, sir, I know I am to see the Italian gentleman only. But I have intelligence this night, sir, that I could scarce convey through him, sir." Luke sidled into the room as he spoke, until he stood, hulking but obsequious, before the captain. "But intelligence, sir, that might be of some service to your mastership. In the matter of this Master Castlemayne."

Sir Malcolm rose deliberately from the low table. He shot out one hairy hand, seized Luke by the throat, and slammed him back against the wall. He held him there effortlessly, helpless as a baby. The eyes beneath the thick black brows bored into the horrified stablehand.

"Have you been given to understand, fellow," he grated softly, "that I have some business with Master Castlemayne?"

"Why—why no, your worship," croaked Naylor, his single eye protruding slightly from its socket. "I have no—I only thought to—"

"Ahhh," rumbled Captain Devereux, jerking his hand suddenly from his victim's throat. He sank morosely back into his chair and turned away, tugging at his stiff black beard. "Come then, rogue, spew it out. Quickly, and begone, or I'll fry your babbling tongue for breakfast meat." Sir Malcolm Devereux had little love for intelligencers, though he paid them well and regarded their use as a prime principle of warfare, too often neglected.

"Aye, sir, and humble pardon, your worship." Luke bowed and pulled his matted forelock. "Well, then, sir, it's—pardon, sir—it's Master Castlemayne's kinsman Langland—and the Italian gentleman's wife, sir." He cringed, half expecting further punishment. "Not an hour since, sir, in my own stables."

Devereux did not even bother to look up at him. "Speak on, villain," he said coldly. "I'll tell you when to hold your tongue." But he did not reach for the wine again, and he sat very still while Luke Naylor told his story.

In his own chambers halfway across the castle, Lodovico Marsigliano struck his mistress across the face with methodical precision. Once, twice. Bianca fell backward across the bed, writhing away from him, the curtains billowing about her. Lodovico reached across, yanked her out and up on her feet. The strength in his wiry arms made the soft-bodied woman quake with terror.

"Who is he?"

She felt bony fingers crushing the tender flesh of her throat. Waves of nausea and faintness swept over her. She could not speak.

Impassively, his face a livid goat-bearded skull, Lodovico increased the pressure. The big arteries buckled, the windpipe closed. He saw her eyes roll up, all whites. He saw the head fall back, the dark hair spilling loose. Her full weight came suddenly upon his wrists and arms.

"Bitch!"

He flung her contemptuously back on the bed. She lay still, her body limp and flaccid. Her face was purplish as she strained to breathe. Minutes passed before she moved at all—one hand, creeping up to touch her brutalized throat. Slowly, uncertainly, she sat up, massaging her neck. She coughed spasmodically and winced at the pain. Then she looked up at him, bodice and sleeve torn at the shoulder, hair wild, eyes brimming with hatred.

"It was Castlemayne's square-headed kinsman," he said flatly.

"It was no one," she managed in a whisper. "I have been dancing only." She had no slightest desire to protect Harry Langland. Only a dark determination to thwart this devil from the icy depths of hell.

"I shall deal with him," said Lodovico, his thin face death-pale in the flickering light. "And the next time, my heart, on the very next occasion that you go baying after some poor villain like a bitch in heat—he will not die alone."

Bianca sat huddled on the bed, fingers digging into the coverlet beside her, watching him. Her dark-brown eyes blazed with animal ferocity. She longed to leap on him with teeth and talons as he turned. To destroy him utterly, and with him all the race of men.

Yet she stared with an awful fascination as he crossed, two short steps, to the cherrywood cabinet. Watched as he opened the door and reached into the obscurity. And saw the first emerging glint of the elaborately wrought hilt of his Picinino rapier.

~ Seven ~

The Furies Are Unleashed
at Exmoor

i

It was the seventh day of Christmas, the very midpoint of
the holidays. A mood of exhaustion had settled over Exmoor.

Outside, the snow fell steadily upon forest and moorland and
the sea, a quarter mile beyond the castle. The roads were
clogged, the woods and fields closed to hunting or falconry or
other outdoor pastimes.

Inside, torpor lay upon the celebrants. They grunted for
speech and moved with deliberate slowness from chamber to
hall and back again. They were in need of nothing so much as
sleep, rest for wit and muscle and weary digestive tract. But
few took this sensible course. Slow of step and somewhat hag-
gard of eye, each man did his weary duty by the full twelve
days' festivities. They would be festive, though they died for it.

This midseason depression was of course a temporary thing.
Once past the middle point, the celebration would spiral once
more upward toward delirium. For the celebrants would begin
to realize that the carefree times were not to last forever, after
all. Ahead lay all the bleak, dull, hungry months till spring. The
guests, alarmed, would fling themselves with new ardor into
the Christmas festival. Twelfth Night would sweep upon them,
joy and folly reigning in absolute supremacy. And when that
inevitable morning after came at last, the departing revelers
would ride away with genuine nostalgia. What glorious times!

What a witty farce! What a mad jester or beautiful woman or brilliant talker was such-a-one!

But on this seventh day, renewed joy and nostalgic leavetaking lay far in the future. This morning, torpor and irritation reigned.

Wisely, the Earl's guests dispersed themselves, getting as far from one another as was possible within the snowbound confines of Exmoor. They explored the outbuildings, the walls, odd nooks and crannies where they had not troubled to go before. They strolled over to the stables to discuss horseflesh. They spent hours in his lordship's armory, looking at swords and pikes and arquebuses, fingering elaborately engraved suits of armor. They went to the kennels to see the hunting dogs, or to the mews to stare at the hawks and falcons they could not use. Even the kitchens might prove a new distraction for jaded palates, or the Earl's library, with its rows of expensive books in monogrammed green bindings. Anything for something new, for some quiet, and to get away from one another.

Women scolded and snapped. Higher servants boxed the ears of menials. Children got sick, hurt one another, screamed with outrage at every imagined slight. In the great hall, swords clashed with renewed ferocity, the young men hacking and slashing at each other with bated blades they half wished were sharps.

The fury of the fencing carried easily to the long gallery on the second floor, where Walter Castlemayne and Harry Langland stood alone, gazing up without much admiration at an oil painting of the first Earl of Exmoor, Lord Henry's illustrious father.

"They are not much alike, I think," said Harry. "There's no uncertainty, none of the rabbit in this old devil."

It was a standard noble portrait, the subject in full face, legs rather belligerently spread, one hand on the hilt of a dress sword, the other on the head of a favorite hound. Barrel-chested and big-stomached, with a full beard and a beet-red face, the first Earl certainly looked considerably more virile and aggressive than his son. Yet there was some similarity in the stubby nose and watery eyes, and in the little Cupid's-bow mouth. One almost expected the pink tongue to pop out and lick the painted lips.

"A man of decision, that's sure," said Castlemayne. "But then, so is the present Lord Henry, despite all his nerves and twitches. A man whose decisions count in this world, at least. As who knows better than I?"

It was some time since he had thought or done anything to influence the Earl's decision on his own petition. He realized this with some surprise, though Harry had mentioned his laxness more than once. In a world that contained Arabella Traherne, who could find time or energy for an aging, paunchy nobleman with nothing to recommend him but coffers full of money?

And yet, on that gray, snowy morning, Castlemayne felt the touch of cold reality upon him. Looking up at the big-bellied dynast in the picture, and through him at his rich and powerful offspring, Walter Castlemayne began to wonder if he should not begin to worry.

Then, above the distant clang of swords, above the moody drift of his own thoughts, a new sound intruded upon his reveries. Boot heels quick-stepping up the staircase from the floor below.

Castlemayne and Harry turned from the pictures to see who moved so briskly this dull, unprofitable morning.

Messer Lodovico Marsigliano strode into the gallery, accompanied by a covey of young gentlemen. Cousin Robert Naseby was with him, and some three or four other gaudily clad young courtiers. Against their rainbow-hued doublets and sleeves, slops and hose, Messer Lodovico's dapper black stood out sharp and grim. Thin-lipped and hollow-cheeked, long fingers gesturing, Marsigliano was a study in anguishingly acute angles, white on black.

". . . An excellent weapon, gentlemen, of course. The rapier is to the broadsword, I may say, as the cannon to the catapult: twice the reach, and thrice the penetration. While your broadsword rises majestically and falls, your rapier will be in and out six times, and leave as many holes spouting blood.

"But only in the hands of the master, gentlemen! An amateur may as well go back to his broadsword, or to a kitchen skewer for the matter of that. To wear a rapier if you cannot use it is sheer brag and swagger, as you English say. But for the skilled practitioner, it is the finest weapon in the world. And the Italians, I say with no immodesty, are the most skillful rapier fighters of this age."

His young audience listened, nodded sagely, looked as knowledgeable as they could.

"But then, what have we here, gentlemen?" Marsigliano interrupted his own flow of discourse. "Two genuine English masters of the art, as I am given to understand. Good day to you, Master Castlemayne—and to you, sir, also."

The two saluted him in silence. Marsigliano's black, dead eyes fixed at once on Harry Langland.

"I say, gentlemen, that Italians are the finest rapier fighters in the world, and Florentines the best of them all. Tell me, sir—do you not agree?"

"Why, as to that"—Harry felt Castlemayne's restraining hand upon his shoulder, and checked himself—"I am no authority on the quality of all the world's swordsmen."

"I further say, sir, that there's never an Englishman can touch a proficient Florentine or Lombard with single rapier."

"And I say, sir, that the world is full of men who talk—but few that act. And there's an end of it." Harry shrugged irritably and turned back to the Earl's ancestor on the wall.

"If I do understand you, young gentleman," said Marsigliano slowly and distinctly, "you say that some men in this world will brag and boast, and then flinch from the test?"

"Such, in plain English, is my meaning."

"I hope there is none here, young sir, of whom you would use such injudicious language?"

Harry shook off his friend's restraining hand.

"By Jesus Christ, Monsignor Jackass," he snapped, "your braying pains my ears! Had I a blade about me now, you'd get answer enough to all your arguments!" Harry Langland was a street brawler and a soldier. He had had enough of elegant hypocrisy and more than enough of the spindleshanks Italian.

"What, boy, would you quarrel?" shot back Messer Lodovico crisply. "Why then, perhaps some friend of mine may oblige you with the wherewithal."

"My pleasure, sir!"

Everybody's Cousin Robert, his weasel face perspiring with excitement, hastened to unfasten his sword belt and hangers and pass them over ceremoniously to Harry Langland. Harry fairly snatched them from his hand. The curly-haired, pimply-faced young men grinned wolfishly as they watched.

"What madness is this, Harry?" Castlemayne whispered urgently at his kinsman's ear. "The points are not blunted, man!"

But Harry, red-faced with anger, gave him no reply. His beefy hand closed about the elaborately worked hilt of Cousin Robert's new, unblooded sword. He drew the long steel blade smoothly from its velvet-covered scabbard.

"Messer Lodovico!" said Castlemayne, turning briskly to the man in black. "Surely, sir, this is unnecessary. If you gentlemen have some real grounds for quarreling, the matter had best be settled at some more propitious place and time. Or if it is truly a mere matter of the fencing skills of the two nations, why I myself—"

"This loud-voiced lout shall answer for the injuries he's done me," said Lodovico coldly. "Here and now. These gentlemen shall witness it."

The gaudily dressed youths were in fact ranging themselves along the wainscoted walls beneath the mullioned windows, their eyes sparkling with savage joy. A short, broad-shouldered youth took up a post at the doorway, alert for interruptions. From the great hall below, the clash of swords and the shouts of fencers rose loud enough to drown the sounds of combat in the gallery.

All planned and laid out in advance! thought Castlemayne, amazed. An ambuscade, by God! But why? Captain Devereux's doing, some devious attempt to strike at me through Harry? Surely not. . . . With nothing but an ornamental bodkin at his belt, he could only stare in helpless horror at what was happening.

The two combatants had stripped off doublets and sleeves. They stood ready, clad only in loose white shirts, dark thigh-length breeches, and silken hose. Each had a steel rapier in his hand, a baleful glitter in his eye.

The steel blades clashed.

There was a sucking in of breath. Glittering eyes followed the movements of the fighters. Castlemayne remembered rings of drunken soldiery, cheering on their favorites when men fought with quarterstaffs or fists in muddy siege-camp streets. He remembered bear-baiting at the Garden, and how aficionados urged on the dogs.

Blades slid and scissored, parted, clashed again. Thrust, parried, feinted, and withdrew. The measure closed, hilts clanged. Muscles strained. A subtle shift of weight, and one reeled back, retreating.

Castlemayne swore silently.

There was no contest. Messer Lodovico's reputation did not exaggerate. Harry raged and cut and drove mighty thrusts that spent themselves in empty air. Marsigliano played, a cat with a giant mouse. His rapier flicked and darted with a delicacy that was beautiful to see. His thin body moved quickly and deceptively as a juggler's, yet always with grace and elegance. Every move was a dancer's figure, precise, perfect. He watched his adversary sweat, watched the furious young man's eyes bulge with anger and exertion. And he smiled, an icy smile that never reached his eyes.

A universal gasp, and startled oaths.

Marsigliano's point had passed as if by magic through Harry Langland's desperate defense, hung poised two inches from his throat—then whisked derisively away. Harry swallowed slowly, his chest heaving.

Once again the hiss and clatter of blades, the stamp of feet. Pause, and heavy breathing. And again the clash of steel.

Messer Lodovico smiled stiffly, like a rusty death's-head. He was ready now. Harry stumbled back and back, defending himself desperately. Castlemayne could see a sudden glint of fear in his kinsman's eyes.

The weapons crossed and clung, ran up each other till knuckle-guards and cups crashed together. An instant's pause. Harry heaved, and Marsigliano faded backward, his blade sliding back along his opponent's, as though to open the measure. It will come now! thought Castlemayne. The instant the two blades part, Messer Lodovico will be back at him like a striking snake! Christ, Harry, can't you see—

Footsteps on the stairs.

Now—

"Malvaggio traditor—"

And a shaky croaking: "By Jesus Christ—"

An instant before the crossed blades parted, Walter Castlemayne had flung himself upon them. He had no weapon, nor even a left-hand gauntlet to catch an enemy's sword. Only the heavy fabric of his doublet to take the edges as he leaped and dragged the poised swords down.

And then:

"Peace ho! Put down those weapons, in his lordship's name!"

"And in the Queen's name too, you idiots!"

Six or eight husky foresters and gamekeepers, the Earl of Exmoor's green-and-tawny livery stretched tight over muscular chests and shoulders, appeared in the great arched doorway.

They shoved the stocky sentinel aside and burst in, shiny-bladed halberds poised at the ready. Behind them, Master Robert Cecil's little black-clad figure scuttled in, immensely irritated. And last of all, the Earl of Exmoor.

Lord Henry Traherne himself, ginger-colored whiskers bristling, face inflamed with anger. At his coming there was a sudden stillness in the long gallery.

There was nothing awesome in his mien. He was nervous, paunchy, watery-eyed as ever. One almost suspected he had just blown his nose to keep from snuffling in company. But when his glance passed irascibly around the room, all eyes dropped before his. And when he said, his fussy voice shrill with indignation, "Put up those swords!" they did. Harry uncertainly, Marsigliano blazing inwardly. But they obeyed the Earl's command. Even Castlemayne, rising slowly, noting that he had not so much as a scratched finger, felt unnerved in that angry presence.

It was a pure abstraction they obeyed. The great Earldom of Exmoor spoke to them through the unimpressive little man who happened to hold that title for this time and generation. And every man of them had known from toddling days that rank must be respected—and that the highest ranks spoke with the veritable voice of God.

"My lord—" began Walter Castlemayne. But the Earl cut him off.

"You are not injured, sir?" Lord Henry asked him sharply.

"No, your lordship. Fortune smiles upon me." Castlemayne essayed a rueful smile himself.

"He ran between the blades!" blurted one young man. "He put his body between their naked blades!"

"Most flamboyant, Master Castlemayne—and most rash." The Earl was obviously unmollified. "In future, you will do better to restrain your hot-blooded young kinsman in the first place. I shall hold you bound for your friend's future conduct in this matter, sir."

His lordship turned brusquely to the two more gross offenders. His little rabbity eyes flicked over them.

"Messer Lodovico Marsigliano, I am shocked at such tricks from a man of your years and responsible position. You are no harebrained boy, to do battle behind the chapel for a lady's perfumed glove! I put you on your parole, sir, to lay no hand to weapon again within these precincts!"

He did not even bother to speak to Harry Langland, but turned instead to the entire group, to all the tense young men. His scraggly moustache twitched once, nervously. He seldom had occasion for such lengthy and forceful declamations. Yet he forged ahead, indignation thrusting timidity to the wall.

"I put you all on notice, gentlemen! I'll have no brawling here. No quarreling, no defiances, no challenges. No swords and bucklers, no rapiers and daggers." He paused once more. But when he spoke again it was with the certainty of a man who knows his word will stand as law.

"The next man that so much as lays a hand upon his hilt, in whatever cause, will have no mercy here or elsewhere. I shall have him taken into custody like a common felon. I shall see to it that the laws of England are executed in fullest measure. In fullest measure, gentlemen!"

Castlemayne, still somewhat dazed, watched his lordship wheel and stride out of the gallery, his liveried foresters trooping at his heel. He saw Master Cecil limp after them, shaking his head and muttering. He sighed and flung a friendly arm across his kinsman's shoulders.

"Come then, Harry, my fine fire-eater. I'm your keeper now, it seems. And by God—if I'm a bit mad sometimes, cousin, you've played the raving Tom o' Bedlam this day!"

Harry Langland shrugged off Walter's arm.

"Ho, lad, give up the business for now," Castlemayne went on soothingly. "He's baited you enough to drive any man that calls himself a man to single fight, I know. But there's no help for it now. Another time, perhaps. . . ." His own eyes narrowed with a half-conscious lust to try the Florentine himself some-time, somewhere.

Harry merely shrugged and strode off, leaving a wondering Castlemayne to follow in his wake.

ii

When Sir Malcolm Devereux strolled into the solar that afternoon with Bianca Marsigliano on his arm, hardly a head turned. For though he might enjoy the Earl's high favor, Captain Devereux had decidedly failed to stir the souls of his lordship's jaded guests.

The older men, used to some respect and deference, found him too taciturn by half, too rough-spoken and arrogant when he did speak up. The young men found him merely dull, a middle-aged, unexciting hero of an earlier generation, with an older man's irritating superiority. Devereux had been punc-tiliously polite to every man there—and he had alienated every one of them by his ill-concealed contempt for them all.

When he strode into the solar that gray-smudged afternoon, only the oldest and most formal bowed or nodded before re-turning to their own dreary round of gossip. Devereux, glad for once of his own invisibility, sat down with his lieutenant's voluptuous lady at the smaller of the two fireplaces that warmed the high-arched room. The two of them sat alone, in intense but unobtrusive conversation. As they talked, he roasted chunks of mutton for her on a long two-pronged fork.

"My lord husband, *capitano mio*," Bianca whispered in high-strung, nervous accents, "he is frenzied truly, *pazzo, furioso.* Full of wild suspicions of myself and that foolish cousin of Master Castlemayne. He paces up and down the room like a beast in a cage ever since the great lord stopped him taking his revenge this morning. I have never seen the fit so strong upon him."

"It will pass," grunted Devereux. "It always has before. This time, God willing, before he slits some poor fool's belly open."

"Mary Mother grant it," Bianca muttered. Ceruse and fucus and other cosmetics, applied with all her skill, barely sufficed to conceal the ravages of the night before.

"Meantime," Devereux's low growling voice continued, "with this jealous rage upon him, he's little use to me. Which is most unfortunate. I have great need of him these next half-dozen days and nights."

"It is a pity, *cavaliere.*" She tossed her head again, this time in irritation. I should have understood before, she thought. His mind runs only on his business. On this cursed ship. "But then, you know my husband lives only to serve you, sir. Perhaps tomorrow even—"

"It is possible, Bianca *mia,*" grated Devereux, his voice darker still. Her heart throbbed suddenly at the unexpected verbal caress. "But it may also be that tomorrow will be too late for me."

"My lord?" she asked, completely off balance now.

He told her. Why they had come so far through the snowy wastes in winter. Why he must have the *Golden Fortune* for his own.

As Devereux spoke, gazing into the flames, he saw in his mind's eye a face.

A gaunt, loose-fleshed old woman in a red wig. Sad, bitter eyes with pouches under them, and an unloving mouth. Bony, dark-veined hands like talons, still strong to clutch and hold. A tall, unwomanly body, poker-thin, swathed in yards of costly fabrics, exquisite white lace, glittering with precious stones. And he heard again the smoothly modulated voice of the great Lord Treasurer Burghley, speaking for this gorgeous, awful apparition: "Her gracious Majesty does not feel . . ."

Devereux could never remember the precise words that came after that, though he had often tried to do so in the months since. But then of course, old Burghley's elegantly chiseled words did not particularly matter. The meaning was clear enough. He saw it carved in Roman capitals on stone, like the decrees of God Almighty:

The English expeditionary force to France has failed. The League remains in the field unbroken, a Spanish sword upraised against the King of France, our good ally.

The English captains have spent several times the estimated charges. Money wasted, money ill spent. Rumors even of corruption, dead pay, collusion between some captains and the paymasters . . .

There will be no more English expeditionary forces.

"Nor has her most gracious Majesty"—the harsh, unfeminine, old woman's face looked stubbornly out the window—"any further employment or command in mind for Colonel Willoughby, or Captain Burrow, or Captain Devereux . . ."

And well enough for Lord Willoughby, thought Devereux bitterly, who was born a peer. Well enough for Burrow, who had half his life ahead to regain the royal favor. But Sir Malcolm Devereux—he snorted sarcastically—Sir Malcolm Devereux was a mere knight only, and a poor one at that. And Captain Devereux—the sardonic smile was gone—was forty-two years old. The autumn of a man's life, as the whoreson poets said.

Age and long experience, still bowing and scraping to royal ministers and fat homekeeping noblemen, still begging for employment at the tables of the great! When by all rights, Sir Malcolm Devereux himself should be among the great men of the realm. A man of wealth and substance, a name to conjure with, a power in the land.

His right hand had fallen upon the hilt of the long, heavy rapier that swung at his side. No dress sword this, but a killing weapon. Toledo steel with a simple Spanish hilt. Plain shallow cup below the crosspiece, the hilt itself of iron ringed for gripping. Unconsciously he gripped it now. His short, thick fingers closed and tightened, till the hairs bristled on the back of his hand and the hard knuckles stood out white and bloodless.

"But—God's wounds—the *Golden Fortune* will do it for me yet!" he rumbled, still not looking at the woman beside him.

"Nothing to rebuild a commander's reputation like a successful sea raid on the King of Spain's golden lifeline. Tow another Great Carrack home to Plymouth—and there'll be no looting on my prizes—and watch her Majesty's gracious favor shine upon me once again. Watch Burghley beam through his noble white beard and bethink him of the rewards and promotions due my long and faithful service. Aye, and watch that overbusy brat of his, this Cecil whelp that presumes to judge me now, fawn and scrape and offer his assurances of friendship.

"They will all bow then, and nod and smile, the powers and names in their furs and velvet robes and jewelry. And the likes of Walter Castlemayne will come to *me* for employment and honorable commands. To Sir Malcolm Devereux, of her Majesty's Privy Council . . . perhaps, with a judicious marriage, a peerage even! To ask and have, command and be obeyed—while the Castlemaynes of this gall-and-wormwood world come crawl and cringe to me . . .

"One more fling of the dice, then! One more chance for what is justly due me, by Christ's blood! This monstrous cockle boat. This arse-heavy, bat-winged thing they're building even now, in Deptford Yards. And then to hell with the wars the politicians will not pay to win and blame us when we lose. . . ."

Bianca listened in a daze, tempest-tossed on roaring seas of her own conflicting passions.

As he began his tale she watched his steady eyes, focused on the fireplace. She listened to his breathing, overloud perhaps, but regular and deep, obedient to his will. She saw his hand go white at the knuckles as it fell upon his sword hilt. Impulsively, she stretched out one soft hand to touch his.

The power in those fingers, she thought. The power in that

body! The Lord God had given her the dark gift of life—but Sir Malcolm Devereux's gift to her had been greater still. For he had the power to extinguish her like a candle. To quench absolutely the fires of lust that burned always just below the surface of her consciousness. Even at the memory, her body seemed to melt, to turn soft and yielding beneath the tight-fitting satin gown, the petticoats, the farthingale and stays.

Then, as he exposed his danger to her, confessed his vulnerability to the jackals of the court, she was thrown into confusion. Was it possible that the life of her Great Captain, jouster with the mighty Guise and the unbeaten Parma, should depend upon one ship, one petty court intrigue?

Unthinkable. And yet . . .

She saw the deep-etched lines about his eyes for the first time. And was there a hint of salt-and-pepper gray in that jutting black spade beard? She looked momentarily away, her lower lip trembling.

Then she turned back to him, her dark eyes full of wonder. For one thing emerged from this tumult of emotions with dazzling clarity—she did not want him less, but more! The cracked idol was more to her even than the unbroken symbol of incarnate power that Devereux had always been to her.

It made no sense, but the blood pounding in her veins told her it was so.

Perhaps in time she would come to comprehend it. But that did not matter. All that mattered now was that slow pulsing in her veins, the flush that spread over her cheeks and throat and breast, the dark passion that no man but Malcolm Devereux had ever given peace.

She remembered that first time, in Avignon, the evening of the day when he had swept the innyard clean and saved her from the scythes and mattocks of the peasant mob. It all came rushing back to her—the swaybacked bed, the sticky heat, the whine of flies in the low inn chamber, the creak of cartwheels on the cobblestones below their window, the laugh of an early drunkard. And Malcolmn Devereux's dark-bearded face, coming down upon her in the darkness. His hands upon her, his rough hairy thighs, his cock driving into her—and into her—until she cried aloud and wept and cried again and writhed and groaned and died beneath the steady driving power of his unending strokes.

Dear God—and my Magdalene!

And afterwards, at other towns, crossing France from Provence to Paris that bright green spring. At country inns, at that chateau outside of Orléans, even in the open fields along the Seine, he had come to her. A dozen times at least. A dozen moments of release for her, of liberation from the rack of a desire forever kindled and forever unfulfilled.

A dozen times—and then no more. As coldly and casually as he had begun it, the Great Captain had ended the affair. Messer Lodovico, he had found, was of far more use to him than any woman could ever be. For Lodovico Marsigliano had rapidly become indispensable to Sir Malcolm Devereux in the primary business of his life, which was killing other men.

So it had ended as it began. A trivial indulgence for the captain—the climax of Bianca's life. And now she sat beside him, older and shrewder by eight years, and put her plump hand on his, trembling like a green girl at the thought that Sir Malcolm Devereux, the closest thing to God that she had ever known, might have some use for her after all.

She moistened her painted lips and listened.

It was a simple thing he had to ask of her, but an ugly one and perhaps dangerous. He would not ask it of his Bianca, he assured her, if he could see any other way out of the forest that pent him in. It would multiply her husband's pain, for a time at least—but had he not deserved some suffering? The sudden feral glitter in her eyes showed him that he had.

Devereux paused to tear a chunk of smoking mutton with his strong yellow teeth. His thick lips smiled at her as he extended half the portion, still impaled on the fork.

"I thank my lord," she said, her brown eyes brimming with sentiment and desire.

Devereux contrived to smile. But his soul was bitter as cold brine within.

Begging was a normal part of Captain Devereux's trade. Under one name or another, it was a part of every ambitious man's career. But to beg and bare his soul before this notorious harlot—only the most painful need could drive him to it. Yet with this woman, there was no other way. This capricious creature of feeling he could neither bribe nor bully into doing what she must do for him. Not her sensible self-interest, but her pure animal nature—what she called her heart—must be won to his purposes. For her soggy strumpet's heart, he thought bitterly, a man can only plead.

"But come now," he said abruptly, rising. "Let us stretch our limbs in the gallery, where there will be fewer ears so late." Best shift to some more pleasant and distracting scene, he grimaced inwardly, before we lay the grimy details out before her. And then, he wanted somehow to distance himself from her cloying passion. Unhealthy, he thought wryly, to sit so close to a bitch in heat.

"Indeed, my lord, your wish—"

She rose also, with creaking stays and rustling skirts, and put her bright-ringed hand upon his sleeve. The few eyes that followed them as they left the solar focused on the woman, with her close-fitting, low-cut bodice, her soft sensual features. For the Great Captain, they had only dull resentment or casual unconcern.

iii

Castlemayne and Arabella stood together, sheltered by the high stone portal, watching the snow that swirled down into the empty courtyard.

It was very late that winter afternoon. The light was filtering out of things, leaving only a gray-white world of gently falling snow. The two young people stood close together in the doorway, not touching, yet close enough to feel each other's warmth. The man tall and wide-shouldered, a short cape flung Collie-Westonward across his scarlet doublet. The slim girl wrapped in a dark-blue cloak that blew about her, uncovering the silver gown beneath. Snow powdered both their fair young heads. Cold drops, melted crystals, beaded both their brows and glistened on their eyelids.

"We must go in, my lady," murmured Castlemayne.

"Yes, Walter," she answered automatically. But made no move to go.

They had been visiting the kennels and the mews with some of the restless younger guests. Now, on their return, they dawdled alone before the great hall door, watching dreamily as their own footprints filled up with snow. Though they hardly knew it yet, Castlemayne and Arabella were utterly worn out with talk and sleeplessness and their own emotions.

They stood now in a strange sort of limbo. Like people that had come to the end of the world—and taken one step more.

Behind them, the great hall. Candles lit along the walls, trestle tables placed, servants larking at their work, steward and butler snapping anxious orders. The heart of the whole vast labyrinth, alive, aswarm with people, balanced at the hinge of the holidays. Warmth and food and drink, and the merry-making that went dreamily on forever in their young minds.

Before them, a wilderness of cold and darkness, falling snow, choked roads and frozen hills, dark barriers of forest. Farther still, and most forbidding, the moorland and the sea. The desolate expanse of Dartmoor, lost in mists and drifts and howling winds, where no living thing would move this night. The roaring wilderness of the Atlantic, monstrous black waves shredded into spray, a tumult where no creature could live at all on such a night.

Here in their limbo stood the two, half protected by the rude stone gateway from the wind. Hovering somewhere between wakefulness and sleep, tingling deliciously at the icy touch of a snowflake on the nose.

A nervous, chafing, fretful day, mused Castlemayne. Marsigliano's fury, Harry's outburst had been rather symptomatic than unique. Even Arabella had seemed distant and preoccupied, vexed over trifles.

But all that was over now.

For Walter Castlemayne, nothing existed now but this timeless, dream-colored moment. The shock of the morning's encounter with the hollow-cheeked Italian was the palest shadow of reality. The great Captain Devereux, the *Golden Fortune*, the Earl who must decide might never have existed. There was only falling snow, the girl beside him, and peace, peace beyond all hope or understanding.

The icy wind reached in to touch the Lady Arabella, and she shivered suddenly. Castlemayne looked quickly down at her blond head, tilted slightly back, shimmering with combs and jewelry. He saw her glistening lashes and her tiny nose, rosy with the cold. He laughed deep in his throat and put a protective arm about her slender shoulders.

"Don't," she said. And then, quite miserably, "Oh dear Lord, please—"

"My sweet lady, what is it then? What can I do—or have I done?" He was stammering like a gawky boy, stricken at the sheer wretchedness in her voice.

"Nothing. Please, Walter. Oh, just—just let me be, for Jesus' sweet sake!" And she pressed her small white teeth hard against her lower lip, to keep the tears from coming.

Arabella had been wracked all that week by strange passions in conflict with a conscience she hardly knew she had.

Day after day, her heart beat more quickly when Walter Castlemayne was near, sharp pangs of anxiety clutched at her breast when he was not. When their eyes met, the blood rushed warmly to her face, so that she hardly dared cast a glance at him when any other eye was on them. And when she dared it, when her heart beat up at the sight of his lean cheeks and smiling lips, his ardent eyes upon her—then at once she heard old Agnes's sharp accents slashing at her ear.

She might tease her old nurse, play worldling by day. But the voice of Agnes Mayhew haunted Arabella's nights. Sometimes solemn and admonitory: "A maid's chaste treasure is God's gift, to be preserved immaculate as it came from the giver." And then, almost as an afterthought: "Until the husband comes whom He shall choose for thee." Or harshly, brutally physical: "The wound of a woman's deflowering, the agony of childbirth, the blood, the pain—these are the heritage of Eve's sinfulness," and, on a dying note, "with God's help only to be borne." Or most horrifyingly, the childish catch from her versified Testament, that had tinkled monotonously through her mind all day:

> Beside the wall of Jezre-el
> The dogs devoured Jezebel.

Jezebel the scarlet queen, queen of courtesans and whores!

The most terrible of all was to be so alone. No mother, no confidante to guide her through this jungle of her own new desires and newly kindled fears. Oh dear Lord, she thought, my Aggie's eyes were ever kind, sharp though her words might be! I do know she loves me, and all the more for every strand of gray I've given her. But what does she know of this—this melting at the heart when his eyes touch me? And how should I dare speak of it to her? Oh God, what shall I do?

Her old familiar world, the world of all-year-round, had faded to a memory, oddly dim, as of a former life. The quiet countryside of Devon, Dartmoor and the red cliffs, even her father's parks and fields seemed to have mysteriously vanished. She was cut off from these simple, safe, reassuring things by the falling snow, the thick-choked roads, and her own hot, bewildering emotions. Trapped in the bizarre new empire of the passions that Exmoor Castle had suddenly become. Locked in alone, or so it seemed to her, with this strange, wild young man.

Who was he, after all, this stranger with the name of a little boy she had once known?

This handsome wizard Castlemayne, she wondered desperately, who has turned order into chaos, and shaken all the castle upside down about my head? This stranger with the bright blue eyes, who fights in my father's hall and comes to my own chamber in the night. Who dances and laughs and leaps on swords—they say he flung himself upon the very blades. And might walk on water next, for all I know. Who was he? And how could she—

His worried hand was on her arm. She shook it off.

"We must go in to supper, Master Castlemayne. We must go in!"

Her voice was clear, her chin was high. It was a supreme effort to escape, to get away from the man who seemed to hold her destiny like a struggling sparrow in his bony hand. She must get away and think, try to put herself and her familiar world together once again.

Castlemayne stared, stupefied.

He saw only her sudden brusqueness, her unaccountable drawing from his touch. He heard only her desire to abandon him for the banquet hall, where the rules of precedence set them a table's length apart. Groggy with weariness, he did not see her brimming tears, her white-clenched fists. Anger flared in him, like tinder-dry pine boughs ignited by a flash of lightning.

"Now by God—by God, mistress, if—"

"You will not raise your voice to me!" Her lips were white now too, her tone imperious. "Let me pass at once!"

She was precisely at the breaking point. Her throat ached to weep. She must escape to her room—God, let him move aside—she could not, would not weep before this stranger.

Without a further word, Castlemayne flung wide one heavy door and stepped aside to let her pass.

For one instant, Arabella only stared, astounded by what had happened. The whole furious exchange had taken place in half-whispers, and had lasted perhaps thirty seconds' time. Then she swept by him, her fair head lowered, clutching her blue cloak about her.

Castlemayne watched with angry, baffled eyes as she hurried up the near side aisle of the bustling hall, her small figure passing pillar after pillar, passing the head table itself, mounting a short flight of steps to disappear at last through a gothic doorway toward the new wing of the castle.

He stood like a man stunned between the lofty entranceway and the towering carved-oak screen, servants moving busily about him. With elaborate apologies, the servingmen shepherded him a step or two farther on into the great hall. The steward closed the door behind him, shutting out the wind. Castlemayne heard nothing, paid no attention to the meaningless activity about him.

He had done nothing to rouse her sudden wrath—nothing. He had not even spoken of that night. Not once, not all that week. He had never dreamed of importuning her that he might come again to her chamber—he was sure of that now. How could she think it of him, that he would lay one defiling finger on his rose, his pale hawthorn flower?

But a cruel thorny rose indeed, to cut me for no reason, for no offense of mine!

He began to move, slowly and mechanically, drifting up the hall, through yellow candlelight and purposefully milling servants. He drifted past his own place toward the high table, where she would sit among the great ones of the county, with Cecil and with Devereux.

"Why then, if she will have it so—so be it!" he muttered half aloud. "But a man can bear so much—no more!"

The great hall seemed suddenly too still, despite the servants' bustle. Fierce urges, firmly held in check these seven days, now clamored for release—flung themselves against the bars. Castlemayne stood for long seconds there, before the high table, the still untenanted tribunal of his betters. Abruptly he reached for the glittering pitcher of Venetian cut glass, filled with dark French wine, that would soon provide his lordship's own opening libation. With a steady yet exultant hand, he poured himself a brimming goblet and raised it to his lips.

For the first time since his return to Exmoor, he drank without a silent toast to the Lady Arabella Traherne.

Sir Malcolm Devereux, standing at the stair head looking down, smiled sourly over his bristling beard. He turned to his dark-haired companion, indicating with a jerk of his thumb the young gentleman below.

"Tonight," he said, as casually as he could manage, "tonight should prove excellent for our purpose."

"Indeed, it would seem so," Bianca answered, watching the handsome head tilt slowly back. With a certain professional weariness, she recognized the symptoms.

"You have only to hold him in that place we spoke of," Devereux reminded her, "until we may legitimately note your absence and send a suitably selected search party to the rescue. It was your lord husband's scheme, though he suggested a chambermaid. And of course we have—complicated the arrangement somewhat."

His hard laugh barked above the growing bustle, the first tuning of stringed instruments, the mingled seeking of the flute and the recorder.

Below, Walter Castlemayne drained his cup and wiped his mouth with the back of his hand. Flung back his head, vertiginous, to gaze up at the vaulting arches and crisscrossing hammer beams far above. He felt a wave of dizziness, heat of red wine in his belly, laughter swelling in his throat.

∽ Eight ∾

The Seventh Circle
of Hell

i

Red flame blazed up a moment, sank to a baleful glow. It flickered fitfully, flared up again, and fell. Resin sizzled in a blackened cresset. There was a drift of smoke against a beam. In the surrounding darkness, a horse whinnied, steam boiling from shivering black nostrils.

There was a screech of frozen hinges, a low chuckle, and a sudden rush of air that bent the flame and sent the shadows wild. A gust of distant revelry and music floated in. Two figures stood silhouetted against the square of night, the gleaming windows of the great hall far off across the courtyard. There was a *screek* again and silence, a murmur in the darkness, the rustle of stiff satin clothing. Velvet slippers stumbled forward over the earthen floor.

Castlemayne and Bianca Marsigliano emerged into the flickering half-light, leaning on each other, laughing thickly. Melting snow still shone on their wet, wind-scattered hair and flushed faces as they came to an uncertain halt. His teeth flashed in the torchlight as he turned to her and gestured vaguely at a glossy horse's rump.

"You see, mistress, there she stands as I predicted, on all four feet upright. Indulging in the sin of gluttony at that," he added, nodding at the crunch of oats. "And all the rest of them the same, I'll wager a crown a head upon it. All firmly planted on four hooves. Nary a one crouching on his hocks and gaskins."

"But, *signore*, we have not examined all the others yet." She laughed unsteadily. Her lips were purple with paint and wine. "This one may be—how do you say it?—the exception of the rule. An impious pagan brute with no reverence for the holy time. A French mare, *per avventura*," she improvised ingeniously, "for they say it's fashionable now in Paris to be an unbeliever."

Her dark cloak fell open as she spoke, revealing shoulders almost bare in the foreign gown.

"No, by God!" stoutly maintained Castlemayne. "Our English beasts are brutes, but they're no unbelievers." He put a stern hand on her olive-tinted shoulder, smooth and full-fleshed above the low-cut bodice, to emphasize his indignation.

"That is precisely what I said, *signore*." She raised her glossy head and touched his wet cheek with a playful finger. "That in a place called Wales, at least, barn and byre and stable are filled with kneeling animals this time of year. Surely, Master Castlemayne, your English farmyard creatures are no less moved to venerate their natural Lord at Christmastime . . ."

"Ah, but I have you now, sweet lady! It is true the Welsh beasts do fall upon their knees to worship, so holy is the season. And so do the beasts of the West Country, I've no doubt. Horses and cattle and sheep and goats even, I'll warrant, in stables and barns and pens and folds through all these snowy hills. All kneeling in humble reverence, with their heads toward Bethlehem." He nodded piously to himself. "A lovely Christian tale, and I do most certainly believe it."

Her eyebrow arched questioningly, and a mocking glance brought him back to the reality of the mare's rump.

"But, mistress, you've clean mistook your time! Aye, there's your error, there's the crux. Our Christian brutes do surely kneel—but only on the holiest of nights, only on Christmas Eve, the night of all the year when the Lord was first made manifest to men. While this present night, my lady"—he fumbled through the calendar and his fading memory—" this is the Eve of the Circumcision merely. An event of unquestioned significance, of course, and one of the fixed festivals required in our church, but . . ."

He paused, steadied himself on the gate of the stall before them.

"Is it so, my lord?" Her rich mouth smiled. Her eyes were wide and dark and fathomless in the torchlight. "The Circumcision merely? Why then, we have come a cold snowy walk for nothing. And had best hurry back before the snow becomes so thick we cannot find our way."

She made as if to close her cloak, but let it slip instead. It fell with a soft plump on the frozen ground behind her. Her breasts, bared almost to the nipple, gleamed dully in the dimness as she bent to pick up the fallen garment.

Castlemayne laughed softly. His eyes were red with weariness and wine, bright with passion too long restrained. His body shook with sexual excitement, the lust of a young hound at sight of a bitch in heat.

Bianca saw, and smiled. Still smiling at him, she turned away and wandered idly off down the aisle between the stalls. Wandered aimlessly, as it seemed, with the young man following eagerly after. But paused at the first empty horse box she came to—a wooden cubicle without a gate, straw heaped far back in its black maw—and turned to him again, and raised her face to his.

Then he was kissing her in darkness. Soft lips and teeth and tongue. Biting, teasing him. Nails stroking gently down his neck. For a moment she drew briefly from him, gazing up, provocative and taunting. There was a gurgle of easy mirth, deep in her dark throat. There was an odor of musk and civet, an odor of woman's flesh. He pulled her back to him, buried his hungering mouth in hers.

Images behind the retina glowed in his seething brain.

Glare of the great hall, howling merriment, viols and tambourines—a moment, an hour ago. Wine trickling negligently
from a corner of his mouth. Wipe it off listlessly. Pour again,
with steady, drunken hand. And watch the dancers, drinkers,
jesters. Hear the senseless jubilation. Feel the anguish—and
the rebellion growing.

Devereux by the Earl's side, square-cut beard jerking as he
talks of campaigns coming in the spring. Skull-faced Marsigliano
listens stonily, adds his bit, responds when called upon. The
icy, perfect ensign once again—he's made his peace already.
And poor Harry pacing their tower room above, chafing, angry,
unfit for company.

Arabella far away, tiny in her curtained bed. She has not
come down at all.

Sparkling purple beads about the silver goblet's brim.

"And enough of this, by God!" Rising in a reeling room,
moving out into the dance.

A swirling galliard, color and light, strength in his tense
thighs, a woman in his arms. Soft cheeks and saucy eyes, a
crimson-painted mouth. Swaying, laughing, touching, dim-
pling, sensuality incarnate. Bianca Marsigliano, warm and quick
and clinging, in his arms.

And Arabella far away, princess of unreal romance, her
large pale eyes and virgin mouth drifting from his blurring
memory. Who is she, Arabella?

Bianca's hot breath was loud against his eardrums now,
mingling with the thunder of his blood. The soft hills and
valleys of her body, satin-sheathed, pressed tantalizingly against
him, slid lingering away. Her deft hands caressed him expertly,
cheek and neck and chest, brushing thighs and private parts.

His laughter boomed suddenly, echoed through the stables.

"Ah, sweet hussy, lovely strumpet—"

He swung her up and carried her into the coal-black stall.

Flung her back into the straw and lunged laughing after
her. Hooked his fingers in against her warmth and tore the

tight bodice, ripping the smock beneath, baring her pale flesh.

"My lord, your cloak to lie upon—I will not be treated—"

No heed—no heed. Only booming laughter, jubilant, almost boyish, as he discovered her nakedness with eager hands and lips. As he groped through satin skirts and silken petticoats, cursing whalebone, exuberantly passionate to possess her.

In her bitter, infuriated mind, a surge of malediction. My gown, you bullnecked English villain—ruined utterly! And when will my magnanimous Lodovico purchase such another? Yet bruise me, bruise me—that is strength at least— Heat kindled in her loins. Half naked in the darkness, she moved her thighs and groaned beneath him.

The ivory hilt of his dress poniard came awkwardly between them. He snapped the velvet hangers like brittle thread, flung the sheathed dagger rattling against the thin planks that separated the man and woman from an excited gelding not three feet away.

She relaxed beneath him then, loose and trembling, wondering wildly if— He no longer laughed, but pressed her deep into the straw, crushing her mouth under his. Their tongues met to tilt and fence together in a counterfeit of combat, till both forgot to breathe.

"You hurt me, sir!" she gasped. "You are so rough." But her heart was racing as it had not in many years.

He chuckled. "You've had rougher louts than I, no question, in whatever sink of Italy you learned your trade, good mistress. Now come kiss me gently, and we'll go on to better sport."

"Indeed, my lord," she said unsteadily, "indeed . . ."

But when he reached for her again, her thighs were closed against him, her body rigid.

"What, lady—no conscience pangs, I hope?" Surely not, my lusty queen, he thought. It would be a great crime, that so gorgeous a sinner should regret it.

He touched one heaving breast. She struck his hand aside.

She had heard what he had not. Creak of hinges, stumbling

footfalls, a muttered curse in the darkness at the far end of the stable.

So soon, then? she thought with a sudden pang. So soon—?

Castlemayne sat happily back upon his haunches, fumbling now with his own clothing. He saw nothing but Bianca, her pale face, the dim outline of her naked torso there below him in the blackness. Drank in the odor of her body mingled with the smells of oats and excrement. Heard only vaguely how the gelding moved suddenly on his left, whinnied, shrill and startled behind the plank partition. Till somewhere a guttering torch flared up once more, lighting the rear wall of the stall, reflecting into Bianca's wide, staring eyes.

Bianca saw his face too in that sudden fitful glare. Saw the ruddy light shine on his left side, illuminating chin and cheekbone, straight nose and forehead ridged with laughter. Saw a shoulder muscle swell beneath his thin silk shirt as he shrugged his doublet off.

And saw the man behind him. A stocky silhouette, heavy-shouldered, outlined against the infernal glow of the distant torch. And gleams of hellish light up and down an eighteen-inch steel blade.

She knew what was coming. Yet she could not help but shriek aloud as the light blazed brighter still.

Wild-eyed, glaring like a wounded bull, Harry Langland loomed above them.

ii

Oh, Jesus Christ—the bitch! The flaming strumpet! And that one-eyed villain swore—

"Aye, master, waiting there for you this moment, hot as a cat in rut! Paid me in good English coin to seek you out and tell you straight—she waits for you alone, for only you can do her business!"

A wink and a leer, diabolic in the hellish glow of the huge kitchen fires.

"You'd know where, she said. And better worth your while too, I'll warrant, than swilling ale here with turnspits and kitchen wenches—"

Harry had tipped the grinning hostler with everything he'd had, and come. Come laughing with anticipation as he plowed through knee-deep snow and roaring wind across the courtyard. Till the heavy door swung open beneath his hand and creaked shut behind him. Till there was quiet edgeless air around him, darkness, the snorts of beasts and scrape of horsetails against wood. And then, far up the hard-earth aisle, where a single torch still burned, he heard a low chuckle and a faint scuffling in the straw.

The exultant laughter died in Harry's throat. His eyes grew suddenly opaque.

He swayed drunkenly and lurched forward through the pulsing darkness toward the telltale sound, the distant torch's glow. His shaggy head swung left and right, probing black horse boxes as he hurried by. Then he saw the crouching figure in the left-hand stall, white-shirted, not alone. Saw dimly through his drunkenness the familiar white-blond head, the lean, wide-shouldered back. And then the woman, wanton in the straw, her bodice torn away.

She made me wait till she had taken off her precious gown!

The eyes of Harry Langland glittered crimson in the guttering torchlight. As of itself, his dagger came into his hand.

Harry could bear no more. He had been bored and baffled by his betters, teased and tempted by the Italian whore, publicly humiliated by the walking skeleton she called her husband. Now he was made game of by a pestilent stablehand—and betrayed by his own kinsman! It was too much. Molten lava surged through his veins, fury blazed up in his drunken heart.

He staggered forward, lifting his dagger with the heavy pommel down, like a club. He had no other weapon. He saw no stick or cudgel or less deadly thing. And this drunken midnight fury must explode in action, or his racing veins would burst.

By Christ, he shall not have it all! Not the Earl's wheyfaced daughter and the whore of Naples too—

The torch flared up. The woman shrieked. And Harry swung the heavy hartshorn hilt, drove it downward viciously at the back of Walter's skull.

Castlemayne, still smiling, saw Bianca's eyes dilate, her mouth fly open screaming. Sensed something move behind him as the first shrill note of terror savaged his ears. And moved himself, started to move, reacting to a blow unseen.

He felt a shock and a blue-white flash of agony—glancing off the occiput, smashing into the left shoulder. Unwinding thighs flung him to the right, half blind with pain, yet diving for his poniard somewhere there. Wild hands fumbled for the glitter in the crackling straw. Fumbled desperately and found it. Wrenched the weapon from its velvet sheath. And then a hail of blows about the head and neck and shoulders sent him sprawling on his face.

He rolled over, rolled again, dodging, twisting, out into the hard-packed earthen aisle. He writhed about, saw two sturdy legs lunge after him. He heard hoarse breathing and a guttural curse. Arms across his face and legs drawn up to protect himself, he aimed a mule kick at an advancing kneecap. Felt his heel impact upon the shinbone—too low for crippling—and rolled away again. But joyed savagely to hear the other man roar with pain and reel back against a rending horse-box gate.

Then Castlemayne was on his feet, half crouching, the poniard in his hand. Giddy, on the edge of falling, still nearly blind with the agony in neck and head. Yet balancing and moving forward, seeking out his foe.

He saw him, sensed him, beyond the dimming torchlight. A hulking shape moving in darkness, glimpsed through scarlet throbs of pain. Heavyset, dagger-armed—but staggering with every step upon the injured knee. Now, by God, we'll see! swore Castlemayne, licking a trickle of blood from one corner of his mouth.

He heard Bianca babble something in Italian, and her sudden silence. Heard the heavy breathing of the other man. Started to circle slowly round him, taut to spring at the first opening.

He did not know by whom nor why he was attacked. He did not even wonder. A dagger fight at close quarters was as dangerous as any fight could be. In the dark, with both men hurt already, someone was very like to die. Stunned and bleeding, Castlemayne felt no curiosity—only a passion to stay alive, and a lust to kill the man behind the other blade.

Toward this simple goal he moved with the coolness and cunning of a man bred up to arms.

The hilt of his dress poniard was of carved ivory, slippery against a sweaty palm. He found an elaborately carved centaur beneath the middle finger that gave him some purchase on it. The blade would sure be inches shorter too, he realized, and delicate, not meant for fighting. Beware the bone, or the thing would snap like an icicle. . . .

He shifted slowly, carefully to the left—the other's limping side. Damn the darkness! he cursed inwardly. If the torch would but rise again, and dazzle him an instant . . . but shuffle leftward, close and open. Keep the pressure on that leg of his, don't let the strength return.

Quick as the thought, Castlemayne lunged through the pain, the muddy half-light shot with crimson, thrusting upward at the other's chest and throat. Saw him leap back out of reach and all but fall upon the gimper leg that buckled underneath him, squeezing out a gasp of agony.

Now move easy once again, he thought. Let the pain fade a bit. Till he forgets the leg again, and trusts it. Then force him once more to throw all his weight upon that knee . . .

He stepped slowly to the left.

But even as he calculated, he felt the hot iron in his own

battered skull. Shuddered under pain that burned like tar upon
a wound.

Waves of blood and nausea seemed to rise in his throat. The
world slipped and wavered, dividing in delicate streamers of
red and black. It must be now, he thought dizzily, now before
. . . O God he hit me harder than I knew.

Now!

He feigned a sudden stroke, clumsy beyond credence, beyond his intent. The other tensed to leap back from the blow
that clearly would not come. Hesitated, while one might draw
half a breath, between a quick counterstroke and prudent holding back. Decided. The half-familiar shoulders hunched, and
the knife shot out.

Castlemayne saw it coming. A beautiful long curving thrust,
sucked in by the awkward feint. A fast hard drive, the right
foot sliding forward, all his body weight flung out upon that
knee. Slashing far across at Castlemayne's retreating forearm,
at the hand that held his weapon. A thrust that aimed to cripple,
to disarm, but not to kill. Castlemayne wondered fleetingly why.
But the longest thrust he could! he exulted, tensing for his
counterthrust. The worst he could upon that battered, swelling
leg!

"Oh, Jesus Christ!"

The joint gave way, twisted outward, and the other man
went down. Pitched forward, to fall crunchingly upon the
knee itself. And screamed aloud, paralyzed with pain, helpless
in an instant.

But for an instant only! blazed Castlemayne. Do it now—
that voice—now get it in—that voice—now now—

Still moving awkwardly and dreamlike, Castlemayne had time
and more than time to counter. Time to step in, crouching low,
closing with the falling man. Swing his left arm, strike aside
the other's dagger. Bring in his own elegantly tapered blade in a
short, upward jab.

Brief resistance of a velvet doublet, solid flesh beneath.

The point is in! Beneath the rib cage—feel the blade in—

And twist it, cutting through softly coiled entrails, the tangle of nerves focused there.

A wild, hardly human cry split the other's throat. Horror and disbelief gathered in one awful rabbit-shriek. The head angled grotesquely backward as he screamed, the throat pulsing with desperate life unwilling to be ended.

Heavy and solid now the body fell, sideways and back, with Castlemayne upon him. A last throbbing heave of the hard-muscled torso almost toppled the victor. Castlemayne jerked the knife in the belly one more time, heard it scrape on bone. Slid out the blade and rose, noting that it was not broken.

Delicate handling that, he could not help but think. By God, I'll make a bravo yet, if the wars should fail.

He stood above his victim, his head still pulsing with pain, but grinning already with relief and exultation. His broad chest rose and fell, sucking in forgotten air. His right hand, that held the poniard, shone wet and red.

At his feet the dying man twitched convulsively, rolled from side to side. Clutched at the hard earth, splitting fingernails. Writhed like an animal with a broken back.

Tried to speak and could not. Twisted more feebly—gave one violent start—shuddered through all his heavy frame. Breathed from his mouth a sudden rush of blood, dark flowing over chin and neck. And did not breathe again.

That's done him!

Castlemayne dropped to his knees, swaying slightly still, astride the corpse. He bent to peer more closely at the bloody face. Friend Luke the stablehand perhaps, he wondered, here in his own domain? Or— The torch behind him sputtered a bit more brightly. He seized a handful of hair and pulled the head up into the light, a twelve-pound weight upon a flaccid neck.

Castlemayne's hoarse breathing stopped abruptly. For an instant there was no sound at all in the dark, low-ceilinged vastness of the stables. Only the wind in the thatch outside. Only the soft patter of snowflakes on loose panes of translucent horn.

Then the earth reeled under him.

The stable, the citadel itself seemed riven like a rock beneath him. Lightning blinded his eyes, erasing for one moment the twisted face before him. Stench of black powder, reek of sulfur and saltpeter filled his nostrils. His eyes strained wide with horror.

And for one fraction of a timeless moment, there was an awful Presence at his elbow. A Person just beyond the corner of one eye, unutterable, unimaginable, yet real and more than real. Reeking, hissing, wriggling there, radiating palpable gusts of evil, unspeakably triumphant. Imagery of a thousand sermons come hideously to life.

And laughter filled the stable. Piercing, shattering laughter, peal on peal. Spiraling demonic laughter that rose past the rafters, through the roof, penetrating storm and storm clouds to jeer the quiet stars.

iii

Still laughing shakily, Bianca Marsigliano staggered from the stall, clutching her ruined bodice close about her.

"Molto subito, signor!" she mocked hysterically. "You are very quick, my lord!" And to herself, shuddering with relief: Such stupid brutes are men, butchering each other for no reason but the joy of it! She had not thought it would go so far, or be so quick and terrible.

Castlemayne still crouched in the aisle, staring at what lay before him.

Harry's corpse lay sprawled upon its back, the head strained far backward, arms flung wide, stiff fingers clutching at the dirt of the stable floor. The dead man's doublet—of soft green velvet, purchased for a single court appearance just six months before —was torn and soaked with blood from the waist halfway up the chest. The lower part of the square-jawed face was smeared with blood, the neck and right shoulder red with it. There was blood in the open mouth, in the nostrils, blood darkening the carrot-colored hair.

Locked in nightmare, Castlemayne bent above the corpse.

The infernal Presence had gone from him, but something of himself had gone with it. What was left of him remained too stunned to move, paralyzed in the battered prison of his own body. He *was* his body, an insensate lump, as lifeless as the thing below him.

He was a bony wrist and hand crusted with drying blood, fingers still curled in the dead hair of his friend. He was two frozen eyes, veined with red, filled with mingled disbelief and terror. He was kneeling shinbones, locked as if from too-long praying, soaked all along in blood.

He blinked and looked about him.

The shapes of things seemed grotesquely warped to him, distorted, deprived of bulk, almost two-dimensional. Colors glowed oddly off key in his eyes, sour as bile, yet preternaturally bright, illuminated from within. Sounds and voices came to him confusedly, with weird fluting overtones and booming echoes, as though heard underwater or in some vast cave. All movements seemed strangely slow and deliberate, yet charged with inexplicable, transcendent meaning. Great waves of horror and exultation swept over him, shaking his body like an ague. A great sob rose unheeded to his throat.

"What, does the paladin weep for his heroic feat of arms?" He heard Bianca's mocking voice once more. "How very pious, is it not? The great hero on his knees, begging for forgiveness for the murder of his brother!" Her tone crested once more toward hysteria.

Castlemayne paid her no heed. When he spoke at last, it was not to the living woman, but to the dead man on the floor.

"God help me, Harry, but I did not mean to cut you so.

God knows, if there is a God in heaven, that I did not mean to do it."

He spoke to no one really, choking on great dry sobs, pawing helplessly at the corpse. Fumbling like a child that has broken some lovely thing of glass or precious metals, striving against all reason to make it whole again.

"A manslayer and a weakling too!" Bianca crowed above him. "And this the man that all the castle worships, the paragon of *cortesia!* A hollow idol truly, that shatters at the first blow of Fortune. But then, so are they all," she added low and bitterly. "All of the wretched sex, poor creatures, cheats and villains, that can never do what they brag on. . . ." And added lower still, with changing eyes, "All but one. . . ."

Castlemayne stared up at the dark woman's face above him, sneering at his agony. Saw her black lips mouth imprecations, her taloned hands twist the ragged stomacher. Saw the tangled thorn-brake hair, jet black, torchlight gleaming redly through it.

Saw this and more.

Saw other faces, real-unreal, peering with flaming eyes from the darkness all around the room. Hairy, hideous visages, long and toothy. Demonic horsefaces, half human and half beast, gibbering and gabbling, pointing long black fingers. Dozens of them peering at him from the stalls and windows, from the rafters, from the shadowy horseshoed recess just above the stable door.

The Satanic Presence that had loomed at his elbow when he saw Harry Langland under him had fragmented. Split into a hundred snuffling, snarling, leering little figures, filling the stables.

Castlemayne flung one arm across his eyes, squeezed them tight enough to burst the eyeballs.

"And this poor wretch would challenge the right of Malcolm Devereux to command in war!" The harpy's voice came to him from far away, drenching him in spleen and passion. "This boy, that falls to slobbering and weeping at the sight of human blood! Dancer, fencer, courtly lover, *per avventura*—but man and soldier never! *Sangue di Dio!* You are not fit to clean the boots of Sir Malcolm Devereux!"

Devereux!

The name sliced through the mists of frightfulness that swirled up about him. The three syllables of that name raced like an explosive charge to his tormented brain. He dropped his arm, his eyes wide open.

It was all there. The dim-lit stable, stalls and implements and tack, a horse's tossing mane—all off color, seen in astigmatic duplicate, the double outlines overlapping. Bianca, dark eyes blazing, with the ruined gown through which bare flesh still glowed. And the man-beast creatures in the shadows, quieter now, but restless, moving about the obscure recesses of the stable, leaping from stall to rafter to that place above the door, red eyes still fixed upon him.

All there, his new infernal world. But ice water in his own veins now, his brain as clear as brittle glass.

Devereux!

He saw the contempt on Bianca's face, saw her turn away at last toward the distant door. Rose slowly as he heard her speak. "No need for me to stay here now," she muttered in Italian. He strained for what words he had picked up at court, at Master Rocco's, at the wars. "Now that things have gone so far. For fighting may go against the Earl's ban at Exmoor, and womanizing affront his delicate English conscience. But murder—murder will hang a man in any shire in England!

"No need for me to stay," she told herself as she moved up the aisle, still fumbling with her clothing, "risk a beating from my loving lord—"

Then Castlemayne's hand closed upon her shoulder, a grip like granite on her flesh.

Her head swung back in shocked astonishment to the man she had dismissed as ruined, broken utterly. She stared, and saw her awful error. In the wild blue eyes that bored into her own, suspicion flamed, blazed to certainty. And carefully then, almost tenderly, the young man placed the tip of his recovered dagger—wet still with his kinsman's blood—against the very base of her throat, in the little hollow where the clavicles meet.

"Now show me the Great Captain's hand in this, mistress," he said softly.

Dumb with shock and horror, she thought only, O my true lord—I have betrayed you!

"Show me his hand!"

She felt a sudden stinging pain. He had punctured the skin very slightly, making a short, neat incision between the two blue arteries that came together there. A thin trickle of fresh blood ran down, over her bosom and between her breasts. The slightest further cutting either way would turn the trickle to a gushing torrent. And there was no relenting in his face, no pity in his hand.

Over Bianca Marsigliano's unheroic soul, like an icy basin on a winter morning, poured liberating fear. Fear that washed away, for now at least, her sentimental passion for Malcolm Devereux—whose name she had already betrayed in any case. That freed her in an instant to save her own life with a spate of desperate words. Freed her to unveil in all its grotesque simplicity the petty plot, the sordid chambermaid intrigue that Devereux had laid against his rival. A plot that had ended so much more violently than she at least had ever dreamed.

Than she ever dreamed, thought Castlemayne distractedly. Aye, verily, I can believe it. But he—*he* dreamed it! Knew it, willed it so—

The horsefaced hairy demons crept nearer now, laughing, jeering, baring yellow teeth.

Castlemayne drew back his knife, long jaw working, blue eyes fixed.

"Christ on the gallows tree!" he whispered hoarsely. "I'll slit his throat in the church!" He thrust the woman from him, his white face filled with light as the resinous torch flared up one last time. "I'll put my sword through his oily guts, my Harry, by God I swear it!"

He was staring past her now. Past her frightened face at something hovering in the air behind her—beard brows moustaches all of jet, thick lips, no-color eyes, hawk nose and chalky skin—

The sardonic devil's mask of Sir Malcolm Devereux.

And the gross lips curled in a contemptuous triumphant smile. Mockery glinted in the colorless unsmiling eyes that peered unblinking from beneath his iron brows. Laughing at me, babbled Castlemayne in his heart, sneering at the tender lamb that thought it was a wolf, and now is come so blindly beneath the butcher's knife!

No, by God! Your throat to the knife—not mine! Yours the carcass that shall roast in hell, not mine—

And the monstrous face, pulsing with unearthly light, posed a mocking question:

The seventh circle of hell, young Castlemayne? The home of the violent men?

And then that short sharp bark of grating laughter, hard as iron on iron, echoing through the stable.

But Castlemayne drowned the sardonic laughter of his enemy —the face now fading, fading—with a roar of vengeance.

"For both of us, sweet Harry! For your death and for the ruin of my life! He'll pay—by God he'll pay—with bile and blood and tears—"

Bianca, halfway up the dimming aisle, heard the voice break off, the cat feet pounding after. Felt herself seized screaming, whipped round, slammed back against a roughhewn pillar. And throttled her own screams, choked off her own breath as the dagger came once more against her throat.

"And for you, mistress—you will speak no word of this! No word of what has happened here to any living soul!"

He spoke low again, almost in the hoarse whisper of some stage-play conspirator. But as he spoke, the gibbering devils drew slowly back into their caves of shadow. And Bianca listened, a bird before the snake's hypnotic glare.

"For if you should speak aught of it, and most especially to Sir Malcolm Devereux, your employer in this, or your lover, or whatever—"

How shrewdly close he hits! she shuddered. They say that lunatics have powers . . .

"—If you betray this night's doings to any but your papist saints in the solitude of prayer, mistress—I shall kill you for it! I shall seek you out in the darkest watches between the night and morning, lady, be sure of it. And this very blade, stained with my sweet kinsman's blood, shall slide between your ribs and seek within until the point of it shall find your fluttering heart. . . ."

He stopped, his mad eyes fixed upon her with a certain cunning. His lean wolf jaw was hard and dangerous, his brow deeply ridged. His teeth and hair glowed in the guttering torchlight. And still the iron fingers crushed her flesh, the blade held steady as Carrara marble at her throat.

"Do you believe me, mistress?"

Bathed in sweat, shaking at his every wandering word, she believed him. Lunatic and frenzied he might be, but he would walk through walls to keep that bloody tryst if ever she betrayed him. She had never been so terrified of any man.

Somehow, in a gasping, faltering mixture of English and Italian, she took the oath of secrecy that he required.

"Excellent, *signora*." There was a surge of exultation in his voice. The hairy beasts crouched silent in the dark. "You are a wise woman after all. Now go, and keep your word. Or fear me, lady, *fear me!*"

The hand that crushed her shoulder opened. Bianca staggered back two steps, turned, and bolted for the door.

∾ Nine ∾

The Dark Night
of the Soul

i

Castlemayne remained alone with the corpse of his kinsman, knowing he must act before this night destroyed him.

On his knees in the horse box where he had touched Bianca's yielding flesh, he fumbled feverishly in the straw. With trembling fingers he recovered his doublet, his bedraggled ruff, the dagger and sheath, a strip of torn black satin still exotic with perfume. Scrabbling about the hard-earth aisle in the deepening obscurity, he found Harry's knife, stuck it through his own dagger belt. Shuddering, breathing thickly, he soaked and scrubbed up what blood he could with his own red-velvet doublet. He hid the rest with earth dug from under straw, and stamped over the dark stains.

Then, in guttering torchlight Castlemayne knelt beside the stiffening corpse. He wrapped the trunk, still bleeding slightly, in his own wet ruined doublet and heaved it up onto his right shoulder. Like a sack of meal manhandled to a wagon, he thought, and grinned a foolish widemouthed grin. Harry would appreciate the metaphor.

After that he thought no more of the man who had been the thing he carried on his shoulder.

He lurched erect beneath his burden and staggered off up the unlighted aisle. He felt the soft velvet and the crushing weight hard across the bone and muscle of his shoulder, the

127

straining tendons of his neck. He heard the piping laughter and the restless scuffling movement of the things that circled round him in the darkness. He saw their red, unblinking eyes, choked on the stinking foulness of their breath, like all the world's sewers ripped open. And—O God!—there came a leathery touch upon his cheek.

Too close, too close! he babbled inwardly once more. I must get out—

He threw all his weight against the wide stable door—his burden thudded sickeningly across the vertical planks—flinging it open against the wind and piling snow without. Then he was outside, over his knees in thick wet drifts, and the cold smote him like an iron fist. Night and storm were absolute around him.

One moment he stood, struggling to breathe and see, glimpsing through the driving snow a flicker of yellow light from one or another of the great hall windows. Then he turned his back upon the unheard revelry and moved awkwardly away, around the stables, into deepest darkness. Beyond the stables, the harness room, the smithy, he knew there was a postern gate. A gate unbarred and never locked these hundred years, that would let him out through the curtain wall, into the woods beyond. Out there, among the looming oaks and towering pines, he knew a place where the thing he carried would be safe beneath the snow.

He struggled clumsily with the latch of the ancient gate, rigid with rust and coated with ice. Managed it, and heaved again.

Then he was through it, lurching through still deeper snow, safe beyond the precincts of the castle. Safe in the close-pressing midnight forest, outside the walls of Exmoor.

Vast wings of blackness beat over the storm-lashed world, tearing at the treetops as he staggered onward, around and down the hill. An earthen bank rose black as basalt on his left. Stygian gulfs fell away on his right hand. On all sides the towering columns of the trees, the tangled canopy of branches filled the forest depths with darkness. The snow itself seemed in that ravine of darkness black as falling ash. Blackness lay over all the world. And in his tortured soul there was a greater blackness still.

Dear God, he groaned as he staggered onward, how many times did Harry swear that heedless ways and reckless deeds would be the end of me? How many times I laughed and clapped him on the back and went my whoreson foolish way. He choked on tears once more. And now we are destroyed, both of us ruined by my hand.

By my hand.

At once the devils were there again, swarming after him through the forest. He heard them shrieking at him from trees and undergrowth, howling at him in the wind. They were in the trees themselves, in the very trunks, slashing at him with taloned branches as he passed, hissing obscene derision in his ears.

And now the path beneath his feet angled much more steeply down, toward his destination. Blind with cold and darkness, gutted by the awful recognition of his own guilt, he must now descend through bracken, saplings, fallen timber, into the deepest vale in all that part of Devon.

Downward then he went, fleeing from his demons. Downward shouting half-remembered phrases, jumbled lamentations of a prophet shattered long ago in Israel. "O God, I am broken in pieces! My teeth are broken by number! I am fed with ashes, and my soul is cast out from peace!"

Beneath loose snow a rotten log gave way. He staggered and almost fell. Recovered and plunged onward, lashed by pine boughs, howling into the wind.

"O God, Thou knowest my folly, and my sins are not hid from Thee. . . ." And then, tears freezing on his cheeks, he heard himself chanting the story of that first murder, as he had learned it from the great Bible at his father's fireside. "O God, the voice of my brother's blood crieth unto Thee from the ground. And now I am cursed from the earth, which hath opened her mouth to receive my brother's blood from my hand. And I shall be a fugitive and a vagabond in the earth . . . and everyone that findeth me shall slay me!"

Night and the fury of the storm were all around him, and primal guilt gushed gall and wormwood from his heart. Thus shouting and weeping to purge the black self-hate that swelled within him, Castlemayne bore his brutal burden down the purgatoried slope.

The crushing weight upon his back was no dead corpse now, but an animated thing that kicked and spurred him, gibbering, shrieking, urging him down into the depths. He felt the heat of red eyes glowing on his neck, smelled the fetid breath of lungs nurtured in the fumes of the Inferno. The man-beast creatures swarmed like bats about him, clutching, stabbing, leaping at and on him, catching at his legs. Until he fell at last, sprawling, rolling, crashing through a screen of briars and bracken out into the clearing at the bottom of the forest gorge.

ii

He lay in a tangle of the living and the dead, half buried in a deep black drift of snow. His thin shirt was ripped almost entirely away, his chest and back and arms crisscrossed with welts and lacerations. Snow coated the insides of his eyelids. There were splinters of ice under his fingernails. Mouth-racked, brain-benumbed he lay, shivering and burning, his limbs awkwardly entangled with those of the outflung corpse.

"O Lord, I am broken in pieces," he heard himself babbling still. "Set in dark places, as they that be dead of old." Then the searing cold stabbed him through, killing the last vestige of his revery, quenching his delirium. Vaguely but with increasing urgency he knew that there were things to do, things that must be done this night.

He rose on shaking legs, into the full blast of the tempest that raged, unbroken by trees or man-made barriers, up and down the Vale of Exmoor. Somehow, in the teeth of it, he heaved his crucifying burden up and struggled from the deep drift, out into the open. Perhaps twenty yards ahead, beyond the howling blackness, lay the stream, the pond—and the little dam, where the water ran deepest beneath the ice.

Bowed down, his strength oozing fast away, Castlemayne moved out into that field of snowy dunes and storm.

Wave on wave of driving snow billowed about him. It dashed into his face, his streaming hair. It plastered his bleeding chest and thighs with molten armor. The blast deafened him, battered shut his eyes, froze in his rattling lungs. His stumbling feet were dead long since. Now his hands, clutching the cloth and the leather belt of the thing upon his shoulders, grew stiff and numb and began to slip.

Then, close before him in the pelting dark, a blacker shadow loomed. The copper beech. He knew its outline well, isolated in the field. Knew its rough-smooth bark when at last he sagged, sobbing from sheer exhaustion now, against its shadowy bulk.

Just beyond and to the right, the pool spread invisibly away, withered reeds along its frozen banks. To the left, the stream meandered off to feed the mill below the castle, where they ground the flour for bread. And just here, where the beech tree shaded the juncture of pond and stream, lay the low stone dam.

Three feet below the bank, a sluice and dam of crumbling ancient stone. An awkward jump, now twice difficult with deep snow over everything. Thrice dangerous with the load he bore, and in that buffeting wind.

He leaped into the darkness. He landed, slid, and fell sprawling across the snow-buried stone. The corpse pitched past him, through loose snow and splintering ice, into the frozen pond.

Into the pond—Thank God! he thought. Where the dark waters lay deepest and most still. Where the thing he had borne so far might be sealed at last from human sight. Might lie undisturbed till spring, beneath the ice and the thickening snow.

The pond's wound at least, he murmured as he staggered to his feet, will be scabbed over and bandaged up by dawn.

Before he reached his bed that night—the solid old four-poster he had shared with Harry—some things came clear at last to Castlemayne.

In action lay his sole salvation—if there was any salvation left for him. In furious activity he might drown the demons that had driven him through the storm. Frenetic labor was his only escape from the furies released in him that night.

But his labor must have some direction. It must be action to a purpose. And before that hallucinatory night was done, the purpose too was clear to Castlemayne.

Revenge.

No more of anguishing self-torment, but revenge. Vengeance for Harry's death, and for his own lost innocence. Vengeance on the man whose scheming had set him and Harry at each other's throats, blind with drink and passion, with daggers in their hands.

Bloody revenge—and victory!

He learned all this as he had learned so much that night—in dreams.

He staggered through his chamber door exhausted beyond anything he had believed possible, with three hours left him of the winter night. He collapsed at once upon the bed, pulled quilts and blankets about his shivering body, and was asleep in seconds. But nightmares came with sleep—to feast upon his life, as the old women say—and filled the remainder of the night with horror too.

Dreams of flight and terror, through all the echoing corridors and rooms of Exmoor. Pounding feet, heart wildly beating, an unseen pursuer breathing close behind. An inescapable pursuer that laughed dreadful laughter at the folly of the fleeing Castlemayne.

Dreams too of the scaffold and the axe. Dun-colored sky above, a surging crowd below, howling jests and curses at the traitor there to die. And Castlemayne himself the headsman, filled with wretchedness and pity for the faceless man—back turned, addressing the unheeding mob—who must die beneath his shaking hand.

Dreams, finally, of burial. In a dim, high-arched cathedral, the ceremonious interment of some great lord and famous soldier of the Queen. Solemn music, musty incense, an archibishop in full panoply officiating. Mourning lords and ladies shaking doleful heads about the carved sarcophagus, open there before them. Throngs of weeping citizens and tearful soldiers that had served with the dead captain. A black-clad, veiled widow shaken by convulsive sobbing. And Castlemayne himself, unaccountably elated, heart beating fast with relief and effervescent joy—and doubly joyful when, with all due pomp and ceremony, to the tolling of great brazen bells, he was himself deposited within the open tomb.

Time after time in the short hours of sleep, these dreams brought him full awake, bathed in sweat and trembling with emotion. And at each awakening, before exhaustion dragged him down once more into the folds of sleep, he felt strong upon him, permeating through his nightmare, the black oppressive presence of Sir Malcolm Devereux.

The laughter of his invisible pursuer was Sir Malcolm's sharp, barking laughter. The jeering iron laughter that had filled the bloodstained stables echoed still through his tormented dreams.

The faceless man upon the scaffold had the coal-black hair and barely glimpsed spade beard of Malcolm Devereux. Though the hands—Castlemayne remembered with a thrill of terror—the eloquent gesturing hands, as the doomed man addressed the crowd, were not Devereux's, square-cut and blunt with the black hair at the knuckles. They were, incomprehensibly, his own long bony hands—the same that held the axe!

The dead captain of his final nightmare was Castlemayne's own self, not Devereux. But the ornate sarcophagus was carved with scenes from the Battle of Coutras, Devereux's most famous action. And the sobbing widow, voluptuous in black, was Bianca Marsigliano, the Devil's chosen instrument!

With each horrified awakening, his obsession with the black captain grew greater. More than once he woke to find himself repeating like a litany the bloody oath of vengeance he had sworn in the stables that night. Or seeing for one vivid instant his own heavy Spanish rapier sliding smoothly into the solid belly of Malcolm Devereux.

One last time Walter Castlemayne awoke in those hours before dawn. Or thought he woke. Seemed at least to waken—to that glowing, warped, unreal world he had discovered in the stable. Rolled over groaning in the dark and tangle of his coverings. And found beside him in the bed, bloody, wet, and icy cold, the dead corpse of Harry Langland.

Blood-smeared hair and dead staring eyes. Black blood, now thick congealed, within the open mouth. The terrible wound in the belly, gangrenous, black-edged already, yet still oozing some dark effluvium out upon the sheet.

A despairing shriek rose then from the depths of Castlemayne's racked soul and brought him bolt upright in an empty bed flooded with gray morning light. And the single word he screamed was a name.

Devereux!

∽ *Ten* ∾

Gambit

i

"The move is yours, my lady," said Sir Malcolm Devereux, heavily respectful, to the Lady Arabella Traherne.

"Your pardon, sir," she smiled ruefully. "My thoughts . . . were not with the game."

"So it would seem," he answered dryly. And then, in the terse but courteous tone he maintained before potential patrons and those closest to them, "Would you prefer to complete the game tomorrow? It is growing late. We shall soon have need of candles."

"Oh no, my lord. The fire will be light enough for me. Besides," she added lightly, "I shall have you check and mate before another dozen moves! There's plenty of time for that between this time and supper."

Devereux inclined his head politely and sat stolidly as before, awaiting the girl's next move.

Arabella's lips compressed into a pout. This taciturn old man was so dull. She could not imagine how she could ever have been frightened of him, that first morning at the fencing. And why her noble father had insisted that she spend the afternoon with him passed all understanding. Truly his lordship's sense of proper hospitality sometimes went beyond all tolerable bounds.

She placed her slim hand uncertainly upon a pawn. A cone of ancient ivory, glowing in the firelight of late afternoon.

Sir Malcolm scratched his jaw and yawned.

The two were alone in the solar. All others had retired to commence the lengthy rite of preparation for the evening's entertainment. The bearded man and the bright young girl sat sedately in low-backed chairs before the fire, facing each other across a richly decorated old chessboard. He wore his customary suit of modest black, the doublet of soft leather. Her gown was bright yellow, square-necked, trimmed with lace.

Arabella advanced her pawn, thinking hopefully that little harm could come from so paltry a move as that. Her sole desire was that the game should last as long as possible. Until dark at the very least, she thought nervously. Surely he will come by then, to see if I am not waiting in our window niche.

"The move, my lady, leaves your bishop unprotected," said Devereux.

"Why then," Arabella answered quickly, "his grace's sacred robes and miter will no doubt protect him from unchivalrous violence!" Her laugh echoed thinly in the empty room.

"I fear not so, my lady." Devereux's black knight moved implacably across the board, and there was the faintest click as the carven horse's head replaced the mitered figure upon the dark-wood square. "But then, the loss is no doubt calculated, and part of your ladyship's plan for a checkmate by supper."

"You do me too much honor, sir."

Why did he not come? All that day she had not seen him, and none could tell her any news of him. Only that the night before he'd been as gallant as ever since he'd come to Exmoor, as though the Lady Arabella's absence mattered not a jot to him. Dancing half the night, she thought petulantly, with that Italian's wife. Holding that gypsy in his arms, laughing into her belladonnaed eyes—I know she does it—while I soaked the bolster with my foolish tears.

Oh, why was I so sharp with him, driving him to that— vixen's arms? I was so weary, and he would not understand. But it was folly and wickedness, to treat him so! It was my

shrewish temper and curst tongue, that Agnes has warned me
of so often. And I shall tell him so, and beg him to forgive me.
If only he will come. She gnawed the tender inside of her
lower lip with nervous milk-white teeth.

Devereux played also with only half his mind. And his
thoughts too ran on Walter Castlemayne.

There had been nothing in the stables. Nothing.

One-eyed Luke the hostler had had some trouble assembling
a suitable search party. It was late, after midnight, before he
could arouse enough concern to move the men he must have,
as Devereux had ordered him. Old Master Norton, shivering
and coughing in the blowing snow, muttering of his lordship's
honor. Messer Lodovico, blue to the lips, eyes blazing with a
dark fire. And three or four of Exmoor's huskiest servingmen,
to do whatever subduing might be necessary.

They had plowed through the snowy courtyard, burst into
the darkened stables—and found nothing at all. No young
hellions locked in violent conflict despite his lordship's explicit
ban. Neither Castlemayne nor Harry Langland, nor any trace
of either. Not even poor Bianca, the pluperfect pawn in this as
in any delicate intrigue. Nothing but horses and straw, hard-
pounded earth and drafty emptiness. Master Norton had been
quite irritable about it.

What in God's name had gone wrong? Sir Malcolm Devereux,
proud of his strategic planning, could not see where his schemes
had broken down.

Bianca. His mind focused once more on the Italian whore.
Could she be lying? Lying to *him*?

What—flee at the first sight of weapons drawn, he mused,
after all she must have seen of such drunken affrays in her
glorious rise from crib to courtesan? It was not likely. Yet she
was frightened badly, no question of that. Devereux had seldom
seen such terror in the whites of human eyes. Something that
happened in the stables last night had terrified the creature to
the point that she could hardly talk or face his gaze. But was

it only two young bulls hacking at each other in the hay? Or
did she see more than she would say? And what in God's name
can have happened to—

"Walter—Master Castlemayne!"

Sir Malcolm looked up quickly into Arabella's face. Trans-
figured, bright with thoughtless happiness, she was gazing past
his head at one that approached behind him, on the right.

Instinctively, the captain twisted in his chair to face his foe,
to free his poniard and his dagger arm for action. Fool! he
thought even as he did it. You're safe enough from ambuscade
in a well-run English country house! Yet the prudent habits of
a lifetime remained strong upon him. And in truth the gaunt
black figure striding across the solar toward them seemed cause
enough for apprehension.

"Walter!" gasped Arabella, so alarmed on closer view that
she abandoned all pretense of a proper distance between herself
and him. "What is it? Are you unwell?"

Christ! thought Devereux. Ask a Cheapside beggar that's had
both legs shot off if he's been at the wars!

Castlemayne did not answer Arabella. His eyes were fixed
on Devereux.

The bearded man and the bright young girl stared back at
him, astounded. The high healthy coloring of his cheeks, once
so striking a contrast to his white-blond hair, had gone chalk
pale, drained overnight of blood. The tall, strong body was
suddenly more gaunt than lean, as though sucked dry of life.
He stood before them hollow-eyed and wasted, as by a long fever,
one hand on his hip, swaying slightly on his feet.

Devereux thought of mortally wounded men that he had
seen. Men that clung desperately to life and breathed in pain
sometimes for weeks before their stubborn wills would let them
die.

Arabella, astonished, could summon up no thoughts at all.
She only trembled inwardly with terror and compassion.

"Will you sit, sir?" said Devereux, emotionless as usual. He rose with calculated deliberation to retrieve a three-legged stool from the hearth. He placed it carefully at one side of the little chess table.

"I will sit," said Castlemayne, as though there might be more to follow—yet said no more. He sank down slowly on the stool, still ignoring Arabella's fluttering attentions, his red-lidded eyes still riveted on Sir Malcolm Devereux.

The knight returned his gaze, steady, ironical, unsmiling. With Castlemayne's strange pallor and unfamiliar suit of black, the two men seemed to Arabella, for one startled moment, like oddly mismatched twins.

"How does the game proceed?" said Castlemayne abruptly. His long fingers drummed on the tabletop. His eyes shifted, wandered over the ancient chessboard. A score or so of pieces still remained on the checkered surface, tiny statuettes of ivory and ebony carved by some long-perished craftsman.

"Not well for me, I fear." The girl laughed quickly, glad of the innocuous line of talk. "Sir Malcolm's experience of martial matters will surely overwhelm me. But then, what would you? When I, poor lass, have only Master Norton's book of theory to defend me!"

Castlemayne pursed his lips and nodded slowly.

"And more than a mere pawn advantage, I should think," he said flatly. "A far stronger tactical position for the black." He had played enthusiastically at this game since he was a boy. The black pieces had been Saracens in those simple days, and the white side the Crusaders.

"Deep strategic wisdom, sir," said Devereux, "especially in so young a man."

"Perhaps I am too young myself," Arabella interjected tartly, "to plumb the depths of such wisdom. To me it seems that Master Castlemayne's wit has sadly declined since yesterday this time." *When we two stood alone outside the great hall door,* she remembered with a pang, *to watch the court fill up with snow. When your eyes spoke cantos of sweet thoughts in per-*

fect silence. And I, with my foolish fears and hateful temper, fled from you. But now—oh, Walter, why do your eyes not speak to me now?"

Castlemayne said nothing. His gaze was fixed upon the chessboard. It was as though the girl were not even there.

She tried once more.

"Surely, Master Castlemayne"—how stiff and unfamiliar the formal appellation sounded on her lips!—"surely, you have taken some distemper. If—if I or my father . . . a physician can be summoned from Exeter . . . I regret there is none closer. . . ." She heard herself stammering and hated herself for it. But his face, his manner, were so totally transformed.

"It is nothing, my lady," he said at last. "Nothing." How cold the voice was! How easily he reverted to formalities! "I fell on the stairs last night. Most foully drunk, I fear, on the Earl's more than bountiful hospitality."

"Oh, but—" My God—had she not seen men sick from too much wine before? Quick tears brimmed her eyes. A whole long day of waiting—and for this!

He paid her no attention. His eyes were fixed on the board.

Suddenly she was on her feet, clumsy in her farthingales, eyes bright with moisture. Before either man could rise, she had turned and fled wordless from the solar, head down, biting her lip to keep from weeping with a mingled sense of misery and indignation.

Christ's bloody wounds! Sir Malcolm swore in disbelief. What mad humor has come upon our puling suitor now? To woo an Earl's daughter under his lordship's very eyes is folly enough. But to reject her publicly—

The rustle of her sweeping skirts faded into silence up the passageway.

Castlemayne rose from the stool on which he sat and took the girl's place opposite Devereux. Sir Malcolm looked at him almost quizzically, wondering what might come next from this daft youth. Then Walter Castlemayne smiled, a crooked parody of his old West Country grin, and pointed one thin finger at the unfinished game between them.

"Shall we play, Sir Malcolm Devereux?"

"Very well, Master Castlemayne. I expect there's time enough to finish the game before the night's festivities commence."

"There's always time for sport, sir." The smile was still there. "And a game begun, you know, must be played out to the end."

The older man raised a heavy brow. "No doubt," he said dryly. "Will you move?"

"Most willingly," said Castlemayne without a shade of hesitation. There was a feverish gleam in his eyes as he turned to the game.

ii

The chessboard between them was large, heavy, and old. It was made of solid oak, the playing surface inlaid with alternating squares of beautifully grained light and dark woods. The wide borders, where captured pieces lay, were painted with martial motifs in the gothic style—clusters of spears and swords, curling scrolls and banners, a plumed and armored knight at each corner.

A fine old board, thought Castlemayne irrelevantly. Surely I must have played on it with Arabella, on snowy days at other Christmases. But that was long ago.

He had played with her upon this same board not two days since. But that had slipped his mind.

Castlemayne's white pieces were of ivory, yellowed with long years. Devereux's black ones were of ebony, or teak perhaps, from the Spanish Indies. All were skillfully carved in the old-fashioned style of a century ago. The pawns were simple solid cones, with knobs on top. But all the others were little statuettes, conventional representations of their namesakes. All four of the mitered bishops, cylindrical in their papistical regalia, had already been captured and lay on the painted borders in a litter of toppled pawns. Most of the castles still stood on the board, miniature stone towers with crenelated battlements and arched portals, waiting undeveloped in their respective first ranks. There were more black knights than white—tossing horse's heads with bulging eyes and saw-toothed manes—all brazening it out in the middle of the board. Both the queens were in the open too: stubby female figures, robed and crowned, seated chin in hand upon their thrones, oddly passive for the most powerful figures on the board. In the far corners of their own ranks, each guarded by a phalanx of pawns, the two royal monarchs sat with orb and scepter, scowling beneath their crowns.

"I do not envy you, sir," said Sir Malcolm harshly. "Her ladyship has left you no very strong position to defend."

"It is most true, sir," said Castlemayne. "And yet not hopeless, I dare prophesy."

"We played at lady chess," Devereux continued coldly, as though there had been no interruption, "where the queen is mistress of the board, and the castles range its length and breadth. The game moves much more quickly thus than by the old rules. It appeals to the bloodthirsty spirit of the young."

Castlemayne did not respond. He found that he could fix upon one thing only now. If he would play, he could not banter. Any division of attention set his mind to aimless wandering, without direction or control.

Perhaps an attack upon the right flank, he thought. Shake loose my castles from the dull corners where they sit. Concentrate what force I have, to compensate for weakness.

He stretched forth a sinewy hand and shoved a small white crenelated tower halfway across the board.

Devereux bent slowly to the game, meditating his response.

The fire crackled and flared as though someone had thrown pine boughs on it. At the far end of the high-arched room, a servant entered upon some minor errand. Performed it. Bowed to the two gentlemen. And departed as quietly as he had come. Outside, the sun was setting, a pale white glow behind the billowing clouds that came churning in from over the Atlantic.

Sir Malcolm was a strategic thinker. Many years of failure and success had schooled his volcanic nature in the necessary patience, the need for caution and calculation. He had learned to plan his enemies' destruction in detail and in depth, well in advance of the action. His famous triumphs in the field, like his defeats, had been characteristic products of the prudently strategic mind.

The brain of Walter Castlemayne, by contrast, operated still on a strictly tactical level. In a hot action, with a handful of pikemen behind him, he had a sort of frenzied genius. He seemed to understand intuitively the best use that could be made of every hillock, every pile of rubble, every wall or doorway or corner of a lane. His voice rang out exultant then, clear as a trumpet over the shouts and curses, the crash of muskets and the clash of steel. Leading and driving his men at once, hurling them against the weakest point in the enemy's defenses. Dividing, splitting, scattering, destroying. For Castlemayne the great moment of the game, the white focus of the hottest fight, came with the sudden fear upon a sweating Spanish face, the shifting of dark Spanish eyes—or French eyes, or Italian—in search of some way out.

Castlemayne played now with some of the nervous intensity of a skirmish or assault, a tense excitement that grew with every move. With genuine fury he thrust the pawns of his own right flank against Captain Devereux's left. He reached, he thirsted for the blood of the king that waited, a tantalizing lure, beyond Sir Malcolm's carefully constructed shield wall.

The pressure mounted.

The wall broke, dissolved before him. Another move and he would have his first check. Then would come another and a third, harrying the ebony king from square to square, from one uncertain shelter to the next, until the final mate. Breathing quickly now, a small red fever spot aglow on each projecting cheekbone, Castlemayne sent his queen into the miniature battle, imperious mistress of the board, to make that first prophetic check.

The dissolving wall suddenly became a net.

The white pawns, the castle, the impetuous knight, even his queen were no longer charging through a demoralized breach in Devereux's defenses. They were themselves enveloped, surrounded by guileful foes. Devereux's thick fingers moved a final pawn, and the trap was sprung.

For Castlemayne, those fingers were oddly fuzzy at the edges; the black pawn had a purplish cast. All about him, colors, sounds, and shapes were weirdly distorted as he slipped into that unreal other world of the night before. And did he not hear a far-off, high-pitched twittering, gibbering, jeering, a sound of restless pattering movement, now nearer and much nearer?

Implacably the ebony pieces engulfed the ivory. Desperately Castlemayne withdrew his queen, a long diagonal sweep back across the checkered field that cost him his last remaining knight. His castle, hopelessly trapped, he maneuvered with such erratic brilliance that a black castle followed his own into oblivion— an unexpected man-for-man exchange that had Sir Malcolm tugging at his beard. But young Castlemayne's pawns fell one by one, and took scarcely a dark pawn with them. The triumphant assault was transformed into a rout. And as his battle hosts dissolved beneath his hands, the real world of Walter Castlemayne slipped ever more rapidly and more wildly out of joint.

Devereux smiled sardonically beneath his thick moustaches. It was surely time for any man of sense to tip his king and go to supper.

But Castlemayne, the strangely damaged man that was now Walter Castlemayne, sat stunned, as though paralyzed by the disaster on the chessboard.

The low flames on the hearth now burned a sickly green. The gray limestone walls of the ancient solar were darkened to basalt black, shot through with shifting crimson streaks, like some infernal living marble. Sir Malcolm Devereux's gargoyle face seemed to take on a sour yellow hue, the color of a wizard's centuries-dead mummy flesh.

Castlemayne knew without turning his head that his devils were back. He felt their presence in the room behind him, the red-eyed hairy demons of the stable, horse teeth grating, talons twitching to be at him when he fell. He could hear their jeering laughter, their shuffling, awkward movements as they crowded closer. His nostrils filled with the acrid stink of them, that mingled stench of blood and sweat and dung that turned him sick and dizzy.

And there was the thing behind Sir Malcolm Devereux's chair.

Bolt upright this time, rigid in the grip of death, and transformed, most horribly transformed already. There was the blood-smeared orange hair, the gaping mouth, the awful wound in the belly. But the skin was gray, blackening and bloating now. The torn doublet bulged, shockingly distended by the swelling corpse within. The wound itself was soft and flaccid and seemed wider, eaten at. The white dead eyes were gone entirely, empty, shredded sockets staring at him.

While one might count to ten, or twenty possibly, the thing was there, concrete and real, in the darkening room. Then it faded, dissolved to gray before his eyes, and vanished. The green-burning hearth fires glowed once more where the thing had stood.

It had not spoken, had hardly moved in fact. But the mind of Walter Castlemayne exploded with sudden comprehension. The message of the dead man. So simple that it flung back his head and twisted up his mouth in a sudden shout of laughter.

And is it all to go for nothing, then? Am I as great a fool today as I was yesterday? As I was before—last night? Before these diabolic gentry, the human and the horsefaced ones, took me under tutelage?

"Ah Harry, Harry—every right to glare!"

Devereux, uneasy hand upon his hilt again, glanced sharply about for Castlemayne's young kinsman.

But I shall learn, sweet Harry, swore Castlemayne, fear me not. I shall yet acquire some smattering of sense. I shall learn—from Devereux himself, by God!

For you're a clever man, good captain. You surely know your business. And I have much to learn, that's certain. And yet—a harder note returning—the day shall come for the great Captain Devereux to learn a lesson too.

The stink of the stables was gone from Walter's nostrils. He knew there were no more devils in the room.

"Do I comprehend correctly, sir, that you concede the game?" A look of irritation had replaced the patronizing smile on Sir Malcolm's face.

"You do not," said Walter Castlemayne. "We have a few minutes yet before supper." The fire burned yellow and orange again, and the walls were gray.

Castlemayne studied the board in the glow of that flickering firelight. He pursed his lips with a certain thoughtfulness over the carnage. He saw and weighed and planned now with an intensity that was at once feverish and icy, ardent and coldly calculating.

He moved his one remaining castle off to the left, into the neutral territory behind his rescued queen.

A ghost of puzzlement passed over Devereux's mind. This was not the style of the Castlemayne he knew. But then, so small an anomaly . . . he shrugged and let it go. With methodical determination he turned once more to the game.

The endgame now, he thought with relish. A victory was always so much easier to devise on a chessboard than on a battlefield, where his instruments must be poor human folk, soft-fleshed, with blood so easily spilled. Here, with hardwood statues to execute his will, it was a mere matter of precise calculations excluding each avenue of escape in turn—geometrically, as Lodovico would say—until the enemy was mated.

Ten moves, a dozen more, what matter? Indeed, it would give him most particular pleasure to roast this young cockerel over the slow fire of a long endgame.

Liveried servingmen came to light the candles in their sconces and went away again. There was an uncertain murmur of activity in distant corridors, the first stirrings of assembling guests repairing to the great hall below. Oblivious to all distraction, Sir Malcolm labored steadily toward the inevitable end.

"Check," said Devereux with slow relish. Three moves now should make it mate.

Castlemayne licked dry lips. He moved his king into the lee of the only pawn left to him.

"Check." Devereux's queen shifted to menace a diagonal attack.

The white king moved quickly up into the pawn's row, momentarily out of reach again.

Devereux shifted a black knight into position for the final stroke.

"Check," said Castlemayne.

Things focused then, or so it oddly seemed to both men. Focused suddenly and sharply, and rushed to a conclusion.

Sir Malcolm Devereux, startled as he had not been since he came to Exmoor, swiveled his gaze back to his own king, and then to that entire left-hand side of the board. To the all-but-empty reaches whither he had himself exiled Castlemayne's two remaining pieces of any strength. With a feeling of total unreality, he unraveled the fatality of his situation.

Castlemayne's queen had abruptly darted across the whole width of the checkered field to pin the black king down in his far corner. To trap him, indeed, behind the little wall of three snug pawns that had been his closest bodyguards. Devereux had but a single piece in reach that was capable of rescue. He could fling one black castle between his king and its attacker. But then Castlemayne's own castle would be free to move. To leap in quick pursuit, destroy his black counterpart, and join his queen besieging Devereux's king. And the next move after that would be check and mate.

Devereux went over the entire board, grimly, thoroughly.

Castlemayne watched with a crooked smile. He knew when the other knew that there was no hope. Knew and exulted, filled with barbaric joy at the humiliation of his enemy.

"It is your game, sir," said Devereux in clipped tones. Though such good fortune, he thought vindictively, will not soon again reward such folly. God's wounds, but I've seen such recklessness kill ten cavaliers for every one it made a hero of.

But had blind Fortune placed the ivory queen and castle there, precisely in position for that last bold stroke? The question struck him suddenly. Was it foolhardy impetuosity—or brilliant calculation that had made possible the coup?

"My game indeed, Sir Malcolm." Castlemayne leaned forward, eyes still fixed on his rival. "As every game shall be from this point on!"

"Your pardon, sir?"

"I'll have the *Golden Fortune,* Captain Devereux." The young man's eyes were blazing now. "I'll have the ship, his lordship's nomination, the Queen's commission—though all the devils in hell should bar the way!" For what revenge could be more sweet, Castlemayne exulted inwardly, and more perfect to the mark, than to have the ship, torn from your clutching grasp—and then your life as well? Honor first, the honor of this fine command. Then life, your life for Harry's, and for what you've done to mine!

"You're an arrogant coxcomb, sir, and a fool to boot!" growled the bearded captain. "One chessboard victory does not make a commander out of a swashbuckling boy!"

"You'll be careful, sir," Castlemayne answered, his voice vibrating with bowstring tension, "not to speak so hardly of a gentleman when others are about as witnesses?" Were there but one reputable witness here, by God, I'd risk his lordship's anger. Stab the spade-bearded villain here and now!

"Careful, boy?" Devereux grunted disgustedly. "Christ on the bloody cross"—incredibly, the bass voice rumbled on as calmly as though he were exchanging pieties with Parson Thwydleton—"I'll birch your backsides if you play with me! Box your ears and paddle your arse—"

By God, it was enough!

Restraint and calculation vanished in an instant. Castlemayne surged to his feet, scattering the chessmen wildly, his big hands seizing on the heavy board.

"What, strike me down with a chessboard, my young hero?" sneered Devereux, still seated.

The dark blood boiled up in him too. Beneath the concealing tabletop, his blunt fingers had half drawn his dagger.

"A judicious move truly, and sure to convince the noble Earl of your fitness for responsible command. Oh, a shrewd move indeed, a master stroke—" His mouth twisted as he goaded his maddened enemy on.

Castlemayne swayed forward—and stopped.

The seventh circle of hell, young Castlemayne? Words that had seared his soul in the low-raftered stable not twenty-four hours before blazed once more across his brain. *The home of the violent men?*

Walter Castlemayne's fingers clutched the wood until his knuckles cracked, then slowly, steadily relaxed. His eyes dimmed from manic rage to that haunted, feverish glint that was normal to him now. He even forced a smile.

"Indeed, you are correct, my lord. I fear I have some lessons yet to learn before my harsh masters let me be. They are most strict, my little masters. . . ."

Devereux's eyes narrowed at the rambling, meaningless remark, by no means the first that day. Mad, he thought, or no more than a step removed from it. By Christ, if that were true!

What claim could a lunatic have upon responsible command?

But it was not possible. What lunatic ever played so shrewd a game of chess? He could have beaten Parma in the field with such a flanking countermarch and enfilade as that—damn him for a velvet-breeched whoremaster!

Devereux shrugged his powerful shoulders.

Well, well, there are other ways to flay a rabbit. And I must to them. If he were raving now, or seeing hobgoblins underneath the stairs . . .

Sir Malcolm Devereux rose heavily. Without a further word to Castlemayne he turned upon his heel.

Walter Castlemayne stood dry-lipped and staring, the foolish chessboard still clutched in his hands, and watched him go. Watched him stride off across the candlelit solar, arms swinging in a military swagger, black shadows capering about him on the floor.

～ Eleven ～

Fair Is Foul
and Foul Is Fair

i

"You comprehend my problem, then, good Master Norton?"
concluded Castlemayne. "I should like to provide an entertainment worthy of the wittiest here, yet acceptable also to the
simplest country gentleman. Something to please his lordship's
taste, and Master Cecil's nice discrimination, and your own
poet's ear, sir. Yet something that will set the lusty squire and
his dame to laughing too."

He spoke with the nervous intensity that was peculiar to him
now. His eyes were lucid, sharply focused. But they glittered too
brightly.

"A worthy object, Master Castlemayne. An endeavor both
becoming in a grateful guest and suited to a Cambridge scholar."

Humphrey Norton chewed at his itching gums as the two of
them strolled up the dim-lit corridor. In fact, he wished young
Castlemayne's febrile energy would find some other object. It
was late in the day, late in the holidays. Master Norton had
eaten and drunk well. His old bones felt the need of a downy
mattress and a feather quilt.

Master Castlemayne placed a helping hand on the old man's
elbow, talking cheerfully, and guided him through a low arched
doorway into the nearest parlor.

"It has always seemed to me, sir," Castlemayne explained,
"that our modern stage has drifted too far from the ancient

models of dramatic excellence. And has paid the price, sir, has paid the price. . . ."

"Indeed so, Master Castlemayne. You are quite right." The sleepy graybeard warmed to the prospect of a literary discussion, particularly with one who seemed to share his own views so completely. "What is our stage, after all, when judged in accordance with the ancient canons of the craft, the models of the Greeks and Romans?" He shook a gnarled finger as the young man drew up a chair for him in front of the small fireplace. "A paltry parade of immoral characters and inane commentary—that is all we have today. Mere vulgarity, without appeal to the discriminating mind."

"Aye, and worse yet," Castlemayne agreed, "corrupting to the innocent, warping the unformed spirit! Before God I am no Puritan, but such stuff as our players put on I can scarce stomach myself without a blush. Naught but murders and adultery and worse knavery. If apprentices are all thieves and rioters, and hardly a lady is both true and fair—well, one cause of it at least is not far to seek!"

Castlemayne did not sit down himself, but paced up and down the little room. His eyes flicked about, probing odd corners and shifting shadows behind the furniture.

"Well may you say so, young man! A ribald jest or two never—hem—never hurt any man. But this sickness that infects our stage—it goes beyond the bounds of toleration!"

"It does indeed," said Castlemayne.

"Consider your *Doctor Faustus,* now," said Master Norton, wheezing, "that has exalted Master Marlowe's reputation to the skies. And what is this Faust, pray tell? A villainous old alchemist that traffics with the Devil—that's your modern hero! Or take this famous *Spanish Tragedy,* that some judicious critics swear has not been matched in our times. Why, so it hasn't—for bloody murders, for diseased morality and raving madness on the stage!"

"Execrable taste," assented Castlemayne.

"Your Seneca or your Sophocles, now—there were tragedians for you! There were poets that could touch a tragic theme with due decorum. For enlightenment and elegance, you cannot match your antique masters with any of your modern playmakers. Mere schoolboys, say you?" The old man snorted. "Why, they have not yet even begun to go to school!"

Castlemayne nodded and bit his lip. He chafed to get the conversation back to his own immediate literary ambition. But he knew better than to cut off the aged humanist's flow of literary talk. For he must have Master Norton's help—or, more accurately, his consent.

And yet the tension built so fast within him. He felt it, he knew the symptoms now. The faint echo after words, the first fuzzing of outlines. And was there a sound of scurrying and scraping in the dark hallway outside the door?

Master Norton paused to draw a rheumy breath, and Castlemayne stepped hurriedly into the breach.

"Indeed, I was sure of your sympathy, Master Norton. And for that reason only do I presume to bring my own poor aspirations in this line to so busy a man as yourself."

The old man's gummy eyes blinked uncertainly, readjusting to the problem at hand.

"Ah yes, this—ah—pageant you suggest for our Twelfth Night's entertainment. Most kind of you to think of it—most kind. His lordship leaves these things to me, of course—entirely to me. Nor is it an easy load to add to my other burdens here. *Magister epistolarum, magister juvenibus,' magister convivii*—secretary, tutor, master of the revels. Too many caps for an aged toiler in the Muses' vineyard." He shook his head self-importantly.

"It was in fact this very thought," interjected Castlemayne, "that even yourself must weary of such labors, that impelled me to dare offer my humble contribution."

"Certainly, certainly. . . ." The note of self-sympathy gave way to anxiety. "But the Twelfth Night revels, now, Master

Castlemayne—it is a heavy responsibility. No light matter to be laid upon a neophyte—if you permit me—"

"Of course, sir. And I make no claim to more than an amateur's skill in such matters. It is honor enough to be allowed at all within the precincts of the sacred grove."

"Well said, Master Castlemayne, well and honestly put! Too few of the young gentlemen, too few men of the sword altogether, show such respect for letters." Master Norton fluffed his robe, like a chicken ruffling its feathers. "But for Twelfth Night, look you, for the celebration of the Epiphany, I have myself prepared two pieces not unworthy, as I dare hope, of that august anniversary. Judicious, balanced fare, do you see, to end the holidays grave and gay at once. If you would care to see my manuscripts—"

"I should be honored, sir. Honored!" said Castlemayne, controlling his perturbation with an effort. "And yet I grieve to lose my own literary labors altogether—"

"Ah—as to that. Could you perhaps have your piece prepared for presentation after dinner two days hence—the night before the Epiphany? There is a gap in my agenda there. I had thought to fill it with mummers from the village or some such foolishness. But a fine masque, now, would be more entertaining and more edifying both. . . ."

"Most willingly, sir!" Castlemayne instantly assured him. "I shall have the script complete by noon tomorrow and ready for the players."

"Excellent, very well done. Our actors are quick at study, especially for anything in the comic or farcical vein. Local bumpkins, most of them, with two or three that have played in some London company or other. At any rate, they'll do your pageant up in proper style. I have trained them to it these last few years myself. In the style of the Old Comedy, do you see—"

Humphrey Norton talked for half an hour more of Plautus, Terence, Aristophanes, the Old Comedy and the New, before a dying fire sent him sneezing off to bed. Castlemayne accompanied him to his chambers to borrow a volume of Plautus "for proper inspiration." He secured also pens, paper, and ink, of which he claimed to be running low. There was no need for Master Norton to know that the elegant entertainment so blithely promised had not yet even been begun. Would in fact have to be completed in less than twenty-four hours of feverish labor.

And by God it shall be finished! thought Castlemayne, as he threaded his solitary way toward his own room, high up in the ancient keep. By tomorrow afternoon, the players shall have a working script at least. Left rough for revision and improvisation as seems best to them. That should please them well enough. And then, I must observe their style, tailor certain passages directly to their special talents. . . .

He hurried on up the dim-lit stair. He was gaunt and hollow-eyed from lack of sleep. But his face was alight with nefarious intent.

ii

Castlemayne pushed open the iron-studded door and stepped into his narrow chamber, lit only by low-burning coals on the hearth. His mind was busy with the task before him as he unloaded paper, pens, and ink upon the small round table just inside the doorway. Humming a bawdy tavern tune whose tetrameter appealed, he closed the door and shot the bolt. It was only then, when he turned to face the room once more, that he saw the Lady Arabella.

She stood at the far end of the room, between the fireplace and the canopied bed. A dim figure in a pale gown, outlined against the dark lancet window behind her.

"Walter . . ." she whispered uncertainly.

"My lady—Arabella!" he gasped.

"Oh, Walter, I had to come!" She floated toward him, fire-light glimmering on her face, skirts rustling across the hard-

wood floor. She still wore the ball gown she had worn that evening—yellow satin, with puffed sleeves and an open-fronted ruff.
Her fair hair was piled high and looped with pearls. Her eyes
were full of anguish.

She stopped awkwardly, a yard or so from him.

"Walter—Walter, are you all right? Are you not doing yourself some—some mischief, to ignore this malady that has come
over you? You seem so ill, so unlike yourself—" She was clearly
terrified at the enormity of being here, alone in his room with
him. Her eyes, her clenched hands appealed desperately to him
for some help, some reassurance.

Without speaking, almost without thinking, he reached out
and caught her to him.

She clung to him, her fingers digging into his flesh even
through the heavy velvet of his doublet. Her whole young body
trembled with relief and joy to feel his arms about her once
again.

"Oh, my love," she whispered brokenly, "that night in the
snow outside the great hall door—it was my curst tongue spoke,
and not my heart! I was so—frightened. Of myself, and of what
was—happening to us. And I have been so fearful every hour
since, that I had lost you forever. . . ."

Castlemayne said nothing. He only held her closer still, re-
learning with his lips the loveliness of her face. Feeling the
eager firmness of her mouth, so warm and responsive under his.
Filling his nostrils with the fragrance of her hair, the freshness
of her linen. He had not known, not guessed until that moment
how much he needed her.

"You will forgive my temper, Walter—always, will you not?
Agnes says it is my greatest fault, my terrible shrewish temper.
But it's only when I am afraid, or weary and alone. . . ."

He muttered some disjointed response, his face buried deep
in her hair. He really had no answer, no thoughts at all. There
was nothing of reason in him now, only mindless need.

For her too there was something beyond words at last. There

was a pure physicality in their embrace that brought a surge of uncomprehending joy to her heart. Clinging, pressing close in the circuit of his arms, she trembled once again to that slow, secret awakening she had experienced only once before, when he had come to her in her own midnight chamber.

"And then," she went on, compulsively explaining despite her longing for nothing but silence, silence and his hands upon her, "then yesterday, when you spoke so strangely in the solar. When I waited for you all day long, only to ask for your forgiveness. And then you came and—and would not speak to me at all, but only Captain Devereux. I felt so—abandoned."

But it had to be, thought Walter miserably. For am I not a homicide, a haunted man whose wits are addled and his future far from sure? A man sworn to a bloody task . . . Christ knows there must be an end between us.

"And the look in your eyes—if you could have seen it! Awful. Awful. Like the damned souls in the chapel window, the big one behind the choir, just below the rose . . ."

Damned souls. He froze at the words, remembering.

The slide and heft of the knife, grating against bone. The wild laughter of the raven-haired harpy rising from the straw. Empty eyes rolling back beneath him, blood upon his hands.

The universe was suddenly unsure about him. Poised and quivering, on the verge of slipping back over the twilight line.

"Walter, I have been so afraid for you. I watched you at dinner, last evening and again tonight, so busy with your petition to my lord father. And I saw you sometimes go all vacant and just sit there staring, with that awful look back in your eyes. I felt like crying for you, Walter.

"I went to my chamber this evening, and I absolutely shrieked at Aggie—though she is not well herself, you know—and I wept a little on my bolster. Then I had to come here. I had to, wrong and foolish though I know it is. . . ."

She caressed his shoulder, avoiding his eyes. When she looked at him again, her blue eyes were bright and misty.

"Oh, my poor Walter, tell me what it is and let me help! I'll go to Father, and he'll do anything I ask. He's so sweet, really, and I know I can. Is it the ship, Walter, and you're too proud to ask me to urge your suit upon him? Because if it is only that—"

But Castlemayne's mind was far from the *Golden Fortune*.

Why must there be an end between us? half his soul cried out. The half that had ruled supreme in his tense young body only three short nights before.

Then this perfect creature had been his. They had laughed, they had danced. Once at least they had kissed, kissed till their two souls rose to their lips, intertwined and blended. He had wanted nothing else in the world. And now all over, ended.

No! Not now, not ever shall we two—

He crushed her convulsively against him, felt her cheek nestle against his chest. Her smooth arms slid around his neck as she raised her face to his.

We two—we two— But his mind stopped and went no further.

For Harry was there.

There in the firelit room with them, the corpse of Harry Langland. Behind the girl's arching back it loomed, facing Walter, perhaps six paces from him. A hulking shadow in the gloom, suddenly visible where there had been nothing, near the shadowy head of the bed. Standing, staring with its empty sockets, swaying slightly on what had once been feet. More bloated still, the skin still further darkened, the flesh sagging softly, loose on the bones. Black holes of shadow for the mouth and eyes, the gaping wound grown larger. Speaking no word, nor moving a hand, beyond that unnatural shift and sway of flotsam on a lifting wave.

It stood there in the shadow staring at Castlemayne with its eyeless sockets while perhaps a dozen seconds trickled slowly through the glass. Then it was not. The slant of shadow beside the bed was untenanted, and the low fire crackled only for the man and woman clinging to each other by the door.

"What is it, Walter?" she murmured against his ear. "Poor sweeting, your hands are so cold—"

He broke from her so violently that she almost fell.

"Walter! My love!" Cold terror closed about her heart.

Fool! Fool! Fool!

Castlemayne pressed his palms hard against his forehead, where blood pounded and pain rolled rhythmically with each pulse of life. The brutal truth poured out in a spate of bitter words behind his sweat-bathed brow.

Twelve days to win a great command, and three quarters of them gone, lavished on a hopeless passion! Lavished on this girl, because she is so pretty, and you pulled her pigtails once, when you both were little. Love! Where will your love be, or hers, when you have no honor left, no chance to dare, no future even to aspire to? When you've been beaten and disgraced by that spade-bearded villain!

By Malcolm Devereux, that murdered Harry through your hand and marked you with your kinsman's blood forever.

The words were blazing sulfur in his brain, coursing through his veins. Consuming passion, tenderness, desire. Freeing him once more for that which he must do.

"Walter," Arabella said again, tremulous with fear.

He lowered his hands and looked at her. He smiled. A smile chiseled in stone.

"My lady?"

"Walter—the strangeness in your voice again. Oh, what is it? The coldness—" Dismay and bewilderment overwhelmed her. There were no models for such circumstances in her poems and romances.

"Cold, my lady? Not so, by Venus Aphrodite!" He laughed, too loudly. "I have been called hard things in my time, but no woman has ever called me . . . cold."

His big hands closed over her delicate shoulders. He crushed her body against his once again, so brutally this time that she cried out. He sank his fingers in the jeweled mass of her hair, pulled back her head, and kissed her cruelly.

No! she thought wildly, oh no! This hard, scornful passion was not love, not the love they had known together. Not the love that had filled her dreams, waking and sleeping, since his return to Exmoor a happy age ago. This clutching, bone-grinding lust of his had no hint of feeling in it. None of the tenderness that had once burned in both of them.

A love that sang like Lancelot's, her young soul cried out, or Tristram's for Isolde, turned to a sweaty barnyard coupling! Oh no, Walter—not this to us! When we had heaven within our hands—

She strained against his arms, broke their kiss. She twisted her face away.

"Let me go now, Walter. It is enough. I only came— Please let me go, Walter."

"Why certainly, my lady! As my lady pleases. I have never yet forced any woman to come to me against her will."

He held her at arm's length and gazed at her. The trembling girl, looking fearfully back at him, saw her own reflection in his eyes. Her flushed face and throat, her loosened coiffure, her shoulders partly bared beneath his hands. Her breast heaving beneath the shaken bodice.

And she saw his face, devouring her. A stranger's face, distorted with lip-smacking relish.

"God, but you're a pretty wench," he said.

"Oh, please—"

He let her go. But he still stood there, between her and the hall door, looking at her. With a sob, she turned her back on him and wept.

Arabella Traherne was nineteen years old. She had no mother, no friend. She had confided more of her half-formed heart to this young man than she had ever done before in her life. And now he had turned lunatic or villainous or both. Bewildered and betrayed, worn out by ten days of unending festival, there was nothing left for her but helpless, bitter tears.

God, but it is villainous to do this, thought Castlemayne. It is foul, foul to treat so fair a creature thus. So fair and helpless and unknowing. As unknowing as he himself had been not three days since.

Dear Lord, let her tears end at least. Let her return with some peace of soul to her bed.

He approached her slowly then. Touched her, turned her small, shrinking figure about to face him. And spoke, kindly but crisply, as one might speak to a temperamental child.

"Come, my lady," he said, "you must be indisposed yourself from too much festivity, too many days of Christmas. You'd best to bed. You are too full of foolish fretting for kissing and caressing this night."

"Walter, you know I did not come for that—but for this illness that has come over you. . . ." She sniffed and dabbed at her cheeks with a loose strand of her own long hair. "And truly, truly, Walter, your speech and manner—oh, you must be grievously unwell. You are—"

"A courtier, my lady!" He presented himself with a rueful bow and a gesture that encompassed everything from velvet slippers through black doublet and breeches to the elegant small white ruff, slightly disarranged, about his neck. "And courtiers, my lady—well, you know them!"

He took her firmly by the arm and guided her toward the door, pattering on the while.

"Your courtier, madam," he quavered in old Humphrey's voice, "is the lowest of God's creatures. A serpent's guile, an adder's sting—low creatures, you will admit—the morals of a rabbit, a mole for burrowing in other men's purses, and a flea for probing his lady's—aye, well, indeed your ladyship may guess better than an honest man may say."

In spite of herself, she gave a little snort of laughter. His wit's not lost, she wondered, but turned satirical. But why, and how—? She dabbed her eyes and clung to his arm one moment by the door.

"Now, my lady, you really must be off. Before some long-nosed servant discovers your absence from your bed and raises a hue and cry."

"No fear of that." She sniffed. "Agnes is retired with a distemper, and I doubt she will be out of her own bed for a week at least. It is her midwinter ague come upon her." She hesitated, then pleaded suddenly one last time. "But what is it, Walter? Oh, please, what has come over you? And what can I do?"

"Nothing, my lady. Nothing. Nothing." He was staring fixedly past her face at the far window, shaken now by a furious gust of the night wind. "Only you must go now, and sleep. Not all of us have license to sleep," he added with a short laugh. "Those that have should prize the privilege."

"Dear Walter, you must rest—"

"Ah, no rest for the ambitious courtier, lady. No rest for the high aspiring mind. He who would rise in this wicked world must labor by day and by night." He laughed again, a harsh unhappy laugh.

"But Walter—"

"Good night, sweet lady!"

There was a shift in the timbre of his voice, an edge of urgency that made her know she must stay no longer. He was staring hard over her head now, his eyes bright, the fever spots glowing on each cheek.

"Good night—my love!" she said impulsively. She smiled and touched his cheek with two quick fingers. Then, before he could muster a jest or a remonstrance, she had slipped out into the darkness of the hall.

Castlemayne closed the door and shot the bolt. He turned deliberately to face the rattling window at the far end of the room.

"Well then, old horsefaces!" he said, not shouting, but loud enough for them to hear. "Come now, I hear you out there in the wind, gibbering and clawing at the panes. Are your lowlinesses and villainships then come to serve as my taskmasters too? Well, you shall see the craftsman at his task this night, by God. The good workman needs no pricking to his labors."

Then in a moment, with a sudden lifting of the heart, "What, will you not enter? Quite stopped by mere glass and leading? With so many chinks in that old lancet, surely Beelzebub's minions can find some way in." Finally, almost with bravado, "Too bad, too bad, gentlemen. I had looked forward to composing an elegy, an epitaph in five acts, to the beat of your dancing feet around my table!"

He stood beside his little table now, arranging pens and paper, humming to himself.

Thereafter he strode vigorously up and down the room for a time. He rubbed his hands together to keep them warm and limber for the writing, while he labored peripatetically at his composition. He deliberately turned each time within a foot of the whispering, shrieking window.

At the fifth turn, he heard nothing but the howling of the cold night wind outside the panes.

After a dozen turns he had his meters fixed and his theme—conventional, but effective—worked through in rough outline. When he reached the round table this time, he sat down and got to work.

His quill raced across the page. His lips moved, murmuring, trying words and phrases, as his point scraped along. His eyes were feverish, glittering in the candlelight.

The hours rolled by, the sun rolled beneath the darkened earth, and Castlemayne's pen flickered across smooth foolscap, leaving black words in its wake.

~ Twelve ~

Men That Are
Born to Die

i

It was quiet in Lord Henry Traherne's dim, dark-paneled library. The whitish light of late afternoon was fading slowly beyond the mullioned windows, where gray clouds rolled over snowy forest and moorland. Inside, shadows thickened beneath the heavy oaken furniture, behind the rows of green-bound volumes on the shelves.

The Earl snuffled suddenly and dabbed at his small red nose. He stood at the head of the long polished table, beneath his own vast coat of arms in colored plaster on the wall, playing absent-mindedly with a pair of compasses. He fretted over his winter wheat and cursed with unnecessary virulence that his sleek cattle must soon be feeling the pinch of winter. And he wished most fervently that he had no more than these familiar things to agonize about.

Little Master Cecil, head slightly tilted on his twisted spine, stood gazing down at the shipwright's drawings spread once more across the table. A cross-sectional view lay under his hand, drawn to perfect scale, with living quarters and storage space, holds and bilge and gun deck all clearly labeled. The floating home that would carry a hundred poor devils down the Thames and out to sea just four months hence. Robert Cecil's eyes gleamed in his sallow, sharp-featured face. But he was not looking at the sheet of vellum before him, nor imagining the tall ship itself, floating idly at that moment in the icy river off Deptford. His thoughts were only for the problem that lay spread out in his mind, and for the ticklish task that now devolved upon him.

Presently he began to speak in even, measured tones.

"So one of these two gentlemen must have this fine new vessel. Sir Malcolm Devereux—or Master Walter Castlemayne."

He paused, dallying idly with the diagram before him. He did not wish to seem to prod his noble lordship. Yet that was exactly what he had to do.

"You have spoken to them both of the matter, I believe, my lord?" he went on respectfully.

"I have discussed the matter with them." His lordship sighed. "With Sir Malcolm on a number of occasions. With young Castlemayne less frequently, and most often in the past few days."

A silence ensued, uncomfortable to them both.

"And has your lordship been led by these consultations to modify his judgment of either gentleman?"

"Oh—consultations," said Lord Henry miserably, wiping his red nose on his sleeve, farmer style. "Not really what you would call in London consultations. A bit of talk strolling in the gallery, you know. Or a few words on the matter over the wine cups, while others indulged in—ah—revelry." The Earl of Exmoor, who had never indulged in revelry in his busy life, really had little idea of precisely what pleasures were indulged in at his own festivities.

"But Sir Malcolm," he went on, "has from the first been more than willing to discuss the command of the ship, and military affairs in general. By way of reminding me of his eminent qualifications, I expect. Most impressive, I assure you, his many wars in foreign parts." Captain Devereux's disquisitions had largely been beyond the unmilitary Earl's capacity to judge. But a peer of the realm, he felt, should never admit incompetence.

"Does your lordship then still lean in Captain Devereux's favor? Have you perhaps decided on his nomination?"

"Well, of course there are—ah—objections to his candidacy too. Objections that you yourself have raised. His age perhaps. And the violent nature of these new naval wars, for which an older man may be ill suited. . . ."

"And Master Castlemayne, my lord?" There was a prickle of irritation in Cecil's dry, clipped voice.

"Ah—Castlemayne. Yes. Young, of course, for so responsible a place. And a bit of a swashbuckler still, no doubt. But a sensible young man at heart, I should think. Or on the verge of being one. Took time off this afternoon from some entertainment he's composing for us to stroll and discourse at length on this very subject of sea fighting. He's had no experience of it himself—he frankly admits as much. Yet he has views that seem most sensible. Most sensible.

"Considers the sea fight to be a fundamentally different thing from a land engagement. Most commanders, so he says, fight them much the same today. But it's a new thing in the world, as he points out, to fight upon the sea with ships for steeds and artillery for swords and lances. Duel of Leviathans, he says." Lord Henry Traherne stoped abruptly, vaguely surprised that he recalled so much of the young man's ardent discourse. "Most pleasant, at any rate, to speak with a young gentleman that's neither too cocksure nor too fawning. Uncommon in these times."

"Very true indeed, my lord," said Cecil. "And does your lordship then incline toward Master Castlemayne?"

"Oh well, for that"—the aging country peer shied away like a timid colt—"we must not be precipitate. He is so very young a man—I can scarce imagine him in so responsible a place. And then, it is only these last days that he has evinced any serious concern. Spent too much time at galliards, when he first came here. Even today, it almost seemed he cared more for this pageant he's composing than for the *Golden Fortune*. . . ."

"Alas then, my lord," sighed Cecil, "I see the hard decision's still to make. I cannot envy you, so excellent are the qualities of each. But I must join my own petition to that of your shipwright Master Hackett, that we may carry your final nomination with us up to London." He paused briefly, to give due weight to his words. "I expect we shall be leaving on the morrow of Twelfth Night."

Two days and two nights remaining, thought the Earl. Confound the ship, and Castlemayne and Devereux as well!

He hardly noticed when Robert Cecil took his unobtrusive leave. The master of Exmoor Castle was gazing unhappily out the window at the gray clouds that loomed above the gatehouse, leaden banks of cloud stretching low and lowering away to the distant hills. He wondered with brooding irritation if more snow was still to fall upon the frozen ground where winter wheat and early peas must somehow be laid down in a matter of mere weeks from now.

ii

"You're a fool, Lodovico!"

Sir Malcolm Devereux slammed the heavy broadsword back into its metal scabbard with a clang. Lodovico Marsigliano, hollow-eyed and more skeletal than ever, stood quietly at his master's elbow, gazing without interest over the antique weaponry that filled the Earl of Exmoor's armory.

"A fool, by Christ!" hissed Devereux. " 'The whoreson carcass is not to be found,' you say! Is that an answer? Langland's corpse to drag before the Earl—that's our only answer. That's our only certain way to make an end of Castlemayne. How dare you tell me then your people cannot find it! As if explanations were any help to me!"

They had the bare, high-ceilinged room entirely to themselves. Swords and lances, pikes and halberds mounted up the walls. Muskets and small fowling pieces were grouped near the door. Massive suits of plate armor, unused this century, stood about the room, and there were dusty pennons hanging from the ceiling. The place was unheated and smelled of sawdust and leather and oiled metal.

"My lord is sure beyond all peradventure," said Lodovico slowly, "that there is a corpse?"

"Beyond all peradventure—beyond all hope of heaven! He's killed his friend!

"What else fits all the facts we have? Bianca saw them locked in mortal combat—so much of her story we may take for true, I think. Bianca saw them in a stabbing fury—and no man has seen Langland since. Now Castlemayne comes forward with some cock-and-bull tale of his kinsman's sudden leaving for a Godforsaken hamlet somewhere south of Truro. Come—it stinks to heaven."

"The fellow was a countryman, my lord. Never happy in the society of gentleman. Is it not possible that he has been injured only, and fled back to the paternal barnyard to lick his wounds in solitude?"

"Pah—you do not know Castlemayne!" Devereux strode restlessly on up the room, hands clasped behind him, his eyes passing malevolently over his lordship's vast array of armament, polished and gleaming, most of it out of date for generations. "Castlemayne's a rapier fighter, Lodovico!" the Great Captain snarled. "All fire and fury—hot blood where his brains should be. He's stabbed his friend, I tell you. Now find me the damned carcass!"

Sir Malcolm's eyes were fierce, brooking no contradiction. Lodovico shrugged slightly, acquiescing.

"I could perhaps," he said evenly, running a sensitive fingertip over the elaborate engraving on a Milanese cuirasse, "pay some two or three of his lordship's foresters to search outside the walls. Every shed and privy inside the curtain wall has been most thoroughly gone over. But he may have flung his friend into a snowdrift outside. Most likely in the shelter of the woods behind the castle."

Messer Lodovico's voice was listless, empty even of the cerebral intensity that usually vibrated below his flat tones. He turned disdainfully away from a French tilting helm.

"But then," he continued carefully, "there is the question of money. We have already dispensed more than was intended—"

Devereux swung round on him, his face flushed with more than the wine he had consumed that afternoon.

"God damn your eyes, what does the money matter? You husband hay while the beasts are dying! Hire the men you need, get them to work. There are only two days left!"

Marsigliano inclined his head in silence, acquiescing, and turned to go. But Devereux stopped him with another angry question.

"That bitch you live with—can you get nothing more from her? Too much of her tale rings false as coiner's metal!"

Messer Lodovico's swarthy skin went darker still. He turned slowly back to face his captain, an odd glint in his eye. But his answer came icily emotionless still in that cold room full of gleaming blue-gray metal.

"She will say nothing more about it, my lord. She insists that Castlemayne drew her from the great hall that night by stratagem. That he then dragged her by main force across the empty courtyard to the stables, flung her incontinent into the nearest stall. When his kinsman leaped upon him in the dark, she fled in terror of her life. So she swears, and will say no more."

"She would not publicly call down Castlemayne for rape?"

"She would not. She was too terrified at the time, and three days after the event is too late now to lay the case before a magistrate. Nor would English justice be likely to accept the word of a foreigner against such a man as Castlemayne." He paused an infinitesimal moment, savoring the bitterness of that fact.

Lodovico Marsigliano was a mercenary soldier. He traveled for his living, and he did not expect to be loved in another man's country. But tonight, somehow, his isolation weighed upon him. For some days now there had been a bitter taste to many things.

"In any case," he concluded, "Bianca refuses absolutely to speak or to act further in the affair. Something, I think, has frightened her beyond all reason."

"And have you no methods of loosening the whore's tongue, then?" Devereux goaded his lieutenant almost deliberately. His blunt fingers and long ape arms ached for some provocation that might release his own mounting fury in a torrent of violence. He yanked a heavy musket off a wall bracket, hefted it, easing his tension in the familiar feel of cold iron in his hands.

"I have beaten her," answered Lodovico in the same dead voice. "But when I strike her, she refuses to speak to me at all. A thrashing only makes her more intractable. She takes her vengeance by divulging nothing of what she may know."

Again he paused momentarily. Then:

"I myself doubt very much that Master Castlemayne compelled the lady to accompany him entirely against her will. Once this affair is ended, I intend to seek out young Castlemayne, in London or wherever. To take up the matter with him further." To run my beautiful gray-steel Picinino through him. To leave him twitching in the new spring grass.

To Messer Lodovico's brooding mind, there was an endgame quality about it all now. Exmoor Castle seemed to him a gigantic coffin. The gentlemen and ladies, squires and servingmen cooped up there together were all tottering, animated corpses to the skeletal Italian.

Sometimes lately, looking at them, Lodovico fancied he could tell the very spot on their bodies where death would strike at them, soon or late. Through the throat or the belly or the groin. Or where death already labored at its task, eating away at liver, lung, heart, brain, killing each man a day's worth at a time. But corpses all of them either way, whether marked for some sudden stroke or half devoured already by the worm.

And yet they fear it, Lodovico meditated. They fear death and all its trappings more than any mortal thing. And they fear me. They all fear me.

"Aye," Sir Malcolm Devereux growled, snapping back the matchlock on the old musket viciously. "Cut his throat for him. Or let him cut yours for you. And the Devil pack the pair of you to hell!" He gave fire on an empty pan and slammed the heavy musket back on its wall bracket. "Filthy world," he spat, "where a man must beg a chance to earn an honest butcher's wage in defense of Queen and country."

"Are there further instructions, captain?" Lodovico asked tonelessly.

"No, no instructions! But do your job, damn you! Do you hear? *Do your job!*"

Messer Lodovico bowed stiffly and turned on his heel. Devereux watched him walk up the empty room and out through the heavy door. The dusty pennons hanging from the ceiling swayed gently as he passed.

"Florentine pimp," Devereux muttered to himself.

He did not know if his lieutenant suspected his own hand in Bianca's rendezvous with Castlemayne. Nor did he much care.

By God, I'll mince the little dancing master if he dares draw his Verdun blade on me! His wits are going anyway, over this strumpet wife of his. And without his brain he's no more use to me. All he ever was, was brains, behind that ugly skull face of his.

But Castlemayne. Now there's another thing entirely.

Sir Malcolm sank wearily into a low-backed chair next to the massive suit of Milanese armor. His left leg ached abominably this evening. A Turkish musket ball was still lodged in that leg. On damp cold days it sometimes ached like a new wound, though fifteen years healed over. Captain Devereux grimaced, but did not deign to seek a more comfortable position.

Castlemayne, he thought bitterly. What the Devil's arse has happened to him? One minute prattling like a village idiot. The next, a shrewd man of business, laboring with his skittish lordship to advance his cause. And then back to babbling words in some deserted hallway, or staring across the table at things that are not there at all.

But Castlemayne was doing better, and Devereux knew it. Lord Henry was listening to him now, instead of simply staring bemusedly as the gallant youth guided his daughter through some intricate court dance. The Earl had even taken to quoting the young man now and again on military matters.

"Now hell roast your bones, Master Walter Castlemayne!" Captain Devereux surged violently to his feet once more. The wine was sour in his belly. "A Spanish fig for your melancholies! And for all you can do to win his lordship's favor now! I'm more than man enough for any two of your kidney. Mincing lace-and-velvet courtiers."

There were rapiers on the wall before him now. Deeply cupped and shallow, edged and pointed only, knuckle guard and filigree. He took one down, felt its weight, ran a blunt finger along the steel blade.

"Aye, fight any two of you in my shirt, by God!"

Devereux had fought his share of duels in days gone by, when he was young and arrogant in London. Younger by half, more arrogant even than he was now. Before he had schooled his choleric nature to the rigid self-control without which there could be no success, for him or for any man, in the violent trade that he had followed all his life.

He had fought and killed in old sword-and-buckler days. And with the newfangled rapier too. The wild charge with an ancient war sword that had cleared a country innyard and rescued Messer Lodovico's mistress was only one of countless half-forgotten skirmishes in the past of Malcolm Devereux.

Killed the first Italian that ever taught his *bottes* and fencing tricks in London, by Christ. He chuckled, remembering. Twenty years ago it was, over a woman. In those days when women mattered overmuch to me.

He saw it in a fleeting vision once again.

The road rising steeply over Shooter's Hill. The carriage creaking slowly upward, the pair of them inside. He leaped out once again before those startled horses, sword in hand, shouting challenges and insults. Till the long-nosed furious Florentine could not but descend and face him.

He heard and saw once more the clatter and flash of blades, feet stamping, leaping in the rutty road. He glimpsed the grinning coachman, and tart Jane peering terrified out at them where they fought. Saw her new lover go down screaming at last, howling wild Italian oaths as he rolled and twisted in the bloody weeds beside the lane.

Broke through his favorite ward, by God! His precious, invincible *stoccata*, that he told his pupils no man could break. And what price then your famous rapier tricks, young gentlemen, when the master of them all lies spouting blood from three several wounds at least, and with not so many days of life left in him?

"Mad whoreson business after all," he said aloud, exhilarated nonetheless by the memory. "But what can our celebrated Master Castlemayne set beside that? What man has he killed in single fight, but his own drunken country cousin? And no carcass to prove even that, by God."

He nodded heavily to himself.

"Fencing is one thing, when blades are bated and it's all in sport. Any nimble quick-eyed boy can do it. But man-killing —that's another matter. Castlemayne and his kind have not the stomach for it."

The bleak, colorless eyes narrowed between deep pouches and thick brows. In his mind he saw the thin, pale face of his rival. Death in that young face, he thought suddenly. No question.

He was cold and weary now himself, he realized. He put his lordship's rapier back and turned toward the door. He moved with some difficulty, feeling the stiffness in his leg.

There are such men, he thought. He had seen them in siege camps and mercenary companies from one end of Europe to the other. Gorgeous young heroes, first to charge and last to fall back in retreat. But too reckless, too dedicated to the swordsman's craft to long survive. The Philip Sidneys of this world, he grimaced. Men that are born to die young, and make good matter for some whoreson poet's maunderings.

Devereux stumped off through the serried ranks of weaponry, glowering at nothing. He remembered how young Sidney had screamed for water as they carried him off the field at Zutphen with a bullet in his groin. And what the whoreson poets had already made of that.

✑ *Thirteen* ✑

The Masque of Glory

i

Captain Devereux, thought the Lady Arabella, has drunk too much wine tonight.

There was a faint odor of stale vintage on his breath, a certain slope to his heavy shoulders as he sat there beside her at the high table. And she had seen how frequently he had signaled the servingman to replenish his cut-glass Venetian goblet.

He has drunk more each night, she realized, since he came to Exmoor.

She saw the black-bearded Great Captain's gaze fixed on Walter Castlemayne, seated just below them, toward the head of the second table. And Castlemayne's deep-shadowed eyes, she saw, swung repeatedly back to Devereux.

She wondered desperately what could be going on.

All about her there was laughter and a babble of voices, the clatter of silver and the clink of glass. Supper was ended, dessert drawing to a close. Busy servingmen moved among the tables, pouring ale nutmeg-spiced, offering beer with saffron cakes, renewing empty wine cups with muscatel or malmsey or claret. There was loud joking and noisy horseplay, a snatch of a carol impetuously begun and broken off. One night only after this remained, and then the holidays were over.

"The masque! The masque! The masque!" chanted three

drunken cavaliers in unison. "Ho, master of the revels, give us th' entertainment you promised for this night!"

Arabella shrugged her slender shoulders impatiently. Masques and music and glittering entertainments were all well enough. But something was happening beneath the joyful surface of these twelve days of Christmas. And she did not know what.

Her father's business was the heart of it, she was sure. But of course he had confided nothing of it to her. One did not confide such things to a child, and a girl child at that. She had always known and accepted this. Only these last days, only since her father's business had become so crucial to the life of Walter Castlemayne, had she begun to care about such things at all.

There was the ship, of course, and whether her Walter or this baleful ogre Devereux was to have it in the spring. That was the crux of it, she had no doubt. Half the castle was talking about that. But what was this strange illness that had so ravaged her perfect cavalier? Why had his country kinsman decamped so suddenly and secretly? What had that fellow from the stables been doing, skulking outside her door that first night, when Walter had come into her very chamber? And more—there was so much more than she had been allowed to know!

Two trumpets spoke abruptly, loud and brazen, from the minstrel gallery above her father's high-backed chair of state. At the other end of the high table, on the Earl's right, old Humphrey Norton rose unsteadily and descended from the dais.

"Your lordship, knights, gentlemen and gentlewomen. Your attention, if I may."

Conversations ended, heads turned. Bleary eyes focused on the master of ceremonies.

"We had at the outset of these holy days a masque—a masque, I may add, excellently well performed by some of the young gentlefolk here present." He paused a moment to let them bask in their own accomplishment. "The theme and title of it, you will recall, was *Antique Chivalry. Or, The Nine Noble Knights and Their Ladies.*"

Arabella's heart quickened suddenly, remembering. Ten weary nights ago—so much longer now it seemed. The singing and the sentimental chivalry. And her triumphant galliard with Walter Castlemayne!

"We offer you tonight," old Humphrey quavered on, "an antimasque, if you will. A pageant or entertainment that treats of this same noble theme, but in a comical-satirical mode. A style highly commended and frequently practiced by some of the most celebrated masters of antiquity.

"The author of this present piece, however, is a young gentleman known to you all. . . ."

She knew. Everyone in the castle knew. She looked down at him once more, her eyes moist with sudden tenderness. Castlemayne leaned forward slightly, his weight resting on his elbows. His thin cheeks were taut and corded, his blue eyes glittering strangely in the dark hollows that shadowed them now. But his gaze was still riveted on the brooding, dark-browed figure on Arabella's right.

"The title of the piece"—Master Norton's peroration wound finally to its conclusion—"is *Glory. Or, The Soldier's Seven Sins.* A masque with a kernel of wisdom beneath the tasty rind of wit."

O Lord, groaned Arabella, he is so tedious.

And yet—and yet! Was not this whole twelve days of Christmas a piece of stage-play pageantry, after all? An allegorical pantomime, all tinsel glitter on the surface while something —she knew not what—moved slow and terrible beneath? For something was moving there, beneath all the feasting and mumming and masquing. Moving heavily and horribly toward its own inexorable climax.

Something was happening, and they would not tell her what. Sitting there in her own father's hall, the great Earl of

Exmoor's radiant daughter trembled in her satin gown.

"I give you then *The Masque of Glory*, whose deeper meaning for these troubled times I commend to your most discriminating consideration."

The vast cavern of the great hall fell strangely silent. The candles fluttered in their sconces along the walls, and the hall seemed somehow to grow dimmer. A nightbird flipped among the raftered vaulting far above. Someone looked up and laughed.

Then drums rattled, horns blared out again. Tripping to a spritely off-key tune, the players scampered in.

Bright-colored masks and garish costumes, nodding plumes, barbaric face paint, mismatched scraps of arms and armor glowed in the flickering candlelight. Half-a-dozen actors first, professionals from Plymouth and Exeter. Then a straggling chorus of half-costumed servants with slaunchways halberds and helmets all askew. Laughing, clowning, exchanging jests and banter with the guests, they came capering and dancing down the hall.

It was Ned Taverner's troupe, the best in the West Country, several of them veterans of the Lord Admiral's company in London. Ned himself rolled and rollicked at their head, all sagging belly and fluttering fingers. His doughy plastic face was made for mugging. As great a comic actor as Will Kemp, some said. Wasting his talents here in the provinces.

To the bray and tootle from the minstrel gallery, Ned Taverner and his company ranged themselves in rough formation facing the tables and began a raucous song:

> "In all countries and all ages,
> Knights have fought for Glory's wages.
> Fought for Honor and for Fame,
> Fought and died in Glory's name!"

Pause. Quick shuffling dance step up and down the lines, clumsily out of time or unison.

"In savage lands, in Greece and Rome,
Knights have fought for hearth and home.
In Italy and Spain and France,
Knights will fight for a lady's glance.

But always Glory is the guide,
Always Glory's at their side,
Leading like a kindly light
To make a soldier's Honor bright."

Glory, grimaced Bianca Marsigliano. The glory of a sword blade through the belly. The glory of camp fever and starving horses.

"It is not badly set forth," opined the supercilious young man beside her. "Though of course there is nothing of the elegance and polish of a court performance—"

The ringleted young courtier, one of Robert Naseby's fencing friends, talked on, but Bianca did not hear him. The fellow had attached himself to her increasingly of late, taking advantage of Messer Lodovico's lengthier absences. Bianca paid no attention to him. He took her silence for attentive interest and boasted to his comrades of how his suit prospered.

The glory of dying in a foreign land, Bianca brooded, watching the players. The Italian woman felt a cold tingle down her backbone. She hated and feared the thought of death with a superstitious terror. Yet dying was forever on her mind these days and nights.

"Here, madam, is Ned Taverner himself," the indefatigable young gallant at her elbow whispered. "He personifies a Savage Man, you see, and offers a song on 'A Soldier's First Duty.'"

Bianca moved restlessly, irritably beside him. Revealing shadows played along her throat and cheek and chin. A softness, a faint looseness showed there now that had not been present even a year ago. But the panting young cavalier saw only the

painted lips and eyes, the swell of her breasts under the black
bodice. He leaned toward her, pressing his discourse more elo-
quently still.

> "A Savage Man from a savage land am I,
> But a paragon of primitive chivalry."

Ned Taverner was singing. He was a hideous, dark, ungainly
sight, grossly fat, his blubber half clothed in animal skins. There
was a horned leather helmet on his head, a club in one hand
and a huge brimming jack of ale in the other. He weaved and
staggered as he sang.

A soldier's first duty, it seemed, was to keep fit:

> "Sound of wind and sound of limb,
> Full of vigor and full of vin—vim—
> A soldier must always be ready to fight—"

Gluttony, drunkenness, and sloth, it turned out, were the
Savage Man's road to soundness of wind and limb. Taverner
illustrated his point by waddling unsteadily up and down the
crowded tables, snatching food from people's plates, gulping
wine and ale alternately from any half-full tankard. He burped
and belched between choruses, drooled red wine into his
whiskers, smeared his face with pastry and marzipan.

The people around Bianca nodded their heads and slapped
their thighs. "By God, it's so"— "Did we not see such a one—"
They had all known soldiers like this Savage Man.

Taverner lurched back to the center of the hall for a final
chorus of "A Soldier's First Duty," and the crowd gave him a
rising ovation, laughing and clapping at once.

It was a historical satire, it seemed. A pageant of military
vices down the ages. There was a Greek and a Roman and a
Frenchman and an Italian. Each personified some notorious
failing of the military character. Corruption, cowardice, strategic
blunders, treachery, looting, rape . . . a parade of harsh realities

to set beside the chivalric idealism that they had all cheered so lustily not two weeks ago.

But poorly mounted really, thought Bianca, watching Taverner and his mates cavort about the hall, singing, dancing, sweating through their pantomimes. There was no splendor, no sparkle or wit to this heavy-footed pageantry. A poor approximation of the fine things she had seen in Naples and Rome and Florence, at carnival time in those warm southern cities, years ago.

Bianca closed her eyes and saw the Bay of Naples, vast and blue, with the purple cone of Vesuvius beyond. She smelled the sweet fruity smell of garbage rotting in the streets, and her ears filled with Italian voices, rich and strong.

Up and down the tables, gentlemen and gentlewomen, courtiers and country fellows alike grinned and guffawed and told each other that it was all true, all true. Ned Taverner was back, portraying the Braggart Soldier this time. A strutting Spanish don, boasting of vast armies routed and golden cities sacked. It was the very essence of all the military brags they had chafed and smiled at politely down through the years. The famous victories that somehow never won the war. The Lord Admirals and Captains General who turned up every spring with hands outstretched for more money, more recruits, more support for their never-ending voyages and expeditions.

The people laughed and cheered and shouted. But Walter Castlemayne had eyes only for the high table, where his chief victims sat.

There in the center slouched the Earl himself, dwarfed by his high-backed oaken chair. Even his lordship, usually so abstracted at his own festivities, seemed caught up in the colorful parade of military follies. His ginger-colored beard was agitated. His pink mouth opened and closed in little bleats of laughter.

There sat the saturnine little Master Cecil, chuckling quietly. But when his restless eyes met Castlemayne's, there was a ghost of puzzlement in them. And you do not like to be puzzled, do you, Master Cecil? Castlemayne smiled to himself.

And there was Captain Devereux.

Elbows on the table, broad shoulders slightly hunched, he sat with a delicate glass goblet between his two blunt hands. His head was down. The shadow of his heavy Roman nose, the black bars of his moustaches, and the coal-black beard hid the lower half of his face in darkness. His eyes were invisible in the shadow of his brows. Only the deeply furrowed forehead and cheeks gleamed in the lemon light of the tall wax tapers.

He turned the wineglass slowly between thick fingers, and he did not laugh. Too much red wine in your belly, Sir Malcolm, thought Castlemayne. And the jest does not amuse you. But perhaps before the night is over . . .

With a heart buoyant as a cork, Castlemayne turned back to the progress of his piece.

The Braggart Soldier was nearing the conclusion of his martial hymn to his own chivalric glory:

> "Without heroes like myself,
> Without victories untold,
> How could any land survive?
> How could any nation hold?"

Taverner preened and mugged and waddled about, warming to his favorite subject:

> "Glory, glory *in excelsis*,
> *Deo gracias* for *me!*
> For without such knights as I,
> Where would any nation be?"

"A far sight better off, God-a-mercy!" called a drunken voice from the low table, and the great hall roared with laughter and approving cheers.

The players bowed and cheered themselves and broke into a

wild dance, an unruly Scottish jig that brought the first half of the pageant to an end.

Servants hastened in to replenish wine and beer and ale, cheese and fruit and sweetmeats. The men in the minstrel gallery played. Castlemayne smiled, lean and pale, the fever spot still glowing in each cheek, as he acknowledged compliments from both ends of the table.

Even Lord Henry Traherne deigned to express his approbation. "Most distracting, most enjoyable, sir, for—ah—for the soul freighted with affairs." He meant it, and the world took note. Castlemayne rose in his place to acknowledge his lordship's praise with a sweeping bow.

"Excellent in its kind," judged Humphrey Norton learnedly, for Master Cecil's benefit. "Really quite good—the true spirit of the Old Comedy. Would you not say so, sir?" The wine glowed warm within him. All his suggestions had been incorporated in the dialogue. Young Castlemayne, he thought, was a man of taste and wisdom beyond his years.

Arabella glowed with pride and happiness, her earlier misgivings all forgotten. Devereux glowered disinterestedly at nothing beneath his beetling brows.

Castlemayne settled back into his seat just as the fanfare sounded, signaling the end of the intermission. Part Two was about to begin.

The axe was about to fall.

ii

"We bring you now the perfect type
Of modern military might:
A knight that lives for Glory's wage—
The hero of *our own* great age!

A captain imperturbable
Whose courage is uncurbable—

Whose hand is ever on his sword,
Whose honor is his plighted word.

A paragon of chivalry,
A hero without rivalry,
For honesty and modesty a knight without a peer—
Behold him come before you now—the Modern Cavalier!"

The ragged line of players parted, and the paragon of chivalry surged forward and fell flat on his face.

To cheers and laughter he staggered half erect, waving a wine bottle, tripped over his own dragging rapier, and went down again. Hopelessly tangled in his weapons, his plumed hat over his eyes, he spent a good couple of minutes just getting on his feet, finding his audience, and striking at last the proper pose of idiotic vainglory to begin his monologue.

It was only then that the thronged and hilarious hall got a good look at him. The laughter sputtered out as they saw, full face and undisguised, Walter Castlemayne's grotesque image of the Modern Cavalier.

Ned Taverner was transformed again. And Castlemayne himself had suggested this costume, this garish makeup. The Earl of Exmoor's guests stared in stupefaction.

The gross belly sagged over his slops as obscenely as ever. The fat fingers waved and waggled as obscenely. The clothes were modern doublet and hose now—black leather and rough black broadcloth, ostentatiously simple and rugged. The ancient traveling cloak was a tissue of rips and smears, relics of many an imaginary battlefield. His plume was bedraggled, his hat shiny with age. Only his weapons were burnished bright— swords and daggers, musket and pike, a gleaming halberd, and an antique longbow and quiver of arrows for good measure.

A soldier's soldier, every inch of him asserted. A man that lived for fighting.

But it was the face that sent stunned silence rippling back

through the crowd, till there was scarce a mutter to be heard, but servants rattling dishes and somewhere a drunken voice, hushed suddenly.

The paint was thick and pasty, chalk white, with bushy black facial hair. A black veteran's spade beard, brows that lay like a black band above his eyes. A nose grotesquely swollen to a huge hooked beak. Thick lips, deep-pouched eyes, and a sneer of idiotic arrogance, of fatuous contempt for any man that had not at least half as many scars as he.

The unaccustomed silence startled Taverner. His jaw dropped, his mouth gaped in a little round O of comical astonishment.

Then suddenly a fuddled drunken squire lifted his face out of a foaming tankard to gurgle his approval. Another braying laugh joined in. Others followed, instantly and eagerly. In a moment the great hall rocked with bellows and shrieks and howls of laughter. And from the bottom to the top of the hall, every glance shot once at least up to the high table.

Sir Malcolm Devereux stared back astounded. His thick-lipped mouth hung open, unconsciously mimicking Taverner's. His hard gut bulged against the tabletop. Inevitably, disastrously, his beaked nose twitched.

Delighted roars of laughter mounted higher still.

When Ned Taverner began on Castlemayne's carefully constructed lines, the joy was doubled and redoubled. The allusions were all brutally clear. The parody was perfect.

> "I am a plain blunt man, my friends,
> And I'll say what I plain blunt think:
> I don't care if thish war *never* ends—"

He winked and tilted up his wineglass.

> "As long as there's plenty to drink."

The goblet in Sir Malcolm's hands glowed red-hot. But he continued to turn it slowly, slowly between his blunt fingers.

> "I've suffered my setbacks, I'll confess.
> In Normandy now, in bloody France,
> My legions met with less success . . ."

Knowing laughter, whispers, nods spread along the benches. Everybody knew about the disastrous Normandy campaign. Everybody told everybody about it. Everybody roared with mirth as Taverner mugged and jigged and waggled his way through a totally unconvincing explanation of his "setback."

The rest of the company capered, charged, retreated around him, acting out the famous debacle. Taverner ended sitting on his arse in the middle of the floor, covered with ignominy, still feebly trying to explain away his unfortunate reverse.

> "The end was somewhat painful"

—rubbing his arse as he rose wincing—

>   "yet
> We'll go down in song and story.
> We did not take the city, but
> We won our meed of Glory!"

> "Glory! Glory! Glory!"

shouted the whole ensemble, surging around him in a wild, ill-patterned dance, nodding plumes and glittering outlandish armor, waving antique weapons and howling at the rafters.

> "The Leaguers birched their backsides blue
> And sent 'em home to me and you,
> Routed, beaten, bloody, gory—
> But they won their meed of Glory!"

> "Glory! Glory! Glory!"

The Earl's guests roared till the tears came.

There was scarcely a subject of the Queen there present who did not have his own reason to hate the Great Captains who lived on military Glory. It was the inevitable other side of the coin whose bright worshipful face was usually presented to the world. The same man that idolized a Raleigh or a Drake could hate and fear the drunken soldiery that shoved him in the street. The chance to voice at last these half-repressed resentments brought a cathartic release that swept the hall toward pandemonium.

"Hee-hee-hee-hee—" A fat old merchant giggled uncontrollably. Somewhere beneath forty years of complacency and calculation, a tormenting memory stirred suddenly to life, escaping in bursts of compulsive laughter.

A big man, rafter-high, filling the door of his father's shop, one huge hand caressing the hilt of a heavy sword. An evil, broad, aggressive grin. Reek of cheap wine and unclean skin. Contemptuous, dirty fingers pawing at the finest fustians, the rich brocades.

His father and his uncles gone, and the two cowardly apprentices pretending business in the workroom behind the shop. Ineffectual protests, ignored expostulations. And shame, shame at his own awkward adolescent body, his soft, helpless, tradesman's hands.

Two other soldiers in the shop now, talking loudly of ravaged towns and foreign women while they fumbled with the goods. Talking of loot, and telling him ironically that he should show more gratitude to men that had bled for Queen and country. And then the new light in their eyes when his mother swept down the narrow stair, clutching up her skirts with one hand, buxom and pretty and too becomingly flushed with anger.

The joy of vengeance long deferred coursed through the fat merchant's aging veins. Vindictive joy to see the archetypal soldier humiliated as he himself had been, that nightmarish afternoon so long ago.

Up and down the tables, laughter rose in gales. Laughter charged with ancient griefs, now unleashed at last.

A sour old maid in a stiff black gown laughed fiercely, like a man. Her withered mouth was hard. Her high-necked bodice tensed with each convulsive spurt of merriment. Her shy young lover had followed a famous captain overseas twenty long, slow years ago.

A solid, honest country squire, wind-browned and gray-eyed, laughed a mirthless laugh, bitter and bleak as a northern winter. He had four sons beyond the seas in this present war. The apples of his eye, the heirs of all his labor on the land. Four tall, strapping sons. And Tom and Will were worm's meat already, fighting to maintain the military reputation of some Great Captain.

Up and down the tables, gusting roars of laughter.

At his seat on the dais, Master Humphrey Norton laughed creakily, shaking his white head. It's Captain Devereux, by all the gods! Captain Devereux to the life. Strange he had not noticed it when Castlemayne had showed him the completed script. But then, the likeness was more in manner and gesture and face paint than in the words. And Master Norton had not been present when the young author had rehearsed the players.

A shrewd stroke, mused little Master Cecil, settling back in his chair, stroking his narrow jaw. One that the gallant captain cannot answer in kind, I think. Unless that Italian ensign of his writes passable English invective? Robert Cecil was a connoisseur of court intrigue. He knew a shrewd stroke when he saw one.

Outrageous! was the Earl's first thought. Outrageous that my noble guest should be made game of under my own roof! But the victim bore it with such frozen-faced equanimity that his lordship slowly relaxed again. No great harm done, apparently. He even smiled himself behind his ginger-colored moustache.

Young and old, country-bred and citified, they laughed. They chuckled, giggled, snorted, hooted, brayed, and howled. Their mockery rolled up in echoing waves, rebounded from the rafters, and crashed down like an avalanche upon the bearded quondam hero at the high table. The Great Captain turned to Braggart Soldier in the twinkling of an eye.

Shoulders hunched, head lowered beneath the weight of their ridicule, Sir Malcolm Devereux stared back at them. Disbelief flickered across his face, and then red fury.

Do you dare then? Do you dare to mock at me? A man of consequence, a name that's known—for some short time obscured perhaps—but Christ, Christ! What no man alive has dared for twenty years, will you fat capons, you shag-haired country louts dare do—

His moorish lips were white as death, his teeth set hard. Not a muscle quivered. Only the eyes glared, pouring basilisk hatred down upon them all. And still the laughter came, again and again. Nor ever after wavered in its object.

Ned Taverner, strutting, gesticulating, mugging, found that the bits of business Master Castlemayne had suggested delighted his audience. Inevitably he repeated them. A short-legged swaggering step, a growling gruffness in his voice always raised a ripple of giggles. A ferocious glare from under lowered brows brought guffaws of happy recognition. A local jest, peculiar to these parts, thought Taverner, grateful to the young gentleman author for putting him on to it.

The Masque of Glory went on, building toward a climax of satirical buffoonery.

The spade-bearded Modern Cavalier won his famous victory at last—by sliding a thin Italian stiletto between the ribs of a pompous, white-bearded royal minister of state. He celebrated his victory in typical chivalric fashion—by reading an order of the day authorizing the sack of London for "gross inhospitality to the heroes of the hour." And while his rabble of a soldiery snatched silverware and chased screaming serving wenches all over the hall, Taverner shouted his final comment on military glory down the ages into a hurricane of jeers and laughter that fluttered candle flames and shook the ancient shields on the walls above:

"I make no brag nor boast, my friends—
You see how the story ends.
Heroes now and heroes then
Are all the same, as you well ken.

Drinkers dicers, lechers, wenchers,
Feebler with our swords than trenchers,
Prudent to a fault, we say:
Live to fight another day!"

And the whole troupe joined in the final chorus:

*"That's our motto, that's our way—
Live to fight another day.
So we'll go down in legend hoary—
So we'll win our meed of Glory!*

Glory! Glory! Glory!"

The company skipped and pirouetted out, waving swords and
clanging shields. A wink, a leer, and Ned Taverner too was gone,
exiting in a finger-wiggling, belly-flapping jig that brought the
spectators to the verge of hysteria. The last glimpse they had
of him was that painted caricature of a face, black beard jutting,
one black eyebrow cocked as he looked back over his shoulder.
He mouthed a cheerful obscenity at them and disappeared.

The audience cheered the players a full two minutes after
they had capered out of the hall.

Liveried servants rushed in with wine and ale and fruits and
cheeses. Lutes and viols, recorders and tambourines struck up
a familiar five-step. Young gentlemen and ladies, laughing still,
rose up to tread a measure.

Young or old, they swore it was the best entertainment they
had yet enjoyed. *Sotto voce* they agreed it served the Great
Captain Devereux perfect justice. They had known, had sensed
from the first sight of him that he was less a hero than a
heroic reputation. Any man could see that this Malcolm Deve-

reux had nothing of true greatness in him. A paltry man, truly. They had known it all along.

In the confusion of moving servants and dancers, Sir Malcolm rose, bowed curtly to his host, and left the hall. He strode out swiftly, swinging his long arms, staring straight ahead with dangerous, dead eyes. More than one startled servingman leaped nimbly left or right, shocked at what they saw on the face of that retreating juggernaut.

Castlemayne watched him go. His eyes burned with an inward fire. *And how many pawns for that, good captain?* he whispered half aloud. *And how many pawns for that?*

~ Fourteen ~

A Strumpet's Bed
Dishonored

i

Sir Malcolm Devereux stood, legs wide-planted, head and heavy shoulders back, pissing tremendously into his own fireplace. Ah Christ, his wine-blurred mind ruminated, that's better! Few better feelings in this whoreson world. . . . The steaming arc of water hissed against glowing coals, drowned the embers in a swirl of smoke. Ah . . . better.

The captain grunted, roughly closed his breeches, and turned back to the table and the wine. Muttering disjointedly, he sank into the low-backed chair and poured, tilting a silver pitcher over a purple-strained tankard.

Good French wine—two, three more hours of it, alone in his dim-lit room—had brought back color to the cruel mouth, the predatory nose. But the shock reverberated still within, like the shock of a wound to the body.

To be mocked before them all, all these fat soft slugs! The image of Ned Taverner, fever-colored and distorted, capered still behind his aching eyes. The raucous gibes, the sneers and jeers screeched across his lacerated nerves.

"Damn Castlemayne," he said aloud, "for a sniveling cowardly carpet knight! Pricking a man to death—with words!" He twined thick fingers in his beard and tugged fiercely, glaring at the single candle flickering on the tabletop before him. His nerves were taut as a drumhead. His mind moved stiffly, like an Italian clockwork toy wound up tight. "Damn his bloody eyes!"

He hoisted the pewter tankard and drank sloppily, soaking his beard. He clanged the empty vessel down on the table and sat brooding, staring at nothing now. He felt the fumes of wine rise slowly to his brain. Perhaps now he would sleep.

He felt strangled, stifled. He shook his head doggedly, but the weight of black oppression would not leave him. The little antechamber itself seemed to be closing in upon him now. He felt the sculptured plaster ceiling press down invisibly. The floor rose up against his feet. The wainscoted walls, alive with linenfold and strapwork carving, seemed to creep silently toward him across the floor.

It—the building—something—was closing in on him.

Might not the whole castle come crashing down upon him? Might not the terrible winds that shrieked outside, the weight of snow upon the roofs bring it all down at last? All those tons of stone, wood, slate, glass, lead, plaster, and brick down upon his throbbing skull?

He would be crushed like an ant between two stones. Like a snail cracking beneath a giant heel.

"Christ's bloody wounds!"

Devereux was on his feet, one arm blurring past his bleary eyes in the act of throwing, his chair crashing over behind him. The pewter mug clanged against the doorframe and bounced away, leaving a sudden gash across a caryatid's oaken face.

The captain stood swaying slightly, eyes aflame. He shook his head and ran stubby fingers through his black hair. He kicked the upended chair aside and strode jerkily up and down the small room.

Trying to clear his head. To think how he might best make use of the single day left to him. Trying to smother the rage that boiled up futilely within him.

The corpse of Harry Langland—there was still the key! Even now Lodovico and Luke Naylor and their unobtrusive army of stablehands and foresters were searching through the night. Skulking through the forest, poking in deep drifts, seeking with hunters' eyes by moonlight for any trace of a rude burial. Report might come at any time—God knew he had promised them reward enough.

And then there was Bianca. Surely she nursed more secrets than she had yet confessed. They had been too gentle with her, surely—too gentle by half.

One way or another, he swore harshly, some proof of Langland's butchery must still be found. Ferreted out and presented to his lordship, as good subjects that come upon a murder are bound to do. And will the great Earl of Exmoor then trust his dignity and honor to a manslayer? To one that's stained his noble house with a kinsman's blood—over an Italian whore?

That will do it. That's bound to do it.

"My lord, forgive me—"

He froze in midstride, wheeled about.

Bianca Marsigliano stood just within the room, looking at him. With one hand she softly closed the door behind her.

She stood almost in profile, her farthingaled gown half twisted round her, a voluptuous silhouette in black. The olive skin of her throat and shoulders glowed darkly in the light of the single candle. A chaste white wimple only partially concealed her shining black hair.

"I could not sleep, my lord." She paused. "For thinking of you." Her lips trembled slightly. "I saw what that devil Castlemayne . . ." She faltered once more into silence.

Devereux stared coldly back at her. "Well, madam?" he snapped. "What do you here, so far from your husband's bed at this hour of night?"

"My husband's bed! *Per Dio!*" she snorted, glad of the distraction from a purpose she herself but half understood. "Small comfort to me that! Lodovico has gone mad, my lord—mad, or near to it. All day and half the night he watches me, with eyes like empty ciphers in that death's-head of a face." She laughed the deep contralto laugh that had once had such power to charm. "Truly, my lord, I fear he'll strangle me in that same bed some night. Nothing but my death will convince him of my fidelity."

"And this is how you calm his suspicions?" Devereux's voice was burred with wine, but peremptory still. "By coming to his master's chamber at midnight?"

Bianca's eyes abruptly softened once again, grew moist with tenderness. Yet she hesitated, uncertain still. She bit her lower lip.

"Malcolm—my lord—I came—"

How could she tell him? How express in words the surging emotions she herself scarcely comprehended?

She had worshipped him for his strength in a world of petty men. Incredibly, she had come to need him all the more when she had learned, that afternoon in the solar, that, for the first time, he needed her. And now, still more bewilderingly, his public humiliation at the hands of Castlemayne filled her with a longing greater still.

And yet she could not speak. Her breast heaved, her lips parted, and still no sounds came. The shell of bitterness and distrust that had grown between her and all the world of men was thick, thick. . . .

"Come, mistress, what's your business?" His voice was hard now, the wine mastered, the furry overtones suppressed. "If you seek your husband—he is occupied on his master's affairs. If it's the master you seek"—he did not offer the faintest ghost of a smile—"I have no strength to waste on strumpets this night."

Her eyes widened. He could see the hurt in them.

But a beautiful strumpet she is, he thought, stirred in spite of himself by a dim spasm of desire. By God, and a hot whore still, I make no doubt. His bleak eyes brushed the soft flesh of her throat, the high-bound breasts, unmoving now as sculptured stone beneath the dark satin of her bodice.

"Well then, mistress?" His voice grated even in his own ears. He was angry at his own weakness. And the accumulated humiliations of that night seethed for release.

"Your pardon, my lord," she stammered. "But I only thought—

that I might bring you some small comfort. Some solace after—what happened this evening."

She paused. His eyes were cold. Yet she blundered on.

"I know this devil of a Castlemayne, my lord. He can be . . . a most terrible man. This thing he did tonight—it was *inumano,* cruel beyond anything. I saw, I heard. And I—I was sorry. For this I come, I risk my lord husband's fury to offer . . . what I can—"

Devereux had risen suddenly, his chest heaving. The woman looked up at him. She threw back her head so that the wimple fell away, uncovering her shining black hair entirely to his gaze. Her dark foreign eyes searched his face. She took a step toward him, and another, swaying slightly as she came. The fingers of one hand reached out to touch his shirt. To feel the great muscles taut beneath, the furnace heat of his body. Gasping like a drowning woman, she raised her face to his.

The butt of Devereux's horny hand slammed into her cheek, sent her crashing back against the door.

"Malcolm, *caro mio!*" She stared at him in horror. "What have I—"

"You pocky harlot! Close your filthy mouth!" He smashed her across the face again, knocking her sprawling in a tangle of skirts.

When she raised her head to look at him again, she was bleeding at the mouth. There was a red welt across her cheek from the square-cut ring he wore. Before she could focus her bewildered eyes upon him, he lashed out at her again.

"Bitch! Drab! Trull!" he hissed between set teeth. "Will you fling his triumph in my face? Will you rehearse before me what he has done to me this night? And will you dare to offer me—your pity? Your pity, whore? Am I to have a strumpet's sympathy, and must I thank you for it too?"

He beat her with his open hand, with his fists, with his booted feet. The whirlwind that night had raised, the wrath building since that first awful moment in the great hall, burst now upon Bianca. All his hatred for Castlemayne, for Exmoor, for years of frustrated ambitions powered every blow.

"Master Castlemayne has put the fear of death into you, has he, mistress? Tell me now, which of us is the more terrible!"

He saw the agony in her eyes, and he knew it was more than mere physical pain. His own tortured soul exulted at the sight.

"So then. Back to the stews of Naples where you belong, *putana* of Italy. And save your pity for what creatures of the dunghill you can find fouler than yourself."

Bianca had pulled herself to her knees and was struggling with the door latch. Devereux stood panting, hands on hips, watching her. She got the door open, pulled herself to her feet. She sagged against the doorframe then, hair and clothing in disarray, choking on dry sobs. He gazed with growing satisfaction on his handiwork.

Well, let her weep, he thought almost cheerfully. A man must beat his whores from time to time, for the good of their souls.

Mistress Marsigliano's dark southern eyes focused on his one more time, full of simple hatred. The hatred of the injured animal for its tormentor. Then she passed through the door and vanished down the unlit corridor toward her husband's chamber.

Captain Devereux slammed the door heartily behind her, grinning savagely. He stretched immensely, feeling pleasantly relieved. He knew he would sleep well that night.

ii

Bianca pushed open her chamber door and stepped inside. Three candles guttered in the wall sconce, where she had left none burning. She paused, wondering dully if Lodovico could have returned and found her gone. Surely not. He had left the castle soon after nightfall, saying in his mechanical, dead voice that he would not be back till dawn. And yet, there were the candles. Uneasily, she closed the heavy door behind her.

Something moved at her elbow. She looked quickly down, wincing at the pain of the sudden movement, one hand rising to cover the welt upon her cheek.

Luke Naylor sat upon a great carved chest just inside the door, grinning up at her.

"What are you doing in this place, villain?" She strove for the strength to be angry, to put him in his place at once. "Who gave you leave to enter here? To lord it in a gentleman's chamber as if it were your own horse stall!"

Luke's ugly grin broadened, revealing broken teeth. The scarred hollow where his right eye had been suddenly winked obscenely.

"I merely do my betters' bidding, mistress," he said in a whining singsong, slouching to his feet. "Poor Luke does as his masters tell him, lady. Takes his pay and earns it fairly, by doing what he's paid to do."

He bobbed his shaggy head obsequiously as he spoke. His shoulders hunched. He seemed to cringe before her, as though he expected any moment to feel a riding crop across his back. And yet the Cyclops eye and broken, grinning mouth looked anything but humble.

"Explain yourself, *briccone,* and at once. Did Messer Lodovico send for you to come here? Because if he did—" Mary Mother, give me strength to get him out, out of here. I must wash, rest my poor ruined body. "Because if he did—" She swayed forward a step or two and clutched for support at one of the ornamentally carved bedposts.

"Is my lady ill, then? And may a poor man that's more knowing of horseflesh than fine ladies—?" He shuffled forward, extending a calloused hand to steady her. The odor of horses and moldy straw clogged her nostrils. These and something else. Something she had never smelled before.

"Get away," she said hoarsely, letting go of the bed and drawing herself up to face him. She fumbled for the English words she needed. "Get away from me, rogue, or I shall have you whipped till there is no skin on your back!" She saw with relief that he drew back at once, obsequious once more. "Now tell me what you are come for. And be quick."

"Mistress, I only do as I am bid," he reiterated doggedly. "'Come at once, Luke Naylor'—those were Messer Lodovico's words—'and tell me when you find the thing. You or your men. And there will be ten golden ducats for you. But only if you come at once.' His very words, mistress, and that's why I'm here."

He stood almost complacently there before her, his ungainly figure slightly bowed, hands folded piously across his belly. His single yellow-green eye slowly opened and closed, like the hooded eye of a turtle.

"*Bene, bene.* Out with it then at once, for the sake of God. I'll see you get your ten gold crowns," she added scathingly, seeing a look of stubborn doubt cross his face.

"But the *signor* bid me most particularly—your pardon, mistress—to report the business to himself alone. Or to his master, if he was not to be found. And to no other living soul. . . ."

"Son of a dog, tell me at once! At once, or pay what penalty I can arrange!" Her knuckles were white. She was at the end of her strength.

"As you wish, good mistress, just as you wish." He spread his hands placatingly. "I am simply come to say, mistress, that I have found the unfortunate gentleman. Master Walter Castlemayne's vanished kinsman. Or what's left of him."

Bianca said nothing. She only stared blankly at him.

"And shrewd work it was too, in the darkness, and with this wind that makes my poor eye near blind with the bite of it." Luke spoke with relish now, conjuring up his exploit for her. "Down at the bottom of the millpond path, my lady, was where I first got scent of him. I could see at once, even in the filtered moonlight, that someone had missed the turn there and fallen, down into the field below. From there, the faintest wandering trench meandered off through the snow. Half hidden by drifting and later snowfall, but plain enough for the eye that was looking for it.

"After that, it was all easy as a game of Where's-My-Thimble. There was only one place the dead gentleman could be. The copper beech by the old mill dam, where the water's deepest.

"Three times I smashed the ice before I found him. Cruel cold work it was too, in the wind and all. And fearful, most fearful, in the dark, when black clouds drove across the moon." Luke laughed, and spat upon the floor behind the chest. "I took him for a tree trunk first, mistress. A tree with some stumpy limbs still on it. But then I felt around a bit, my hand near frozen down in that black water, and touched his face. And then the hair, all icy even in the water, and stiff as wire."

She shuddered in her warm gown. "Get on with it, for sweet Jesus' sake." Her superstitious soul revolted at such talk of the dead. And now she knew what that other stench upon him was, that she had never smelled before.

"Why, there is only this to say. That it would be well to move the gentleman from where he lies—or rather, floats—to some place more commodious for accidental discovering. For such, by your leave, I take to be Messer Lodovico's purpose. Pitch the carcass under a bush, where a man might stumble over him by accident. Hard to explain the face, of course—the fish have been at him some. But then, crows and rooks might account for that. And freezing for the water's work."

A faithful dog indeed, she thought, abashed at bringing home a damaged bird.

"But the wound is clear enough," he growled, brightening. "No coroner but will see it for a stabbing—and I've seen some stabbings in my day." He nodded complacently to himself. "All in velvet he is too, with one sweet dancing slipper left. No likelihood he ever set out for Land's End in such clothes. Or Truro, or wherever it was Master Castlemayne gave out."

So there it is, thought Bianca, weary and bitter beyond words. Sir Malcolm's victory after all. As usual. As always.

"But mistress, if you will, be sure to tell the *signor* the carcass must be moved. . . ."

Through the haze of her giddiness and pain, Bianca saw the black-bearded face of Malcolm Devereux. The pale cheeks corded with laughter. The colorless eyes kindled suddenly with exaltation. It was a savage face, ablaze with triumph. As she had seen it not half an hour since.

The image had scarce faded when she knew what she must do.

"I shall convey your message," she said, smiling for the first time, almost dreamily. "Now go. And do not come here again until my husband sends for you."

That, of course, must never happen. She would see to it. She would devise something, she knew not what. But there were not thirty-six hours more before they would all be gone from this Aladdin's cave. Surely she could devise something to keep Devereux from knowing until then. Until it was too late to matter.

Her eyes had glazed over as she stood there. She swayed, and her hand once more reached out to the bedpost for support.

"Surely my mistress is not well," said Luke Naylor. "If I can be of help—"

"I need no help from you, villain." She strove for a note of command. She was astonished when her words came out trembling, on the edge of hysteria.

She swayed again and almost fell. Luke's heavy hands shot out. He caught her, held her up with muscular ease. She felt his hands on her body and saw in his narrowed eye a light that was no longer calculating greed, but something far more immediate and compelling.

"By God—" she swore.

He pulled her roughly to him. Crushed her delicate lace against his leather jerkin. Pressed his dirty mouth avidly on hers.

By Jesus, mistress, he swore excitedly, but I'll take those high and holy airs out of you! Italian drab, that goes about prim as any Puritan, and then plays the beast with two backs in my stables!

Bianca heaved once, wildly, against his encircling arms. And then let go.

His kiss savaged her battered mouth. His hands hurt her bruised and lacerated body. Yet she did not fight him now. She let him have his way with her.

Why not? Why not? she wondered dizzily, laughing and weeping at once. Why not this filthy shoveler of horse dung, as well as any other man? Has not my lord—she saw his livid face once more, felt his blows and curses—has not my true lord called me whore? And is it not a whore's vocation to give herself to any man that beckons, smell he of rich Eastern scent or horses and moldy oats . . . ?

She dug her fingers into his matted hair and pulled his face down to hers.

Luke swept her up in his powerful arms and flung her back into the canopied bed. In a moment he was on top of her, tearing at her clothes.

What lovely dugs, truly! And what a pillicock-hill for mounting! He reared back, pulling his jerkin over his head. O your Italian for a copesmate every time! I'll play the goat tonight, by Jesus. And fair pay too for ten days of cringing to her stick of a husband.

One of the flickering candles guttered out, and it was darker still.

Then Luke came sprawling across the bed after her, naked, dirty, reeking with lust. Bianca stopped her very breath to close out that which she was welcoming to her arms. Since her childhood in the stinking alleyways of Naples, she had loved soaps and strong perfumes. In her own house in Venice she had always made her clients bathe before they came to her.

Luke clawed at her, felt the nippled hills of flesh through the thin silk that still covered them. He swore delightedly and tore her shift away.

Then he came over her. She spread her thighs and turned her face away.

And even in that dark rocking bed, with Luke's hoarse breathing in her ears, she saw the eyes of Sir Malcolm Devereux upon her.

So I am *putana* in your sight, my lord! Pocky whore, harlot, strumpet, punk, and drab—all the lovely things you gallant soldiers call us, the women you cannot do without. Why then, if I am naught but a whore to you, then see me as I am. See me, damn your granite eyes—see what I can do!

Her hands, her thighs did wonderful things. Luke Naylor cried aloud and rolled on to his grunting climax. Sobs and crazy laughter mingled as the bed shook mightily and he expired upon her breast.

"Enough, woman! Christ—enough!"

She collapsed then too, all her fury blown away. She felt befouled and limp and helpless, staring emptily at nothing. God damn them all. Mary Mother damn them all.

Luke rolled away from her, one arm flung across his face, still breathing heavily. Jesus, he thought, but these Italian guinea hens—

There was a silence in the tumbled bed. Silence, while a man might draw three slow breaths.

Then, with a jolt of terror, Luke knew that he and she were not alone.

Some part of his still-spinning brain must have caught the faint sound of a lifting latch. Or perhaps his cooling, sweaty skin felt the surge of air from a briefly opened door. For all at once, and from no conscious cause, fear drained his body.

Then he heard quite clearly the stealthy scrape of a boot. The rasp of metal upon leather.

His one good eye flew open. His languid arm jerked away from his face. He strained frantically into the gloom, where a single candle still burned. Where a dark thin figure now moved with sudden awful purpose.

Luke saw the skeletal shape, like a vision in a nightmare, loom shockingly close above him. Saw the thin arm go back, the dull glitter reflecting up and down the blade.

He screamed as the stiletto cut into his naked flesh. He howled again, like an animal, at the second blow, and at the third. Then his throat was neatly slit. A precise incision, from one ear to the other, just below the hairy jaw.

His powerful body still writhed on the bed, but silently now. Like a cock with its head cut off, that still races frantically about the yard. For Luke was dead already, struggling against a fate that had already fallen.

The lethal hands reached over him, toward the woman next to the wall.

Bianca knew that skull-like face. Knew the bony fingers that closed upon her arm. That yanked her, shrieking, half out of the dim cavern of the bed.

"No no no—Lodovico my love—"

She struggled wildly against his icy grip. She saw the inexorable dagger rise again.

"Lodovico, my heart, my husband," she cried in Italian, "please—"

For one unreal instant she wrenched free.

But as she leaped up, he caught her by her flying hair and flung her back upon the reddened coverlet. There he held her for a long moment, leaning with all his weight on the hand that pinned her heavy, soot-black tresses to the bolster. She lay helpless, panting, staring up at him.

His eyes were two black hollows in his head. His clenched teeth flashed. In the half-light, he seemed oddly lipless, like a fish. Slowly, as though obeying a will of its own, the stiletto rose once more.

O Mary Magdalene O Mary Mother of God

He drove the dagger into her just above the trembling, dark-nippled mound of her left breast. She stiffened at the blow. Her eyelids fluttered, her lips still moved, muttering incoherently. She raised one feeble hand, as though to catch his wrist, to prevent the blade that already transfixed her. But her fingers only brushed the back of his hand very gently, and fell away.

Lodovico Marsigliano was alone in the room.

~ *Fifteen* ~

The Picinino Blade

i

So you have stooped even unto this, *signora!* To couch with grooms and stablehands. To do the act of darkness with this dungy-handed wretch a chambermaid would spit upon!

Lodovico turned away, his thin lips reflecting the contempt, the loathing that welled up in him.

Mechanically he went on with what he must do. He cleaned his blade on the bolster, examined his clothes for any traces of blood. But his soul shuddered at the spectacle he had seen. The lady who had taken his name—the ancient name of the Marsigliani—in fornication with a stablehand! Death was a meager recompense for such a stain upon his honor.

"Unnatural," he said aloud. "Unnatural. To offer herself to such an upstart as this Castlemayne is insult enough. But to give herself to this—"

Then came a further thought, and a shock of cold horror.

How many other such menials have enjoyed her body? How many others, here in my own bed?

He remembered an aging gentlewoman of Pisa who had sunk to this perversion. Rumor swore she had slept with every servant in her house and half the peasants in her fields. But he had never thought Bianca—even Bianca—capable of this.

Bailiffs? Body servants? Footmen? Foresters? Waiters at table

206

and turnspits from the kitchens? How many of them will smile at me tomorrow, and see the cuckold's horns?

For the first time since he had entered the room, sweat broke out on his swarthy forehead.

The sweat turned cold. There was moving air against his skin. He blinked, and saw a candle flame bend double.

How long then, and who—?

He spun like a thin, goat-bearded dervish to the door behind him, dark cloak wide-billowing, one hand flying to his rapier hilt. And even as he turned he heard the voice and felt the first stab of joy. The one man of all others to make this night complete! The one man whose undoing might turn his thoughts from all those nameless others . . .

"Jesu!" gasped Walter Castlemayne.

For Castlemayne, the manic exultation of that evening came crashing to an end. He stood stunned, dislocated, staring into an inferno he thought to have escaped forever.

He had come with a heart swollen with the triumphs of the hour just gone. He had come remembering his victim, the wounded bear that had gone lurching from the jeering hall, red-eyed and white to the lips. Remembering himself victorious, striding through a sea of murmured congratulations, allusive jests, reminiscent laughter. All signs and recognitions of his victory.

He had danced and laughed and smiled easily thereafter. He had held Arabella in his arms once more, moving to a brisk French galliard. "Oh, Walter," she had smiled radiantly up at him. "You're yourself again!"

But his mind had been busy all the while. Thinking, scheming, elaborating on his next bold stroke.

Devereux would drink himself to sleep. He was halfway there already. Messer Lodovico had left early for some strange Tuscan sport of night hunting in the snowy forests. That left the weakest link open to his blows. The fading Italian strumpet who called herself Marsigliano's wife would be alone and unprotected in her chamber.

The fear of me is strong in her, else she'd have cried rape and murder long ago. Who knows but what a midnight visitation might bring her quaking to her knees before the Earl, to tell all she knows? To betray her master once for all, and bring this silent struggle of words, innuendo, intrigue to an end at last?

Why not? Why not?

Scenting victory, he had come by labyrinthine ways to the isolated chamber of the Marsigliani. Had pushed open the door with a feverish eager hand. And had stepped back into his recurring nightmare.

Two candles wavered in the brass wall sconce to the right of the door through which he entered. The rich, dark furnishings showed dimly, the tapestries and curtains glowing green and scarlet in the shadows. The man and the woman lay naked on the bed, tumbled hideously together. He saw contorted limbs, wild hair, dark blood still flowing over bare white skin.

One-eyed Luke the groom lay on his back with his throat cut, head lolling over the bed's edge. His single empty eye stared inverted up at Castlemayne.

Bianca, her shining black hair spread wide upon the bolster, showed white teeth all around her open mouth. Blood coursed down between her full breasts, flaccid now in death. There was blood everywhere, more blood than he had ever seen, even on a battlefield.

In the middle of the long narrow chamber, between the blowing candles and the bed, stood Lodovico Marsigliano, the regnant demon of this lurid corner of hell. His dark riding cloak still swung from narrow shoulders. His long rapier, with the ornately fashioned hilt, hung at his side. Flecks of unmelted snow still gleamed on his boots and shoulders.

"Master Castlemayne."

The Italian's hissing intonation seemed almost to caress the name. His face cracked at the mouth into a death's-head grin. And Castlemayne, standing weaponless before him, tasted brass beneath his tongue.

"If it's to visit your mistress you've come," Marsigliano continued smoothly, "I fear you arrive too late. She was incapable of fidelity, as you see—to husband or to lover. But do come in, sir. We have things still to say to one another, I think." Or will you have me chase you howling down the corridor and run you through the back?

Castlemayne stepped in. For he saw the same green fires flickering behind Lodovico's eyes as had lighted his insane attack on Harry that afternoon in the gallery. He saw the bony hand fondling the sculptured sword hilt—the same dueling rapier he had worn that day. He had no choice. He stepped into the room.

"This is a fortunate meeting, Master Castlemayne." The voice was flat and unemotional, as though they met over foaming jacks of ale in some Cheapside ordinary. "I had intended to seek you out in days to come, for further discussion of this very matter. In fact, sir, I had thought"—his toothy smile grew fixed—"to make a point of honor of it."

Point of honor! thought Castlemayne, staring at the naked corpses. This is bloody butcher's work!

"Indeed, I had intended a formal challenge. In defense of my wife's . . . good name. But now, as things have fallen out, the slut is dead. And alive or dead, so false a whore is scarcely worth such ceremony." His hollow grin was wolflike now. "The differences between us can surely be settled more informally. Here and now, where the wench herself has suffered for her infidelity."

His fingers closed about the hilt of his long Verdun blade.

"The ground," said Castlemayne, dry-lipped, "seems cramped and incommodious." The room was long and narrow like his own, far too confined for normal swordplay.

"It is," assented Marsigliano. "But both of us, I'm sure, have

fought on less convenient ground. And as it happens, the circumstances compel me to insist on an immediate settlement."
The dead must be disposed of, after all, and some excuse found
for their precipitate departure. And all must be done posthaste,
before that night was over.

"And then," said Castlemayne evenly, "you see I have no
weapon." He spread his arms slightly. He stood silhouetted in
black doublet and hose, not even a dress bodkin in evidence.

Lodovico laughed, an ugly sound, like an iron gate swinging
slowly open. And behind the Italian's inhuman mirth Castlemayne heard other laughter, horribly familiar. It was the high-
pitched piping of the demons, the horsefaced haunters of the
dark he thought he had mastered once for all.

Young Castlemayne fully expected to be murdered where he
stood. Marsigliano had given the other two no chance. Why
should he do more for Castlemayne?

But Lodovico, still laughing, reached into a tall cherrywood
cupboard and drew forth the silver-mounted ceremonial rapier
he had worn when he first came to Exmoor. The weapon he had
abandoned when the castle had become a battleground. He extended it hilt first, with the faintest of flourishes.

Castlemayne, after all, made some pretense to gentility. And
a gentleman must be killed properly, according to the code.

Hardly believing his good fortune, the younger man hefted
the sword and drew a long, slow breath. With four feet of steel
between him and this bloody murderer, he felt some semblance
of hope returning. There was the taste of brass in his mouth still,
the unfamiliar taste of fear. Fear of the Italian's formidable
reputation, and of the creeping devils whose first warning laughter he had heard a moment since. If they were to rise up to taunt
him even as the other man attacked, he would have no chance.
But with a sword in his hand, Walter Castlemayne felt his confidence seeping back.

Across the room Lodovico Marsigliano methodically unhooked
his sword belt, slid the rapier from its sheath, flung the harness

casually on the bed. The belt and hangers draped themselves grotesquely over Bianca's sloping thighs. But Messer Lodovico did not notice. With the sensual pleasure of a lover, he was running his long fingers over the elegant shell guard and the fluted blade made for him by Antonio Picinino, the finest of that family of famous swordsmiths.

"The blades," he said, "are of a length. Or will you measure?" he added, with a shade of mockery.

Castlemayne shrugged irritably and did not reply. Marsigliano's blade had not been of a length with Harry's. But there was nothing to be done about it. He shook his head to clear the shadows from his brain.

Now, he thought, and quickly. Before the room blurs out of focus, and they come.

He stepped out from the wall and fell into a wary guard.

"Come then, sir," he said tensely. "Let us see your *passado!*"

Messer Lodovico stood easily still, his point lowered, observing his opponent. He had the air of a professional horsetrader appraising the jades and hacks at a local fair.

"It is not bad, Master Castlemayne," he said slowly, "for an Englishman. Though the stance is a bit too wide. And you are a shade too close for single rapier, I think—"

Castlemayne lunged, thrusting at the narrow chest.

But something happened.

A dark cloud swirled out of nowhere to intercept his thrusting point. Caught it. Swept it aside.

For an awful fraction of a second, he simply froze. He hung there, off balance, at the extremity of his lunge, wide open to a counterthrust. Then his trained fencer's muscles seemed to operate of their own accord. Back and to the right he sprang, flinging himself away from the riposte, sending a stool flying.

But the riposte never came. Marsigliano simply stood there, the hilt of his rapier lying almost negligently in his hand, the arrogant smile unchanged upon his lips.

Only his left arm had moved. For while he had talked with

Castlemayne, he had draped his cloak with casual elegance over that arm. When the other man lunged, he had expertly flicked the velvet cape up and over to entangle and brush aside the impetuous point.

Back against the wall again, Castlemayne crouched panting, clutching his weapon like the rankest amateur. Fear surged up in him once more.

He had no cape, and no skill in manipulating it in any case. It was an Italian fighting trick his masters had not seen fit to teach him. Even on equal terms, he knew, the Italian ensign was a striking cobra. With the advantage of the cloak for ward, the Florentine was beyond a doubt his master.

And Walter Castlemayne had never in his young life faced an enemy that was a better fighting man than he.

"And now, sir," said Messer Lodovico, "let us to our business." He fell into a fighting posture, his cloak gathered about his left arm. With quick sliding steps, precise and delicate as a dancer's, he advanced on Castlemayne.

Behind the lithe oncoming figure, the room seemed to draw in, to lose its clear defining outlines. The candles burned a bilious green. There were strange movements, low down, in the shadows of the cupboard and the bed. There were fluting, piping noises, and the scrape of talons on the floor.

What happened then—if it happened, for he was never sure—came very fast, and was gone as quickly.

Crouching there, sweating like a green recruit in his first affray, Castlemayne felt a hand on his shoulder. A hand that could not be there, for his back was only inches from the wall. But a firm, familiar hand nevertheless, falling heavily on the big muscle of the shoulder. A comradely, reassuring squeeze, and then a long moment's steady pressure.

Nothing seen, no words spoken. Only the steady, reassuring pressure slowly fading. The fingers icy cold and thinner than they should have been, but *his* hand, no question. His hand, as on the eve of how many wild skirmishes and desperate assaults?

The brassy taste of fear faded. The room swam back into focus, the demonic piping died away. And the hand was gone.

"Let us see," Lodovico was saying, "what my compatriots in London have taught you, that they deemed worthy of the title of master of fence." He took another quick step forward.

"Most willingly, sir," said Castlemayne.

And if he kills me, he added grimly to himself, why then, it is a soldier's death, dealt by the defter hand and quicker eye. Not by devils. Not by dreams.

He crouched on springy knees, raised his ward a fraction of an inch. And the Picinino blade came flashing in.

ii

The blue-steel blades clashed, slid scraping, parted. Young Castlemayne thrust deftly, driving low, inside his adversary's guard. The Italian eluded it with almost casual ease, and flashed in a quick riposte. Castlemayne parried, feinted, drove in a second thrust. But Marsigliano's cape flicked out, caught his point, entangled it, almost tore the sword from his hand. Only a strong wrist saved the weapon. Only a wild leap to the side eluded the vicious counterthrust.

Both men paused, breathing quickly.

"*Bene,*" whispered the Florentine, "a strong young bull for goring." His flat, dead voice vibrated with the instinctive superiority of the Italians.

"Perhaps," Castlemayne responded crisply, "but the bull has horns!"

Instantly Messer Lodovico closed the distance once again. Thrust high and low, inside and outside the other's guard. Chivvied the younger man back one step, two—till Castlemayne's heel caught on the stool he had himself overturned. He kicked it aside. But the moment's distraction was enough. Marsigliano drove in.

A simple, clean, and beautiful *stoccata,* low and from the

Englishman's left. Castlemayne did the only thing he could. He flung his whole body desperately to the right. But even as he leaped away he felt the steel point rip open the flesh of his left forearm from the wrist to the elbow.

His back slammed against a bedpost with a jolting, dizzying impact. The whole bed shook, the corpses jerked grotesquely. Then he was reeling farther backward, dodging frantically to avoid a second jab of that lethal point already glittering with his blood.

A third and yet a fourth time the Picinino blade lashed out.

The fourth time, Castlemayne caught it on his own blade, deflecting it upward and away. The two swords rasped together as Marsigliano's momentum carried him in against a Castlemayne who no longer backed away. The basket hilts clanged furiously.

For a timeless moment, black eyes glared into blue ones at less than a foot's distance. Both faces were wet already with exertion, both pairs of eyes inflamed with bloodlust.

Then Castlemayne heaved mightily and flung his skeletal opponent away from him, back half the length of the room.

Amazingly in that narrow chamber, the two men had exchanged positions in the scuffle. Castlemayne now stood in the interior of the room, in the open space before the mullioned window. Marsigliano, poised and ready, stood beside the door.

Messer Lodovico saw the blood that soaked Castlemayne's left sleeve. He grinned his death's-head grin.

But Castlemayne had already determined that none of the big veins were cut. Since he held no weapon in that hand, it was no crippling injury. Far more important to his skirmisher's eye was the reversal of the ground. For Marsigliano was now hampered, as Castlemayne had been, by the clutter of furniture that filled the other end of the room. Most crucially, the cupboards and chairs and bedposts would hinder the free manipulation of that flicking cape. And if its folds could be fouled completely on a chair back, or even momentarily caught on the corner of a table—

But for now, hold him there! thought Castlemayne. Keep him there, where fortune, if she's kind, may deal with the cape. That will be work enough, God knows.

They closed the measure almost simultaneously, eager for each other now.

Their two swords closed like scissors, crossing with a clang. They broke apart, flashed and darted, met shatteringly again. They rasped edge to edge across each other, parted, hovered, clashed once more. Their feet moved quickly, almost geometrically about the floor, sliding, leaping, pausing, springy on the instep.

But both chests were laboring now, both men breathing hard.

Lodovico Marsigliano's attacks were theoretically brilliant, conceived and executed with mathematical precision. Castlemayne's defense—for he still fought on the defensive—was by comparison slapdash and improvised. But the younger man was stronger and faster despite his bleeding wound. Half-a-dozen times he saved himself by sheer dazzling speed from the most devious of traps. And still he did not retreat. His flashing rapier proved impenetrable as a wall, penning his enemy into that cluttered corner of the room.

Messer Lodovico's expression was unchanged, but he was cursing inwardly. This business should have been finished long ago. How long could it go on, even at this time of the night, before they were discovered? The walls, the floor, the ceiling were solid and thick enough. But any late reveler passing by the door would surely hear some muffled sound of conflict.

This fool must die quickly. He must die now.

Yet the Florentine went about it calmly, rationally, as he had always done.

With bewildering rapidity he released upon his wounded enemy a lifetime's accumulation of subtle maneuvers, *bottes*, tricks of all the mankilling trades. For he was master of them all. Walter Castlemayne, as both men realized at once, was a rank amateur beside him.

Duelist's tricks, things no fencing master taught.

A feint and a quick recovery. A second feint at once. A third. And then a lightning lunge that drew his opponent into an impatient counter—and turned out to have been only a fourth feint after all. But a deadly counterfeit this time. For the other's premature response exposed his whole left side, and Lodovico's fourth feint developed suddenly into a vicious stab aimed precisely at that opening.

Castlemayne saw his error, but too late to check himself. He ducked wildly, almost fell, and heard the blow thud into the wall on his right.

Soldier's tricks—simple, but highly effective in the fury of a skirmish.

Marsigliano, his rapier poised, suddenly closed the measure. As he did so, he shouted loudly, a sharp, angry noise like a man frightening away a dog. Inevitably Castlemayne blinked. He escaped execution by two inches and a fraction of a second.

And then—hired bravo's tricks.

Castlemayne thrust low over a squat tabletop, alert for the first movement of the velvet cloak. He saw it swing up, almost sure to catch on a high-backed chair. Too late he realized that Marsigliano's guiding hand had released the cape. And then the startling wrench as that bony hand closed suddenly on Walter's own thrusting rapier blade! And from the right, the shimmer of candlelight on steel as the Florentine's own sword came circling in.

Castlemayne had sometimes fought with the thick gauntlet on the left hand in friendly fencing bouts. He knew too that in brawls men had been known to catch an opponent's blade in a bare hand, to snatch away the sword or to hold it till they could get a cut in themselves. But he had never seen a man drop a cloak and use his hand instead.

Taken utterly unawares, Castlemayne could only depend once more on speed and strength. With a savage twist he wrenched his weapon free. Simultaneously he catapulted his whole body sideways to escape the Italian's *mandritta* as it came slashing in upon him.

Castlemayne crashed bruisingly against the wainscoted wall. But Marsigliano's rapier stroke had missed. And as Walter recovered his defensive ward, he saw Lodovico stagger back against the chest beside the door. His left hand was torn open, already bright with blood.

Disabled! Castlemayne saw instantly. He'll not use that cloak again, not with a hand ripped apart like that. And then, more in amazement than in jubilation: By God, I'll beat him yet!

The blood on Castlemayne's own injured arm was congealing, stiffening. His right shoulder throbbed from the brutal crash against the wall. But Lodovico's ravaged hand bled profusely, trembling visibly with pain. The breath wheezed and rattled in his bony chest. His strength was running out more rapidly than Castlemayne's.

Damn this bull-necked Englishman! the Italian cursed under his whistling breath. He'll do for me if I'm not careful!

In his rigidly rational soul, he knew that it was worse than that. Superior skill and vastly greater experience were still his. But these had not brought him victory when all else favored him as well. The odds were tipping in the Englishman's favor now.

But there were still ways to kill him.

And then, between one labored breath and the next, a strange thing happened.

Honor is courage! said a prim, dry voice. *Honor is justice! And the Marsigliani are an honorable race!* The voice of that unbending old aristocrat who had once only deviated from the path of honor—when he had sired the bastard Lodovico, the black sheep of the clan.

There is no question of courage, Lodovico found himself answering sharply. No man living can reproach Lodovico Marsigliano with any want of courage, sir! And as for justice—he glanced expressionlessly at his handiwork on the bed—all men accept the justice of summary execution for a woman taken in adultery.

There was no answer. Instead a picture formed, filling the eye of his imagination. A vivid image, bright with sunshine and color. A rare thing indeed for a man who normally thought only in words and abstract concepts.

Now, for half-a-dozen heartbeats, he thought nothing at all. He simply stared at the familiar scene thus miraculously conjured up before him, exact to the tiniest detail of brickwork, the most delicate streamer of cloud.

The courtyard of the Palazzo Marsigliano, four o'clock of a spring afternoon, rapier play and quarterstaffs just ended. Heat and healthy sweat and the sharp tang of triumph in the air, for he had bested both his half-brothers that day. The two of them, hard-voiced Antonio and grim Sebastiano, both stiff-necked as their father, had just turned away from him to hand their weapons to the hovering servants. Behind them and above, colonnaded porticos ringed the courtyard, with columns and stringcourses on the upper stories, carved capitals and marble facings everywhere. The bright blue sky shimmered overhead. The rose-colored bricks of the courtyard were dusty beneath his feet.

All perfect, just as it had been. The harsh mutter of Antonio's voice, talking to his brother. The clack of the quarterstaffs as a servant took them in his hands. The flash of sun off an upstairs window as Lodovico tilted back his head to look up at the sky.

And then the old gentleman's voice. "Honor is courage. Honor is justice. Remember then the formula, live by it absolutely." The elegant, aging master of the house, lean-jawed and hollow at the temples, white hair lifted by the wind, his tall imperial figure framed by the Corinthian columns of a Roman arch.

Ah, well enough for you, thought Lodovico bitterly, as he had thought it on that long-vanished day. And well enough for your true sons, who will pass your name on to their sons in turn. But how shall I live up to your nobility? How shall Lodovico do it, a bastard born, tainted from my first hour with my mother's primal sin? How shall a bastard then maintain the ancient honor of the gens Marsigliano?

One instant more the old man's face glowed in Lodovico's mind. The tight-lipped mouth, the hawk's beak of a nose, the silky white hair blowing in the breeze. Lodovico looked and knew the answer to his question. It was there, a simple imperative, in the harsh nobility of that deep-lined face.

"You are tainted, you are warped," the old man's eyes mercilessly agreed. "And still I say unto you: Honor is courage. . . ."
A man must obey the Commandments, though they come from an evil God, and reach only a hunchbacked heart.

Lodovico Marsigliano blinked his reptile eyes, and faced his enemy. He was smiling still, but no longer with contempt.

A man must obey the Commandments, though he cannot do so.

For the first time, as it seemed to him, he truly understood how foul this world was. He knew now why every man was for him but a walking corpse, whose death's man he must be, or die in the attempt. And he knew whose death he had really sought down all the twisted years. Whose liberation from the prison house of flesh and bone he had so long labored to effect.

He faced Castlemayne across the Picinino blade and smiled as the young man's point leaped at him.

The swords clanged once again in the dim-lit, cluttered room where two corpses lay already stiffening.

Castlemayne bored in coolly, fiercely now. He watched with cold blue eyes for the opportunity that must open up, if only for an instant, under the unrelenting pressure of his sword.

The moment came quickly.

The slightest of miscalculations. An upward slashing parry, off by no more than a quarter of an inch. But it was enough. Castlemayne slipped his blade free and down for a backward thrust. The Italian started to leap back. Too late.

Messer Lodovico grunted as the point of the heavy rapier drove through his velvet doublet and into his hollow belly. He gave an odd little groan as Castlemayne whipped out his blade and stepped quickly back, alert for any counter. But Marsigliano's swarthy, emaciated features barely managed a cold smile, and his rapier sank slowly to his side.

He sat down heavily on the low carved chest beside the door. Nausea and a queer numbness swept over him. He doubled over, his sword cradled crosswise on his knees. But only for a moment. Then he drew himself up again, fighting down the radiating waves of pain from his punctured stomach. He fixed his cavernous eyes upon Castlemayne.

Breathing already with difficulty, he sought the proper words with which to take leave of the world. Something decorous and elegant, with just a touch of wit, that men might remember. For a gentleman of Florence must die with due dignity, even in this barbarian land.

His lips moved, but he could speak no words. There was only a harsh gurgling sound, ugly to his ears. Then something seemed to break inside him, and the room funneled into darkness.

Walter Castlemayne watched the Italian slump sideways, till he toppled off the chest and sprawled out upon the floor, his rapier clattering down beside him. He lay unmoving, a bag of spindly bones, staring sightlessly up at the sculptured plaster ceiling. Only then did Castlemayne lower his own sword.

The breath of life was strong in his young nostrils. The smells of blood and death and guttering wax candles were sweet as Arabian perfume to him.

He knew that there was much to do. His wound must be bound up. He must arrange this carnage so that his own hand would never show in it. He must get away, separate himself entirely from this bloody stage-play tragedy. All these things must be done, he knew.

But for that moment Walter Castlemayne simply stood there, his rapier in his hand, listening to the beat of his own heart.

∽ *Sixteen* ∾

Point of Decision

i

Slowly and deliberately, the aged porter emerged from his cramped quarters just inside the castle gatehouse. Half-a-dozen plodding steps from the massive walls he stopped and stood, blowing on chapped hands and squinting up at the sky. He was a hale old man, long-headed and bald but for a few wisps of white hair, with a red face and long white moustaches. He squinted up at the sky with the heavy seriousness of one who was well-known as a local weather prophet.

Such unheard-of weather this past week, he ruminated to himself, narrowing his eyes into the creamy whiteness that closed the castle in. The awful snows last weekend, cutting Exmoor off from the outside world. Then these past three days of tremendous threatening clouds and howling winds—but not a snowflake falling. Now this strange day just ending, absolutely still, with the white haze over everything. Ghostly hills and shadowy headlands, silent seagulls floating by. A hush over all the still, white world. And yet an odd sense of expectancy, of impending violence, like the exhausted pause at the height of a storm, before the thunder crashes.

Let these mad folk but begone tomorrow, the old man muttered in his feathery white whiskers, and a blizzard may bury them all betwixt here and Exeter, for all of me. Only let me bar the gates of Exmoor behind their backs, that a man may sleep again o' nights. . .

"Faith," he said aloud, "another day and they'll burn the castle round our ears!"

The porter had seen many holidays come and go, and many a holiday gathering of his betters assemble to partake of Lord Henry Traherne's hospitality. He had seen them ride gaily in through this great, twin-towered gate, laughing and chattering expectantly, the bells jingling on their bridles. And he had seen them leave, sometimes openly irritable, sometimes forcing their frivolity, but always glad to separate and be off for home. But this Christmas feasting had been something beyond all his experience, something almost beyond imagination.

The old man shook his head.

"There do be devils here at Exmoor. I'll swear upon the Book."

Too many unheard-of things had happened for it to be natural. The rumors about young Master Castlemayne and the Lady Arabella, for instance. Incredible even to suggest it. Or the fight in the long gallery between Castlemayne's kinsman and that spindleshanks Italian, blades unbated and both hot for blood. Or the public insults heaped on that famous old soldier Sir Malcolm Devereux by the players. A shocking breach of hospitality, truly.

And then, to cap it all, the terrible bloody business of last night. Of course it was the Italians' doing, no doubt of that. And like them too, scurvy villains all, these foreigners. He had never heard the like. And the gatekeeper knew every scandal in South Devon, back to his great-grandfather's time at least.

The old man turned and stumped back toward his porter's lodge, still shaking his white head and clucking to himself. Just outside the little door, his mind already warming to the acrid-smelling fire on the grate inside, he paused for one last glance about the empty courtyard.

On the south wall, just this side of Saint David's Tower, a tiny figure moved. The gatekeeper shaded his eyes against the opalescent glare of the haze that hung over the sea, wondering who could be so foolish on such a bitter afternoon.

He sighed and clucked and turned back to his narrow door.

Across the court and thirty feet up, Sir Malcolm Devereux watched the molelike figure pop back into his hole. The faithful keeper of the gates, he said acidly to himself. And no shadow of an enemy to close 'em against in his lifetime, I'll warrant.

He stood on the windy rampart scowling down, his broad-brimmed hat low upon his brow, his dark cloak flapping about him. He paced a dozen brooding steps along the wall, then stopped again to lean on the battlements and peer out toward the sea.

Six feet before his wind-battered eyes, a seagull hovered in the air. For a long moment it hung balanced there on broad white wings, the black feathers of the wingtips bristling, its eyes and blunt beak fierce as any hawk's. Then with a mournful cry the big bird tilted, turned, beat its wings twice, and slid away, fast and faster down the wind. Devereux watched it go.

Cold as a witch's shriveled tit up here, he thought. But at least it's open and unpopulated. None of those bleating sheep, with their darting, smirking eyes. Always watching when your back is to them, but never facing you when you turn.

There was little enough to see beyond the parapet. To the south, mist and snow and sea still blurred together in a milky haze. High up, a few black dots skimmed and floated—more sea-birds flying. Westward, to his right, there were glimmerings of color where the lowering sun settled toward the gray outline of distant cliffs. That was all. A vast emptiness, illimitable and utterly lonely. Then the sloping stone, rough beneath his forearms, and the sharp wind on his face.

"God damn them all!" he shouted suddenly into the gale. "Roast their bones in hell! Capons and peacocks all of them!"

But he knew he had not come to this deserted place to curse

his enemies. He had come for a summing-up. And for a decision.

Sum and substance of it all? he thought bitterly. That's easy enough. The popinjays have it. And the old hawk had best begone, before meaner fowl peck his eyes out in the yard.

His people were gone, to the last pawn. Bianca was good riddance. But the two men were vital losses, irreplaceable. Without Messer Lodovico's tactical genius, without Luke Naylor's contacts among the underground army of serving people who ran the castle, Devereux was helpless. And he knew it.

Of course no breath of rumor connected Castlemayne with the triple horror. It was Lodovico's dagger that had stabbed Bianca and slit her stablehand lover's throat. Lodovico himself had been found just inside the door, doubled over, his own court rapier rammed through his belly. But Devereux knew better. Disgrace might drive Messer Lodovico to murder others, but never to disembowel himself like an antique Roman. Someone else had done that for him.

Sir Malcolm staggered in the sudden gusts that shrieked about his ears. The sun had vanished behind the distant cliffs, and the sky grew darker every moment. Through the windows of the great hall below him, he could see the yellow glow of tapers being lighted.

It was done, over with. The game lost. There remained but the gall and wormwood of his future.

They will be most polite at first. Obsequious, even. Especially the serving people, the ale wenches and the tavernkeepers. "May we serve you with another flagon, sir? And is that how you like your haddock?" Point me out to strangers come for an idle jack of wine. "Indeed, sirs, it is the celebrated Captain Devereux. Comes here every afternoon. Often stays for supper." And some young visitors, and old topers too, will even ask respectfully how I view the progress of the war. And then, most deferentially, when I expect to be off myself to the wars once more.

But they would all soon understand that there would be no

more wars, no more commands for him. Then young gallants would no longer ask for his opinions on military matters. Only tosspots, seeking an excuse to sit and doze, would slouch over to his table to ask about some long-forgotten battle. And when his shillings and pence were low, not even these would come.

Just sour wine and a dusty windowpane and strangers jostling by outside, seen through the slight intoxication of early afternoon.

The mist was freezing in his beard as he strode along the parapet. His nose and ears were numb with cold. Ah God, he thought, let there be red wine. Sweet red wine from the south of France. There's life in that.

Life!

The wind screamed. Black clouds scudded overhead, tatters and streamers. The man stopped and stood—cloak, plumed hat, spade beard, and fierce mustachios—rock firm against the gale, solid as the battlement itself.

By Christ, there is life still! There is strength in me still to stand against the natural elements—or any natural man! Strength in these hands to smash the life out of that lace-and-velvet-breeches coxcomb!

He held up one heavy hand, balled it to a fist. Blunt, stubby fingers, broken-nailed. Curling black hairs that ran along the tendons, tufted at the knuckles. No old man's palsy in that hand! He swore. The power of his will flowed outward from the center of his being, calming limbs that trembled in the chill. Neither cold nor weariness could stand against the unbending will that had carried him through a quarter century of war, had made him a commander and a twice-dubbed knight.

He remembered the bloody field at Coutras, the windrows of corpses in the mists of Zutphen.

Captain Devereux laughed aloud, his harsh, barking laugh hard against the wind. He plunged on once again, lurching along the narrow parapet toward the Margaret Tower. Burst

through the empty archway into the dimness of the ancient
fortification. Wiped his face and beard on one damp sleeve, and
grinned like a wolf in the dusky half-light.

"What, turn my king and end the game? Not while I have
a move left in me, by God!"

A dangerous move, certainly, far from the prudence and the
caution that were his hallmark. A wild young man's gamble,
even, sharply against his grain. But the only move left to him
now.

He must kill Master Walter Castlemayne.

He would need men to swear that Castlemayne was the
aggressor. Not easy with his own people gone, destroyed, and
time so short. But there were always men to be had, for money
or for promises. A name or two, an ambitious hungry face
flicked through his mind already.

The killing—that he must do himself.

Then let the Earl decide. With little Cecil clamoring for a
name to take back to his almighty father at the court. With
Castlemayne removed, and no time left to seek out a third choice
for the command. Lord Henry must take Captain Devereux
then. Must take him, or miss the year's great venture against
Spain, with all its hopes of a golden harvest.

A chance. A chance. If the witnesses were well chosen. If
lust for profit overbalanced in the Earl his sense of due decorum.
If—

No time for ifs. He must act now. At once, before the
Twelfth Night festivities began. And the musicians even now
were tuning up their instruments, the servants laying table.

It must be set in train.

One last brief glance out through the arched doorway of the
little tower. He saw a wide band of clearing sky, free of clinging
mist and lowering cloud, above the vanished sun. He saw the
hills, rolling range on range away to the north, white with snow,
then gray, then blue in distance. By nightfall tomorrow, he
realized with sudden savage joy, I'll be riding through those

same far hills. Climbing toward Dartmoor, on to Exeter and
London.

With the *Golden Fortune* or without. In triumph—or in
absolute disgrace, perhaps even in Master Cecil's custody. But
either way, out of Exmoor! Out of this crypt where he had been
entombed alive for surely many times twelve days.

Out of it all! he thought fiercely, groping toward the stairhead. And then dimly, as he descended one more time into the
bowels of the castle: These walls can crush a man's soul.

But his face was hard, his eyes expressionless as he went down
the winding stair. His boot heels hit each stone step with sharp
authority as he descended into darkness.

ii

"It is decided, then!" intoned the Earl of Exmoor. He spoke
firmly, in a voice pitched louder than his usual uncertain snuffle.
"And I thank you, gentlemen, for your attendance and advices
in this most pressing matter."

Down the long table, they inclined their heads with proper
dignity, accepting their dismissal. There was a shuffling of
papers, a rustle of stiff formal clothing, as they rose to depart.
A scraping upon the polished floor, a murmur of ceremonious
leavetakings, as they retreated down the high-paneled room and
bowed themselves out of his lordship's presence. The master
shipwright Hackett and three of the Earl's chief proprietors
first, glad to be away, knowing they had been summoned primarily to swell the formal council. Master Norton and Master
Cecil last, the two who had most often spoken, both glad of the
decision finally arrived at.

Through these concluding ceremonies, Lord Henry sat unmoving, the still center of this bustling world. His face was
impassive, as befitted his rank and dignity. An artist's study in
calm arcs and circles: plump chin and round ginger-colored
beard, downward curving moustache, full flushed cheeks, pug

nose in the center. A face all harmonious benignity, nobly set
off by his large wheel ruff and the black skullcap on his head.

He watched the last of them pass out beneath the orna-
mented lintel—old Humphrey, pausing to bow one final time.
Then the carved oak door closed behind them all, and the Earl
was alone in his dusky library.

Abruptly then, he pushed back his chair, rose, and stood
teetering ecstatically back upon his heels, his plump face radiating
happiness.

Castlemayne.

His lordship turned almost friskily from the long polished
council table and stepped over to the nearest window bay. He
stood there, legs astraddle, hands clasped behind him, gazing
out upon his vast domains.

Castlemayne it shall be, then, he thought, self-satisfaction
mingled with relief tingling through his body. Master Walter
Castlemayne it must be. In fact, it could be no one else.

The warm glow faded somewhat at the latter thought. His
lordship of Exmoor did not like to feel compelled.

Yet surely one should feel nothing but gratitude that Master
Castlemayne's pen had ripped away Sir Malcolm's mask of military heroism. The Earl grimaced. Master Norton said small boys
about the castle were already aping the quondam Great Captain's
stiffly swaggering martial step. The short, sharp stride that seemed
to say to all honest men: One side, fat whey-faced citizen, for the
Queen's only true servant! As though the Earl's own more
mundane labors on the County Commission of the Peace, or his
services as Lord Lieutenant of all Devonshire, were not as worthy
as any soldier's rollicking in Dutch taverns or Paris bawdyhouses!

Lord Henry's lower lip projected irritably as he thought of it.

And then Master Cecil had surely been correct when he
pointed out that *The Soldier's Seven Sins* would make a great
success in the London playhouses, or even at the royal court.
Should Castlemayne decide to have it played—anonymously, of
course—before such discriminating audiences, the famous Cap-

tain Devereux would be the laughingstock of London in a month. And a disgraced commander would make recruiting for the *Golden Fortune* well-nigh impossible.

Worse yet—far worse—would be the dishonor to the Trahernes of Exmoor.

The Earl bit his lip, vexed at the very thought. To have the mere tavernkeepers of Southwark, the boatmen that punted playgoers across the Thames, repeating it with grins and winks. "Yes, sir, an excellent witty farce, as all say that have seen it. About Sir Malcolm Devereux, the Earl of Exmoor's man. You have heard—the swaggering captain that has the command of his lordship's new-built ship? Will Kemp most comically portrays him to the life, they say. As clownish an old Braggart Soldier as ever walked the London stage." Lord Henry shuddered, hearing the gruff guffaws as clearly as if he were there. "The Earl of Exmoor's man . . ."

But far more terrible, and more decisive, was the ghastly business of the Italians.

Captain Devereux's foreigners—and his own chief groom! It was the sort of thing one saw in a play. A newsbook sensation about some shocking murder in Kent, or on the Scottish border. But that it should happen here, in his own tidy, well-run house!

He turned from the window and paced the room, his face beet-red, tugging nervously at his drooping moustache. In his mind he saw again the sight that had seared his eyes that very morning. The two naked corpses tumbled in the canopied bed. The skull-faced Marsigliano curled over his own rapier on the floor.

He thought of the inevitable inquest. No question of the verdict. No coroner's jury in this quarter of the kingdom would dream of challenging the word of the Earl of Exmoor's servants. Murder of the wife and lover, taken *in flagrante*. Suicide of the disgraced husband, no doubt in fear of English justice. That would be the last word officially, duly attested and engrossed, sealed and submitted to the proper clerks on timeless parchment.

But the rumors—the rumors would not stop. Exmoor Castle was stained forever by this bloody deed. And Sir Malcolm Devereux had brought this horror to the house of Traherne.

"Will my lord have the candles lighted now?"

It was almost dark outside the wide mullioned windows. The library was full of shadows. An aged manservant stood in the doorway with a long glowing match, his shoulders hunched obsequiously.

Lord Henry blinked, recollecting himself.

"Light them at once," he said brusquely, stumping back to the head of the table. He sat down again, as though he had more business. He wondered if he had been muttering aloud. He felt foolish and uncertain—his old self again.

He must soon retire to prepare himself for dinner. Twelfth Night, the last night of the holidays. No doubt Master Norton had some fine entertainment for his guests. Old Humphrey always saved his best things for the last—and his dullest, most sententious speech.

While the white-haired servingman went methodically about his task, Lord Henry bent over the plans of the *Golden Fortune* there before him as if he were studying them. Idly he traced the smoothly curving line of the gun deck, running from stem to sternpost. He read the inboard longitudinal dimension, neatly inked in above the drawing. Mildly interested now, he pushed aside the top sheet and fumbled out the plan of the midship section to check that dimension too. The width of the vessel amidships, its broadest point, would be not three times Castlemayne's own height across the open deck.

And all those scores of men would be cooped up together on this floating chicken coop for weeks, perhaps for months. Why in God's name, the Earl wondered, would any man trust his life and fortunes to such a frail contrivance on the sea? A flimsy structure of wood and canvas, at the mercy of winds and waves that made the very cliffs of Devon shake.

The old Earl shook his head, bewildered at the follies of his fellow men.

iii

Castlemayne stood once more at the altar of the little chapel, staring at the loot of Spain—and into his own future. But he was a different Castlemayne than he had been ten days before, and it was a subtly different future that he saw before him now.

He seemed more gaunt than he had been even twenty-four hours before. Paler, too, with fever spots on each pointed cheekbone. His eye sockets were dark and deeply shadowed by half-a-dozen sleepless nights. He held his left arm gingerly to ease the stiffness and the repeated throbs of pain.

His fingers clutched the same massy Indian idol, glowing dully in the candlelight. Once more he gazed into and through that tantalizing lure to the great voyage that waited for him in the spring. The command that must be his now, beyond all peradventure.

Once again he felt the deck of the *Golden Fortune* heave and sway beneath his feet. Heard the sea hawk scream, saw green combers rise beyond the low poop rail. Smelled the tar and the salt wind. And then the sudden reek of powder, the stench of singed wood and blackened flesh.

Once more artillery crashed like the crack of doomsday against his eardrums, and he felt the ship reel to the thunder of her own huge guns. The high-castled galleon filled half the sky, smoke billowing around her, one mast shot away. And then he was on her slippery, tangled decks once more, shouting, thrusting savagely, driving on, with a horde of English freebooters screaming at his back.

Again, as in that earlier vision, he felt the joy of it—the wild joy that had carried him to glory at Doesburg and Rouen, in a dozen bloody skirmishes already in the Low Countries and France. He felt the tingle in the eyes, the power in his arms and wrists, the tumultuous exaltation in the veins. The joy of absolute endeavor, of everything upon a single cast. The mad joy of battle.

But now—he felt the terror too.

The stomach-turning sight of a red wound opening under his own flashing blade. The shock of death on a swarthy stranger's face. The disbelief, perhaps a wrench of pain, and then the blankness as he fell. And the brassy taste of fear in his own mouth as another man's weapon reached out for his own unprotected eye or sinewy hand.

The possibility of death for Walter Castlemayne.

The possibility of death.

Strange that he had never felt so obvious a truth before last night's encounter with Messer Lodovico. Strange how many young cavaliers knew the mad intoxication of battle—and how few its terrors. And a sad thing too—he wondered at his own emotions—how many of them died without ever having known that humanizing taste of fear. The fear of death that gave life acid-sharp new meaning. That gave a man new courage after all. The courage that comes from knowing in your bones the worst thing that can ever happen. Castlemayne looked down at the golden idol in his hand, turned it over slowly.

The remembered taste of fear was strong still in his mouth. Yet in his ears there sounded the roar and wash of the sea on distant shores. And he knew that whether he found those beaches strewn with orient pearl, or left his own white bones to bleach there in the sun—yet he would surely go.

He put the garish heathen figure back on the table and turned away, thin cheeks smiling faintly, eyes burning with a somber fire.

He turned and stopped, one hand upon the altar rail, staring back up the length of the little chapel.

Three men stood in the arched doorway, looking at him.

Three black silhouettes against the gleaming tapers in the lobby just beyond.

Sir Malcolm Devereux closed the doors himself, before the others thought of it. He wanted no witnesses to what was about to happen. None except these two men, of course, handpicked for their malleability, for the moral softness that bent so easily to his will. He let the ancient latch fall and turned to face Master Castlemayne, now sauntering up the aisle toward them.

As Devereux turned, his two companions drew back left and right, leaving him alone to face his foe.

"Master Castlemayne!" said the knight.

Captain Devereux's black beard and sharp moustaches were stiff and neatly combed. Above the hawk's nose and the enigmatic eyes, his bushy brows met in a black bar. His thick, square hand was steady on his sword hilt.

"Captain Devereux," responded Castlemayne.

He bowed very slightly, without speaking, to the lesser fry who flanked his enemy. Robert Naseby, nervous and perspiring, every man's cousin and any master's man. And the plump nonentity who clung to Cousin Robert like a leech—Wilton, was it? John or William Wilton? Surely a decline in quality, Castlemayne thought wryly, from his Florentine professionals to these poor creatures.

"You are pious, Master Castlemayne," said Sir Malcolm, "thus to seek the Lord's House on this last night of the holy festival." His voice reeked of studied sarcasm. "But then," he added slowly, "the greatest knaves wear sometimes the most pious masks."

"I beg your pardon, sir?" Castlemayne spoke crisply, almost pleasantly. His blue eyes were bright and still feverish in the caves beneath his brows.

The situation was clear at once to him. They were performing a ritual act, he knew. He felt that he must be very careful not to fail in his responses.

The code of honor was a stern, exalted mistress.

"Beg my pardon, Master Castlemayne? And well you may, indeed. But this is no papist country, sir. Mere confession will bring no remission of sins here."

"Speak plainly, sir," snapped Castlemayne," and I'll know how to answer you!"

An instant of silence, teetering on the brink of bloodshed.

Cousin Robert darted out a nervous tongue to moisten his dry lips. Wilton breathed in little gulps, watching with all his eyes.

"Why then," said Captain Devereux with deliberation, "I shall speak clear enough for the most spineless slave to understand.

"I say you are a liar and a coward, Master Walter Castlemayne. I say you use a fat actor's voice to speak those slanderous untruths you dare not say to my face.

"I say you are an insolent boy, that deserves rather a birching on the backside than a sword blade through the gut. And you shall have one or the other—by the Christ on yonder cross—if you do not apologize most humbly here and now, before these witnesses."

At last! breathed Castlemayne. At long and bloody last!

He paused one heartbeat only before he took the last, irrevocable step.

"To be brief, sir," he said then, "I say to every several one of your most foul and dishonorable accusations, that you lie in your throat!"

The lie direct and unequivocal.

"And I, sir, in defense of my sorely wounded honor"— Devereux smiled sardonically at the words even as he spoke them—"I must demand that you make good that foul allegation of the lie, with arms and to the utterance." His thick fingers caressed the hilt of his rapier as he spoke.

"Gentlemen!" protested Robert Naseby. He intended an authoritative tone, but the word emerged as a shrill squeak of alarm. "Gentlemen, I beg you! This is not the place, or an appropriate time—"

"Evidently not," said Devereux dryly. "But it must be soon. At once. As the aggrieved party, furthermore, I must insist—"

"It would require the whole College of Heralds to discover which is the aggrieved party here, sir," said Castlemayne tersely. "But let it be as you wish. I shall most willingly consider myself the challenger and you the injured party, with full choice of weapons and all other particulars. If one of you gentlemen will act for me in this—?"

He fixed his eye on the pudgy nonentity that was Cousin Robert's cousin.

"Indeed, sir—willingly—" young Wilton stammered. "I shall be honored . . ."

Robert Naseby smiled, not a pretty smile. For one moment he fixed his beady eyes on Castlemayne's, and the perpetual mask fell away. The vengeful hatred of a man humiliated glared out through the perfect courtier's all-forgiving affability. Of course, thought Castlemayne suddenly. The bout in the great hall that first afternoon. With all his fickle followers looking on.

But the mask was back in place. Naseby turned suavely to his principal for instructions.

Captain Devereux's words were curt and to the point. Time, place, and weapons. Naseby formally relayed the information to his unhappy cousin. Wilton then turned shakily to Castlemayne, but the latter cut him off with a brief assent.

And the thing was done.

"Until the morning, sir," concluded Devereux, his bleak eyes fixed on Castlemayne's, his voice flat and expressionless. Castlemayne looked back at his enemy and bowed without reply. He knew his own eyes were as empty of emotion now as the older man's, impersonal and cool.

Then Devereux was gone, striding out through the gothic portal with his minions in his wake. The doors swung to, the click of boot heels died away.

The vaulted chapel lay dim and empty once again, save for the gaunt young man in black. Young Castlemayne in the shadow of a clustered pillar, listening to the beating of his own heart. Feeling the chill of the unheated chapel penetrate through his clothing and his flesh to the center of his bones.

It was decided. Time and place and weapons, all arranged.

Tomorrow, in the frozen dawn, when the sun rose red, turning the sea to blood. Tomorrow, while the castle slept, exhausted by this last night's revelry.

Outside the castle walls, on the knoll behind this very chapel choir. A safe place, utterly unvisited, nor overlooked by any sleeping chamber or service building.

With rapiers and daggers. His weapons—but was he man enough to wield them now? He looked down somberly at his own ravaged body. How many pounds lighter was he now than the man who had ridden into Exmoor not two weeks ago? He closed his left hand tentatively about the hilt of his poniard and felt the pain shoot up his injured forearm, the feebleness of his grip. He felt from head to heel the deadweight of his exhaustion, of too many haunted nights and frantic days.

A brief tremor ran through his wide shoulders, a spasm quickly gone. He glanced hurriedly at the nearest carven devil, leering downward from a pediment three feet above his head. But the demon made no sound. The half-human face of pitted stone remained unmoving. Castlemayne remembered then, almost with surprise, that there had been no fluting laughter behind Sir Malcolm's hard, phlegmatic challenge.

So I am beating them, he thought. Slowly, but I am beating them. Whether devils from hell or creatures of my own melancholy madness, yet they fade, they fade. . . . He would sleep this night, and there would be no devils tomorrow, no touch of a dead man's hand.

He heard the sound of lutes and viols, hautbois and tambourines. Music drifting through the open doors, summoning him to the feast.

Dim candlelight glimmered on the ghost of his old West Country grin. Before he slept, before he rose to face the dawn, there was still this night to live. Lute music and foolish laughter, tender meats and good red wine. And my Arabella.

His wavering, shifting shadow followed him on up the aisle and out through the ancient doorway, toward the Feast of the Epiphany.

~ *Seventeen* ~

High Festival

i

For Arabella Traherne, that last night of the holidays had about it a dreamlike, mystic quality.

A shimmering veil seemed to hover between her eyes and the brightly lit hall, the laughing, gorging people, the carolers and mummers. A strange veil that made the world, not dimmer and hazier, but preternaturally brighter, clearer, more distinct. The red wine, the steaming meats, the silver and crystal, the soft gowns and particolored doublets down the board all seemed to glow with color, illumined inwardly, like images in a dream.

Above all, it was a night radiant with secret, throbbing meaning. Every gesture, every glance, every turn of a head or negligent position of a hand seemed somehow infused with heart-stopping significance. A casual, meaningless word, caught out of context, made her want to laugh or cry out with joy. It was a Twelfth Night such as she had never known before.

Walter Castlemayne sat beside her at her father's high table.

All about her, they were singing the very old songs, as they always did on the last night of the Christmas holy days at Exmoor. They sang them with verve and vigor, for almost everyone knew them by heart:

> "Adam lay a-bounden,
>   bounden in a bond,
> Four thousand winter
>   thought he not long;

> And all was for an apple,
>   an apple that he took
> As clerks finden written
>   in their book.
>
> Ne had the apple taken been,
>   the apple taken been,
> Ne had never our lady
>   been heaven's queen.
>
> Blessed be the time
>   that apple taken was,
> Therefore may we sing
>   *Deo gracias.*"

Arabella had sung these quaint old tunes since she was a tiny girl, a plump, pettish little bundle of silks and laces sitting proudly at her father's side. As she sang them now, her eyes filled with tears for those lovely times that seemed so far away tonight. But she sang with gaiety nonetheless, with joy for this night, this moment, with Walter by her side. She put her small hand upon his arm and sang, laughing up at his grave face through the foolish moisture in her eyes:

> "The time came that was chosen
>   for Arthur to be born;
> As soon as he came on earth
>   the elves took him.
> They enchanted the child
>   with enchantments strong."

She looked up at him again, to see if he remembered the lines they used to chant together, all those years ago, singing fast and faster, sparkling eyes fixed on each other to see if either faltered:

> "They gave him might
>   to be the best knight,

They gave him a second thing,
  to be a strong king,
They gave him a third thing,
  that he should live long,
They gave to that king's child
  gifts that were good;
These things the elves gave him,
  and the child throve."

Old Humphrey Norton had found that song himself, in an old monk's book in Wales, and had copied it down for them. Arabella had sung it for the first time the Christmas that Walter Castlemayne had first appeared at Exmoor. She had always connected the song with him. Indeed, she had somehow heard "Walter" for "Arthur" that first night. She had sung his name right lustily for years, till someone had caught her up and corrected her with laughter. But in her heart she had continued to identify her Walter with that legendary King of the old Britons.

"There was a blast of horns,
  and men most glad.
There they raised to be king
  Arthur the young."

He did not look young now, she thought. He sat quietly, very straight, eating and drinking little. The light of the waxen tapers threw moving shadows on his corded cheeks, into the hollows about his eyes, the cleft in his long, lean jaw. His stillness and the gauntness of his features made him seem much older than he had looked even the week before. He is a man grown, she thought, vaguely surprised in spite of the obviousness of the fact.

They were singing another old hero song now, but this a sad one. A song from the wild Scottish border far to the north, where the weird skirling pipes could still call the clans to war.

"The king sits in Dumferling town,
  Drinking the blood-red wine:

'O where will I get a good sailor,
    To sail this ship of mine?'

Up and spake an eldern knight
    Sat at the king's right knee:
'Sir Patrick Spens is the best sailor
    That sails upon the sea.'"

Some of the joviality seemed to go out of the cheerful holiday throng as the grim tale of loyalty, shipwreck, and disaster unrolled beneath their mingled voices. When they reached the tragic denouement, Arabella's beautiful eyes were blinded once again with childish tears for the martyred hero:

"O long, long may the ladies stand
    Wi' their fans into their hand,
Or e'er they see Sir Patrick Spens
    Come sailing to the land.

O long, long may the ladies stand
    Wi' their golden combs in their hair,
Waiting for their own dear lords,
    For they'll see them no more.

Half over, half over to Aberdower,
    'Tis fifty fathom deep:
And there lies good Sir Patrick Spens
    With the Scots lords at his feet."

Even as a girl she had always cried at that part. The image of the faithful Scottish knights dying each at his post, grouped about their liege lord, seemed to her the quintessence of chivalry. And Arabella, like Castlemayne, immensely admired chivalry, that unique mingling of courage and grace which the greatest of the old heroes had achieved. She liked to imagine Sir Patrick Spens seated stern and upright in his great oak chair of state, there below the waves, with his vassals grouped symmetrically about his feet.

"Fifty fathom deep," sang the intertwined voices, dark and

light, booming bass and childish treble, and young girl's soprano like her own. "And there lies good Sir Patrick Spens . . ." Hearing the words she sang so sweetly, she gasped in sudden horror, one small hand leaping up to cover her mouth. She darted a quick glance at Walter, to see if he had taken this ballad of lost ships and heroes dead as an evil omen. But he sang steadily on, with only slightly sharpened shadows at the corners of his mouth to indicate that he had caught the alarming parallels between Sir Patrick's case and his own.

"With the Scots lords at his feet." Foolishly, unreasoningly, she felt a quick urge to cross herself, as a chambermaid had taught her once, to ward off evil. But old Agnes Mayhew had said that was papistry, and had so punished her little hands that they were red and swollen for a week. So now she rather bit her lip and pressed her knuckles hard against her mouth, as though she could force the offending words back into her throat again.

Dear God, she prayed hurriedly to herself, I did not mean it, nor wish any such fate—to any man that sails upon the sea.

Or will sail. Or will sail in the spring.

Then she saw Walter gazing down at her, and smiling. And could that be amusement she detected in the laugh-wrinkles about his shadowed blue eyes?

"No fear, sweet minion," he whispered quietly. "Unlucky words can have no power to hurt on such a holy night."

It is true, she thought gratefully. On this night our Lord the Holy Child was first shown to the Three Kings. Surely on this night no evil thing will be shown to any man, in prophecy or omen.

But it was Castlemayne's easy smile and the gentle pressure of his hand that dashed her fears like bubbles into nothing. She smiled trustingly up at him, and proudly too. He squeezed her hand once more and turned his thoughtful face away, his mind apparently full of some great matters.

She let her little hand lie under his big one, there upon the table between the greasy silver plates and stripped chicken bones, as long as she dared to. It was warm and dark and secret, to have her small curving fingers thus completely covered by his strong, hard palm. It made her feel again that strange stirring of excitement deep inside her. She flushed and slipped her hand quickly out from under his, lightly caressing his bony fingers as she fled away.

Inside all the layers of stiff clothing, she stretched her tight girl's body, voluptuous as a cat before the fire. Surely no woman had ever had such a perfect cavalier, or known such inexpressible happiness before, outside of tales and poetry!

She loved him, she loved herself, she loved all the world. She trilled the last carol before dessert with the natural, full-throated joy of a lark in springtime:

> "Make me merry both more or less,
>   For now is the time of Christymas.
> Let no man come into this hall,
>   Groom, page, nor yet marshal,
> But that some sport he bring withal.
>   For now is the time of Christymas."

ii

The singing ended in a burst of applause, laughter, cheerful talk up and down the tables. Servants passed among the guests, carrying fragrant sweetmeats, fruity pasties, tarts, puddings, and sugared marzipan. Brown ale and red wine and good English beer flowed freely.

The gossiping was more intense, the wit was brighter, the boasting and the laughter louder this last night. Country youths and soberly clad students sought more hungrily for the glances and the soft responses of the shy, uncertain girls about whom their ardent universes turned. Flamboyant courtiers groped more eagerly for the flesh of moist-eyed matrons, hoping they might yet enjoy the favors so often promised and so seldom granted.

Tomorrow they must go. Tomorrow they must all go, back to the real world outside the castle, beyond the tinsel holidays. To the hard, dull winter months ahead in lonely hall or grange. Or back to London, with its intrigues, feuds, backbiting, and too-often futile aspirations.

For now, it was Christmas still. High festival, and the more exciting because the dissolution of their fairyland lay so close ahead.

Each was consumed with his own holiday affairs, with love or lust or merely chatter. Yet almost everyone found a moment to turn speculative eyes to the head table, to the lean young man who sat beside the Earl's daughter—where Sir Malcolm Devereux had sat before. Some envied, some adored, but no one could ignore him. The affairs of Castlemayne seemed somehow everyone's concern.

In Castlemayne's large-featured, handsome face, in his wit and strength and skill, these people saw what they could not live without. They saw the man that they would never be. The man their lovers were not. The son they had not raised. They saw the eternal hero, young Achilles, the boy David, and exulted at the sight.

Only here and there did some somber soul turn away with a sigh, remembering that Lord Achilles died in the pride of his youth. Or that, more lamentable still, King David did grow old.

Walter Castlemayne at the high table saw neither his enviers nor his worshippers. Their voices reached him as distorted sounds from under sea. Their faces were uncertain blurs in the far background of his world.

Even those who sat beside him on the dais were strangely unreal to him. He answered the Earl of Exmoor's occasional remarks respectfully enough, and Master Cecil's, and even old Master Norton's witticisms. Yet he scarcely saw or heard them.

Castlemayne knew that in the morning he must draw his sword in a fight that was at once utter folly and the sternest

duty. For who but a fool would risk all he had won on the slip
or thrust of a rapier blade? And yet—how could any but the
most arrant coward retreat from a fight with the enemy whose
scheming had destroyed his dearest friend?

He did not fear the outcome, though he had no idea what it
would be. That morning sun also seemed oddly detached from
his real self. As impersonal to him as the sea wash of murmurous
voices, the shifting faces of the crowd in his lordship's hall.

That night once again his whole being was absorbed in Arabella.

She was no longer perfection itself to him, no longer his fair
Aphrodite, the creation of his passionate imagination—though
she still seemed very fair. Nor was she the little girl he had
known in his vanished childhood, the Maid Marian of his
forest games—though she was still very young, God knew. She
was his Arabella, and his longing for her was a sword's longing
for its sheath.

When he turned to soothe her fears about the silly song, to
touch her hand and smile, he saw Arabella Traherne more
clearly, it seemed, than he ever had before.

The carefully coiffed hair looped high upon her head, glinting
with pearls, still mesmerized him like alchemical gold. The
wide mouth, full and softly sensitive, and the long-lashed pale-
blue eyes still seemed to him the most beautiful he had ever
seen.

But he saw other things now too, things to which he had
been blind ten days ago, when she had been his half-imaginary
Queen of Love and Beauty. He saw the thinness of her throat
—no tower of ivory, alas—and the bony sharpness of her shoulders. He thought how slight must be the body beneath the richly
brocaded stomacher. He noticed with his new clarity of vision
the nervousness of her long pale hands, the tiny line of imperious
vexation that once or twice appeared between her brows. He
wondered what conflicting surges of uncertainty and arrogance
trembled within this charming girl.

And yet he loved her more, and in a surer way, because of her very human meagerness and fallibility. To smooth away those childish fears and furies, to open that fresh heart to the profusion of real life—what happiness that might be. What joy, what frustration, what incalculable rewards.

The bearded face of Malcolm Devereux blazed up for an instant on his retina, the heavy brows and the pale eyes waiting. Then the white flash of the seagull's wing against blue skies, and the crash and slip of the sea beneath the bows.

But Arabella was here beside him now, no vision, no fantasy, but real, all warmth and breathing happiness. Let what might happen tomorrow or thereafter come. He was ready. For now, there was only Arabella, filling all his universe.

Lord Henry smiled down upon his guests, flushed with wine, happy in his temporary freedom from the awful burden of decision. Twisted little Cecil nodded and smiled at a bawdy jest, contriving at the same time to answer with due gravity a garbled inquiry from a tipsy magistrate at the second table. Aged Master Norton brushed the crumbs of meat and pasty off his belly with a faintly trembling hand, pale and delicate as tortoiseshell. He cleared his throat with a scraping sound, preparing his peroration.

Castlemayne saw them all, and did not see; heard, and did not hear. His senses and his soul were full to overflowing with the girl beside him. Her slight, graceful body and bright hair. Her laughing voice, the quickness of her half-awakened spirit. The love shining in her eyes when she looked up into his face.

Old Humphrey rose creakily to his feet. The steward called for silence, that the worthy Master Norton might be heard. Amid the muttering and laughter of ending conversations, Arabella touched Walter Castlemayne's hand a second time, and whispered up to him, quick and shy:

"Walter, I am so happy!"

The face of Devereux rose briefly, and Harry's empty eyes. The seagull called, the sea crashed and swept by.

Her eyes, her mouth, her uncertain hand on his. The knotted fist in his belly, the heat rising in his loins. The tiny hollow at the base of her throat, where a secret pulse throbbed.

O Christ I love this girl.

~ Eighteen ~

O Western Wind,
When Wilt Thou Blow?

i

Old Agnes Mayhew felt a strangeness in her young mistress that last night.

The aging nurse's arthritic fingers moved with their accustomed deliberation, unlacing, unhooking, slipping the heavy velvet and satin and starched lace off the young girl's body. It was traditionally their quiet time together. Agnes permitted herself a softness at the child's bedtime that she otherwise strictly eschewed. "Softness and discipline are no good yokemates," she would say, puckering her withered lips. And again, "Without discipline, no virtue. Without virtue, no salvation." But in this last quarter hour of the day, she allowed herself to be gentle. To use the childish pet names that Arabella had fixed upon herself. Even to croon a barbaric Scottish lullaby to the sleepy girl.

"There now, Bella, we'll have that sleeve if your ladyship has no objections."

And the Lady Arabella would extend a languid arm, limp-wristed, to be divested of its finery.

"Here, Aggie. You may burn the old thing for all of me. Truly these sleeves are stiff as leather. They have chafed my poor arms terribly all evening. Let some accident come to them,

dear Aggie, do! Father has promised me three new gowns for the
holidays, and he may as easily buy me a new pair of sleeves as
well. Violet is so ugly with my eyes."

"Ah now, my young mistress, you wouldn't be leading an
old woman into trouble with his lordship, then?"

Arabella's face would light up wickedly. She would purse
her lips and speak with mock severity, parodying Agnes herself.
"Yes, Aggie, do remember your place and mind your manners.
Or I shall have you whipped through the village at the cart's
tail, see if I don't!"

They would laugh together, away there in the night, teasing
and affectionate at once. Then the dry unmusical voice would
sing some incomprehensible northern song of her forgotten
childhood. Arabella would smile sleepily and stretch her healthy
young body. She would gape and yawn, and the lids would
droop over her lovely eyes as the last comb was deftly removed
and the glowing weight of hair came tumbling down around her
shoulders. Perhaps the old woman would allow herself a single
quick squeeze of her mistress's shoulder, or an awkward caress
of the drooping blond head. Then she would withdraw, leaving
her ladyship to prayers and candle snuffing and the big four-
poster bed.

But tonight there was a strangeness.

Nothing obvious. No bad temper or petulance. No nervously
concealed misdemeanor awaiting discovery and penance. None
of the things that did occasionally divide them at this hour.
And yet there was a distance, a cool obliviousness about her
charge that baffled and disturbed old Agnes Mayhew.

She had risen from her sickbed to do for Arabella this last
night of the holidays. The girl had been glad and grateful—for
perhaps ten minutes. After that, she seemed to have forgotten
that Agnes was ill. Almost, that she was there at all.

Lady Arabella spoke but little now. Her pale-blue eyes were
vague and dreamy. She answered her nurse's questions and dry
essays at humor absently or not at all. She seemed to want no

more than to be left alone as quickly as might be. Alone with her dreams in the great canopied bed.

"And did you enjoy Master Norton's device of the *Three Kings?* Most apt for the season, or so I thought it."

"Yes," said Arabella, vaguely nodding. "Yes, it was excellently well done."

"I do not believe Master Norton's health is what it was," Agnes went on in her precise, gossipy, old woman's way. She paused momentarily to cough, almost apologetically, under her breath. "His liver is very bad, I understand." She shook her head, looking rather disapproving than disturbed. "It's the black bile, they say. Not enough of it." She coughed again.

"Indeed," said Arabella slowly, "I'm sorry for that."

The old Scotswoman wondered if the girl had even heard.

Agnes Mayhew thanked her stiff-necked Calvinist Divinity that the holidays were ended. For many weeks there would be no more excuse for sinful finery and wordly entertainment. No temptation to unchaste thoughts and immodest deeds.

Above all, the evil influence of Castlemayne would be removed upon the morrow—God grant forever. Surely the man had bewitched the girl. Beglamoured her heart with some witchcraft brought home from foreign lands. The way she had behaved this night, there at the high table, for all to see. Making sheep's eyes at him, paddling with his hand . . .

Then Goody Mayhew looked more closely at her mistress, and her wrinkled hands twisted tightly together at what she saw. She was not so unworldly that she could fail to see the meaning of that slow burning flush, of that languorous abstraction. Dear Lord, she said in her heart, it is truly time the child was married.

But my lamb, my little lamb, another voice cried loudly in her soul, so young, still my wee one yet—

"It is enough, dear Agnes," Arabella was saying quietly. "You must retire and . . . conserve your strength till you are full recovered. I shall have Nance to do for me till then. . . ."

She did not even raise her eyes to her old nurse as she dis-

missed her. She simply sat there in her smock, dreamily con-
templating her own face in the Venetian hand mirror. The old
servant, with a pang of fear, could only curtsey stiffly and pass
slowly from the chamber.

May Jesus Christ protect her, she whispered as she went.

Arabella laid aside the glass and sat quietly for a time, hands
folded in her lap, alone in the candlelit room. At first her mind
remained almost totally blank, empty of all memory, all thought.
She was conscious only of the slow, radiant happiness that filled
her whole being.

She had hardly dared look at her father, or even at Walter,
when she left the hall, for fear that her joy might blaze up in
her eyes and reveal her hapless, hopeless state. She did not dare
let even Walter know how utterly she was his.

Slowly, as she sat there, the use of her senses began to return.

There was the odor of a guttering wax candle in her nostrils
and the sizzling sound the shrunken taper made as it expired.
There was the darkness that abruptly filled the far end of the
room, where the ornately carved old four-poster stood, the curtains drawn aside, the coverlet turned down. She saw that the
fire was dead on the hearth and felt the touch of the chill night
air on her bare arms and face. She felt the chilliness penetrate
her thin silk smock, felt its icy fingers on her body, sensed goose
bumps forming and her nipples hardening at its touch.

She shuddered with a vague voluptuousness and experienced
her first conscious thought of the past hour. I must get into bed,
or I shall come down with a cold myself, and probably sniffles
tomorrow. Then, passionately, Oh no—I mustn't sniffle when I
say good-bye to him! When I press his hand in secret, and tell
him low that I shall wait! She had been through that final
scene so many times that it was almost history to her. Oh please,
God—she recalled her prayers now too—don't let that happen!
Please, please, dear God—

Arabella fairly flew across the room, her hair floating out

behind her, the loose-hanging shift billowing like a sail, to kneel beside her bed.

Dear God, she coaxed, dear Jesus, please not that. I shall see him only this one more time perhaps before he sails away. I have no miniature of myself to give him. He will have only a memory to carry in his heart. O Lord, don't let him carry away the image of a red-nosed little girl with a runny nose!

But that picture touched her mischievous imagination, and her mood exploded into a sudden smothered laugh. Mildly shocked at her own desecration of the sacred moment, she stiffled her giggles against the heavy hangings of the bed—and found that she was crying.

For a time she laughed and cried quietly together, kneeling there in the obscurity beside the tall four-poster. When it was over and her spasmodic breathing calmed, her cheek dried on a cool lavendered corner of a sheet, she felt much better.

But I must get into bed, she thought, feeling the cold rising through the small carpet on which she knelt. Truly now, I must get into bed at once, this instant!

As if in answer to her unspoken words, she felt strong hands touching her shoulders, lifting her up.

"Oh!" she said, in the strangest voice.

She twisted about, melting into the circle of his arms, pressing herself tight and tighter still against him.

"Arabella," he whispered very low.

"Oh, my Walter," she said, suddenly a girl no longer. "Oh, my darling Walter."

There was no need for words between them. For long minutes he simply held her, pressed close against his chest, while she warmed herself against him, joying in his bigness and his strength. He held her, caressed her, breathed in the fragrance of her hair. His palm and fingers tingled to the smoothness of her body beneath the thin silk.

Then, still without speaking, he lifted her in his arms—a

flash of pain passed unheeded up his injured wrist—and laid her in the dark recesses of the bed.

She slid quickly between the icy sheets, beneath the heavy quilts and blankets, and lay still, shivering slightly, her eyes tightly closed. She heard the wind softly sighing, gusting suddenly, sighing and whispering again. She heard boards creak: frozen beams in the ceiling, polished floorboards depressed by his foot. She heard the soft rustle of his doublet as he dropped it on the dark oak chest at the foot of the bed.

Within her the blood began to rise in slow, heavy waves, throbbing in her temples, heating her body. Old Agnes's voice —exhorting, warning, moralizing—was blotted from her mind. There was no fear in her now, or any sense of shame. Only a rising, quickening excitement. Like galloping along the river, following a soaring hawk high in the summer air.

When the mattress gave suddenly under his heavy frame, she turned to him at once, welcoming him joyfully.

He gathered her small body against him, feeling her heart beating against his chest. His caressing fingers traced her spine, a row of pebbles down her back. He felt the sharpness of her shoulder blades, even through her shift. She slipped her arms about his neck and put her face close to his on the long, cool bolster. They kissed then, slow and searchingly, sighing into each other's mouth.

And there came stealing over them both a slow, glorious, tingling relaxation. There was relief at last from the endless round of artificialities, a closeness beyond all words.

Then, as her fingers followed wonderingly the hard muscles of his naked chest and shoulders, as his hand slid underneath her shift, brushed her hip, touched her tight little breasts— there came for both of them a magical release into joy.

"Oh, my Walter," she whispered close to his ear, "this is love. This is really love."

"This is love, sweet Arabella," he answered quietly, smiling

invisibly in the darkness. "This is the ascent the poets write of.
Up the slanting world together, bodies twined like fingers of
two hands. Up and upward, if not to the seventh heaven of the
philosophers, then to each other. To the discovery of ourselves."

She laughed low, delightedly, and kissed his nose.

"You talk such silly lovely nonsense!" she whispered back.
"I always loved your talk, your lovely words. But"—she sighed at
his wandering fingers—"don't talk now, Walter. Only touch
me."

He pressed himself more eagerly upon her then. He was
amazed to find such ardor in her.

For she offered her body to him, pressed it passionately upon
him, with the pride of some dark innocent savage girl from the
jungles of America. She thrust her pointed breasts up for his
kisses and laughed aloud with pleasure at his eagerness. She
cried out, a plaintive, amazed little cry from the depths of her
throat, when his hand passed gently between her thighs to touch
her trembling loins.

Her heart beat faster, faster. Her body moved of its own
accord, responding recklessly, all unbidden, to his most passionate caresses. A dam had broken somewhere deep within her,
and she raced tumbling onward like a river at the flood, bound
she knew not whither.

His own heart thudded like a rattling drum as her soft mouth
opened under his. His hands felt her kitten softness, moist and
warm beneath his fingers. Felt her long limbs loosening, loosening to admit her lover.

O my darling O my love

He never after knew which of them said the words. Both
bodies trembled with the one desire. Either might have voiced
it. It seemed almost, not that he took her, but that they took
each other, so naturally and completely did they cleave together.

Castlemayne groaned joyfully as his blunt shaft broke into
her. Groaned aloud, with an aching cool shudder of fulfillment.

Arabella cried out at the pain, at the bruising bigness of the thing that forced itself inside her. She clenched her fists and moaned. The old Scotswoman's voice shrieked once: *Beware his reechy kisses—the blood, the mutilation—* But then came pleasure back again, pleasure growing, rising, surging high within her.

Awkwardness still and broken rhythms, perspiration, hotly clinging bodies, limbs entwined. Choked sobs of effort, gasps and little helpless cries of gladness. Yet high and higher, the world crumbling, breaking apart, vanishing behind them, leaving only the two together, mounting on trembling chords of sensuality.

O my love

And then at the last, two unwinding endless moments of self-transcending joy. Two moments merging into one. The two of them united at the zenith, bodies locked and fused in love, souls melting one into the other.

Then plunging down together still through endless depths of space. Down through translucent spheres of fire and air and water toward the earth. Down into the darkness where they lay, naked together in the big four-poster bed.

For a time they were conscious only of their own individual bodies, of their breathing, of the beating of their own two hearts. They saw that the last candles had gone out, leaving them in almost total darkness.

Walter sat up then, letting a gout of cold air in beneath the heaped-up quilts and woolen blankets. At the touch of the winter night, Arabella came out of her lovely revery with a startled gasp. He chuckled and drew the heavy hangings closed about the bed, shutting out the cold night, leaving them alone in their own warm nest of darkness.

Arabella giggled and turned to him again.

"My lord, what would you do?"

She wondered at the cheerful coquetry in her own voice. I really should be weeping, she thought. Or crying rape and violation. Or pleading to be made an honest matron of. But old Agnes's warnings were all forgotten now, reduced to arrant foolishness by the joy that had been theirs.

"What can be in your mind, my lord?"

He would have wagered a thousand pounds that her eyebrow was cocked at him in the blackness.

"My lady, I propose—to kiss you once again! This time in perfect privacy, and more properly, as you deserve." His fingers touched her face, caressed her throat.

But she laughed softly and rolled away. He caught her shoulders, found that she was trying to smooth her shift back down, and promptly pulled it off over her head.

"My lord, I do protest—" she spluttered, laughing. "Truly, sir—"

"My lady, I do insist!" he answered. "Absolutely, madam!"

He bore her down into the bed once again, smothering her laughing expostulations with quick, light kisses. He kissed her lips and eyes and cheeks, the tip of her nose, her fragrant hair. When his lips sank to the base of her throat, she sighed with happy anticipation. He kissed her bare shoulders, and they moved voluptuously beneath his roving mouth.

"And how if Agnes should come?" she murmured, her thighs shifting softly to admit his ardent hand. "My old nurse that raised me and believes most rigidly in the moral law of Moses—and John Calvin of Geneva?"

"Alas, my lady, I fear she must draw what comfort she can from whichever of those two learned gentlemen pleases her. For I am well enough suited here this night, and have nothing over to spare the poor lady."

They laughed together, and kissed each other again. Their bodies moved together once more beneath the sheets in the warm enveloping darkness.

Afterward he slept, as he had not slept in many days. A strengthening, healing sleep, no longer nightmare-haunted. She lay awake beside him for a time, unthinking, only feeling his closeness, listening to his steady breathing. Then she slept too, more soundly than she had since he had come to Exmoor. The long winter night rolled over them.

ii

" 'Tis a beautiful ship, Arabella. I saw her in the Deptford Yards, the day before I left London. A month ago today."

Castlemayne smiled, remembering.

"Sweet curving waist amidships, with gently rising fore and after castles. Three tall masts, do you see—" He drew diagrams in the dimness. Square sails on the main- and foremasts, a spanking lateen aft . . .

"Oh, but she will be beautiful at sea! Like a great white bird upon the Bay of Biscay. Hovering about the Azores, gliding majestic as a gull over the Atlantic. Swooping like a sea hawk upon the coasts of Mexico and Panama and the islands of the Spanish Main."

He laughed at his own enthusiasm. Laughed, but more in exultation than derision. For he knew now, as that morning came upon him, that it was really going to happen. Dreams of love, dreams of glory—they were dreams no longer to him, but hard realities, with odor and sound and touch, trembling within his grasp.

He stretched his sinewy arms up into the gray pre-dawn, stretched his muscles till they cracked, and yawned mightily. He turned then with a chuckle to the drowsy girl beside him and swept her, sleepily protesting, up against his chest. He kissed her tenderly on both closed eyes.

"My love," she murmured contentedly, curling up against him.

"Like a great gull, I say!" he hissed into her ear. "Have you no soul, mistress? No sense of glory?" he nibbled gently at her ear.

"Indeed, indeed, my Lancelot," she mumbled, snuggling sleepily closer. "My Roland and my Oliver in one. My Palmerin of England. But it is so chilly, and you are so rough. . . ."

A long looping tress of her hair fell across his face as she settled herself against him. He gave it a gentle yank, and she yelped like a tiny puppy when its tail is pulled.

"Villain!" she grumbled. "Have you no respect for your betters?"

He slapped her small buttocks, a slap that ended as a caress. She scratched feebly at his shoulder, weak as a kitten still with sleep. They laughed together and murmured each other's names. They warmed each other with their bodies. About them the icy gray light spread slowly—he had opened the bed-curtains once again—gradually driving the blackness from every corner of the room.

Walter spoke on, slow and harder now, gazing up at the canopy above, stroking her hair while he talked. She lay half over him, her breasts flattening against the hardness of his chest, floating deliciously between sleep and waking.

"These Spaniards are a fearsome race, dear heart, make no mistake. These are not pasteboard Saracens I go to fight. Not some poet's mustachioed villains, with paper scimitars and picturesque speeches ever ready on their tongues. Nor yet the stable boys, with wooden swords I routed so heroically those other Christmases at Exmoor.

"Men like myself. Shorter, many of them, than we Englishmen. But tough as leather and hard as flint. They stand together in their squares of pikes and arquebuses better than any soldiers in Europe. They kill efficiently, and they die very hard. Aye, and kill you while they die, if they can manage it."

He was silent for a moment then, remembering an incident in Normandy a year ago. A thing he had managed to forget from that day to this, now clear and vivid in his mind's eye.

A fierce-eyed, stocky man with a stubbly black beard and a white scar zigzag across his forehead. Sprawling on his back in the lee of a great yellow boulder, a casualty of that day's fighting. His liver had been hacked open and he was bleeding in great gouts—dead where he lay, no question. Yet as Castle-mayne passed by, the dead man heaved up on one elbow and slashed viciously at the moving legs. Trying to hamstring him and bring him down. Trying to cut the big tendons at the back of the knee joint, to bring the Englishman's throat down within reach of his dagger as he lay there in the blood-spattered grass.

And Christ, he thought, how near it came to happening! The tug and rip as the blade tore through his woolen hose were palpable still in his memory. The scratch across his flesh, the finest fraction of an inch beyond the Spaniard's reach.

Castlemayne had turned and seen and leaped back beyond a second stroke. In a fury then, he had kicked the knife spinning from the fallen soldier's hand. The fellow had shrieked like a woman when the booted toe smacked into his knuckles. But it was no womanish heart that fought like that, to the last drop of his ebbing blood. No man could call the Don Diegos cowards.

"And they will be waiting for us, Arabella," he went on, almost meditatively, to his beloved's sleepy ear. "Wherever we go, they will be waiting. Since Drake has shown them they are nowhere safe, from Cadiz to the coasts of California, they are everywhere prepared and ready. Waiting for the Englishmen to come. For of all their enemies, they say, it is the English they most especially desire to kill.

"Harbors are fortified, bays and even creeks patrolled. New galleons are built to guard the great plate fleet. It will be much harder now, my lady, to get you pretty baubles from the mines of America to deck your ears and fingers."

He paused in his meandering discourse to tickle Arabella's ear until, incongruously, she sneezed. She muttered against his chest, something incomprehensible, but she was more awake than before. He grinned and kissed the top of her head, drawing the sheets and quilts and coverlet more closely about them both.

"And yet, by God," he concluded then, "we'll have our way in spite of all! The strutting dons will learn that Drake is not the only Englishman can singe King Philip's beard!"

"And you'll come back a hero!" the girl's muffled voice agreed enthusiastically. "The Queen will knight you, as she did Sir Francis Drake—on the deck of his own ship!"

"Not likely, alas," he replied with too quick realism. "That ship was the *Golden Hind,* that he had sailed the whole world round. What can the *Golden Fortune* perform in a single cruise to merit such reward?" Yet his eyes sparkled as they had the night before, when he had held the Aztec idol in his hand.

"The crowds will cheer you through the streets," she went on blithely, "and fling their hats into the air for joy. The Queen will grant you private audience to solicit your advices on how the war proceeds. And in public she will call you her well-beloved faithful servant." She raised her head from his chest, thoroughly awake now, and entranced with her own word picture.

But Castlemayne shook his head.

"Not for a long time, my sweet. Her Majesty dispenses trust and honor with a miser's hand, and then only after years of signal services." He sighed almost inaudibly, reining in his imagination with a stern hand.

"And yet—a knighthood, even now? That's not beyond the range of possibility, perhaps. Her Majesty sometimes grants her supreme commanders authority to dub a man knight banneret on the field. My lord of Essex has more than once rewarded some heroic exploit thus. And he will most probably be Captain General of the troops this spring.

"Would you like that, lady? To have me visit Exmoor next as Sir Walter Castlemayne? Come, sweet lady"—he rolled her over and kissed her—"would that not please you?"

"Oh, Walter, you know it would!" Her face was radiant at the prospect. He shook his head at both their folly. But he kissed her on the cheek and tousled her hair. Nor could he cast the thought, the wild hope, entirely out of his mind.

"The Earl my father," she said, slowly and more seriously now, "would like that too. A knighthood from the Queen would please him mightily." A pause. "You know he values rank and high position above all earthly things."

"Indeed I do, my lady. And to please your noble father, what prodigies would I not perform? For should his lordship not approve my conduct as commander of his ship—why, I might not see Exmoor soon again, or the treasures that my lord keeps here." He tweaked her nose and gave her hair another grinning swipe.

She lay quietly after that for a while, nestled in the crook of his arm, listening to him while he talked.

He spoke of strategy and tactics now, ways to beat the Spaniard on the sea. He was more serious and thoughtful than she had ever seen him. And she found herself listening carefully, though two weeks ago she would have been bored to tears by such dull, unglamorous details of his craft.

As the light grew about them, she drank in the outlines of his face. The strong line of nose and chin, the firm, wide mouth. The forehead faintly lined, his pale hair falling over it. She could see the shadowed caves beneath his cheekbones, the hollows of his eyes. He has had a hard time of it these holidays, she thought.

Her fingers traced the sloping muscles down his left arm to where the bandages began, running from the elbow to the wrist. He said that he had injured it at wrestling. But she had never seen a muscle strain like that before.

I do not understand it all, she thought, as she had thought before. And I know that I have brought him suffering too, with my temper and my follies. But I at least shall be no further trial to him! Not now, when he has need of all his strength and wit for this great adventure. Now I must make it easier for him, as easy as I can. Afterward when everything is better for us both, he will love me the more for not . . . hampering him now.

She realized that Castlemayne would be gone for months.

Until the spring at least, she told herself. Perhaps he will be back by then, at any rate. But she knew in her heart that he would not be back so soon. He would be rushing about London until the very moment of departure, pouring his very soul into every detail of the venture. How could he hope to find time for a trip to Devonshire, ten days on the road each way?

Then he would be gone from England.

How long? Weeks—months—all the summer surely. And I must sit and wait and not know how it fares with him. There will be word, of course. The fleet will send back word to London, and father will know because he has a ship and an interest in the expedition. But all that time he will be gone away from me. I will not see his face or hear his voice or feel his hand upon me.

She felt the agony of her loss already grip her throat. Two drops of moisture welled out upon her cheek. But she made no sound. A soldier's lady must not show such weakness.

But bleak and hard within her, she knew and feared—her heart stopped at it—the farther thing, unthinkable. Even as she pressed herself against him there, felt his warm hand upon her hip; even as she wept quick tears because he might not come till distant fall; beneath it all lay the bright hard knowledge that he might not come at all.

Might never come again.

Not that he might perish in the wars, as so many had. She believed utterly in him and in his destiny.

Nor that he might prove unfaithful to a poor deflowered maiden. That was not possible between them.

But: O God, I must be married to an Earl's son at the least— to someone called a lord, with half a country's worth of lands. Father will never have it otherwise!

No one too ill-favored, probably, nor an aging lecher for a young girl's bed—nothing so obviously unjust. But some pleasant, plumpish youth—she writhed inwardly at the image of her future lord—that led a steady life. That promised to become a solid man of business and affairs, to become a magistrate, and serve on royal commissions. And was a peer's son at the least.

So ran the class-conscious code of her age—the code that had been part of the catechism for the Earl of Exmoor's daughter all her life. The code that had become as solid a reality to her as the ancient stone of Exmoor Castle itself.

Arabella gazed up stricken at her lover. Her fingers dug involuntarily into his shoulder. He took it for play, and responded with a playful caress. She gave a tiny choked cry and jammed her knuckles into her mouth, to keep from weeping.

Master Walter Castlemayne would do to sail her father's ships. To advance her father's honor in the world. To bring in still more money to swell his lordship's coffers. But to marry the Lady Arabella Traherne, to marry the great Earl's daughter? What chance of that, dear Lord? she wept silently. O God, what chance of that?

And, oh my Walter, you must know it too. You must know it in your heart. That this is only lovers' talk, of coming back to me.

Only lovers.

For this was love, so much at least was sure. Not French romances, nor mythic chivalry in rhymed and rhythmical Italian. Not pretty, witty words at all. But just this warm bed on a winter morning, and the two of them together. Just this man's steady, serious voice, his long-jawed face in profile, his hand on her thigh. This, and the taut longing in her breast. The joy that had been and might be once more between them—before he rode away.

Dimming memories would be all she had of him before this very day was done. When he was gone, and she sat alone in the solar where they had been together, reading, playing, talking through the long afternoons. Where she had trembled at his voice scarce a week ago, and had not yet known why.

Her heart was pounding as it had not even at the zenith of their passion the night before. Tears coursed unnoticed across her cheeks.

For now she knew what love was. And it was very real.

Walter had stopped talking. His head had turned to look at her, and he saw her pale, wet face. Saw and knew what she knew. That this must surely be the very last for them.

With a cry of pain he clutched her to him.

They made love slowly, with an ardor intensified almost beyond bearing by knowledge of what lay ahead.

There was none of the awkwardness of the night before. No fumbling or uncertainty now. Under his hands, the joyful sensuality surged up in her like a replenished fire. She laughed and sighed by turns, reveling in the wonderful physicality, the capacity for sheer pleasure, that had lain undiscovered in her through all her nineteen years, until this single night.

They made the sweetness last for long, long minutes. Minutes that were not theirs to spend.

His face was suffused with his old high color. His shaggy white-blond hair got in his eyes, unkempt and wet with perspiration. More than once he groaned aloud.

Her eyelids, dewed with tears, were almost shut as her small head rolled helplessly on the bolster. Her lips moved soundlessly, saying his name.

The moment came for both of them, the moment out of time. The dim swaying world vanished away. They soared into constellations of darkness, to heights beyond sound or sight or dimension. They were one, for one last, unending moment.

Then they were two once more.

He returned to life hearing her voice husky against his ear.

"Walter, Walter, I do love you so."

Her cheek was wet against his, her slender arms locked tight around his neck. He tasted her pale-gold hair across his mouth. "Arabella," he said, unable to say more. "Arabella. Arabella." There were only minutes left to them now. The gray light that filled the room was paling rapidly into dawn.

"Dear heart, I must go," he said at length, low and not quite steadily.

She nodded slowly, her large pale eyes fixed on his.

By God, I must—I must.

But he only kissed her instead, and pressed the warmth of her body tighter still against him.

Outside that door, beyond her antechamber, the corridor lay dim and deserted. No devils waited for him now. Halfway across the castle, his own room awaited him. His clothing partly packed away. Icy water in the basin. Razor, clean linen all laid out.

Beyond the castle walls the snow was still knee-deep in places, and there was some wind. He heard it rattle and whistle suddenly at the casement. Out there, beneath the clump of pines and oak that stood behind the chapel, they would be waiting for him. Three, four men if they had brought a surgeon. Five if they had brought a priest. And one among them waiting with a sword and dagger.

I must go.

The sea wind struck again at the mullioned windows, white now with morning. Struck with a shriek and a dying moan as it swept away inland toward the moors.

Then Arabella saw his suffering, and wiped her eyes, and spoke.

"Does my lord remember the song of the lover in winter," she asked quite cheerfully, "waiting for the winds of spring?"

His gaunt face broke into a broad smile, the West Country grin she loved. They said no more, but sang. Sang together in low tones, with elaborate harmony and great seriousness, the single stanza of the old lute song:

"O western wind, when wilt thou blow
  That the small rain down can rain?
Christ, if my love were in my arms,
  And I in my bed again!"

They ended laughing, and he kissed her nose. Then he flung
back the covers and stood up, naked in the cold air, and reached
for his clothes.

ᑪ Nineteen ᑭ

The Blades Are
of a Length

i

Castlemayne pushed open the postern gate, heaving against the wet, banked snow outside. Ducking his head, he stepped across the high stone sill, through the mighty walls of Exmoor and out into the dazzling morning.

He saw white snow heaped and drifted, black towers of trees, scattered explosions of green pine, and over all the pale-blue sky of dawn. Three long startling streamers of orange cloud knifed across the blue, lit by a just-risen sun still invisible behind the forest. High above the treetops, a curlew hovered for a long moment, then dipped and wheeled and slid away crying toward the sea. In a dry bush close at hand, a sleepy bird chirped twice. Farther down, something moved suddenly and scuttered off through the bracken.

Behind his back the great gray walls loomed darkly. The roughhewn stone was wet, patched with moss, crisscrossed with a tangle of leafless vines. Castlemayne stood a moment longer in the shadow of the walls, the narrow gate half open still behind him, to drink his fill of blue sky and black bare trees, of whiteness and wind and scuttering things and half-awakened birdsong. Excitement filled his chest and flooded through his veins.

A fine day for riding, he thought cheerfully, if it does not melt too fast.

Standing shin-deep, he shifted his weight and felt the snow

crunch easily under the arch of his foot. The bird in the gorse bushes chirruped again and flicked away, a flash of brown and yellow, through shaken branches and sifting puffs of snow. Then again it was so quiet that Castlemayne could hear his own blood pulsing, could feel the throbbing of the great muscle in his chest. He smiled broadly at the steady beat.

And a fine day for fighting too!

Walter Castlemayne had never set out in cold blood to kill a man before.

There had been incidents, of course, passionate exchanges exploding into violence. A drunken quarrel with two Germans in an Antwerp tavern, settled with swords—and jacks of wine. A wild affray in a Cheapside street, that left a ruffling play-wright of his acquaintance sorely hurt. A blow and a formal challenge, most ignominiously avoided upon the very field of honor by his antagonist, a Frenchified hanger-on of the Earl of Cumberland's. But this was young Castlemayne's first proper duel. He was pleased to find no slightest tremor in him anywhere. Only exultation that the end of it all was in clear view at last, only a few minutes, a few strides away.

He exhaled slowly and watched his breath boil out in vapor, stream away and vanish on the gentle breeze.

Gentle but steady, gusting sometimes. The ground would be blown almost bare on the knoll behind the chapel. Good. Wet snow was dangerous footing.

He turned and set out briskly then, along the wall to his right, wading knee-deep through virgin drifts. The snow was thick and heavy all about him, piled against slanting trunks, splashed over bushes, half burying the red clay banks that showed here and there down the forested slope. Sharp-needled pine boughs, pressing in from the left now, brushed his shoulder and spattered him with snow and icy drops. He dashed the moisture from his hair and chuckled to himself. He plowed on, batting branches aside with his sheathed rapier, smiling to feel so little pain in his wounded forearm.

Even half a night of sleep had done much for Castlemayne. There were still dark hollows beneath his tufted brows, but his eyes had lost their restless fever-glint. His big-boned frame, still thin and wasted, yet was animated by a healthier, more durable vitality than he had known for many days.

"I shall beat you, Captain Devereux!" he said aloud. "God damn me if I don't!"

He rounded the southwest corner of the bailey wall, treading cautiously on uneven ground, and looked up to the knoll behind the chapel. There was the rear of the ancient Norman church, towering above the crenellated wall. There were the three tall gothic windows of the choir, their bright stained glass appearing mere grisaille from without. The spire that rose above the crossing was visible for half its length above the wall, culminating in a simple cross, black against the morning sky.

Here outside the castle, just below the choir windows, the trees drew back in a semicircle from a bare, windblown hillock. This knoll loomed up before Castlemayne like a natural stage, bounded on his right by the centuries-old battlements, on the left by the still more ancient forest. And there, stage left, beneath the branches of a naked oak, four men stood waiting. Four black stick figures, silhouetted against the incandescent red-orange disk of the rising sun.

Castlemayne stood for a moment, squinting across the shadowed vale that separated him from the waiting men. They moved slowly about, rubbing chilled hands to keep the blood flowing, the fingers limber. They had not seen him yet.

Robert Naseby and young Wilton, the two seconds, approached each other and seemed to exchange a whispered word. Captain Devereux, his stocky body and long swinging arms readily recognizable even at this distance, paced restlessly back and forth under the wind-stripped oak. Now and again he seemed to tug at his jutting black beard. The fourth man, clutching a long cloak about him, turned to speak to Cousin Robert. The reedy fluting of his voice reached Castlemayne's ear. Master

Norton, by all the dead Olympians! Ever willing to lend his dignity to any ceremonious occasion! Castlemayne smiled wryly and started down into the draw that lay between him and the waiting men.

He knew with a sudden certainty that he had been moving all his young life toward this spot, this single sunrise. From Land's End, from Cambridge, from the court, from the Netherlands and the fields of France, moving inexorably down the years to this crossed point in space and time.

Exmoor Castle in Devonshire, he told it over to himself. The morning of the seventh of January, the year of our Lord fifteen hundred ninety-two. Master Walter Castlemayne hastens to his meeting with Sir Malcolm Devereux, that they may settle their differences as befits gentlemen of honor, with rapiers and daggers.

Will the learned chroniclers of our age record the moment for posterity? Not likely, alas. The talk of St. Paul's for a day, court gossip for a week, then into limbo, down to Lethe, and forgotten. He shook his head, half serious, half satirical. That such a landfall in this life of mine should go unremarked of any save the rumormongers of the capital! Purveyors of dangerous tales indeed, he added more thoughtfully, whom, should I survive, I must do all possible to silence.

He was deep in the last little hollow now, where cold night shadows lingered still. He took a dozen long strides across the bottom—sudden faint smell of urine here, an emptying jakes on his right—and started up the farther slope. There was less snow and firmer footing as he climbed. A cold wind blew, and then he felt the sunlight on his face. Off to the left, through thinning treetops, he caught a glimpse of red cliffs and glitter of the sea.

The four men were close above him now, their features clearly visible despite the ruddy light behind them. Ratlike Cousin Robert and plump Wilton stood nervously together, striving after unconcern. Old Humphrey Norton shivered in his cloak, his untidy gray beard lifted by the wind. Captain Devereux stood alone beneath the gnarled oak, one hand resting heavily on the hilt of

his rapier, his black-bearded face tilted down toward Castlemayne.

ii

Christ's bloody wounds! Behold the swordsman—swaggering
like a crested cockerel in his own barnyard!

Sir Malcolm Devereux looked down upon the climbing man.
His heart was full of hatred. But his eyes were as expressionless
as ever beneath his bushy brows.

Sir Malcolm Devereux.

Dark wide-brimmed hat and traveling cloak, black doublet,
slops, and hose. Square-cut beard and thick moustaches, black
hairs mingling now with gray. Heavy lips, chapped and cracked
and wrinkled at the corners. A big Roman nose, beaked like a
hawk's, with hairy nostrils. His face was pale and seamed with
tiny lines, creases, crow's-feet. His colorless eyes were set between an old man's wrinkled lids, though these went generally
unnoticed below the fiercely jutting black brows.

A man forty-two years old, who took no pleasure in his food
and felt a growing hankering for wine. Eleven scars upon his
body, half-a-dozen ill-knit bones—and a shrewd lesson learned
with every swelling and white scar. A quarter century of killing
men. Yet no qualm had ever stirred his self-made, self-absorbed
soul. A man who lived on hate, contemptuous of his fellow men,
ambitious only that he might visit his wrath more furiously upon
his enemies. And all mankind was Malcolm Devereux's enemy.

Devereux did not feel the breeze, or the warmth of the sun's
first rays on his back. He did not smell the freshness of the
morning. He scarcely saw the brightening world about him, beyond the bare slope and the man who climbed, who stepped out
now upon the dry ground of the knoll.

Young Castlemayne, broad of shoulder, thin of shank. The
man who dared to challenge the Great Captain for honors and
dominion.

By God, swore Malcolm Devereux, he'll fry in hell before this hour is done!

"Good day, gentlemen," said Castlemayne with a sweeping salutation. "A rare day for such honorable work as ours. But then, if June's the month for lovers, look you, then January—"

Devereux stared back stonily, his lips pressed heavily together. Then, with an insolent shrug of his shoulders, he turned his back on Walter Castlemayne.

"My lord!" murmured Robert Naseby, astonished at so uncourtierlike a gesture. Master Norton, his sense of decorum deeply shocked, raised one pale hand in protest. But Devereux's fierce glance silenced both at once and swung them into line. Neither spoke further, and no one answered Castlemayne.

The young man flushed dark with anger, bit his lip, and said no more. Inwardly he cursed his idiotic banter, the voice of the frivolous boy he had been, that had opened him to such a cut.

He stood alone, so much was clear. Cousin Robert had hitched his own rising chariot to Captain Devereux's star. Wilton, though Castlemayne's second, was Robert Naseby's satellite, and clearly in the other camp. Old Humphrey's ineffectuality left him weightless in the balance. Not one of the three would do more than murmur a mild protest if Devereux should run his rival through the back this moment. Castlemayne grinned sourly. But then, it was always well to know how the world lay.

He turned unspeaking then to the ritual prescribed, to the technicalities of his craft. Handed his weapons to his pudgy second—stiff blades in soft leather cases, tangle of belt and hangers—to be measured against his opponent's. Began the business of removing his velvet sleeves and doublet, that his skin might face the other's point with the thinnest of silk shirts between.

Sir Malcolm Devereux swung heavy arms, feeling the skin pebbling into gooseflesh beneath his shirt. Far off, through the gap between two scraggly evergreens, he saw a tiny peasant's cart crawling toward the crest of a distant hill. He grimaced sud-

denly, his lower teeth flashing strong and yellow, as the sight
triggered a flash of memory.

Strange dreams, repeating, oddly horrible, had woven through
his sleep that night just past. He who never dreamed at all had
twice awakened shouting, drenched with sweat. Denying something—what? He could not remember.

Only this was clear: All night the wheels of an unknown
coach had rumbled past a tavern window.

A nameless tavern, Southwark, near the Bear Garden. A place
where hopeless men fetched up to die their tedious slow deaths.

Himself sitting there, staring out through dim windowpanes,
wavering bottle green, at the passing feet. Drinking bitter wine,
taste of vinegar. Smell of malt and ale, dirty rushes on the floor.
Then, always and inexorably, came the rattling of the coach, so
rare in these narrow, dangerous slum streets. Coach wheels on
the cobblestones, coming quickly closer.

And after that? He could not remember, though it had happened all night long, again and yet again.

"The blades are of a length, my lord." Robert Naseby, in his
elegant knee-length Venetian breeches, licked dry lips as he re-
ported on this vital ceremony. "The rapiers, I mean, my lord. In
the dagger blades, his poniard has perhaps two inches more of
length. If my own poor weapon will serve you, sir, I should be
most honored—"

Devereux nodded brusquely and took the dagger from Cousin
Robert's outstretched hand. Couched the hilt against his horny
palm, tested the edge, and found it cutting sharp. Nodded once
again and retained the weapon in one hand, his own iron-hilted
rapier in the other.

His shadowed eyes were on his enemy now, observing every
slightest move with riveting attention.

Castlemayne. Nodding with minute impatience to Wilton's
stammered words as his weapons were returned. Turning, whistling through his teeth, to survey the ground. Testing with uneasy feet the slipperiness of the dry, yellowing grass where the

snow had blown away. Noting carefully the two or three sizable patches of snow remaining, near the base of the wall, under the trees. The eye of a professional skirmisher.

But worn and wasted with his illness—and he clearly knew it. The dry whistling, the overbusy hands. And was there a faint stiffness in the left arm?

Satan's arse, what matter? Devereux shrugged heavy shoulders, impatient with himself. I'll skewer our bantam cock as quickly as may be, through the belly or the throat. And then before the Earl. Present him with his chosen commander, dead as a capon on a spit. Three witnesses to a fair fight, and two who will swear he forced me to it. And myself all humble dignity beside the bloody corpse—another reckless young fool of a rapier fighter whose hand itched once too often for his sword.

Thus petitioned, what else could his lordship do but give the whoreson ship to Malcolm Devereux?

It came back suddenly then, with a rush of blood to his pale cheeks. After the rattling carriage wheels—his own name spoken! And then the rest of it, leaping into painfully sharp focus. Sharp as a surgeon's cut, the shock and then the pain.

Four young gallants at a table half across the empty tavern parlor. Four pairs of eyes swiveling at the sound of wheels, to see whose coach passed here. Arrogant young eyes seeing for the first time the slouching figure by the big bay window, the drooping hat and soiled ruff. And the familiar whispering began:

"Sir Malcolm Devereux, or I'm a Yorkshireman!"

"A celebrated soldier once—my father spoke of him."

"Yes, gentlemen, he takes his wine every afternoon at my humble house. If you would care for the honor of an introduction—?"

"No no, thank you, host. He was . . . my father's hero."

Muted, supercilious laughter, more it seemed than so few men might make. Laughter rising to a dream-crescendo, higher and louder, louder still. Ending with a crash as the coach drew up, creak and nicker and a coachman's cry.

Through the dark-green diamond panes he saw it. A fine new coach with matched black horses and a noble crest. Unfamiliar heraldry—a Castle planted on the Spanish Main. And a face peering out, long and lean, grinning like a young satyr beneath a gout of white-blond hair.

A coach and four—a gilded crest! "It is Lord Castlemayne," they whispered, "just back from the Bermoothes!"

Dear God—Lord Castlemayne!

Darkness and confusion after that. With laughter roaring like the sea. Until he found himself again seated by the window, watching moving crowds through wavering green glass, waiting with a thrill of horror for the first faint rumble of carriage wheels on ghostly cobblestones.

And for that, Master Castlemayne, Sir Malcolm thought savagely there upon the hilltop, it shall be through the belly, where life ebbs slowly!

"Gentlemen, if you are ready," fluted old Humphrey's exquisite musical voice, barely audible in the thin winter air, "with your gracious leave, I shall take just two words to propound my own humble office and duties here."

Castlemayne nodded curtly, repressing a brief smile. Master Norton will bid the seven angels pause as they lift the trumpets to their lips, he thought, and offer a few choice words on the Last Judgment. In most elegant Ciceronian Latin too, no doubt, in honor of so august an occasion.

Devereux responded not at all. He hardly heard what followed. He had heard it all before, too many times to care.

"I shall consider this to be a judicial combat, gentlemen, of the sort sanctioned by the highest jurisprudential authorities and by numerous precedents in all ages. . . ." He paused and chewed his gums a moment, evidently tempted to cite at least a precedent or two. But his sense of the temper of his audience urged him to get on with it. He sighed and continued, briskly businesslike.

"The weapons are these basket-hilted Spanish rapiers and these two daggers, here compared and found equal by your two seconds, and no other weapon of any sort. Is that understood and acceptable to you both?"

The two men nodded.

"The place shall be this present ground, and the time this present morning. The combat to continue until the quarrel between you shall be settled honorably to both. And rightfully, by God's grace, we pray. Is this also understood and accepted, gentlemen?"

Both indicated that it was.

"In the event of a hit in which blood is clearly drawn, I shall separate the two combatants with my own sword extended thus." He raised the weapon awkwardly and held it out in front of him, shoulder high. The cold breeze blew a sudden gust that flapped his black robe about his bony legs.

"I shall then ask each of you in turn whether the demands of honor are satisfied, or not. In the event that either gentleman does not feel the debt of honor is yet fully paid, the combat will be resumed. And will continue until such time as both gentlemen shall be content that the quarrel is honorably settled, or until one or both shall be unable to continue. Is this understood, and will you both abide by these?"

The two men nodded rather more briskly than before.

"You will not be unaware that there is no physician presently here at Exmoor. None, I fear, this side of Exeter. I have, however, myself some small store of surgical skill, sufficient to bind clean wounds until the injured gentleman may be transported there, or a physican summoned here. This I propose to do if called upon, and if acceptable. . . ."

Neither bothered to respond. They stood looking quietly at each other past the man in the middle, who always did talk one minute too long.

"Finally, Sir Malcolm Devereux and Master Castlemayne, it it my duty to attempt to reconcile you one to the other, here and now, before a weapon has been raised in anger. This is, I believe, the general practice at such formal combats even in this degenerate age. If therefore I may by any means arbitrate, compose, or quench this quarrel . . ."

"You may not," said Devereux sharply.

"You may not," said Castlemayne.

Humphrey Norton sighed, rather in irritation at their folly than in sorrow for their impending fate.

"In that case, gentlemen, I shall separate your blades."

The sun had cleared the hills and hung, a ball of orange fire, in the east. The two men raised their weapons and stepped forward.

~ Twenty ~

Blood on the Snow

i

Pipe-piping of a bird, urgent with alarm, shrill from the forest's edge. Cold arms and legs, painfully nipped ears and noses on all five men. Naseby and Wilton, ludicrous in foppish lace and padding. Norton like a paunchy windblown prophet, long-bearded, sword held out as if it were a wand. Three pairs of eyes unblinking, staring, mirrors with red suns in each. Eyes reflecting Castlemayne and Devereux, approaching armed to the center of the knoll.

Each with a cup-hilted rapier in his right hand, four feet of tempered steel. Each with a dagger in his left, a tapered blade eighteen inches long. Holding the weapons loosely, easily, hilts nestled in their palms, balancing the heavy blades. Thumb and index finger of the rapier hand slipped over the crosspiece for a better grip, dexterity in thrusting.

Swords much alike. Both long hilted, shallow Spanish cups below undecorated crosspieces, with a knuckle bow from cup to pommel to protect the fingers. Both rapiers and both daggers double-edged, brightly pointed, sharp as shaving razors.

Moving in, half crouching, boots scuffling over brittle grass, scraping frozen earth. Touch of frigid wind flapping their loose white shirts, ruffling the blond hair and the black, stirring the captain's square-cut beard. Crimson sunglare flickering along their swords, as if each pristine weapon already ran with blood. Quick breathing, a sudden throb in each chest as their blades extended slowly, touched, metal clacking sharply on metal in the stillness.

Then, with an awkward rustling movement, Master Norton struck their points apart.

Three pairs of red-reflecting eyes.

Now taste it, Master Cock-o-the-Walk Castlemayne! hissed everybody's Cousin Robert in his heart. The brine of humiliation, the shame of helplessness before us all!

Castlemayne for youth and skill perhaps, old Humphrey estimated, lowering his weapon, stepping hastily back. But Sir Malcolm for experience and shrewdness. No easy match to judge. For all his ceremony, his palms were wet as any man's, his breath wheezing in the chilly air.

Jesus God in heaven, Wilton almost gasped aloud, this is no game for a man of delicate humors and an uncertain stomach! His puffy cheeks quivered, and he prayed for the courage to turn his eyes away before—

A whistling thrust—

A savage, slashing dagger parry—

Clang and screech of blade on blade shattered the stillness of the morning.

All four weapons at once engaged, and neither man retreated. Four-foot streaks of hardened steel clashed, slithered, parted, and clashed again, with a ring like silver. Long, flat knife blades darted in to bat aside cut or thrust of the rapier, or to jab wickedly at a momentarily unprotected belly. Still neither would step back. The scissoring blades played about them in the sunrise like streaks and wheels of fire.

Then suddenly the rapiers were locked, hilt to hilt, each man straining for advantage. The two daggers played a brief insidious game below, each man lusting to rip the other open. For one quivering moment the two men glared at one another, unspeaking, eyes boring into eyes, testing, probing, seeking weaknesses.

Abruptly, with a mighty mutual heave, they flung themselves apart, opening the distance to begin again.

A general gasp.

"No hit either way!" declared Master Norton. But his words were lost in the clang of steel on steel resumed.

Little joy of war in this, Castlemayne though wryly. Here was no pell-mell charge, no fanfare of shouts and trumpets. No startled men-at-arms breaking and scattering before the shrewdly calculated onslaught, or going down under the sheer weight of the attack. The great Captain Devereux would not flee or fall, but Castlemayne must put him down.

Brace to it then, as old Master Rocco said. Drive always for the face and belly. Rapier for the attack, dagger for your guard. But Christ knows he is strong!

Walter Castlemayne lunged like a striking snake, again and yet again. Sir Malcolm Devereux smashed aside each thrust with the fury of a baited bear. The trained fencer fought always with the point, in the best Italian fashion. The older man attacked with point and edge at once, unorthodox and sometimes wild, but with an unleashed passion that threatened severed limbs and disemboweling. Breathing hard, they broke apart, circled slowly, crouching low, watching for an opening. Leaped at each other again, stabbing and hacking, parrying, dodging, slashing at each other's limbs and body. Sprang apart once more and in again, eyes aflame, snorting like two stallions.

To those who watched, they seemed hardly men, but fighting animals possessed by primal bloodlust. Yet magicians too, their charmed skins emerging miraculously unscathed from their most furious exchanges. Old Humphrey's jaw hung slack beneath his beard. He had witnessed duels before, even street affrays—but never a fight like this. Young Wilton, with bulging eyes and churning stomach, knew that he would never see the like again.

Then, suddenly, a break.

Serpent-quick, Castlemayne lunged the whole length of his

body in a low, crippling thrust. Devereux's dagger was there in time, driving down with paralyzing force, enough to send the rapier spinning from the hand of a lesser man. An instant later, Devereux's own sword flashed down at his antagonist, caught momentarily off guard at the extremity of his futile thrust. Castlemayne took the devastating cut on the crossbar of his dagger hilt. Caught it, held it, turned it off, and leaped away—with a gasp of pain.

A flash of agony all up and down the bandaged left forearm, from the elbow to the fingertips. Jolting shock, sickening feel of blood oozing beneath the bandages, an instant weakness in the hand and wrist.

Captain Devereux saw, and his yellow teeth showed suddenly, like a hunting carnivore.

As his enemy backed away, Devereux bored in, swinging his four-foot rapier as if it were a Scottish claymore. Castlemayne, his defensive arm all but disabled, could only reel backward, parrying frantically with his sword, before the momentum of Devereux's assault. Back and back, till his booted feet were in soft snow, his back scraping the great limestone blocks of the castle wall.

While a man might draw three breaths, Devereux pinned him there. Boxed him in against the wall, threatening with both hands, first with the rapier, then with the dagger. Then, feinting savagely with his left, he swung an overhand cut at Castlemayne's blanched face. Swung and missed, striking blue sparks from the squared stones where the head had been. For Castlemayne had broken out—knocked aside the confining knife blade and escaped, out into the center of the knoll.

Sir Malcolm wheeled after him—too late. His elusive prey stood a full two swords' lengths away, on guard. It was all to do again.

The two men wiped their faces, glistening with sweat despite the cold. Their chests were heaving, their hair wild, both shirts wet and dirty. Devereux's heavy countenance was mottled from exertion. Castlemayne's thin face had gone dead white again, all his recovered color drained away. Yet they crouched and closed once more, their hands minutely trembling on their hilts.

The younger man moved hotly in, heedless of injuries and weakness. So, villain, would you bay me in? Chest of a bull, arms of a Barbary ape—but short of wind already, Captain Devereux. By God, I'll let the wind out of you—

Cursing the light-headedness that seemed to mar his judgment, frantically working his left hand to restore strength to the enfeebled fingers, Castlemayne drove in against his foe. His single rapier, inspired now by an anger as hot as Devereux's own, stabbed and chivvied with a dazzling deftness that brought startled oaths from those who watched.

And this time it was Sir Malcolm Devereux who stepped slowly backward, moving cautiously over frozen earth and uncertain grass. Back and backward from that flickering, dancing point, maintaining distance, avoiding fight. And was there a tiny tremor in those solid tree-trunk thighs?

Has the pace already worn you down, old devil? exulted Walter Castlemayne. By God, I'll rest you, Mephistopheles!

Come to me, Master Castlemayne. The one thought burned behind Devereux's dark brows. To me, my young cavalier. If I cannot catch you, come you then to me! Come . . . come. . . .

With a single smooth professional stride, Castlemayne closed the distance, thrusting high for the right shoulder. Devereux parried hectically, feinted a counterstroke, leaped sideways out of reach. Castlemayne closed again, prodding with quick short thrusts at his enemy's defenses. Still Devereux defended merely, a trifle less effectively it seemed, and withdrew once more.

The younger man pressed in yet more impatiently, watching lynx-eyed for an opening. Then Devereux, close beneath the trees, set one backward reaching foot into a patch of melting snow. Felt his weight shift back upon insecurity—and saw that

Castlemayne saw too. The heart dropped out of Devereux, but no flicker of alarm showed on his face. Luck favored him. The black-shod foot slipped only an inch or two before it found firm ground. His sword and knife points wavered not at all. No harm done, he thought succinctly, and the accident may help our purpose.

Castlemayne released his sudden tension in a long slow breath. Well enough. A few minutes more to rest the dagger hand, where strength flowed back already. But assuredly the old man was getting careless. The next time, now, the next such slip . . .

Devereux sidled to his right, feeling his way along the forest edge. Eyes fixed on his antagonist, he moved cautiously and slowly.

But not quite cautiously enough, Walter thought, tensing to attack. Two steps more and his leg will surely brush that clump of snow-laden bracken. A small, a tiny thing. But it should suffice. . . .

Crackle of dry twigs, half-glimpsed fall of snow, a rasping touch across the calf. What man born of woman would not cast one quick, furtive downward glance?

Will that bring you, Castlemayne?

ii

No one saw clearly everything that happened in the next half-dozen seconds.

Castlemayne's thrust came beautiful and deadly, straight for the unprotected throat. Wilton, watching, cried aloud. Even Robert Naseby gasped. Then suddenly, confusingly, the struggling men were jammed in close together, the crosspieces of their rapiers grinding hard, briefly locking. Castlemayne had someway missed his mark. And Devereux had snared him.

One moment the captain seemed to hug him close. The white-faced youth jerked, staggered in that embrace. Then wrenched himself free and took two fast dancing steps backward and away.

Devereux lunged wildly after him, jabbing, hacking for a finish. But Castlemayne, bent almost double, erratically retreating, held his quivering point in his assailant's eyes and somehow kept him off. Until the older man slipped himself, fell almost to one knee, and saw his man escape. In the center of the windy knoll, the distance opened wide between them, the two men stood baffled once again, gasping, glaring at each other.

Blood glittered wet and running on the dagger in Captain Devereux's left hand.

Walter Castlemayne straightened slowly up, his left arm clutched tight about his body. Palm and fingers were smeared with blood. His silk shirt was ripped all up the right side, torn open to the armpit. The white cloth, where it hung in rags, was quickly turning red.

"Gentlemen!" cried Master Norton hastily, thrusting his foolish sword between them. "Is your offended honor not now satisfied on both sides by the blood thus shed?"

Norton's rheumy old eyes shifted anxiously, almost fearfully from one man to the other.

"It is not!" breathed Sir Malcolm Devereux. Step to one side, old fool! he snarled silently.

"It is not," said Castlemayne. Even as he spoke, he explored the wound with trembling fingers. A shallow cut up across the surface of the rib cage. Certainly not mortal. Not even crippling, if no muscles— Rapidly he tested the mechanism of his right shoulder, arm, and hand. He found no numbness, only minor hampering of dexterity. Though it will be worse, he admitted, as the blood cools, tries to congeal into a scab. And the blood itself that's lost will take its toll.

He bent wincing and fumbled up his dagger, bruising his uncertain knuckles on the ground. But came up poised and ready once more, low-crouching, long gleaming blades extended. Only then, while the fussing old referee drew back, muttering at their madness, did Walter Castlemayne begin to comprehend what had happened to him. How it was that he, whom the Italians had dubbed a master of the art of fence, should be so close to dying.

How in the Devil's name? he wondered. My point went true. But his counter was swifter than I looked for, deflecting, locking hilts. And then the daggers. Had I been whole-handed, my bodkin had been as quick as his! Damn you, Marsigliano, who serves your master even from the grave.

Yet—that short upward stab tearing across the bone. . . . He must have held his weapon higher than I saw, ready for the stroke when I should be lured within reach! Some tavern fighter's trick I have not come upon before.

And how many more such *bottes,* in a quarter century of practicing the soldier's craft?

A spasm of nausea twisted the young man's stomach, tightened his lean jaw. His body still reacted to the shock of violation. Pain shot up and down his left arm. There was pain across his torso. Shafts of pain with every move.

Christ—this old man will kill me!

Pain and fear of death welled up in him, seemed to suffocate him. Familiar enemies to him now. He set his teeth to drive them down.

But the foul injustice of it!

That he should die thus, to no purpose. Die fighting neither for glory nor for England, but stabbed in a stupid quarrel in the depths of backwoods Devon. Never see the *Golden Fortune* full-rigged and sails unfurled, never ride her down the tide past Sheppey to the sea. Exact no single drop of blood in vengeance for poor Harry, floating in the frozen darkness under a coffin lid of ice. While this spade-hearted villain, whose plots and minions brought it all to pass—

Castlemayne shook his head violently, striving to clear his brain of its terrors.

Aye, look at him! he said sharply to himself. Look at the

swordsman who's going to lay you in your grave! Is this the man will cut down Walter Castlemayne?

Devereux's pale eyes still gleamed granite-hard beneath his brows. Still, prudent, calculating, deadly. But his face was flushed with exertion, blotchy and congested in his rage. His mouth gaped open, and his hoarse breathing was the loudest sound upon the hillock. And there was pain there too, each separate muscle strained and wincing with every sudden move. Pain in Sir Malcolm Devereux as well, though it showed only in a twitching eyelid, a spasm in the cheek.

Why, his wind's all but gone, and his legs! His old body has been suffering since our blades first crossed, even as mine does now! And half consciously, at the back of his clearing mind: If Malcolm Devereux can play a soldier's part, can bear the pain and fear, the living with his own mortality—can Walter Castlemayne do less?

Then, as his tactical intelligence began to function once again: Can he last another quarter of an hour at this pace? Surely he'll not do better now than he has done. And I cannot do worse!

Captain Devereux thrust at Castlemayne's face, hard and vicious, grunting with the effort. The rapier point flashed past his victim's ear as Castlemayne leaped sideways and away, opening the distance. Another moment for recovery, Castlemayne thought prudently. And to exhaust the old villain further with pursuing me. Then back at him—anger kindling once again—and vengeance for my Harry, and for the mark of Cain upon my brow!

Almost at once he found that he could bear the pain of rapid movement. He felt the nausea and shock ebb from him. His terror was gone, his fury surging back. He felt only humiliation at the wound, hunger for revenge, the bloodlust of the fighting animal within him. No hot, heedless anger this time, but the cold rage of the hunting tiger, its cunning unimpaired.

He met Sir Malcolm's next attack with a favorite defensive ward of Master Rocco's—and flung him back.

The great circle of the sun was paling, from searing orange-red to rose to merest yellow, twice its own diameter now above the hills. The sky was turning blue again, as the red glare of the sun's first minutes faded. The hills were dark purple in the east, the sea bright orange now, glittering behind the black branches of the trees. High above a seabird called, banking about the chapel spire. Graceful balancing of wings—raucous, blaring, predatory cry. A fish killer, feeling sudden hunger.

"Now, Sir Malcolm Devereux!" said Castlemayne, speaking low, his fury grimly disciplined. "Now, old ironguts, let's see how well you fight! For I've learned much from you and yours, nor has it been an easy schooling. But now it's time you had a lesson in your turn."

Devereux saved his breath. But there was contempt still about his mouth for the bantam cock called Castlemayne.

The younger man raised sword and dagger as though in invocation, ignoring pain along his flank, and closed once more with his enemy.

iii

Sir Malcolm Devereux would not break.

His huge strength and driving will stood up unbending against Castlemayne. In the old man's iron thighs, steel springs still tightened and released. Beneath his sweat-soaked shirt, heavy shoulders still heaved mightily. Thick wrists and hairy, slug-white hands, gripping sword and dagger hilts, still jabbed and cut with paralyzing power. He seemed to draw upon some primal fount of dark energy, some deep-burning passion for destruction. His courage was unfailing, his lust to kill and maim unslaked.

Again and yet again he charged like a battering ram against the wall of flashing steel flung up by Castlemayne. Repulsed, he stood like a wall himself, nor ever gave an inch of ground before his furious attacker. Behind his dark brows burned a single-souled, maniacal desire: to smash this young man to his knees, and in this idol of his age to crush the age itself beneath his heel.

It was no longer for the *Golden Fortune,* but for revenge upon a brutal world that Devereux now fought. To overwhelm, humilate an age that could so cheerfully consign yesterday's Great Captains to the dunghill of oblivion. For such a moment of gut-filling joy, his old man's life was all too cheap a price to pay.

Relentless, unflagging, he stood his ground and fought.

And Walter Castlemayne attacked.

Around, around his enemy he moved, thrusting, feinting, parrying, lunging in again. His teeth were set. No flash of agony diverted cut or thrust by a fraction of an inch or a particle of time. Every foot of the low hillock—withered grass, dark earth, smears of trampled snow—was etched into his brain, at the service of his skirmisher's instinct for terrain. This was his country now. He was master of it. And if fantastic strength and desperate activity saved his antagonist a few moments longer, yet the end seemed certain as tomorrow's sun.

Castlemayne's thin face smiled ferociously, cording cheeks, ridging his pale forehead. His blue eyes were as opaque as his opponent's. But in his two sinewy hands he wielded lightning bolts.

Thudding feet on frozen ground. Ragged breaths in agony sucked in. Sweat-blinded eyes, sweat-soaked rags of shirts flapping over naked chests. Wrists and shoulders strained past numbing weariness to the perfect strength of artificial things, powered by will alone. In both men, the triumph of the will incarnate, towering over mere mortality, flaying flesh and bone to the ultimate exultation of unbending pride.

Minutes after first blood had been drawn, both men were hurt again: Devereux with a slicing gash upon his arm, Castlemayne a bloody cut across his dagger hand. And only seconds later, Sir Malcolm was hurt a second time—an ugly stab wound, not deep but painful, high on his left shoulder.

Humphrey Norton's vain expostulations were drowned out by the clang of weapons.

Two pairs of aching eyes, frozen, expressionless. Seeing only flashing, bright steel blades moving in a geometric dance. Seeing only naked flesh to slice and slit and stab. Bloody clothing, dark-stained boots, blood-spattered weeds and clods. Racing hearts, fast-pulsing veins, pouring life out upon the ground. No longer fighting for a ship, a friend, a future, but to kill some primal enemy each saw incarnate in the other.

Centuries and millennia seemed to melt away. Two fierce-eyed dragons fought, wet scales glittering in the ancient rain forest. Two stags crashed together in the forest night, white antlers shaken, breathing blue in moonlight. Gashing, ripping, ravaging with horn and talon, stripping bushes, tearing up the smoking earth. Two unvanquishable wills in conflict, past fear or pain, past calculation, living only to humiliate, obliterate, destroy.

Slice you into quarters, my prancing cockerel—gut you like a slaughtered piglet, eat your entrails for black pudding—

Jam you down the Devil's jakes, old whoremaster—by Christ I'll nail your hairy hide to yonder oak—

Gleaming sword blades, russet-stained, clash and slither rasping, part and clash again—shock of iron against a knife, slanting sliding up and off, into empty air—rapier blade up blade, to a crash of cup hilts and crossbars one against the other—heave and thrust and break away to come again like tigers at each other's throats with four-foot metal fangs—

Until the moment that must come, when the most unbending will succumbs at last to the fallibility of flesh. When young muscles hold firm, while hoary fur soaks red and ancient antlers droop and crack.

When Devereux's blotchy face turned slowly chalk-white. And at a given belly-level thrust, no more and no less powerful than another, he faltered, parried with a sudden awkwardness —and staggered backward.

Castlemayne advanced one long stride forward, closing the distance instantly, giving not a second's respite. Another thrust from Castlemayne, an answering cut taken easily on his poniard —despite the wounds upon his dagger hand and arm—and Devereux stumbled backward once again. Castlemayne, inexorable, took another sleek stride forward.

And stamped his seal upon the turning tide.

Moved suddenly and beautifully, graceful as a leaping panther, too quickly for the eyes of the three spectators to follow. Swung his rapier in a sweeping arc that struck aside his opponent's sword, opening the line for one rapid dagger stroke. An awkward and unlikely crossing cut, upward beneath the ribs—ignoring the other's knife, no longer fast enough to counter. An altogether unlikely bit of swordplay, dangerous but perfect for that moment of crumbling defenses and incipient collapse. And brutally successful.

Castlemayne leaped back at once, out of reach of any possible retaliation. But Devereux could only stare in sick surprise at the long gash that ran from the hard fat of his belly halfway up the rib cage. Not a deep or a disabling wound, but wide-lipped, quickly filling with blood that flowed down over white, creased flesh to his velvet breeches. And most awesome, the very twin of the first blood Devereux had drawn from Castlemayne.

Both men saw and understood—the older with a hiss of indrawn breath, the younger with a laugh. Both the bleeding, gasping men shuffling and fighting over the brittle grass could now clearly see the endgame coming.

For Sir Malcolm Devereux, there was no hope now of victory, the *Golden Fortune,* and the future. He had lost his gamble.

For he knew he would never again pierce that wall of shifting steel. He dodged and parried his enemy's incisive razor strokes rather from an instinct in his bones than from any hope of parrying the last. Yet there was one hope in him still, one last scheme taking shape in his weary brain.

If I die now and in this place, he thought, young Castlemayne dies with me!

Let Captain Devereux die here, on the blade of the ambitious courtier Castlemayne. And what will they say then? He grinned savagely, sucking a tortured breath over jagged teeth. "Old soldier of the Queen, on the eve of some great service"—so the rumormongers would retail it in St. Paul's—"most shamefully cut down by a courtier that sought for his command." And would Lord Henry then bestow that command upon the man-slayer?

It was his last hope. His only chance for vengeance, and a kind of victory.

It was one thing for the great Captain Devereux to kill an almost unknown youth in a duel forced upon him. Quite another the reverse. A risky gamble for Devereux was for Castlemayne sheer and certain suicide. To defy his lordship's ban, to murder the Great Captain, to fling his bloodstained ambition in the face of the world—not the most glittering career could survive it.

Trust Castlemayne to do it! exulted Devereux. Trust your mad-brained rapier fighter to see no further than his nose, and cut it off to spite himself!

And there was pleasure for Devereux himself in such a termination. An end to it, at least. The surcease of an honorable death. He grimaced wryly. Surely some hack poet, that sees a few shillings in a eulogy, will so describe my passing. And truly death . . . death at least will kill the rattling carriage wheels. The wheels of the crested coach that comes clattering over cobblestones beyond the green-glass panes . . .

And trust Castlemayne to do it!

Wheezing, lurching back beyond the reach of a vicious thrust,

Sir Malcolm Devereux laughed aloud. A single bark of jeering laughter, harsh and strange in the thin cold air.

For Castlemayne, the dagger stroke that raked up the old man's ribs, ripping through fat and muscle, brought a surge of savage exultation.

The fighting animal within him screamed, trumpeting primeval joy at the feel of rending flesh. There was blood upon his tongue, sweet as pasty to the taste, and a ravenous thirst for more. There was a lust to bring the old buck down, unseam him thigh and belly and breastbone. Cock of the walk, king of all mountains, brought down into the dust.

And then the joy of vengeance realized at last.

For one fleeting instant as he moved in against his enemy, the morning sunshine dimmed. The sharp stench of mud and slime, the stink of corpse gas swept against his nostrils. In the flicker of an eyelid, something seemed to reach over his left shoulder. A human hand, all skeleton and tendon, tattered fragment of a shirt flapping wetly from the bone. A hand the color of gray fungus too long hidden from the sun. A hand that pointed at Sir Malcolm Devereux.

Then the voice spoke, close beside his ear. For the first time that voice six days vanished from the earth, now cold and grating, harsh with victory.

"See him now, Walter, see him back away! See the death-pale face of the devil that jeers no more. Break it—smash it! Smash the face that laughed us both to scorn, that made you kill your Harry. Stab Satan to the heart, as you swore upon my corpse to do!"

And soft and sibilant below the voice of his dead kinsman, the self-extenuating Cain within himself echoed lower still: Vengeance for yourself, for your lost innocence, for Walter Castlemayne!

But it was to the ghost of his dead friend that he spoke his

answer, half aloud: "Aye, Harry, blood for blood! Ram it
through his oily guts, as I swore to do!"

He moved in fast and mercilessly, weaving, jabbing, pushing
his panting victim back. The spectral figure hovered at his
shoulder, exulting at every wicked thrust and forward gliding
step. A crimson haze seemed to close about Walter's brain, narrowing his vision to the livid face, the torn and punctured flesh
of his foe.

Then suddenly there came from the grim-faced man before
him that short, sharp bark of derisive laughter.

And even as the grinning captain thought, *Trust Castlemayne
to do it,* the final change came over Walter Castlemayne.

The swordsman's furious rapier paused, wavered, froze in
air. While a man might tell a dozen seconds, he was a statue—
crouching, blades extended, with blazing eyes that slowly,
seraphically cleared.

Between one heartbeat and the next, the crimson mist was
gone, the roaring beast abruptly stilled. One blink of an uncertain
eyelid, and the vengeful ghost had vanished down the wind.
Over him like a wave of cold seawater, salt and green, swept
realization of the time and place and of the problem.

What—kill this toothless devil, he asked himself amazed, and
so lose my *Golden Fortune* forever? Risk a lifetime for one
moment's pleasure in the death of this old villain?

A tight smile split the thin pale face.

Why, Devereux himself would teach you better, Walter
Castlemayne! And Devereux will jeer at you once more, even
as he feels the suicidal blade sliding through his belly. "What,
boy, have you learned nothing yet?" he'll say, and die laughing
up at you.

Then, squeezing out the smile: No, no, old limb of Satan—
you'll spit no blood on me!

Cool-eyed at last, in control, Master Castlemayne proceeded

then to the check and mate. A problem in tactics first, then one in swordsmanship. And for each a clear solution. Dangerous, but logical and likely, and capable of execution.

Late, late, he thought. The sun is thrice its own width above the hills. Few servants of his lordship ever pass this way. But a forester might come, or some early-rising guest. And one witness beyond my power to control, one pair of eyes I cannot blind or buy—

Quickly then to make an end, and set us all upon our ways.

One moment more he paused to survey his shattered enemy. To choose, with an icy swordsman's eye, the target for his final thrust.

Sir Malcolm Devereux stood swaying slightly in the blue shadow of the gnarled oak, both feet uncertain in the trampled snow. His ravaged face—the hollow eyes, the furrowed cheeks, the gray in his coarse hair and beard—made him seem half again his forty years. His blood-smeared body, half naked in the cold tree's shadow, shuddered with a sudden ague.

But he held his weapons ready. In his cold expressionless eyes there already glinted a first shrewd doubt at this strange holding off. . . .

The big muscle of the thigh, decided Castlemayne. That will bring him down. But outside the bone. Avoid the artery.

He closed the distance, crouching low, for the last engagement.

Three pairs of eyes watched hypnotized as young Castlemayne stepped in. His lithe, blood-spattered body moved easily, breath coming deep but calmly now. His knotted arms and shoulders, gleaming in the sun, passed in bright silhouette against the gray walls of Exmoor. The last exchange was sharp and lovely, the last thrust went cleanly home.

Castlemayne jabbed high up, drew an easy parry. Then a backhand cut, slashing at Devereux's throat, to jerk his head back and pull all his defenses up. And instantly the long clear downward slanting thrust.

The point of Castlemayne's Spanish rapier went in just below the padded slops, hardly tearing the black woolen hose. The narrow blade slid easily through the thickest part of the thigh. Castlemayne felt it graze the bone. He jammed it well through, till the point protruded six inches or so behind. Whipped it out at once, widening the wound. And stepped swiftly back, out of reach, his weapons still prudently raised and ready.

Devereux bent over with the pain. Tried to take a step forward. Fell face down in the snow.

Both the gorgeously clad seconds rushed forward, Cousin Robert with a courtierlike oath. Humphrey Norton followed hastily, clutching cloak and robe about him.

Naseby and Wilton fumblingly turned Sir Malcolm Devereux over and disarmed him, slipping the hilts from his nerveless fingers. Master Norton, functioning now as surgeon, knelt with trembling knees in the wet snow beside Sir Malcolm.

Castlemayne dropped his own rapier and dagger in the grass and joined the group about the fallen man.

"No fear, Master Castlemayne," rasped old Humphrey in his reedy voice. "He'll do well enough, in spite of your best efforts." Then, unable to contain his irritation at all the mad fraternity of swordsmen, "He'll live quite long enough, I have no doubt, to see you in like case."

He dabbed at the big cut up the side and belly, cleaning out dirt and bits of dried grass, muttering to himself. But he said no more aloud. For he knew the prudent respect that was due the victor.

Walter Castlemayne stood looking down at the Great Captain. At the gray in his hair, the wrinkles around his closed eyes, the deep trenches in his cheeks. He looked at the sagging, bearded jaw, listened to each thick whistling breath. He did not think that Devereux would live so long.

But he will recover from these wounds of mine, he thought with satisfaction. Beyond that is his own affair.

Walter stood waiting quietly for Master Norton to turn to his own still bleeding wounds. His battered body was relaxed, at ease, letting the pain pulse through him. But his mind was busy. So many things must be done within this next hour.

Cousin Robert's cousin Wilton, looking sicker than either of the two wounded men, made a sudden retching sound in his puffy throat. He was staring in fascinated horror at the ground beneath Castlemayne's feet.

Castlemayne looked down.

Red drops from the fingertips of his own left hand were falling noiselessly into a patch of snow already dark with blood from Devereux's last injury. The red stream flowed through winking crystals into a darker pool. Castlemayne was standing boot-sole deep in a glittering puddle of their mingled blood.

◦ *Twenty-One* ◦

The Road to London

i

Castlemayne reined in on the lip of the vale and looked down. He sat straight in the saddle despite the pain that coursed through his damaged body. The castle loomed behind him, tall and dark, half seen through the trees. The Vale of Exmoor fell away before him.

His gaze moved down the thickly forested slope to the white slash of the clearing at the bottom. There in the open, squat and black against the drifts, the copper beech spread its tangled limbs above the milldam and the frozen pond. Winter sunlight glinted faintly on bare ice.

And who was it truly, then, Castlemayne asked himself, gazing down at that cold tumulus, that killed my Harry? Whose the guilt, when all is done, for the blood that glittered red upon my hands—dear God, not seven days ago?

The blood of his kinsman, his comrade, the only brother he had ever had. Or ever would have in this life.

The big Sussex mare moved restlessly under him. A cold wind touched his gaunt cheeks, watered his eyes. Behind him, shaggy stone pine and fir cast cold shadow over horse and rider, pausing there on the forest track. The woods were silent around him, save for his horse's sudden snort, his own steady breathing.

Was it truly Sir Malcolm Devereux's doing, after all? He plotted the rendezvous that brought us both to grief, that's sure.

Yet it was not his hand that jammed the knife in Harry's belly.
Nor was it his soul the demons that slaver after guilty men
pursued.

A sudden spasm shook his sinewy frame. Tattered memories
of flight through the storm-wracked forest with his dead friend
across his shoulder came briefly back to him. "O God"—his own
wild lamentations echoed in his brain—"the voice of my brother's
blood crieth unto thee from the ground. And now I am cursed
from the earth. . . ."

But there was a new clearness in the icy blue eyes now. Nor
was there any touch of madness in the brain that coolly asked:

And did I kill him, then? Am I my brother's murderer?

When it was Harry leaped first upon my back, as mad for
blood as I? As mad for blood as his poor ghost was for Devereux's
this very morning? For truly, though he was slow to anger, yet
Harry was as violent as any man when the fighting rage was on
him. He would not have been the soldier that he was, if he were
not capable of fury.

He knew that it would be many a long and lonely day before
he ceased to suffer for the brother he had lost. Before he ceased
to miss that hearty slap upon the shoulder, or the strong arms
at Doesburg that had braced up the ladder that brought him
help at last on those bloody walls. Before he could put out of
mind the red-lit stable at Exmoor, the wild affray, the feel of
his own knife going in.

But he knew too that he no more than Devereux bore all the
guilt upon his soul. He knew that, if Malcolm Devereux had
presided like some tutelary demon over the affair, yet it was
Walter Castlemayne and Harry Langland, fighting drunken in
the stable, that had contrived between them to stab poor Harry
dead.

Forgive me then, sweet Harry, Walter's lips said silently, as
I do you. And God forgive us both.

And Devereux?

Castlemayne saw Sir Malcolm's bleak no-color eyes look up

at him from the back of the covered cart, that last moment before the crack of the groom's whip set the ambling plow horses into motion. Eyes cold and hard as ever, but truly empty now, emptier than Castlemayne had ever seen them. Void of hope, of lust, even of hate. The eyes of a living dead man beneath those bushy brows. The old man's mouth had moved slightly, and there was a trickle of saliva on his grizzled beard.

Castlemayne had dropped the canvas flap and nodded curtly. The whip had cracked, the horses had begun to move.

A long hard road for you, Malcolm Devereux, he had thought as the wagon jounced off, the two horsemen following slowly in its wake. Two days of rattling about in a country cart is bone-shaking enough for a man with a whole skin. For your poor battered carcass, I fear it will be purgatory.

Castlemayne's big horse nickered and tossed her head, eager to be gone. He short-reined her to uneasy quiet, meditating still.

Simple expediency had dictated the hasty dispatching of the injured man upon the road to Exeter. The hacked and bleeding carcass had to be gotten out of Exmoor before any whisper of his guest's indisposition should reach the Earl's indignant ear. Master Norton's judgment that surgeons should see to Devereux's injuries had provided a rationale for the journey—but a rationale only. It was the need to preserve his hard-won victory that had dictated Castlemayne's course.

As for the witnesses, the three men whose testimony could be as damning as the captain's living wounds—all had been almost fawningly cooperative. So easily manipulated, so eager to be used. Castlemayne had only to look them each in turn between the eyes. To speak with due authority—a touch of menace, a hint of patronage and promise. And the thing was done.

His eyes glinted in the chill air, remembering.

He had but to suggest that the wounded gentleman should have an escort on his journey. Robert Naseby instantly volunteered himself and his cousin Wilton for the merciful errand. The trip would take them several days out of their own ways home, of course. But that was a trifling inconvenience, they assured him, if it would free Master Castlemayne to make best speed to London in the Queen's service.

Only old Master Norton would be left behind, the one man in Exmoor who knew of that morning's bloody work. But Castlemayne had spoken to him earnestly, if obliquely, for some ten minutes after the other two had hurried off to prepare for an immediate departure. A mere ten minutes' talk to the Earl's best advisor, yet Castlemayne would go bond for the old man's silence now.

All had been so easily accomplished. Within half an hour from the moment Sir Malcolm had pitched forward helpless in the snow, the little cavalcade was assembled. Two riding horses for Naseby and Wilton, a covered cart and team, and the dullest groomsman in the stables as a driver. Devereux, half conscious now, had been bundled in with little ceremony. And before the sun had risen another diameter above the hills, the creaking wagon had vanished down the forest track, the two horsemen following in its wake.

"God rest you then, Sir Malcolm Devereux," said Castlemayne aloud, flicking his horse into motion at last, "Great Captain that was, and never will be more." But he added silently as he rode off under the dripping trees: So long as you give the wall to me if ever we should chance to meet in any narrow London lane!

ii

When next he reined in on a windblown hilltop, the castle and the Vale of Exmoor lay far behind him. He sucked a chestful of cold air into his lungs and smiled.

All about him, round hills fell away, heaved up, rolled on to the misty wastes of Dartmoor on the far horizon. There were patches of forest here and there through the white hills. There was a vast cold blue sky above. The road ahead was a ribbon of reddish mud, churned to a quagmire by the wheels of country carts and the horses of those departing guests who had preceded him out of Exmoor.

He turned in the saddle to look back.

The castle was still there, huddled darkly on the forested ridge above the vale, miles behind already. The massive walls and towers, the great hall and the keep hoary with age, the gate-house and the outbuildings that ringed the courtyard. All blurred with distance into a single chunky mass of dark stone looming above the forest. The whole intricate complex of chambers and passages, galleries and stairways and chimney flues that was his lordship's pride. It seemed unreal somehow to Castlemayne as he sat his horse, looking back.

Unreal—but for one bright presence that dwelt there still. One that grew more real to him with every hoofbeat that carried him away from Exmoor.

But he would not think about that.

He kneed the big mare into sudden movement. She missed her footing momentarily in the slushy mire, and Castlemayne, tensing, felt a stab of pain across his bandaged ribs. He knew his wounds would begin to hurt in earnest before nightfall. They would plague him unmercifully all those weary jogging miles ahead, along the road to London.

Best to concentrate on that, he told himself. Best to brace himself for the road ahead, ten long, grueling days from here to the capital. And for all that would come thereafter. For the busy weeks, the months of labor at the court, at the shipyards, seeking through the city for the men he would need, stout swords to second his own in the great adventure.

He had earned it fairly, this chance for fortune and honor and all good things. Won it by the devious, violent rules of the game as they played it in his own violent day. It was his now— the great chance, the main chance, the one wild reach for glory.

Why could he not enjoy it?

Why did his heart not beat as it had when he had dreamed

of it in the chapel, a golden idol clutched in one lean hand?
When he had talked of it this morning in Arabella's tall four-
poster bed?

He had but to think the name, and Arabella's face was instantly before him.

He saw her fair head on the bolster by his side. Her profile,
clear and lovely in the gray pre-dawn light. The upward-tilting,
small girl's nose and the womanly mouth, lips softly parting as
she turned toward him.

He saw that face swim close through the veils of memory. His
dimming eyes caressed the long line of her throat, the tumbled
masses of her wheat-blond hair. He felt the fine bones of her
shoulders, trembled at the small, firmly nippled breasts that
moved beneath his hands. He heard the little strangled cry she
gave as she pressed desperately against him at the last.

Dear God—what was the great adventure, glory and fortune
and all good things, without his Arabella?

"Yet I will come again!" he cried harshly to the empty sky and
the snowy hills around him. "Sweet Jesus, but I will come back
to her!"

It was a denial of truths that were as much a part of his own
mind as of the world he lived in. It was a rejection of the great
reality of caste and class which they both had recognized that
moment when she cried out and clung to him—when he had
felt the wetness on her cheek, the ache in his own throat. And
yet he denied it now. Denied it fiercely, powerfully, with all his
passionate being.

And with that denial, a dazzling hope surged up in his heart.
The boldest dream that even he had yet dared conjure up:

Might there not be a possibility for them after all?

A possibility for the threadbare swordsman Walter Castlemayne of Land's End—and the great Lady Arabella Traherne?

His mind began to work upon it, the mind of the new Castlemayne he had become. A passionate dreamer still, but something

of a calculator now as well. A brain fit to master the harsh facts
of life he had so painfully learned to recognize.

For Master Walter Castlemayne—folly to think it! But for
Sir Walter Castlemayne—for the scourge of Spain and a rising
man at the Queen's Majesty's court—

It would require shrewd planning and hard work, as well as
wild courage and a quick hand on his sword. And yet it might
be done. Men no more daring than he had made their fortunes
in the Spanish wars, had risen at the court and married above
their station on the strength of it. Who was that upstart
Raleigh before he went off to the wars? Who was Sir Francis
Drake before he put to sea?

For a man may climb, with brains as well as nerve to carry
him—and such a prize to reach for! A man may climb as high as
the highest! And why not Walter Castlemayne, as well as any
other?

His eyes blazed with the old fire. He heard the sea surge and
break beneath the bows, and saw the face of Arabella smile.

Why not Sir Walter Castlemayne, as well as any other?

And then he heard it.

iii

"Walter. Walter."

It was her voice.

A real voice, no drift of memory. Faltering but clear in the
crisp cold air—and Arabella's own.

"Walter—here!"

He wheeled in the saddle, startling the big horse beneath
him to a whinnying uncertain quickstep on the slippery road.
There, in a clump of oak and furze halfway across the snowy
slope, he saw her. The Lady Arabella Traherne on horseback,
one hand half raised to him.

She wore a hooded blue riding cloak over her white gown.

The hood was thrown back, and the wind had ruffled her yellow hair. She sat a sleek chestnut mare in the shadow of an ancient oak tree. The horse moved nervously, its flanks gleaming with sweat. A hooded gerfalcon stirred restlessly on her gauntleted left wrist.

Arabella, he breathed in wonder and disbelief. He whipped his heavy mount around and pricked her to a wild gallop across the hillside toward the girl. The big horse's shoulders heaved, snow swirled around the plunging hooves.

And then they were together.

Her eyes were blue and bright with the wind, her cheeks glowing from the long ride. Her lips parted, the syllables of his name still trembling there. He saw a single gold comb gleaming in the wind-loosened golden cataract of her hair. He saw the white outline of her throat flowing down into the ermine hood, flung back now in heavy folds upon her shoulders. He saw how her taut young body molded the blue cloak in the wind, and the white gown beneath.

Her hand reached out and touched his arm.

"Walter—I know I should not have come. They will be wondering where I have got to even now, be looking for me already. And yet—oh, Walter, I could not but come, to see you one more time—"

The words came tumbling out of her. Castlemayne's sinewy hand closed reassuringly upon hers.

"Dearest Arabella. God knows—"

"Really, you left so quickly," she hastened on. "After your last talk with Father—the commission and—and then I did not see you at all, but riding out through the gate. Your back, your hair—your head was up—and then you were gone. There was only the shadow of the gatehouse, and hooves on the bridge beyond. And then that fat silk merchant came riding after and blocked out—your image—"

A shadow passed across her face at the memory.

"And I ran and called for hawks and horses—a dozen of us rode out. And I left them when I could, slipped away, hoping I might catch you here, or this side of Taunton anyway. I had" —she finished awkwardly—"I had to say good-bye."

Castlemayne looked at her, his face alight.

The Lady Arabella Traherne gazed back at him—and snuffled. Her small nose, rosy with the cold, wrinkled up suddenly, and she sneezed.

"Oh, Walter!" She burst out laughing helplessly. "I knew that would happen. I knew it last night, when I knelt on the cold stone floor to pray. And now you'll take away a red-nosed *child* in your memory—"

And he laughed too, pitching back his head and roaring gusty laughter into the wintry air. It was the first time he had laughed in many days.

With a quick movement he reached out and took the small gray hawk from her wrist. He deposited the hooded bird on a low branch of the mossy oak. Then he swung down from his horse and reached up for her.

She came into his arms with a rush, a flurry of hair and cloak and hood and rustling gown. Then they were kissing, warm faces together, their two mouths moving eagerly against each other. He felt her slenderness through the heavy winter clothing, and she felt his strength. For long moments they clung together, kissing and holding each other close.

Time passed, murmurous and warm and fierce, totally together.

Their horses moved restlessly in the snow. The abandoned falcon turned his hooded head left and right, quick nervous jerks, seeking his invisible mistress. A squirrel leaped somewhere in the bare gnarled limbs above them, and snow filtered down, glittering in the pale afternoon sunlight.

They drew apart at last, still holding hands, looking into each other's eyes.

"Red-nosed perhaps, my lady," said Castlemayne gravely. "But not a child. Dear God, never a child, Arabella mine."

She laughed delightedly again. Swayed back, then toward him. Pressed herself once more tight against him, her head against his chest. He wrapped her close in his heavy traveling cloak. And then he began to talk.

There in the shadow of the old oak tree, he told her everything. All that had happened at Exmoor those twelve days of Christmas. And all that might yet be, if Fortune favored and his courage did not fail.

The chill that reddened her cheeks and nose faded when he told her what horrors had been unleashed there beneath her father's roof those two weeks past. She pressed closer still against him, comforting and warming, as he told her of his madness— melancholy, haunting—whatever it had been. She looked up at him in fear and wonder when he told her what had happened that very morning on the snowy knoll behind her father's chapel.

But it was only when he spoke of the future, of plans and possibilities for them both, that she bit her lip and looked away, quick moisture welling in her eyes.

"Oh, Walter," she said bitterly, "you know my father. You know it is quite impossible. I should not be here even now. God knows when we two shall even see each other again. And as for —more than that—"

She stumbled into silence, stricken with misery.

"Oh, my dearest Arabella!" He all but laughed back at her. "Impossible is too mild a word! It is unreal, it is not happening. It cannot be by all the laws of logic and all the rules of human intercourse. That you and I—a common squire's son and the great Earl of Exmoor's daughter— Impossible, incredible, not to be tolerated!"

She blinked up at him uncertainly. Uncertain as only he could make her feel, with his wild dreams, his strange convictions, his audacious certainties.

"And yet you are really here, my heart." He touched her hair,

and his blue eyes smiled down at her. "You are here, and this
—is really happening!" He bent to her once more, and put his
lips on hers.

"For all things are possible in this world," he whispered
softly then, close against her ear. "My own, my Arabella."
And she believed him.

She watched him ride away from the hill's high crown, above
the oak coppice and the furze. Watched the Sussex mare's big
shoulders churning up the opposite slope beyond the shadowed
hollow in the hills. Watched him urge the great beast on with
the pressure of his powerful thighs, the touch of a roweled spur.
Saw the moor wind pick up his white-blond hair as he neared the
summit.

I must get back, she was thinking vaguely, still dazed and
full of wonder. I shall say I lost the hawk. Say I followed him
halfway to Taunton before—

Then Walter Castlemayne rode out upon the hilltop and
turned back toward her, and Arabella thought no more.

He raised one arm to her. He reared his huge mount suddenly
in a graceful salute, there on the sunlit hilltop. He waved to her
again, then wheeled and was gone.

She stood beside her horse's head, a gold comb in her golden
hair, and watched him go.